Everyone knows it's wrong to kill.

WRONGFUL DEATH

PRAISE FOR
WRONGFUL DEATH

Selected as one of the *Chicago Tribune*'s Twelve Best Mysteries of the Year

"Dramatic and intelligent . . . Kerr is a talented writer."
—*Houston Chronicle*

"Populated with memorable and finely fleshed out characters that add to the impact of the narrative . . . [Kerr] give[s] the story the chilling ring of truth."　　—*The Denver Post*

"Baine Kerr is simply one of the best lawyer-novelists out there, and *Wrongful Death* is further proof of the fact."
—Scott Turow

"This is a terrific book—smart, fascinating, and a rare look at how the mechanisms of the law have to fit themselves around moral ambiguity . . . a gold mine of information and wisdom."
—Molly Ivins, nationally syndicated political columnist

"[A] strong and very moving tale . . . The book's climax is a superbly rendered trial sequence . . . a stunning, inspiring read."
—*Publishers Weekly* (starred review)

"Kerr puts a sinister twist on the age-old problem of evil . . . will likely keep readers guessing as to the true culprit's identity well into the novel."　　—*Colorado Daily*

"A tour de force cross-examination and a provocative meditation on vanity, betrayal and evil."　　—*Kirkus Reviews*

"This is one of those rare works by a writer who's been there. He writes with style and skill and an astounding knowledge that far exceed the demands of the usual thriller. The book has a powerful ring of truth because it is true."

—Gerry Spence,
author of *Half-Moon and Empty Stars*

"A masterful tale."　　—*Honolulu Advertiser*

continued . . .

Books by Baine Kerr

JUMPING-OFF PLACE AND OTHER STORIES
HARMFUL INTENT
WRONGFUL DEATH

WRONGFUL DEATH

BAINE KERR

JOVE BOOKS, NEW YORK

WRONGFUL DEATH

A Jove Book / published by arrangement with
Scribner, a division of Simon & Schuster, Inc.

PRINTING HISTORY
Scribner edition / May 2002
Jove edition / July 2003

For information address: Simon & Schuster, Rockefeller Center,
1230 Avenue of the Americas, New York, New York 10020.

ISBN: 0-515-13574-7

A JOVE BOOK®
Jove Books are published by The Berkley Publishing Group,
a division of Penguin Group (USA) Inc.,
375 Hudson Street, New York, New York 10014.
JOVE and the "J" design
are trademarks belonging to Penguin Group (USA) Inc.

PRINTED IN THE UNITED STATES OF AMERICA

10 9 8 7 6 5 4 3 2 1

For Dara and Terce,
and your generation,
to whom the world belongs

. . . *farewell Fear,*
Farewell Remorse: all Good to me is lost;
Evil be thou my Good.

—JOHN MILTON
Paradise Lost
Book IV, lines 108–10

PART I

THE CONSERVATORSHIP

In re June Stillwell
96PR172-5

CHAPTER 1

Trials can have moments of truth—subtle, unexpected, even magical. Like the sudden stillness of songbirds or animal tracks filling with water or a name called from a dream. All at once a meaning comes to light, if you're paying attention. If you're not so taken up in the action you miss it, a revelation that flares and blows out.

I was incidental to the action in *Stillwell v. The Western Pacific Railroad.* As the court-appointed conservator for Dale Stillwell, my only job was to approve a settlement between the company and the injured brakeman and his wife. Ten minutes into Stillwell's testimony, the adjuster for the Western Pacific's captive insurer had seen the writing on the wall. The robber barons were going to get hammered again. It was settlement time. Given Stillwell's impairments, the judge and lawyers wanted a conservator to bless the negotiations.

As a piece of legal work the Stillwell case made no particular impression, but I'll see the facts of the accident as long as I live. I probably would even if they hadn't led five years later to the Colfax Center for Rehabilitation, where June Stillwell was warehoused in Denver with other hopeless patients.

December 25, 1993. Triple overtime at the Western Pacific switching yard in Laramie, Wyoming, for the unsentimental few who'd service locomotives on Christmas Day. June Mooney might as well sign up. Her daughter was spending the day with June's ex. Her father was snowed in seven hours away in Lander. Dale Stillwell showed up too. A loner, that was no surprise. Christmas was just another day.

June was the only female engineer at the Laramie yard. She put Stillwell on the lead of the three-engine string she was hostling in to be serviced. Dale Stillwell was quiet, good-looking in an offbeat way. Wiry, tough, aloof, he'd worked June's trains once or twice, rarely talking, always moving, quick as a cat. June liked to know what made folks tick. She'd wondered about his hidden depths.

From the cab of the trailing locomotive June couldn't have seen much in the ground blizzard tearing by. Her task was to nose the string through the maze of track and on into the roundhouse. The yard was backed up with cars going nowhere on Christmas. Stillwell stood outside atop the lead engine, checking switches and hand-signaling go-aheads back to June.

The yardmaster in the diesel tower radioed permission for June to come inbound. There shouldn't have been any other power out there—any other locomotives, cranked and manned. June's engine started down a line that curved, then converged with a cutoff spur, the two lines merging to form a curving Y, a gantlet. Neither knew it but an outbound coal train was standing on the cutoff, fouling her tracks, the brakeman working the switch instead of protecting his power. Stillwell scampered down the front steps and hung off a grab iron to check what lay ahead. From back where the curve began, back in the cab and behind the string, and through the plumes of snow, June couldn't have seen a thing.

I imagine, in the two seconds when calm turned to terror, a weightless feeling. Stillwell'd trotted up the lead engine's hull like a sailor and dropped down the right side for a look. Bent and leaning, one bulky glove hooked on the angle iron, balanced on the ball of a boot. Lulling sounds of rolling wheels and wind-rushed snow. No sky or ground, as the locomotive burrowed into the storm. Straining through the spray at the shadow taking shape ahead like a rockfall blocking the road.

June kept the engines coming though he hadn't waved her on. The cowcatchers closed with six inches to spare. Stillwell raced up the rungs but missed one, cracked a knee, lost his hold on the frozen metal. He slipped between the locomotives as they nearly touched, rolled like a rag in a wringer, dropping when they parted, with two collapsed lungs and eleven snapped bones and a penetrating head wound from a bolt that had jammed his skull like a geartooth. June said she never saw the standing power until she passed it. She never saw Stillwell until the yardmaster called her to stop, she had a man on the ground.

June Mooney was the ace switch engineer of the Laramie yard, envied for her gentle throttle. A "Casey Jones," in railroad lingo, she could close on a coupling at a quarter mile an hour, so smooth that water wouldn't tremble in a cup. But the switchman is the engineer's eyes, clearing the track and signaling forward. Nothing's worse in a yard than a curve where a hand signal can't be seen. A radio would have helped, or a relay crew, but they hadn't been assigned.

June was running her string without a go-ahead from Stillwell, but the yardmaster shouldn't have let the outbound power leave. They should have kept the gantlet clear. There were no clearance markers. In zero visibility, how was she to know a locomotive would have to be cleared inside the curve?

She did know. She "sixth-sensed what was going down before it did. Everything, Dale bleeding in the snow and me running at him screaming. Something kept the power on," she later typed in her journal, "like I froze up too, paralyzed by fate."

Guilt is a dangerous motivator. Sometimes it leads to breakthroughs. More often it takes you places you've got no business going.

While Stillwell was hospitalized, first in Cheyenne for six weeks of drug-induced coma, then down to the brain-injury unit in Boulder, through months of hysteria when he was strapped down, and finally the faltering baby steps of therapy, June was there every day, feeding him, reading, singing, whispering prayerfully, unfolding his balled hands. A year into his recovery she married Dale Stillwell in the Boulder hospital chapel. They got an apartment near the brain-injury unit once Stillwell was discharged to outpatient care. They filed suit in Boulder, kept it out of federal court when the Western Pacific tried to remove, and in Boulder—my town—it came to trial.

Four days into the plaintiff's case Dale Stillwell took the

stand. For his wife, for his lawyers and the house counsel for the
WP, and surely for its adjuster, the moment of truth had arrived:
halting answers to simple questions that built into a pressured,
panicked rush of scenes of snow and steel, agitation, then incoherence that flew apart in convulsive stammers and shuddering
tears of frustration and shame, and then the moment. The agonized silence that hung in the courtroom when he gave up trying
to speak.

     Their moment of truth, not mine. I was called in afterward,
and I caught sight of a very different man.

CHAPTER 2

•

Before going further I should declare a bias. Most of my career I was a railroad lawyer. I defended the robber barons. I guarded their deep pockets against featherbedders with sore backs and the bereaved families of kids at crossings who'd tried to beat a train. I wonder sometimes what I was thinking, even who I was. At the time, I liked the work as a type of cerebral sport, but I never shared the true believers' scorn for greedy plaintiffs. Lots of the claims were worthy and lots of the losses tragic, more so than money could begin to make up for, as the Stillwell settlement would prove.

Stillwell's claims were brought under FELA, the Federal Employers Liability Act, which governed on-the-job injuries to railroad workers. As regional general counsel for the Missouri and Santa Fe, I knew FELA law. As a trial lawyer I knew the vagaries of litigation. I knew traumatic brain injury from four or five dozen cases of heads whacked by trains. I had the time, mid-1996, to come down to the Flatirons County Courthouse, learn the case a little, sit through negotiations, and tell the judge it was squared away. But I'd have to be persuaded.

Paige Jorritsma, lead counsel for the Western Pacific at Stillwell's trial, was in charge of the persuading. I owed her a favor, Paige thought. We'd appeared together at the Public Utilities Commission on grade-crossing protection hearings for the double tracks from Denver to Pueblo. My railroad had the north-bound; Paige had the southbound, and she'd kept both of our maintenance costs to a minimum. Paige proposed my name to Hancock, the Stillwells' FELA lawyer, as a conservator her company could deal with. Hancock and I knew each other as opposing counsel in a half dozen hard-fought trials. He thought he'd rolled me settling a spine case in the eighties. He actually left a quarter million on the table. Still, I was a little sur-prised he'd hand over the reins of the Stillwell settlement to a railroad lawyer he'd fought with before. After all, I'd be signing off on his fee.

I gathered from our telephone conversation Paige also thought she was doing a favor for me. She knew I was quitting the railroad and heading out of town for a midlife change of practice. I suspected her for one of those semicolleagues I'd come to think worried I was falling to pieces. She suggested a no-brainer, one-shot conservatorship to approve a settlement as a healthy diversion, something therapeutic.

I wasn't inclined to agree. Working for a plaintiff—even just as a conservator for just a few days—was something I'd never done. Working with Hancock—the thought made me squirm. But Paige pushes hard. Everybody thought I was perfect, including Stillwell's doctor, Hans Leitner. With that I gave in. Hans Leitner clinched it—not only a respected physician and renowned expert witness, but one to whom I owed a real favor for his help with my new appointment in The Hague. If Leitner stood behind Hancock's client, the case had merit. And if Hans thought I should be his patient's conservator, who was I to argue?

There were "personal reasons" for my professional turbu-lence. Two years earlier, my wife, Kathleen, had died unexpect-edly. I spent months afterward in a trance, the next year hiding in work. By degrees I realized I had to break free, like an animal seeking safety in the open, a deer in flight rather than a rabbit trembling in its hole. We had no children, no other family nearby. I could change everything, I realized. Seek the haven of the unfamiliar.

By the time I got Paige's call about the Stillwell case, I'd wound down my railroad practice, grown a beard, signed a ten-ant, and booked a business fare for the end of the month to the

Netherlands, where I knew no one and no one had known Kathleen. I'd pulled every string, including Hans Leitner's, every school-tie connection I had to join the prosecutor's office at the United Nations criminal tribunal for the former Yugoslavia.

"Personal reasons" can be a rationale of convenience for politicians and CEOs. I needed work I could believe in. I vaguely hoped it would lead to a judgeship. But the true reason was acutely personal. I wanted to get over Kathleen.

Once she'd talked me into it, Paige brought me up to speed. After the agonized gap in Stillwell's testimony, Judge Otero had dismissed the jury and called the lawyers to the bench. It was conceded all around that settlement should be explored. Because Stillwell did not appear legally capable of signing off on a deal, a conservator was needed. Conservatorships are opened when a legally binding agreement must be reached on behalf of someone not yet twenty-one years old or unable to manage his affairs due to disability. Conservatorships can be ongoing or, as in this case, for a single transaction. The conservator owes fiduciary duties to act in the best interest of the ward. Court was adjourned until the following morning. Everyone huddled and came up with my name. Paige set in twisting my arm.

When I got to court, the Stillwells weren't there, though I knew, in varying degrees, everyone else who was—Paige, Stillwell's lawyer, Hancock, Judge Otero and his staff, and Dr. Leitner, next to whom I took a seat in the gallery. "What are you getting me into?" I whispered. If only we'd known.

The judge made short work of the appointment. Since I was the plaintiff's choice, and lawyers for each side agreed, as did the plaintiff's physician, the judge found me suited for the job. Given what he'd seen the day before, he found Stillwell incompetent and me qualified to manage his affairs. Testimony from Dr. Leitner on the plaintiff's mental capacity wasn't even needed.

Both attorneys attested to my fairness of mind and experience in such cases. I agreed to serve if I could study Hancock's file over the weekend. The judge ordered the probate clerk to issue letters of conservatorship and guardianship. Four pages signed and sealed and I was empowered to authorize settlement on Dale Stillwell's behalf. Empowered in fact to decide all questions of his material and physical well-being. They were godlike powers in hindsight, the like of which otherwise fall to no one in a free society.

Hans Leitner gave me an elbow. "Elliot Stone," he said, smiling. "Friend of the oppressed." He clapped my shoulder. "I welcome it."

Leitner and I set to gathering and packing Redweld files in trial bags. Files bagged, he raised a finger. "Soon you will find oppression, injury, and injustice like you really can't believe," he said. "You will grow. You will never see the world the same. And the physically and psychically maimed will be looking—to you. As does this couple now."

Between us we lugged four fat leather bags of Stillwell case documents to my car, Leitner regaling me all the way with tales of Yugoslavia, the accursed land.

Monday morning I arrived ready for negotiations, the jury out till after lunch. Hancock briefed me in private. Always an edgy guy, with a jumpy little mustache and restless eyes, he seemed particularly tense. In court he had a disconcerting examination style. He'd ask a question and stare, mouth slack, peering over gold-rimmed spectacles as though they were bifocals, snapping off and on the cap of a gold metal pen. His conversational style was roughly the same.

"Settlement offer eve of trial was five point five," Hancock said, speaking of millions of dollars. "Railroad laughed. By yesterday I'd proved up eight. Stone-cold solid." He gave me his peering look.

I could see $8 million in wage and medical losses with a thirty-two-year-old senior brakeman permanently, totally disabled and a lifetime of therapies to pay for—occupational, physical, speech, psychiatric, and cognitive. Physically, Stillwell had had a change in handedness, right to left, and his right-side fine-motor dexterity was shot. He showed a host of lesser neurological signs—tics, gait, and balance. But the prefrontal divot the bolt blew out had actually left him, after a hell of a comeback, more judgment- than cognition-impaired, according to Hancock. Stillwell was moody, easily overstimulated; he fixated on irrelevancies, his impulse-control gyro spinning out of orbit. He had a "tendency to catastrophize."

Minor setbacks were calamitous. There was profound sleep disturbance, and a question of depression. He had deficits in word-finding, turn-taking, and topic maintenance. To let off steam he'd shoot baskets incessantly, autistically, and with surprising finesse. Morbidly, he dwelled on the accident.

Because the brain is incapable of recognizing it's been harmed, Stillwell lacked insight into his losses and therefore into how to compensate for them. The speech/language deficits grabbed your attention, but the interesting part, Hancock said, was that Stillwell remained intellectually intact—which didn't mean his thinking was sound.

Hans Leitner had spent a full day the first week of trial testifying to the medical overview. Jock Beck, a life-care planner, put unit costs for an expected future life of forty-nine years on everything from therapy sessions to medication to neuropsych software. The economist crunched out a present fund to cover it all just shy of 8 million bucks.

"You know Leitner," Hancock said. "Killer witness. Jury lapped it up like dogs." He giggled to himself, lost in his war story, a trial moment not of truth but conquest. "She came after him. She can't help it." Hancock was referring to the hard-driving Paige. "Leitner threw her cross back at her like Dr. God. Like fucking Thor, man. Slinging bolts of lightning."

The image wasn't so far-fetched, given Hans Leitner's size and air of comfortable majesty, and his leonine thatch of thick white hair.

Hancock smirked and peered, inches from my face. "Cool, it was," he whispered. "Dr. God on my side for a change."

I knew Hans Leitner's testimonial skills. I'd hired him fifteen or twenty times to pick apart brain and psych claims against my railroad. He'd been treating Stillwell for close to a year for brain-injury coping and, most recently, post-traumatic stress. Leitner told the jury Stillwell's was the worst case of PTSD he'd seen in a career that included working the ward where the syndrome was first identified in Vietnam vets. In Dr. Leitner's expert opinion Dale Stillwell would relive the moment when he slipped between the engines for the rest of his life, with crush nightmares, phobias, dissociation, and anniversary panic. Christmas would be dreaded all year.

Hancock's settlement pitch was that Leitner had made the

case, especially once he'd jujitsued Paige. Paige's haymaker cross-exam had put out her own client's lights. After that, how could the railroad question damages with no less than Colonel Hans Leitner backing them up? He was chief of the Forensic Service of the Department of Veteran Affairs for starters, founder of the American College of Legal Medicine, and past president of the American Academy of Forensic Sciences, if anybody doubted. He had three Johns Hopkins degrees and a fellowship at the Armed Forces Institute of Pathology, an international reputation for forensic human-rights investigations, and was on staff at each of Denver's teaching hospitals.

The first time I'd marveled at Hans Leitner's accomplishments was shortly after transferring from Chicago twelve years before. An annual listing, "Best Doctors in Colorado," put him at the top of three specialties—psychiatry, pathology, and forensic medicine. According to the magazine, everyone who was anyone in medicine and law, and international justice too, knew Hans Leitner, both a "distinguished scientist" and "medical moralist" who remained a "doctor's doctor."

Most impressive, both to juries and me, Leitner had been a founder of Doctors for Human Rights. He'd team-led, at that time, medical investigations of killing fields in El Salvador, Guatemala, and Eritrea. I'd always felt a tug of envy for this man of parts who, at the peak of his profession, retained the balance and values to apply his skills to justice and the general good.

I took the listing of best doctors to my new boss, Henry Steele, who'd defended the railroad since the days, it seemed, of the James brothers and the Dalton gang. "You know this doctor?" I asked. "Is he for real?"

Henry looked up with his fastidious frown and nodded. "Top doc all round, though he's spread a little thin. CV that'd choke a horse."

"It says 'forensic medicine.' Can we use him?"

"Can and do. He belongs to the railroads."

If he ever did, he didn't anymore, as Paige Jorritsma had just learned.

Dale Stillwell was one of Leitner's half dozen ongoing patients. He maintained a tiny psychiatric practice in Boulder to keep his hand in clinical medicine. When a patient needed medical testimony in court, he was there. Otherwise, he appeared as a retained witness for the defense in civil cases, for the prosecution in criminal ones. His occasional testimony for patients who were plaintiffs added a little balance to his horse-choker CV, insulating him from attack as biased. With two tough defense types like Leitner and Beck on Stillwell's side, instead of touchy-feely plaintiff's treaters, even as hard-hearted a cynic as Paige Jorritsma might not haggle over an $8 million price tag.

So why discount to five point five or less?

Hancock stared at me and blinked, chuckled, and darted a look at the jury room, where he'd parked his clients. He pushed his glasses against the bridge of his nose. "She was driving," he said. "The engineer."

"So I gather."

"That is a problem." He smiled painfully. "Human error. Why'd she enter the curve without a signal? You got a woman driver, jury could hold it against us."

That sounded a little candy-assed. I'd read the file. The company had violated a half dozen of its own operating rules. If the engineer was negligent as well, under FELA that was the railroad's responsibility too. Paige would try to imply, in closing, the injustice of rewarding a couple with millions of dollars when the wife was a cause of the damages. But June's fault was legally irrelevant to Stillwell's damages. Even on her own lesser claim for emotional distress, blaming June could be a hard sell.

There was a photo in the file of "J. Mooney, Senior Engineer" of June in workboots and coveralls, perched on the platform of her cab with a cocky grin, waving a cap. Projecting strength and assurance, as I saw it. Less Error than Competence.

"What kind of money do the Stillwells want?" I asked.

"Got an offer from the railroad this morning. Two million, structured. I'd be happy to split the baby from our five point five pretrial. Three point five, and everyone's a winner. Let's see if the railroad goes for it."

"What do *they* want? Your clients?"

"Ask." He grimaced strangely. "Your job—am I right?"

The psychology of my assignment was coming into focus. The judge wanted to close the file without Stillwell coming back and claiming he hadn't understood. Paige didn't want Stillwell

saying he'd been railroaded, as it were, into settling. Hancock
wanted a done deal that secured his seven-figure fee.

"Show me your people," I told him.

Shaking pocket change, Hancock flipped through the clerk's
door at the rear of the court. He bore down a short hall to the jury
room, a DELIBERATIONS IN PROGRESS sign stowed in its door
pocket. He paused, drew the door ajar, and breathlessly
announced my arrival.

The Stillwells sat alone at a long, battered table facing an
empty wall. June Stillwell turned, our eyes met. Hers widened
and held with the same sting of recognition I felt for an instant in
my own.

In the ready sincerity of her look, the turn of her throat with
lips parting, the vivid coloring and the gloss of her hair, and the
white skin faintly freckled, like specks of light, like stars by day,
I recognized my wife. An illusion, of course. I didn't know this
woman. She didn't know me. Though, for a moment that raised
hairs on my neck, I could swear we'd each seen ghosts.

"You—look familiar," I fumbled. "Mrs. Stillwell? And
Dale?" Stillwell nodded without looking up.

"We've met somewhere." June Stillwell tracked my eyes as I
rounded the table to take a seat, Hancock heading the other way.
"Do you shop at Wild Oats?"

Hancock made a hilarious face and noisily sat down. I shook
my head and smiled back. "Ideal," I said. "King Soopers when I
have to."

Opposite her now, with an objective second look, there were
unmistakable similarities, but differences too. I considered them
as a couple, the sort who, side by side, exaggerate each other's
physical differences. June was the tall and sunny one, with her
blue eyes and pale complexion and fine auburn hair. He hunched
at the table while she sat composed and erect. She threw her husband's mood into shadow. Long-boned and old-fashioned handsome, less dreamy than Kathleen, more Wyoming than Ireland.
In her mid-thirties, June Stillwell might look awkward in an
evening gown but wonderful in jeans. That day she was dressed
for court, like a lady, in a blue skirt and pleated white blouse,
hair drawn neatly back from her face, fingers clasped precisely
in front.

Hancock sat at the other end of the table, rolling his pen back and forth between his palms, clock-click, clock-click, against a fat wedding band.

I reached across and shook their hands in turn. Stillwell had a stiff and formal grip. I set in explaining my role. I was Dale's fiduciary, appointed by the court. That meant my duty was to look after his interests. The judge had ruled Dale couldn't settle his claims himself, and June couldn't do it for him. As a coplaintiff she had a conflict of interest. So someone like me had to stand in for Dale. I wanted to know their wishes and to get their consent to any settlement. I assured them I would only approve a deal if I thought it was as good as they'd get from the jury, discounted for the risk of losing, and as high as the railroad would go.

I explained the advantages of the future-payment structure Paige had put forward—annuities paid over time rather than a lump sum up front. The $3.5 million settlement Hancock recommended would generate, after fees, roughly $12 million in annuities over the next twenty years, all of it tax-free under Section 104(a) of the Internal Revenue Code, AAA-rated and guaranteed, and exempt, under state law, from the claims of creditors. The money would be safe. It couldn't be squandered, and no one else could touch it.

I finished a little expansively. "My objective is nothing less than an adequate amount of money to meet your medical and personal needs for life."

The silence grew uncomfortable. June broke it, less to respond, it seemed, than to put me at ease. "I think," she said almost confidentially, "money is essential, like you say, as a means to an end. Our goal is to bring Dale *all* the way back. *We can do it,* Mr. Stone, and the WP can help us get there, is how I think." She stole a smile at her husband, tentative but intimate.

Stillwell sat expressionless, absorbed in the drips and blemishes on the bare white wall. June's long-fingered hand slid down the tabletop and swallowed his fist, gathered the keys he was clutching, and slipped them into her lap.

"Dale thinks different." She exhaled and shot another look his way. "Men are fighters. Women are healers. Like the thing with the glass, is it full or nearly empty? I try to be forward-looking. Dale can't stop thinking about the past. Dale thinks the railroad should pay for what they did, for what we've been through and what's been taken. And he's right." She touched his arm. He let her fingers stay. "The railroad should pay for his torment."

"You're both right," I said earnestly. "Dale is entitled to compensation for everything he had to endure, pain and suffering, mental and physical. The settlement should also cover what you're talking about, June. Everything that could help Dale overcome his injuries."

"You come with him?" Stillwell suddenly asked me. The reference was to Hancock. "This w-weasel?"

"How's that, Dale?"

"Joke." Hancock chuckled, clock-clicking his pen. "Word for lawyers."

"With Hancock? Not on your life," I said.

"You w-work with him?"

Hancock and I laughed falsely. "Hell no," I assured Stillwell.

"I told you," June said to her husband. "Mr. Stone's got nothing to do with Neil Hancock. He's mostly against him."

Now Stillwell smiled, a subtle tightening of closed lips, disarming it was so unexpected. "You don't-don't like him either," he said to me.

More awkward laughter. I nodded and shrugged. Stillwell's expressive black eyes caught mine and I gave back equal intensity, trying to gain his trust.

"Mr. Stone's all for us," June whispered. "He'll do it right." She squeezed Dale's arm and held it.

Dale Stillwell's pain was so palpable the first impulse was to soothe him, the next to pull away, for touch could torture the wound. But clearly June could touch him, and together they made a kind of sense. His dark masculinity and global distrust, his heaving mix of strength and impotence might appeal to her. She'd want both to subdue and to enable him. Each might fear that, separately, he could flounder in his losses and she sink in her guilt, while together, they might float to shore. They seemed needy and credulous, in June's case to the point of a leap of faith, a blind belief that devotion could heal a damaged soul.

But you deserve better, I wanted to say. A full life, the pride and contentment implicit in the file photo of the cocky engineer and not now to be seen in the desperate, handsome woman sitting across from me.

And Dale Stillwell, what did he deserve?

"We getting out of here today?" Hancock blurted from his end of the table. This was for me and I got the message: Get 'er done. My boy might bolt.

"W-weasel." Stillwell glared in Hancock's, not my, direction.

FELA weasels—I liked the ring of it. Why *had* Hancock gone along with me?

I never envied union-designated FELA counsel like Hancock. The way to get cases was to cozy up to the locals, keep scouts on retainer. The most shameless repaid favors with women, underwrote Las Vegas boondoggles, took bosses to dinner at the neighborhood Delmonico's and cut them in on fees. At one end they had to curry favor with plug-uglies who wanted a cut. At the other end, they had to deal with cold-blooded railroad claims agents. Then they had to deal with me. In '08, Congress passed FELA, after the Pullman strike and Clarence Darrow's defense of the unions, to redress robber-baron outrages. By the nineties, as elsewhere in late-twentieth-century America, it was hard to say who was exploiting whom.

Physical danger remained an enduring truth. Trains deserve your respect. A single road locomotive can put out forty-five hundred horsepower and weigh four hundred thousand pounds. A hundred-car coal train can top thirty million pounds. At twenty-five miles per hour on a level grade it takes interlocked air brakes simultaneously blocking all the wheels of all hundred cars a mile and a half to drag them to a stop. It pays to keep out of the way.

Hancock clicked nails on the tabletop. "Let's do it, folks. Let's wrap it up."

Across the table June Stillwell searched my face. "Mr. Stone," she said softly. "Can you help us?"

Her appeal felt liturgical. I saw she didn't mean "Give us a hand." She meant capital *H* Help. Help us make it. Save us.

The hold June Stillwell's gaze exerted had a lot to do with her splendid delft eyes. Larger and rounder than Kathleen's and less veiled, haloed by flocked brows, bright with intelligence and burning with need. June's power was her look. Kathleen's had been her voice.

"You have to understand." I put my bias forward. "No amount of money can change what happened."

Stillwell abruptly stood. He rammed his fists in his trousers. "I think you're right," he said loudly. "I don't want their money."

Hancock rolled his eyes, cursed me under his breath. I cautioned that a jury might come back with nothing.

"I can live with nothing." He rocked on his feet from ball to heel. "I'm a St-Stillwell. I'll make out."

June's composure broke. She looked on the point of tears.

"I don't need their goddamn money." Stillwell's eyes were glistening, wild. "You can't just t-take money and go away. It doesn't go away. It never goes away." His lips trembled and I looked off, embarrassed for him. Wondering what I'd gotten myself into.

June then stood and closed her arm around him, as a mother calms a child. He twisted in her embrace. "Go on out," she was saying. "Go on. It's okay. We can do this. I'll take care of you."

He pushed back from her, eyes darting. "This is why you t-took up with me." And he was out the door.

June looked exhausted. She closed the door and sank back into her auditorium chair. "I'm sorry," she said. "He doesn't mean it." Her composure, I saw, had been baled together by force of will. With Stillwell gone, she collapsed into herself, into self-awareness.

"I know," I said, though I didn't.

"I'm scared." She looked up. "I think the jury's gonna blame me."

"They won't," I assured her, under the power of her look, "and it doesn't matter." It was legally irrelevant.

Hancock sighed, intending a message of exasperation, but trailing off roundly into relief: his client had left the room. "Help us out, amigo." Hancock addressed me. "And remember whose side you're on."

Neil Hancock's side, is what he meant. More specifically, Neil Hancock's fee. If the principals in the case went along with the settlement the WP seemed poised to accept, Hancock would clear a million bucks. If one of the principals balked and it played out instead to an unpredictable jury, Hancock might not get anything. A million bucks or more versus maybe nothing at all. I'd never had to face anything like the double-or-nothing that beaded Hancock's brow. A million-dollar pot, playing against the house. Paid by the hour like a plumber, I could only marvel. No wonder the man was a bundle of nerves. Still, his nervous tension was annoying.

"I want this over," June said. "You see the stress on Dale—"

"Man's out of his loving mind." Hancock patted out a broken tattoo.

"What?" June looked annoyed.

"It's hard." Hancock frowned. His mustache humped.

She watched him skeptically then slumped into herself again. "So—we have to settle. Don't we have to?"

"I strongly recommend it," Hancock intoned, suddenly hunching toward her on his elbows. "If not now—never. Last chance, June. You'll regret it for all time."

"Mr. Stone—"

"Elliot can seal the agreement regardless . . ." Hancock trailed away.

"Mr. Stone. Tell me about after. This gets done, what happens then?"

"My appointment is for what's called a single transaction." I was leaving the country in three weeks and couldn't continue even if I wanted to. The terms of any agreement should antici- pate a substitute conservator who would continue until Dale could independently manage. After settlement June wouldn't have a conflict. She should step in as substitute conservator and guardian.

"So let's do it." Hancock snapped off the cap of his pen and broke out cost reimbursements and his one-third for fees at $2.5, $3, and $3.5 million. He circled the net remainders and passed the page to June. She said go ahead, get what I could. I shuttled to and from Paige and her adjuster, bumping them up. Eventu- ally we split the baby the way Hancock wanted, a settlement with a present value of $3.5 million for Stillwell plus a hundred K for June, which included $1.2 million in a lump up front for Hancock's fee, then monthly annuities and five-year balloons. The guaranteed future payments would come to $12 million over twenty years, payable to the order of June Stillwell as sub- stitute conservator. June found Stillwell, we notified Judge Otero, and I walked it through in open court.

At counsel table there were white plastic water pitchers and Dixie cups stacked on end. I poured four. No one sipped but me. Hancock rolled the gold pen in his palms, clock-click, clock-click, against his ring, a domestic anchor, a talisman. Stillwell sat board stiff, lips pursed, not there.

As soon as we adjourned, Stillwell headed for the courtroom door. June thanked me copiously, both her hands on mine. "You've given us a new lease on life," she said. "A new beginning." What I was soon leaving to try to claim for myself. She hugged me. I didn't feel deserving.

I was glad it was over. Helping plaintiffs carried a weight that could make you gasp. Against the railroad, the hostile world, Hancock and I were all these people had. I wondered if we were up to giving them a new lease on anything.

And something else was off. I gave it a minute's thought.

If Stillwell was incompetent and needed a conservator, why had the lawyers waited until now? If incompetent, how could he legally have hired Hancock and authorized suit at a time when his impairments were presumably worse? What persuaded Hancock to go along with this late demand from Paige for a conservator to secure the settlement? And why me, from the enemy camp?

Maybe Hancock wanted a conservative like me instead of a plaintiff's lawyer who'd overvalue the claims and put settlement out of reach. Hancock was in it for the fee. He'd settle on the short end if he had to. He cleared a million two as it was. He was getting rich off Dale Stillwell.

Hancock might also have thought I could better deal with Paige. Paige had a damn hard edge. She hated midtrial settlements like coitus interruptus. But the adjuster makes the call to settle and he must have seen enough. Stillwell made him nervous.

Hancock probably thought I could keep Paige in the game, maybe bluff her without getting called. Hancock had used Drs. Leitner and Beck, ordinarily defense witnesses, to build credibility with the railroad. Bringing me in was consistent.

But what explained his agitation, pressuring me to get on with it?

In the end I did the job expected of me. I knew what I was there for. Hancock wanted his fee. The railroad wanted to cut its losses and close a claim. The judge wanted to clear his docket. June wanted resources to help her husband. And she didn't want Paige condemning her in closing argument and a jury judging her actions that Christmas Day.

I was there to rubber-stamp the deal. As a money deal there was nothing much wrong with it. But they never were just money deals. Indeed, money, as my bias and the Bible would predict, was the root of the evil to come.

I was there to cover everybody's ass. Everybody except the guy to whom my duties ran.

Hans Leitner had said this couple was looking to me, and I left the courtroom worried I'd let them down. I didn't know exactly why and wouldn't for a long time, if I understand it now.

Outside the courtroom's double door a narrow hall led to a sort of reception area with docket postings, security gates and belts, chairs and benches, and milling, anxious citizens enmeshed with the law. Passing through, I noticed Stillwell on a bench next to the probate window, muttering to himself. Doreen, the clerk at the window, caught my eye and made a silent gesture down in his direction, eyes rolling and brow raised. I drifted nearer. He didn't see me, and I paused a moment, *my* moment of truth, when songbirds went silent and a name was called: "I'm going to k-kill her," I heard Stillwell mutter. "K-kill her."

I looked back then and saw June coming, darkening the narrow hall.

CHAPTER 3

I reported to Hancock what I'd overheard. "I know," he told me, "he says stuff. He doesn't mean it. You should hear what he says about me." He chuckled and I got it—why he wanted a conservator; his twitchy nerves. It wasn't only anxiety that Stillwell would back out of the settlement. Hancock wanted a shield. He wanted me to protect him from his client.

But my bit part was done. I was gone at the end of the month. I was getting off the train and flying to another world. Hancock remained both the Stillwells' lawyer. He should do what he needed to do. I wouldn't have given them further thought except for the weird, reverberating vibe I overheard him muttering, and the fading image of a face I'd mistaken for Kathleen's. With time the vibe and the image grew faint. Hancock was out of the picture once he banked his fee. And June Stillwell was left alone with sole control over annuities belonging to her disabled husband that would run to $12 million.

Two years later I was back from Europe. Within three weeks I'd been appointed conservator by Judge Otero again, but this time for June. Once or twice a week I kept June company in her double room in Denver with a view of the White Spot diner. I shared my thoughts, between her roommate's interruptions.

From the wheelchair where she was strapped, June's room-mate made a mooing noise. Her head, bound like a papoose, strained against a Velcro strap. A pink-socked foot on a pencil-thin leg arched and pumped against her footrest. I've never heard a more doleful and baleful sound—without content, devoid of meaning, not bawling for food, or crying from pain. It would fall in cadence and stop. It would be quiet awhile. Then it would resume.

The MRI brain scan of June's roommate revealed white globes of ruined tissue blooming throughout the cranial cavity. I never learned what had done that—overdose, aneurysm, near-drowning, trauma, a nasty toxin? I'd heard but didn't use the roommate's name. A name would imply humanity.

June's MRI was dramatically different: dark swells at the outer vesicles from fluid buildup a shunt might drain, but only one spot of traumatized tissue, a dime-sized white blotch at exactly the worst place—the reticular activating formation, the subcortical mechanism that regulates consciousness. One vicious blow to the face had kicked her brain stem exactly wrong. The cortex was intact. She was there, receiving messages, but unable to respond. As Silverman, the rehab-center doctor, explained, a single, focal brain-stem bleed "switched her off" and "locked her in" a coma.

June could hear my monologues. To some extent she could understand me. She no doubt looked forward to her daughter's arrival that afternoon the way a conscious person would. Surely she heard the mooing. But there was nothing she could do to shut us up.

When I visited then, I'd talk and talk, as I am now. Something in June led me to confide about the last two years. About the Balkans, the Serb I'd tried for mass murder in The Hague, the shock of *his* moment of truth. About Quierin, the woman I'd met there, and the complexities of a cross-cultural, interconti-nental love affair. About that summer of 1998, the unprece-dented heat, the boudoir farce in the White House being exposed by a corporate defense litigator turned prosecutor, just like me. At least I'd been given real crimes to go after.

And I told her about my wife. Maybe it was the illusion of familiarity—the auburn hair, the palely freckled skin—but being with June let me verbalize it. June even heard about Kathleen's death—what I'd told few others. She heard how, on a sunny May day in 1994, Kathleen had stepped out the kitchen door. In the kitchen garden a tennis ball lay among the poppies. Kathleen picked it up, turned, and threw it hard at a squirrel ascending the bird-feeder pole. As she threw the ball, which missed the squirrel, the bone in her upper arm snapped. It snapped because inside it was a tumor. On the X ray it looked like an insect's chrysalis.

The surgeon who set the break thought it was benign, but we found out differently ten months later. By then the insect had escaped. Chemotherapy was begun for spots on her liver while she still convalesced from surgery. The drug treatment allowed an opportunistic infection to reach her lungs. She was moved to the ICU, sedated to unconsciousness, and propped up in bed to keep from drowning. Tubes ran down her throat and her face was taped over. She'd lost her long hair from the cancer treatment. She couldn't breathe on her own. She couldn't even glance my way. She was unreachable and I began to lose it. A nurse held me as I shook. If only Kathleen needed a kidney so I could give her mine. There was nothing I wouldn't give her. They could have transplanted my heart.

As I talked about it, June would observe me with her powerful look. I began imagining, then half believing, I saw the light of sympathy in her eye.

"The hard part," I told her, "was that I couldn't speak to Kathleen at the end, not even how I speak with you. We couldn't say good-bye. When I asked if she could hear me, Kathleen couldn't squeeze my hand or close and open an eye," I said, "like you can." Which made it worse than either a lingering death or a sudden loss, the call from the highway patrol. Highway mayhem is expected; death is the expected end point of terminal illness. Nothing about Kathleen's leaving made sense.

In the ICU the intensivist was professionally detached. He explained ARDS and septic shock and DIC, when the blood stops clotting. It just runs and runs. We kept a sacramental distance from Kathleen, ghostly in the bright light, motionless, bald, bound in tubes and tape. The nurse steadied my elbow. We focused on the green lines and readouts of a stack of monitors. Like watching a tragic accident from afar, the stunt plane at the air show spinning toward the ground. Train and car meeting at a crossing. Red stains spreading in her bedding. Green numbers that blinked and dropped. Oxygen saturation at 70, 45, then 0 percent, then a dead, gray screen. Heart rate falling: sixties, then forties, then ERROR flashing like the plume of smoke where the plane went down.

For a long time, years, I looked on our marriage in soft focus, arcadian pastels. I saw us as the lovers of "Dover Beach," true to each other in a faithless world. As might be guessed of a "Dover Beach" widower, her death left me bereft. Among colleagues my shell-shocked daze was mistaken for composure. I dropped friends. I blamed myself, I said, just as you did, June, for what happened to Dale. I hadn't insisted on second opinions. There was so much more I could have crammed into our eighteen years. For a long time I lost interest in love, all forms of love— romantic and physical, brother love, love of God. Of adventure. Of a good book or bottle of wine or end-of-season picnics on Pawnee Pass.

Twenty months out I fumbled through lunch with a medical malpractice–lawyer friend. Moss thought there were issues— missing a malignant tumor, starting chemo despite a pleural infection, gaps in antibiotic coverage. Kathleen wasn't killed by her cancer but by treatment. Her doctor the night she fell into septic shock was an unlicensed intern on the teaching service.

Moss said he'd look at the records, send them out for review. "Of course, the defense will be 'So what? She was Stage four as it was. So she went a few months early.'"

"I could tell them *what,*" I fumed. "What we could have made of those months." I stopped. This was lawyer to lawyer, and I was venting like an aggrieved plaintiff.

I never followed up with him. I was too defense-minded. I knew what wrongful-death cases were like. I didn't need the money and I didn't have the strength for it. I'd barely gotten through lunch.

When the two-year statutory period for bringing wrongful-death claims expired, perversely I felt relieved. One day Moss ran me down and left a message: "A tip, from a plaintiff's lawyer to a glorified Pinkerton guard. You need out. Run for it

while you can." He was right. I'd been working on the railroad
too many years. All the livelong day.

It was time for the next blind swerve in a twisting career:
a Yale BA; theoretical moral philosophy (all-but-dissertation)
at Corpus Christi College, Oxford, where I met Irish Kathleen;
Harvard Law; a quick Wall Street turn at Skadden Arps; in-
house for a Chicago client, the Missouri Northern Railroad;
transfer to Denver as regional general counsel for what came
to be known as the Missouri and Santa Fe, handling much
of our litigation myself, mostly FELA and grade-crossing
cases.

I began in the securities department, moved to quasi-judicial
hearings before the Federal Railway Administration, then PUC
hearings, finally jury trials, for the theater and the moments of
truth.

I went in-house in 1984 to get in on the deregulation boom
created by the Staggers Act. The Reagan years were the railroads' second golden age, a freewheeling heyday of mergers
and downsizing and glorious profits guarded by immunity
from antitrust laws. A laughingstock, moribund industry
became the apple of Wall Street's eye and more monopolistic
than the robber barons' wildest dreams. Employment was cut
by two-thirds in five years. From a peak of 2.2 million
employees in the 1920s just two hundred thousand remained
by the mid-eighties to man the most extensive and least safe
advanced railway system in the world. But that vestigial work-
force earned on average the highest wages in the country. June
and Dale Stillwell were in high cotton, but nowhere near as
high as mine.

My first years in Denver I worked under Henry Steele, an
old-school railroad lawyer, a lifer. Henry's code of loyalty
meant not reflecting on the consequences of your labors except
as they advanced your client's cause. Always be ethical, he
taught me, and always be mean as hell. I was not an employee of
a corporation. I was a lawyer, goddammit, with a single client to
whom every obligation ran. We were Steele and Stone, railroad
lawyers and tough as railspikes.

Before he retired to Vail with golf clubs, Telemark skis, and a
forty-year railroad watch, Henry Steele bestowed on me a little

molded-plastic figure with bright red skin, a fiendish grin, horns and tail and pitchfork, and a brass baseplate reading:

Elliot Stone
DEVIL'S ADVOCATE

Henry was gone and the eighties were over, but I stayed where I was. My income kept climbing. I could do the work in my sleep. I indulged the conceit I had railroading in my blood. One grandfather was an Irish-American switchman for the Illinois Central, the other an assimilated German Jew. My Dutchess County parents in their IBM retirement community preserved little from either heritage, which freed me to indulge sentimental notions of railroads and old-world origins. The railroad work got harder and harder to sentimentalize.

From where we lived on Mapleton Hill, in Boulder, in five minutes I could be running a bluestem meadow trail or alongside a white-water canyon or up a knife-edge sandstone ridge. Kathleen taught fourth graders in a historic stone schoolhouse with a bell tower and a hilltop view of the Flatirons. Between finger math, cursive, world capitals, and environmental indoctrination, she played guitar and thrilled them with tales of leprechauns and banshees. On Sunday nights she sang at Wandering Aengus with a Celtic band. For her students and also for me, Kathleen created a safe place filled with song, an Irish fairy ring that walled out my increasingly demoralizing occupation.

For years I'd pipe-dreamed about an appellate judgeship. It might have gone no further except that Kathleen died. The fairy ring was breached and I faced what my work really meant. With Moss's prodding I applied and came in second—nominated by the commission but passed over by the governor. The bulk of the state supreme court's caseload was criminal. I'd tried only civil cases for only one corporation since I'd been in Colorado. The governor urged me to broaden my experience and credentials and try again next vacancy.

Coming up with impressive criminal-trial experience midcareer in Colorado looked next to impossible. Then, one winter evening in 1996, I sat in by chance on an Amnesty International film about the Omarska concentration camp in the Serb Republic in Bosnia. Afterward, three former inmates spoke, Muslim women who'd been made to witness their husbands' executions, had themselves been raped for months on end and then forcibly exiled. Shame as an instrument of ethnic cleansing—they'd never return to their places of violation—but, in their cases, a miscalculation by the psychotechnologist, Dr. Radovan Karadzic, president of Bosnian Serbs. All three were en route to testify in The Hague in the first trial in history of sexual assaults as crimes of war.

I was stunned by the understated courage of these widows, the taboos they'd overcome "to let the world know," as one said in a quiet voice, with downcast eyes. Here was strength in the face of such suffering and loss my own should be comfortably borne.

I was ready to enlist. My first foolish thought was, Kathleen would want me to. Kathleen would be proud. My next foolish thought was of Dr. Leitner, whose weaving of the humanitarian with the professional I'd long envied. My most foolish thought was that, part Irish, part Jewish, I could understand sectarian and ethnic conflict as well as anyone.

I read up on the region and human-rights law. I watched CNN as the massacre of eight thousand at Srebrenica came to light. I looked up Harvard connections in the State Department. A former colleague at Skadden Arps was recruiting prosecutors through the American Bar Association, and I renewed his acquaintance. For a promise to reciprocate when I had the chance, I got a strong reference letter from Hans Leitner, well known at the UN. Things fell into place. I got the job, with a two-year commitment. Trial attorney for the Office of the Prosecutor for the International Criminal Tribunal for the former Yugoslavia. The OTP of the ICTY. I loved the ring of acronyms, the sense of mission.

The problem I'd studied in philosophy at Oxford was whether Kant had successfully answered Hume. Hume proved not only that we cannot know the truth, but there is no truth. No causes and effects, only antecedents and consequents. Meaningless sequences of disconnected experience. In other words, shit happens. Kant championed the truth-finding faculty of intuition, the model of democratic freedom, the authority of subjective knowledge. He proposed a universal moral standard, the categorical imperative: act as you would have all others act.

Yo, Kant. My man. The man, that is, of my sunlit youth.

But my defense of his idealism against Hume's nihilism ultimately failed to convince my thesis supervisor—or me. Kant and Hume came to represent the irreconcilable duality of Europe itself, both shining model and cautionary tale. I left Kant's ideals for Harvard Law, and Hume had been stealing back ground ever since. The categorical imperative doesn't hold up well in the adversarial system.

Then there I was back in Europe trying to find a place for Kant's ideals again. By August in The Hague I was scrubbing at cigarette stains inside a brick canalhouse with bay windows and beveled mullions and a twenty-foot rhododendron in back. Around me was the sunken land of children's stories, Frisian cattle and barrier dunes, egalitarian cyclists with regal bearings, the artificial forests of the queen.

In September I made my first trip to the former Yugoslavia for an exhumation outside of Vukovar and got my first stomach-turning blast of Balkan reality. As lead prosecutor on the Vukovar case, I could express a preference in expert witnesses, and I did. Hans Leitner was as well credentialed as his handful of rivals, maybe ten in the world, an obvious choice as medical examiner for the mass grave site and a personal touchstone for my new career.

After the exhumation I continued intermittently to work with him both in Vukovar and The Hague. Leitner's Boulder patient, my onetime ward, came up briefly only once. Otherwise, in the dying bale fires of the Bosnian war, the strange, sad story of June and Dale receded entirely from view.

By December in The Hague it was dark by four. All that first winter the canals never froze and colorful Dutch on silver skates never glided down them. In the gloom I passed their uncurtained flats, North Sea gusts tugging my umbrella like a fish on the line. In a flat, gray, wet country, chockablock with people, I missed the West, that clear and sunstruck land.

But by summer Dutch days were eighteen hours long. The trial of Darko Jovanovic, the Serb mayor of Vukovar, got under way with a short-lived fanfare of media attention. The morning of opening statements I was intercepted at the base of the double spiral stairs by the CNN correspondent, emerging insectlike from a nest of technicians with boom mikes and cameras. I deferred her questions to our press officers. I had a case to try. In a black robe with a white bib, I had a stand to take for moral idealism in the late twentieth century.

The war crimes tribunal was an exercise in applied philosophy, the categorical imperative enforced by UN bureaucrats like me. Cases were assigned by ethnicity. I got Serbs—the plum, or so I thought until I went to the Republika Srpska. Serbs put a Balkan twist on the hoary problem of evil. *Why,* the philosopher inquires, did God create a world in which evil happens? Serbs complicate the inquiry: *How* could otherwise admirable people who mostly share our values commit such savage acts?

The Serb conundrum: *How can the good do evil?*

To which the Stoics had a simple dodge: It doesn't matter. Only one thing matters: how to lead your life. Pay attention to the things you can change; ignore the things you can't; have faith in knowledge.

In other words—*get real.* Facts are your friends, as Moss liked to put it. My version, framed on the wall in my home office, is *Quantum Scimus Summus.*

We are what we know.

June Stillwell lay on her side facing the wall, motionless as a rock in a stream as the mooing and monologues passed over. At my request Rico, the day nurse, a big guy with a pigtail, had brushed and spread across the pillow June's long, Pre-Raphaelite hair. Red-brown and woven with gold, gleaming like fine wire. Luminous, weightless, timeless, as I imagine the hair that grows after death.

I tacked a color copy of a photograph of June's daughter, April, at the spot on the wall she faced. Blue eyes, white smile, purple gown, gold honor student tassel on a black mortarboard. I reminded June of the visit planned for that afternoon, April's first to Colfax Center for Rehabilitation.

I looked forward to April's coming, for June's sake, and to spell me. I'd returned from two years in Europe at something of a loss. The Vukovar case had not ended well. I wasn't going back to the railroad, but that's about all I knew. I had time on my

hands and little desire to spend it in a makeshift home office
among memories of Kathleen. My surprise appointment as
June's conservator required some visits to Colfax, and I welcomed the excuse to be in Denver. June could use the company,
I thought, and she couldn't contradict me.

Three weeks after my return, and two weeks after June was
injured, Judge Otero had asked me to serve as temporary conservator. I called April, a twenty-year-old college student in California, to explain my role and report on her mother's status.
Now legally responsible for June's well-being, I needed to know
her life story, who she was. April and I had rambling weekly
conversations. Distraught people, I'd learned in the former
Yugoslavia, sometimes speak more freely by telephone. It's an
ordering process, and April got into it. She tried to bring her
mother to life for me.

April was two years and half a summer session into a BS in
biochemistry at Santa Cruz when she was notified by Boulder
police that June had been found unconscious in bed with no sign
anyone other than Dale Stillwell had been with her. April flew
back for a three-day vigil in the hospital. June was ventilated,
and most of her face and head were bandaged. Stillwell
appeared once in the waiting room, and the bad blood between
April and him was such that a guard was called. When June was
out of danger and breathing on her own, April returned to her
dorm to finish the session and save what she could waiting
tables at a crab joint on the boardwalk for an extended Colfax
visit. Each week I filled her in on her mother's subtle signs of
progress, careful to lower expectations, and she filled me in on
her mother's life.

April was the only child of an abusive first marriage of high
school sweethearts. June, herself an only child whose mother
died young, had been raised by her father on a ranch at the foot
of the Wind River Range. She had gone to school in Lander and
was head cheerleader her senior year. Buck Mooney was an all-
Wyoming outside linebacker with a chip on his shoulder, and a
long-haul trucker for a yogurt company after he and June moved
to Cheyenne. The marriage lasted eleven years, in the first of
which April was born.

Her childhood had been okay, regular, April told me, up
until first or second grade. Her father was nice enough when

he was around. June worked back then in the deli at the IGA. On weekends she showed Yuma in horsemanship events around the state. Yuma was a dark palomino with a cream mane and tail, black saddle and bridle, a martingale with silver conchas on the breast band. The three of them trailered Yuma all over Wyoming, June driving because Buck was off. June had a gift with animals, April told me, and again I thought of Kathleen.

The last years of the marriage weren't okay. "Dad got to be a serious asshole." Buck accused June of affairs while he was on the road and beat her for lying when she denied it.

A weakness for destructive men was June's undoing. For spite, she began seeing a Medicine Bow forest ranger who liked to cut loose when he came to town. Buck found out. The ranger got scared and stayed away with his own wife, and the beatings June half believed she deserved began in earnest. Buck sent her three times to the ER with broken ribs, a broken wrist, and a torn spleen. It took April, their pastor, June's father, horse-show friends, friends from work, a lawyer, and a quarter bottle of Maker's Mark before June could call the sheriff. After that she was on her way, pressing charges and filing for divorce.

Within a week of the restraining order June gave notice at the IGA. Acting on a notion she'd long entertained, she applied for the Western Pacific's engineer school in Laramie. She got the high scores of the year on the entrance exam and the cab simulator, and a leader's profile in the personality survey. An aptitude for multipart mechanical tasks had been waiting to be discovered. She didn't even need the gender preference. As she saw it, a fifty-ton GE switch engine couldn't be that great a step from a twenty-foot Diamond D horse trailer. Not for a liberated woman. You need to watch out for your freight and be careful backing up.

June swore off men for a time. She promised April she'd never again be with someone who hurt her.

She was soon a favorite at the WP yard, a Casey Jones, making twice what Buck got moving yogurt. She and April had some good years in their man-free home, hitting the weekend horse shows, making big travel plans that never quite came off. But April was different. A 4-H dropout and a 4-point scholar, she dreamed of cities, coasts, careers. Jocks and cowboys weren't for her. She got a reputation as the class feminist. She bragged about her mother's job while secretly feeling like her guardian.

Then, for reasons unknown, on a Christmas day, June crushed a man while driving her engine into a storm, and her scaffolding of independence and self-reliance came to pieces like matchsticks. How could she, in the job she was so good at, have done something so awful that caused such terrible harm? She gave up everything, even her daughter, to devotion to the man she'd hurt.

April stayed in Cheyenne to finish high school while June followed Stillwell from hospital to hospital. She sold her horse and trailer and took disability leave from the railroad. She kept a journal on her computer of Stillwell's recovery. She obsessed on his getting better. To April's horror, they married in Boulder April's junior year. She drove down from Cheyenne, hysterical, confronting Stillwell for deceiving and using her mother, and Stillwell locked her out of the apartment. After that she and June would meet halfway in Fort Collins at the Olive Garden near I-25. There was always some tension. June visited once in Santa Cruz after April went to college. Parents' weekend. June didn't seem real interested. April felt abandoned and let it show. She scoffed at June's grim mission to save Dale Stillwell, her anxious news of the progress of the lawsuit, the idea that settlement money could change anything.

April saw June's devotion as servitude. She despised Dale Stillwell, a good-looking bad guy who'd taken her mother away.

It is a commonplace that coma simulates sleep. The comatose, when not aroused, resemble dreamers, peaceful, even blissful. Their tranquillity can seem enviable to the conscious, until a shudder or grimace or the opening of an eye, myoclonic tremors, or the smacking of gums compels you to remember the life locked inside, clawing against the portal.

Except for two days a month, when Ivan Silverman, its outside medical director, made his hurried rounds, Colfax, nominally a hospital, was a doctor-free zone. Everyone in Colfax was a Medicaid patient, a ward of the state. The state had decided its wards did not require personal physicians. According to Silver-

man, though June's prognosis was guarded, she was healthy.
She might stay this way who knew how long. A living death, not
a peaceful sleep.

But anything could happen. Two weeks after she was hurt,
June's decerebrate posturing stopped. Her clutched hands and
bent and twisted wrists relaxed. Her fingers rested lightly in her
lap. She grew able to move them, especially a thumb, sometimes
on command. She began to move her right foot, her mouth, her
eye. In her eye I could see a knowing light. I began to recognize
a struggle to continue—pain, sorrow, and not happiness, but
interludes of peace.

June was admitted to Colfax at the beginning of August with
a coma/near-coma rating of 1.5—extreme, like her roommate.
Ten days later she'd progressed to level 2.5 on the Rancho Los
Amigos scale—intermittent responsiveness to one-step com-
mands. The week before April's visit, Jasmine, the OT,
recorded, for the first time, greater than 50 percent accuracy
responding to simple instructions: raise your foot, move your
thumb, move your pinkie, close your eye, open your mouth,
lower your foot. Levels 3 to 3.5—near-consciousness.

June looked healthy, lovely really, except where she'd been
hurt, which was remarkable since she was being nourished
with nothing more than liquid feedbags and cans of Nutren
1.5 through a G-tube into her stomach. Every four hours
another can down the hatch; once a day at the midnight check
the feedbag of colorless fluid draining to the feeding pump
from an IV pole; once a week after the Sunday feedbag Rico
plunging a piston syringe into the stoma to her stomach to
draw out 60 cc's of gray-green bile to refrigerate for laboratory
evaluation.

The day of April's arrival I approached with a sponge stick
and toothbrush to touch up June's mouth and lips and teeth. It
had taken a while to master this chore, but now I found it oddly
gratifying, the kind of care I never got to offer during Kathleen's final illness. The mouth goes to hell when it stops pro-
cessing food and fluid. Oral hygiene is a grind. Swabbing the
inside of June's cheeks with a sponge cube and twisting up the
coating from her gums and lips was difficult enough. Brushing
her teeth stimulated an involuntary response, forceful chewing
with bared teeth like a tasteless parody of poor table manners.

It needed doing twice a day, and the staff couldn't be relied on. What got to me, though, was working close around June's face where I couldn't help confronting what had been done to her. Her crushed orbit and shattered porcelain eye.

I patted June's cheeks and chin with a damp cloth and reminded her how special today was. Her skin was baby soft and white, "blossom pale," like Yeats's Maud Gonne's. Her left eye watched me, expressive, sentient, I would think at less judicious moments, running to clichés: a well of feelings, even of wisdom, a window between worlds.

Someone was at the door. "Knock knock." It pushed open. April, whom I recognized from her picture. I said how pleased I was to finally meet her.

"Yeah? Same here." She started in, then stopped, taking it in. "Hey, Mom."

In the photograph April's hair hung straight below the mortarboard. There in the room, loopy black curls sprang in all directions from under a black cap. She had a dusky complexion, high cheeks, bright lips—almost Latin. Rings on each hand. Tight jeans and a jean vest over a T-shirt with a photo-transferred likeness of—could that be Madeleine Albright?

Not whom I'd expected from our weekly conversations. I'd expected a college kid, bright and stressed, and she was. I hadn't expected a force to be reckoned with.

"I feel like I know you," I said anyway.

"Yeah?"

"All those phone calls, and—here you are."

"Here I am." She smiled quickly and came past me into the room. Her black cap, brim backward, was lettered GODDESS.

"Wait. Wait a minute. She's sleeping."

But April had reached the wall that June lay facing. She edged between it and the bed.

"Wait."

"I never saw—her hair. Like that. It's—beautiful." April nodded vigorously in my direction. "It's great."

"April, wait. Have you seen your mother's face?"

"Not since"—she shook her head—"a million years?" She leaned close and extended her right arm like a priest. She lowered it softly, caressed the riffles of hair. She collected some strands stuck to her mother's brow and pulled them away. She

kissed June's cheek just below the ruined eye and drew back to
contemplate the damage.

Then the mooing started.

"Oh my *God.* Shut *up.*" April gave me a desperate look. She
had her mother's fragile blue gaze. "Can you make it *stop*?"

CHAPTER 4

I never doubted what had happened to June,
because I had witnessed the moment of truth.

The details of her life, as known to April, were sketchy and
gap-ridden after she'd married Stillwell. June's Wyoming support group didn't follow her to Boulder. Some, like her father,
had died; others scattered or just lost touch. The best record is
in the journal in the hard drive of her laptop, confiscated by the
police and printed out at my request. It consists mostly of personal observations about Dale's progress mixed up in self-help
bravado and New Age koans, I Ching throws for a brighter
future. Behind its rose-colored self-deceptions a shadowed
authenticity comes through, the true emotional colors of their
lives.

What bound the Stillwells seemed to be the unstable compound of his needs and her guilt for creating them, together with
a physical attachment that sounded genuine. Dale's injuries
appeared to exaggerate somewhat antisocial tendencies. While
sociable enough—leading cheers, showing horses, bantering at
the switching-yard beanery—June did not seem like much of a
social person herself. She was sentimental about isolation.
When she fantasized it was of lonely rides on the prairie or trav-
els in exotic lands with April or alone.

In Boulder, June and Dale Stillwell kept their distance from caregivers and apparently had no close friends. Only April, it seemed, would try to break into their shuttered world. April was largely cut off herself, except for twice-monthly phone calls. She never set foot in their house.

Turning inward after a traumatic loss and losing interest in the company of others was something I had no trouble understanding. I was also coming to appreciate how helping someone who'd become disabled can help you piece your own life together. Through four years of marriage, June was Dale's caregiver, secretary, bookkeeper, and, as a matter of my legal succession, his guardian and conservator. Certainly, she cared for him profoundly. She fell for his cryptic intensity, his almost charismatic differentness. But she also seemed to be doing penance. "I can tell when he's thinking about the accident though he denies he is. I can't believe I hurt him so bad. We're going to make it, Dale."

I tried to imagine this woman of high, wide Wyoming in her confinement, pouring out her hopes at the laptop, while, outside, her husband ceaselessly shot baskets at the carport hoop and backboard—bup bup k-*thong,* bup buppa-*thong*—until the neighbors called. Five houses were jammed around their cul-de-sac keyhole, and sometimes Dale kept at it into the night. The neighbors understood, June wrote, and Dale would make it up to them.

June's journal is a record of hope always rising. She remained the optimist I'd met in Judge Otero's jury room. She insisted Dale would work again. That he was getting so much better. That she understood why some blowup wasn't his fault. But she left out all distressing facts—what the blowup was, how he acted when he was worse.

At her urging he began volunteering at the Boulder Shelter and they loved him. Aloof, dignified, diligent, hashing beans and wieners for the homeless schizos and heroin washouts, the Khe Sanh cases among whom he was not disabled, to whom his abilities mattered.

A trait emerged in June's descriptions of Dale. He liked to do favors. He shoveled every driveway and sidewalk on the cul-de-sac every time it snowed. In the summer he hauled off everybody's yard trash. He pitched in on weekend chores. He built back self-worth by helping others. At home he was a ceaseless

handyman. He did all the housework, except for anything that
had to do with money.

June began to volunteer too, as a two-day-a-week assistant at
the Therapeutic Riding Center on Dale's shelter days. Within
the year she was NARHA-certified by the North American Riding for the Handicapped Association to instruct the disabled and
train therapy horses. She taught grooming and tacking to those
in wheelchairs and coached ring games and obstacle courses for
kids with cerebral palsy. In the foothills, she led trail rides for
adults with brain injuries or multiple sclerosis.

As in all her occupations, with the disabled June was an
unqualified success. She mounted her CP riders as young as four
or five to stretch calves and heels, strengthen muscles, and
rotate pelvises. Some even learned to post at the trot, and a few
were show-ready by season's end. "Breaking barriers," she
wrote, "is my job." She and her horses transitioned two
teenagers, wheelchair-bound all their lives, to walking with
crutches. To "the miracle of walking."

Back in her rodeo cap and jacket, June was at home. She
knew what horses teach of freedom and bonding with nature.
She knew the rhetoric of body language, the magic power of
reins. She had faith that an easy-gaited plug could teach a CP kid
more than any clinical therapy. That plodding around the ring on
the massive back of a slow-moving beast would realign his
brain/body relationships. That afterward he'd plant his braces
with heartbreaking new confidence.

The center asked June to be program coordinator, a paid
position. She turned down the salary, which she didn't need, but
accepted the job and expanded her hours. She began to write
excitedly of her kids, her horses, her trainers, Anna—her Special Olympian—a circle ride the highlight of the week for her
Down's boy, Danny. She wrote about the sense of mastering the
physical, and thus the promise of overcoming injury or disease,
that could be gained from reining and turning a creature the size
of a horse. "I was born a caregiver and never knew it," she
wrote. "Going back to where I came from, I discovered myself."

Then, according to the center, four months before she was
hurt, June quit. I wondered if it was at Stillwell's insistence. I
guessed he might see it, paid or not, as a real job, and that he
couldn't bear for the person who had disabled him to work,

though the journal doesn't say so. About Stillwell, June was
never critical, always upbeat. She allowed herself one forlorn
complaint—"Why can't I live my life?"—for which she quickly
upbraided herself. "Remember to see it Dale's way too. Life's a
process. It's a journey. A partnership." The cops, who were after
a history of abuse, found the journal worthless because of this
kind of thing. Its one telling line—"Why should I have to live in
fear?"—was written twenty-seven months before the assault
and didn't reference Stillwell.

I read the journal as a between-the-lines story of deepening
codependent distress into which the ever-sunny author had little
insight, a subtle foreboding that got more ominous when the
writing stopped. I saw it as the veiled narrative of a marriage
that had spiraled inward and compressed, like a dying star, until
its impacted density could no longer be sustained.

My duties as June's conservator included inventorying and
marshaling her assets. I visited their cedar-shingled cottage-
with-carport on the cul-de-sac in their north Boulder look-alike
development. I videotaped her rooms of things—"June's junk,"
Stillwell called it, trailing behind me. Tyrolean cuckoo clocks.
David Winter figurines from her favorite shop, the Mole Hole.
Ceramic replicas of the Grand-Place in Brussels, the Arc de Tri-
omphe, the Bridge of Sighs. A cabinet of onyx bears and seals,
ivory scrimshaw and netsuke. A case of soigné dolls, Infants of
Prague in spangled dresses, holding silver globes.

One hamper contained at least a hundred caps—feed caps,
baseball caps, caps reading Chugwater Round-Up and Big Tim-
ber Stampede, and zebra-hatched railroad engineer's caps like
Bob Dylan and John Lennon had affected, but which, in June's
case, were earned. There was a wall of framed pictures—June
astride Yuma, the palomino; her engineer's diploma; a glassed
case of horse-show ribbons; April's graduation photograph; a
wedding photo in a hospital chapel as stagy as a Reno drive-in
nuptial.

June's tastes spanned the map from Old World to Wild West.
The more I found out about her, I told April at the White Spot,
where we'd gone to talk, the more interesting she seemed.
"Yeah?" April looked dubious, but it was true. June struck me as
someone whom, at a different time, and in a different life, I
would at the least have wanted to get to know.

Stillwell said he didn't want June's junk around, meaning the figurines, clocks, dolls, and onyx animals. I cataloged and boxed and moved them to a storage locker Stillwell agreed to rent. At the police station, I looked at photographs and read the field reports. At home, I tried to make some sense of June's financial records, bank statements, credit card receipts. It looked as if the money she spent on curios and collectibles, and generous donations to the Therapeutic Riding Center, had all come from her husband's account.

In the corner booth at the White Spot, April's arms lay across the booth back, black cap snug, the determined features of the secretary of state thrust in my direction. Face-to-face, April was more guarded than she sounded voice-to-voice. As, perhaps, was I. We were feeling each other out, interviewing each other. April's was the more focused interest. She burned to know what had happened the night before June was found.

On White Spot breaks I preferred the corner booth my wait-ress buddy, Darla, tried to save for me. I sat toward the window with an encompassing view of the neo-penal architecture of Colfax Rehab—an in-your-face cube of blue-brown brick in a lake of asphalt. Rarely more than a handful of cars parked in the unstriped lot. At the far end homies played pickup at a lone bas-ket, negotiated the sale of goods, and manned an isolated pay-phone hood. The severity of the place commanded your respect—treeless, grassless, the loading bay black as a cave, the fourth window on the ground floor where June's room was, the signs of decay, weeds in cracks and crumbling mortar, the tar-nished metal letters—C LFAX. Dark, mean, and brutal, Colfax mocked as weak and bourgeois pretense our soft desires for pleasant places.

"You like caps, like your mom," I noted awkwardly, tracking from back- to foreground.

"Mom's thing," April replied. "Cap queen of the north. The Imelda Marcos of caps."

"Like mother, like daughter?" I wondered. She looked blank. I tapped my head.

"Oh." She tapped hers.

"Your names too," I said. "I like that. I like 'April.' Very pretty. Very positive associations."

"Like showers. Like ape."

"April-June, June-April, was that the idea?"

"You think that's funny?"

I said I didn't. I thought they had really great names. Simple springtime names that made me think of birds and blossoms, seeds sprouting, days getting longer.

"Simple," she said. "You think my name is stupid."

"Not at all."

"Yes, you do. You think we're hayseeds with funny names."

"I like funny names."

"See," she said. "Funny."

April removed her GODDESS headgear and shook her springy, black hair. She smiled sideways to let me know she was teasing, then, in what I'd learn was a characteristic turn, retracted, soberly introspective.

"Mom'd tuck her hair up in a cap." April frowned. "Mom never did anything with it. Her hair." April made a crown, then thumped it out. "Stillwell have, like, a record?" she asked abruptly.

I told her no criminal history was summarized in the reports in the police investigation file. What did April know about him?

"From Nebraska someplace. Foster home I think I heard. Railroader out of Alliance. Had a reputation is why I asked. Supposed to be a 'hat,' a troublemaker. Ladies' man. Had to have come to Laramie to get away from something, which probably appealed to Mom. You know, dangerous fun. Goddamn Mom."

April spoke with a flatness that was troubling, though she had cause. She thought her mother had broken her promise, then cut April out of her life. I asked if she was upset with June. I tried for delicacy but still provoked tears.

"I shouldn't have let her marry him. *I'm the one who went away.*" She was suddenly disconsolate. "How could she stop him by herself?" She huffed and blew her cheeks. "God." She got up for the ladies' room. Darla eyed her, then glanced at me.

When April returned, I tried for reassurance. "Your mother is an amazing person, you know. Not just compassionate, but strong, heroic even. You should be proud of her."

"Yeah? Well, I am." She drew a tangle of hair across her face and inspected the ends. "Let's talk about the night in question."

• • •

I told her what I knew.

For the ten months before June's injury, the journal was blank. The cops hadn't been able to flesh out much of anything of the last year of their lives together. No one from the riding center, the shelter, no one who'd treated Stillwell, seemingly no one at all had known them the final year. It was as though June and Dale Stillwell had dropped off the face of the earth.

In the detectives' reports April was quoted as having called her mother at ten the night she was assaulted, and again at eleven, and at midnight, and no one ever answered. Why, I asked, had she been trying to reach her?

"I was worried from the night before," April said. "She seemed, like, depressed for months. She used to be so—posi-tive. We talk usually two times a month. When I'm home, I call Mom and hang up after one ring so she knows it's me, and Mom calls back so the call's on her. When he's there listening, we had this code way to talk. I talk and Mom goes 'yes' or 'no' so Still-well's just, duh.

"So the night before the night Mom gets hurt I do the usual one-ring hang-up and Mom calls back and we do the code. 'Is he there with you?' I say. 'Yes.' 'Can you talk?' 'No.' But she sounded kind of funny. 'Is he treating you okay, Mom?' I ask real soft. She says, 'Okay,' even softer. 'But something's wrong?' 'Yes,' she says. 'How's he doing? Worse?' She says, 'Yes.' 'Is it worse than it was with Dad?' I ask her, meaning my dad, and she says, 'Yeah, it is, different but worse.' I ask if she's worried and she says yes. I ask if she's afraid and she says yes. Then she says she has to go.

"*Worse than Dad.* That's, like, nearly the last thing Mom ever said to me." April shivered from her moment of truth. "So that was too scary. So I called the next night and all night I kept calling. It must have been while he—was doing it."

April wore her emotions on her sleeve. A human mood ring. Her present mood was stricken.

"But she said he was treating her okay?"

"He was sitting right there." April knocked a nail against a tooth. "What else do we know he did?"

"He attacked your mother once in the hospital in 1994. Doc-tors said he was delusional from brain injury. He attacked a cog-nitive therapist in 1995. In 1996 he attacked a veterinarian when his dog was hit by a car and they hospitalized him on a seventy-two-hour hold. Apparently he threatened Hancock. The cops don't know about that. But . . ." I shrugged.

"What?"

"Except for the one delusional attack, there's no history of violence toward your mother. Just what I heard him say and what your mother seemed to be telling you. You and me—we're it."

"So—what do you think?"

"I think being crushed between two engines left your stepfather a dangerous man. The compensation—the money—for his injuries made things worse, magnified the dangers." Indeed, in my view it was a case study in the smoldering resentments of codependency fanned to flames by money. Blood money I'd cavalierly approved.

"I *mean,*" April repeated, leaning forward, "what *exactly* happened that night? I can take it. And please don't call him that."

"I hope you're ready." I took a breath and gave her the story according to the cops. At 8:01 A.M., July 15, 1998, Dale Stillwell called 911 to report his wife had fallen and was bleeding. At 8:05, emergency personnel found her covered with blankets, though it was July, unconscious, on her back on a blood-soaked mattress, a gaping bell-shaped wound to the right side of her face. The blood in the wound was crusted. The bone of the orbit was shattered and exposed, the globe of the eye dislodged.

April flushed and looked away. Out the window a Falcon delivery truck for durable medical equipment was backing into the Colfax loading bay. Its beeper sounded like a tolling bell.

The state criminalists and blood-spatter analyst thought June Stillwell had been rendered unconscious by blunt-force trauma from a single blow with an instrument with an irregular edge. The edge appeared beveled with a hollow center. Given the pattern of depressions in the bedding and pillows, the pooling of blood into the mattress directly beneath her head, and the lack of blood elsewhere in the house, June was struck while in bed. She may have been sleeping. She never moved after she was injured. And the blow was inflicted from a standing position with considerable downward force.

In the police photo taken that morning, Stillwell, who doesn't drink, looked like someone on a bender. A small red lump was on his right-center forehead. He told the detectives he and June had stayed up watching a *Northern Exposure* rerun. Then he thinks he watched the news. Maybe CNN. Something on the news. After leaving a note for the milkman, he joined her in bed, he said. He woke at seven-thirty after an uneventful sleep. He went out to walk Monty, their pug. Maybe fifteen minutes later he returned to find June hurt and bleeding. He thought she must have fallen then staggered back to bed. So he called for help.

Stillwell didn't believe he'd locked up behind him when he took Monty out to "do his business." Something might have happened then, he said. Had the door been locked throughout the night? It might not have been, Stillwell nodded. The cops found no signs of a break-in. No neighbor had heard a dog barking. Except for the front door the house was shut tight, every window bar-locked and clasped.

"What else have they got?"

"Not a whole lot." The blunt instrument hadn't been found. Detectives had swept the ground with metal detectors, dug up Stillwell's garden, crawled the neighbors' roofs. But there was a gap in the row of knickknacks on the fireplace mantel. They took photographs and diagrammed a pattern of dust surrounding a clean, irregular, nine-centimeter oval on the mantel's smooth, black marble.

April shifted in the booth, agitated. "Want to tell me why he's still walking around? It's obvious, right? I mean, Jesus."

"It's obvious he's lying, which helps, of course. But—he's a head case."

April rolled her eyes.

"It's what Stillwell's lawyers will say, and you need to know where they're coming from. They'll say Stillwell gets confused. You can't hold his grief-stricken babblings against him. I know his doc, Hans Leitner. He's dynamite in a witness box. He'll say Stillwell has a heart of gold and couldn't harm a fly. Plus, he's *adjudicated incompetent.* Plus, your mom can't tell her side. Plus, his neighbors all think he's the greatest, at least when he's not shooting hoops."

"So we just need to show he's the worst."

"Not *we.* The DA, who can be faint of heart. He wants to send the blankets down for hair and fiber analysis. Knowing him, he probably hopes to find signs of an unknown third party so he'll never have to charge."

"But this is, like, so—*duh.* Man." She sighed. "It's open and shut."

"It's circumstantial, as DA Tucker sees it. And it doesn't quite add up. And with a maybe unlocked door an intruder can't be ruled out. And it's not the expected pattern, Tucker tells me. Wife beaters use multiple blows. Batterers batter. Striking a single time doesn't fit the profile. And there's always some kind of history, he says." I opened a hand. "It's how these people think."

"How do we change how they think?"

"Find witnesses. Like somebody who could say what their lives were like their past year. Better yet, find the weapon."

April nodded. None of this did she find daunting. "What happens if we don't?"

"It's an ongoing investigation, is how Tucker puts it."

"Meaning?"

"Meaning Stillwell remains under 'an umbrella of suspicion,' as he calls it, but he and the cops suspend activity on the case so long as it's an assault."

"You're saying—if Mom doesn't make it—"

"They might take it more seriously. Sorry. Otherwise we need some kind of unified theory Tucker will buy to move him off square one. He's scratching around in all the usual chicken crap. The crime scene's not clean because she was carried out to the ambulance before they could photograph her. No weapon, no confession, no witnesses. No physical evidence tying him to the blow. No history of abuse. Supposedly no motive."

"Yeah? He's crawling with motive."

"Tucker doesn't see it, I guess. He's a cautious man. Gunshy, according to his critics. A dishrag DA when a suspect's got money."

April swallowed distastefully. "What do you think?"

"About motive? Everything fits."

I thought June's control over Stillwell's money probably became unacceptable to him. He'd been getting better, which only increased his frustration. He thought he could run his affairs himself and his resentment mounted. He had reason to resent June for all kinds of things: his injuries, his constricted life, her spending his money on herself, her legal authority over him, the emasculation all of that entailed. He couldn't sign a check. She was detaching from him and engaging the world again, while he was still trapped and dependent. He was jealous of her success and afraid of losing her too.

It appeared from the journal that Stillwell had stopped treatment close to a year before. With nobody to reason with him, calm him down, his resentments may have become unmanageable. Something June did—a complaint, a request, an expenditure, a slight—may have sent him over the edge. I imagined her sleeping as he brooded. Brooding progressing to rage. He took the receiver off the hook. He found a hard-edged object and approached her. He watched her, swelling with envy and hatred. The cause of all his losses. Why he couldn't do as he liked, spend what he wanted, be who he was. And his hand rose and with all his strength he shattered his sleeping wife's face.

He must then have done something with his weapon and returned. Next, probably, he waited, afraid to approach, letting her life recede. Hour after hour he waited. She never moved. Day broke. Figuring her for dead, he finally called for help.

The mystery to me was not who'd done it. The mystery was why Stillwell seemed unaware of what he'd done.

CHAPTER 5

"I'm not sure I understand—you? How you fit
in."

April rested her chin on a palm at the Formica table at the
White Spot booth. Darla brought a second round. "Cuppa joe for
Gramps," she said. "Pepsi for the younger set." April stayed
locked on me, skeptical but connected. An evaluation was under
way. Sincerity and commitment were being probed.

She'd heard about her mother from a lot of people. She'd
spoken with the chaplain at Flatirons Community Hospital.
Detective Roybal had interviewed her twice, as he had me. She
had had a long, supportive, inconclusive conversation with a
victim's advocate. Millsap, the chief deputy DA, was earnest
and brief. He had given her to know he was doing his job. That
the district attorney made crimes of domestic violence his personal priority. Teachers and classmates counseled patience: let
the system take its course. April's father had called to say, as he
often had, how sorry he was. And of everyone she had talked
with, only one had felt the way she did. Only one shared her
certainty that Dale Stillwell had attacked his wife. Hence our
connection, bridging the Formica gap. We'd each known
moments of truth.

"How I fit in." I frowned. "You want recent history? The
long view?"

"I've got the time." She sucked a line of cola up a straw.

I hadn't been two weeks back when Hancock had called. The catalyst to return was the passing of Justice McGrath of the Colorado Supreme Court, though I'd already decided to stop trying to save the world by prosecuting crimes of war.

In our state a commission of legal and layfolk reviews applications for judgeships and recommends candidates, three per vacancy. At that point politics takes over from merit. The governor interviews the short-listed three and picks the one he wants.

Governor Tom Turner had a lock on his office but, from habit, took nothing for granted. A wiry-haired martinet, he passed himself off as a populist on the strength of a family ranch-equipment business. Except for boosting large public works, he didn't have much of a program. He didn't need to, our constitution having prudently limited the powers of his office to a figurehead's prerogatives. He seemed content to bide time between elections waiting for disaster-scene photo ops—trudging to an avalanche site in snowshoes, puttering across the swollen Platte in an outboard, laying into the fire line with a Pulaski in his yellow protective suit. Governor Tom looked good in a hard hat with choppers juddering overhead. I voted for him too.

One of the few arenas he ruled unchallenged was judicial appointments. The first time I made the commission's final cut for the Supreme Court, I knew it would go no further. Photos of the three nominees looked like a lineup of aging Benetton models. Thomas Garcia. Susan Wu. Me. The governor was candid in our interview. The political pressure was intense, though he insisted his decision would be qualifications-driven. A bunch of letters said I was qualified. But the DAs questioned appointing someone without a background in criminal law.

That became his hook, and who could deny the man the opportunity to place the first Hispanic in state history on our Supreme Court? He led me to understand the next white-male seat was mine. "It's important to me personally that you reapply."

I got the E-mail in The Hague of Justice McGrath's death the same week the Vukovar case I'd worked on for nearly two years finally came to an ambiguous close. My first significant relationship since Kathleen had also reached a turning point, possibly a stopping point. A stupid argument over the usual issues—professional versus personal priorities, career versus commitment. I weighed in for commitment, but on my turf for now. Quierin was commitment-averse. She worked for the tribunal herself, a well-regarded forensic anthropologist. She liked the work and the regard.

Quierin is a difficult person. In Europe it is not a vice to be difficult. It is expected of intelligent people. But Quierin in Boulder? Smoking Gauloises?

It blew up at a good-bye dinner at the Goude Hooft. Quierin fell into addressing me as "you Americans," as though I wanted to be the relationship's only superpower. Then she blurted it out, her direct Dutch side: "You are in love with your wife. She is more alive than me. You are married always. I am your *maltresse,* the kept woman. And *this*—" Her hand flew away. Ash from her cigarette powdered the floor. Gleaming black eyes lit on mine. *"This,"* she hissed, "is adultery."

Outside, the number 3 tram rocked past, ringing its farewell. The stylish *burgerij* strolled and shopped in the endless evening light.

"You've got it backward," I told her. I meant, my problem was not that I was still in love with Kathleen. My problem was that I couldn't love anyone else. That I might not be up to it. Volatile Quierin might vanish so I should go only so far. If I went further, and Quierin left, I might be wrecked again. Irrationally, I feared that Quierin might die too.

"Go home," she commanded, as though I were a child. "Go be a judge." She held a drag, then sighed it defeatedly away. Then she looked up and smiled ambiguously, a person who enjoyed being difficult, who preferred complexity. "I might like you being a judge. I even might come see."

Until Europe brought it to earth, my appellate-judge ambition was basically an escapist fantasy of a quasi-academic life—researching and writing, Socratic exchanges on esoteric abstractions, jurisprudence informed by philosophy. Elevations to the bench by tradition crowned distinguished legal careers. By tradition more than practice, as judicial salaries became less elevated, though that was not an issue for me.

But two years abroad dealing with war crimes had refined my thinking considerably. Professional vanity and social cachet had little to do with it anymore. I wanted to do the work of justice. Without justice, the wasting of democratic freedoms, leading even to Bosnian savagery, was inevitable anywhere. Even here, complacent countrymen, without sure, fair justice vigilantly enforced.

I faxed my application to the judicial nominating commission, gave the UN notice, boxed my belongings with DHL express services, and caught the *sneltren* to Schiphol Airport. I had to get back from Europe to conduct the political campaign the governor's pro forma letter prohibited judicial applicants from engaging in. I managed to be nominated again, and this time with two other white guys. One was politically connected but weakly qualified. The other was Jewish and smart but had enemies.

"Have you always had the beard?" the governor's interview began. "Maybe it's longer?" he said. "Or different? Wasn't it a Vandyke before?"

I smiled and shook my head, already at a loss.

He acknowledged he'd gotten positive letters. "What makes people think you're so smart? Yale, Harvard, Oxford, is that it? What do you think?"

A modest demurral was called for and given. I had no idea where he was going and soon neither did he. "Help me out, Jerry," he said, turning to the kid legal aide sitting in. "You got any questions for Mr. Stone, fire away."

The kid frowned and jotted a note. "Not really, no."

I couldn't take my eyes off the governor's Brillo-pad hair, his metal spectacles, his box-shaped head. I much preferred the hard hat.

"So they all say you're smart." He found his thread. "But some folks wonder about your commitment to justice here in Colorado. They wonder how in touch you are with ordinary people."

They who? The DAs? The criminal defense bar? The FELA weasels?

I tried to explain my views on justice. I told them what I'd seen in Vukovar, Prijedor, Brcko, the extraordinary promise of a world in which courts of law could be instruments not of justice alone, but of peace, reconciliation, and democratic reform. It fell

on deaf ears. Political ears, deaf to reports from beyond the elec-
torate's borders.

"What I need to know," he said, smiling darkly from within
his box, "is why should I pick you?" Code, I realized, for the
crucial question he'd never directly ask: Forget qualifications,
ideals, justice, what can you do for me?

The underqualified guy with connections got the job. His
prohibited political campaign had been managed by Governor
Tom's former finance chairman. I and the smart Jewish nominee
commiserated at the Ship's Tavern about our naïveté and the
death of merit in the legal system.

By then Hancock had called to bring me "up to speed.
There's been an accident. Pretty bad. The Stillwells need some
help. It's—messy."

"Where do I fit in?" I asked, as April would.

"Don't know, but the judge wants you there."

So I end up conservator, I told her. Hanging out with your
mom, licking our wounds, forty-five years old and staring down
the short end of a legal career.

"You mean"—April high-signed Darla for a third Pepsi—
"you're here with Mom 'n' me because you're not a judge?
This isn't a bill-by-the-hour deal, is it?"

I winced at the cynicism of the young. "I'm not sure exactly
why I'm here." I took a sip of tepid coffee and reflected on my
lot. "But no fee till we know where we're headed."

It was peculiar being back. The Balkans don't let go easily.
The best work wasn't in the high-tech courtroom in The
Hague, costumed and encased in grenade-proof glass, putting
on testimony simultaneously translated, transcribed, and
broadcast in three languages to computer monitors, radio
headphones, and closed-circuit TV. The best work was in the
vale of tears, scrounging evidence and chasing down witnesses. I started off expecting bloodthirsty Chetniks who slit
their neighbors' throats. I left bonded to the southern Slavs
who'd captivated Rebecca West. A cultured and tragic race,
Slavic-poetic and Mediterranean warm. Croats, Muslims, and
Serbs too.

The little secret of those who've worked in the former
Yugoslavia, from Bob Dole and Richard Holbrooke, I suspect,
to on-the-ground "internationals" like me, is that the Balkans

are—a high. The place delivers mainline hits of fear and pity, adventure and enlightenment. The legal work was leading edge and righteous. Our express assignment: to fix individual responsibility in order to avoid collective guilt. Break the revenge cycle so that ethnic cleansing will happen, as is said of the Holocaust, never again.

Leaving the hyperstimulating Balkans meant going from Technicolor to black and white. At the far end of the spectrum lay Colfax on the edge of darkness, and the deep night where June Stillwell dwelled. But that's where I was drawn.

Giving up the tribunal, missing out on the judgeship, left me, I thought, at loose ends. In hindsight I was treading water between what I used to be—husband, railroad lawyer, prosecutor—and whoever I really was. I was spending time with a comatose woman I hardly knew to try to figure it out.

I scheduled a round of lunches with hiring partners at the silk-stocking firms on Seventeenth Street and, for the meantime, fitted out a home office I hated spending time in. As soon as I'd opened the door to my house I knew Quierin had been right about me and Kathleen.

After two years away prosecuting war crimes Boulder felt shallow and self-absorbed. Everywhere I found the opaque, searching-elsewhere gaze of the personally trained, striving after personal bests. The wandering look of benign disinterest if I brought up, say, the disappeareds rotting in Bosnian earth. Like the oblivious joggers in a Nike commercial, passing through Y2K Armageddon, aware of nothing but themselves.

Though I was there with them, on a compulsive first-light running regimen, as a sudden sunburst hit the foothills like thermonuclear wind. This was stalking hour in lion country, and running a mountain trail at dawn could approach a Balkan high. Logging twenty-five, thirty, forty miles per week—I had the time and, hey, I lived in Boulder.

Our Boulder friends had all been couples. My guy friends were mostly Denver lawyers. Not yet up to the company of either, and without much steady work despite a halfway horse-choker CV, I found myself often alone. Alone felt right running a trail, but wrong in an empty house, and I visited Colfax more than duty required. I had sound reasons to be there, but a secret reason too. I sought the company of June to commune with Kathleen.

There it was. With unclosed grief you get neuroses.

I wasn't yet ready to confess such things to Quierin. Let her reach her own conclusions. *Hah,* Quierin would say when she thought she had my number. I wanted no *hah*s, or the electronic equivalent. I wrote her matter-of-factly of how I passed my time. It is revealing, Quierin E-observed, that an unconscious person had become my valued companion. The equivalent of a *hah* and a jokey echo of our last argument that pierced my secret and described my plight.

Quierin was unfazed by the lost judgeship and my troubled prospects. Little fazed Quierin. Quierin knew corruption, of the body and the soul. "So what? It is par for the road. Do something else."

"Oh, sure," I E-replied. "Like what?" Hapless gringo-ese.

"Consult is best," she wrote. "Consult is the really rum job. Write books is good too and helps consult. Plus teach, be a lobbier, be elected, go work in your government. Or just go out to make the voyage of spiritual discovery and things like that. Jesus, Elliot, like you say to me. What about travel just to travel? Why so much purpose anyway?"

"So *much*? I feel perfectly purposeless."

"That's talking! Perfect purposelessness is the holy state. You are free. Open up your eyes."

Quierin was only half Dutch, but she had the Dutch compulsion to preach. She had all the Dutch paradoxes—naive sophistication, anything-goes Calvinism, tolerantly didactic, bluntly complex, concretely abstract. Quierin thought America, as she imagined it, endlessly entertaining, especially our commander in chief. *Clean tone,* as Quierin pronounced his name.

"I hear Bill walks around the White House with a pair of women's panties on his arm," she concluded her message.

I knew the drill. I E-replied, "Why is that?"

"He's trying to quit," Quierin E-responded. "He says it's a patch."

●   ●   ●

April was staring at me like a Netherlander and I looked away. I'd lapsed into the confessional with someone I hardly knew. Some Colfax orderlies and Rico, with the pigtail, were rolling wheelchairs like supermarket shopping carts from the Colfax bay into the trailer of the Falcon truck. That seemed kind of backassward. The ghetto streets had been emptied by El Niño's heat. The boiled sky was milky and curdled with clouds. I closed my eyes and the afterimage cooled to purple.

"Your age," I said, "was a problem for Judge Otero at the hearing Hancock phoned me about. One of the problems." April would turn twenty-one in December. Until then she was disqualified from managing her mother's affairs. June had no other living relatives apart from her husband. As a named suspect in her assault, her husband wouldn't do.

A hearing was called in the old probate case opened to approve the FELA settlement, over which Otero retained jurisdiction. The judge faced a nice legal problem, a law school exam question in Trusts and Estates: What do you do when the protector of an incapacitated person herself becomes incapacitated? At the hand, perhaps, of her ward? Two conservators now were called for—one for June because she could no longer act for herself, and one for Stillwell because his conservator, June, could no longer act for him.

At the time of the hearing June lay under intensive care at Flatirons Community Hospital. She was not expected to recover for months, if ever. Monthly annuity checks would be rolling in, uncashable. Enormous physical and financial needs promised to go unmet, and the judge declared his grave concerns.

As he studied the file, forehead propped on his hand, I wondered if Otero harbored second thoughts about what had happened two years earlier. That he might have overreacted to Stillwell's trial behavior then and would feel bound this time to be more particular.

"Mr. Hancock," he said. "As far as I can see, the only person who can legally speak for Dale Stillwell, or hire you to do so, is his wife, and she is unable to speak."

Hancock stood and jangled the change in his pocket. He unfurled a finger and drew a breath, the better to argue the point, but the judge had already moved on. "In these circumstances," he said, "I'm not sure anyone but Mr. Stillwell himself can address his interests. Mr. Stillwell? What do you think?"

Stillwell uncoiled and stood. He wore a blue-checked shirt, jeans, boots, a tooled belt that read DALE in the back. For all his churning intensity he looked pretty cool. Next to Hancock's fluttery unease, he projected a crude dignity. A suggestion, I thought, of poise.

"I'm a whole lot b-better," Stillwell said. "I can take care of me and June both."

Hancock sat muzzled, fidgeting with a cough-drop package. He rattled a couple in a fist and popped them in his mouth. If he hoped, in the event of assault charges, to argue impaired capacity, it looked as if Stillwell was about to blow his defense.

"I know a *lot* more than these *lawyers*," Stillwell then declared, "what these f-fellas give me credit for."

Hancock threw up his hands, half stood, half sat—"whoa, whoa"—but Otero had heard enough.

"Dale Stillwell has today placed his capacity in dispute. A competency hearing is therefore required. This time medical testimony regarding his recovery must be presented. As to Mrs. Stillwell, her need for a conservator is obvious and I so find. But in light of the daughter's age and the husband's adverse interests, no one on the list of statutory preferences qualifies.

"Mr. Stone. You know the case and the couple. You were qualified for a like role already once by this court. Literally no one else is available. June Stillwell's needs are urgent and immediate. I'd like you to step in on a temporary basis. Meet with the daughter, sort it out, come up with something for the longer term. If Mr. Stillwell agrees, can you handle it?"

I glanced at Hancock. He tossed down another cough drop. I said I'd be honored to help but only if Dale Stillwell waived any possible conflicts of interest since I'd acted briefly on his behalf before.

Otero explained to Stillwell at length why he could object to my acting for his wife since his and his wife's interests might now conflict. Did he object?

"I don't have a p-problem with Mr. Stone helping June."

"Mr. Hancock?" Otero said. "Objection?"

"No sir." Hancock grinned as if he'd nailed me.

"No objections noted, the appointment is approved. The clerk will set forthwith an evidentiary hearing to determine Mr. Stillwell's competency. If I find him not competent, his waiver and your temporary appointment will be void, Mr. Stone, and you all will be hearing from me again. Understood?" It was. "Court is adjourned."

As the judge heeled toward the door to his chambers, Stillwell made a further point. "Her k-kid should keep out of this," he called to Otero as his door closed after him.

"Woo," April said. "Beautiful guy."

"Something else came up earlier." My inflection hinted it wasn't good. "Visitation."

"By him? Here?"

"Stillwell claimed he wanted to spend time with his wife. Otero thought it over. Suspect in her assault but he hasn't been charged. Presumed innocent. Presumed grief-stricken spouse. So he decided to allow visits but only on reasonable notice to me as June's conservator, and Stillwell has to be accompanied by a health-care provider who understands his condition."

"Oh my fucking God." April trashed a napkin and flipped it aside. "Fox in the henhouse. He gets to be with Mom?"

"Sorry, April. It's a free world. We've got to adjust."

Before we left the White Spot, April came back to a couple of points. She wanted to know what I was working on that might interfere with working for her mother. And she wanted to know more about Quierin.

I ticked off my modest client list—neighbors with a fence-line dispute, a would-be liquor licensee, an internist fighting former partners over a covenant not to compete.

Cat crap, I told her.

"I'm impressed. Why not go back to suing Serbs? Has to be more interesting than . . . whatever. Not competing."

"I'm looking around. Something will break. Anyway, I can stick it out four months until you replace me."

"What's the real deal, Elliot? Why not go back and sue more of those guys?"

I shrugged disingenuously. There were problems with going back. One I didn't want to talk about was how the Vukovar case had ended. How I wasn't ready for more prime-time mass-murder prosecutions just yet.

"You have a girlfriend," April observed, as though there lay the answer to it all.

"And you have a boyfriend." A plausible conjecture.

"Who? *Kimo?*" She laughed off at the window. "I am way moved on, believe me. I am way grown past Kimo."

I had no idea who Kimo was. "What's he up to?"

"What else? Steamer's Lane. In the puka-shell necklace, waiting for the wave." April struck an illustrative pose. "Kimo in a nutshell. Nutshell's all there is, actually. But, *c'mon.* Back to the point. Quierin the girlfriend. Out with it. Describe."

"She's tall. Chic. Multiracial. Too much perfume. Digs up bodies for a living."

It stopped April cold. "Bodies?"

"Dead people. You asked."

"Oh. Ah. So—the perfume relates?"

"Who knows?" I knew. After working mass graves you need stronger stuff than Shalimar. I tried to explain Quierin. I talked her up, anthropology Ph.D. from Leiden, talented testifying expert, important work for the war-crimes tribunal's Exhumation Unit. A leading taphonomist—a specialist in the analysis of biological remains. Hoping to celebrate her thousandth body later in the year.

Now April really was impressed. She flashed me a glance that felt minutely more admiring.

"What I still don't totally get, though, is why you're, like, honored to do this for Mom." Her brow creased sincerely. "I mean, you can decline. Judge didn't, like, order you to."

I looked into June's daughter's vivid blue eyes, considering my place in her life. I'd helped set in motion a train of tragedy that had to be brought to a stop. Quierin had said, Open your eyes, you're free, but I wasn't. Not yet.

"I signed the settlement agreement with the Western Pacific," I said. "I spoke for those I was appointed to serve. Your mother and her husband. I testified it was in their best interests. And I was wrong."

"I guess."

"I heard what Stillwell was muttering but I was off to

Europe. I couldn't be bothered. I learned a few things in Europe, and I want to make up for it. I owe it to your mother."

I said something right. The blue eyes were shining.

"I can help," she whispered urgently. "*We* know what happened, don't we? We just have to prove it. You sue war criminals, for God's sake. Tell me what to do."

CHAPTER 6

Darko Jovanovic served as mayor of the
ancient ecclesiastical city of Vukovar during its Serb occupation
in the early nineties. Control of Vukovar, on the west bank of the
Danube, has been contested for centuries between Croats and
Serbs. In the fall of 1991, the contest culminated in Vukovar's
destruction in a three-month siege by the federal army of
Yugoslavia, the JNA, and the Serb takeover that followed.

Two days after Vukovar fell, the most grotesque atrocity of
the Serb-Croat war occurred. JNA units entered the Vukovar
Hospital and ordered the medical staff to leave. All of the non-
Serb male patients were rounded up from their hospital rooms.
Not just combat-wounded, but heart, stroke, and cancer victims,
day patients for minor surgery, the direly ill in intensive care
were mustered then bused under JNA guard to a farm near the
hamlet of Ovcara. There the patients were divided into groups of
ten to twenty, systematically beaten, and taken, one truckload at
a time, up a dirt track along a cornfield to the head of a wooded
ravine. They were hustled from the truck, lined up, and shot
from behind, mostly to the head. A bulldozer tumbled the bodies
down a deep cut in the gulley.

Two months after leaving Colorado, I found myself in a
sycamore grove at the top of the Ovcara ravine trying to fathom the
evil that could command the mass murder of hospital patients in

the late twentieth century. The Stillwells were far from my thoughts, though I knew Hans Leitner was en route, at my request, to supervise the identification of victims. The Ovcara grave site would be Leitner's first in Europe. Like me, he was probably attracted to the case partly by how a European war-crimes prosecution would look on his CV. But his commitment to human rights was actually central in his Renaissance sweep of interests. Human-rights medicine, Leitner told me, is the Way of Participation, in Mahayana Buddhist terms. Joyful participation in the sorrows of the world.

My role at Ovcara was to supervise the team of anthropologists from the tribunal's Exhumation Unit in The Hague and protect chains of custody in the tagging, logging, and videotaping of evidence. Leitner would conduct and testify to the identification of the bodies. Seven of us stayed in the Hotel Slavonija, an empty, darkened relic of central tourism planning with a turbofolk disco that ruled the Vukovar night.

A year after the Dayton Accords, Vukovar was like Paris in August, but for different reasons. With 95 percent unemployment, every day was Sunday. Teens in tracksuits idled at cafés sipping Turkish coffee. Crowds gathered on the *korso* at poolhall doors listening to Aerosmith or Pink Floyd or "Achy Breaky Heart." But they were picnickers at a landfill. The five-thousand-year-old city was no more. Its Baroque and Ottoman arches and facades, its monasteries, the Austro-Hungarian river fortress, all were rubble. Every one of the houses of the forty-six thousand residents had been damaged or destroyed. Rats ran among the ruins as squatter camps of refugees scavenged for pantiles and strung their wash. The Serbs had gone on to lose the war and eventually withdraw, and now the Croatian *sahovnica* was everywhere—on banners, handbills, and police uniforms—the red-and-white checkerboard shield that means genocide to Serbs.

After a day digging and bagging remains, our crew socialized with other internationals on the *korso* or caught a bootleg Hollywood movie in the makeshift opera house. Hans Leitner, the veteran among us, encouraged long hours of labor followed by brief, intense carousing as part of what he called all-expenses-paid adventure travel to a former war zone. Back in the hotel at the end of the evening, the clopping of horse-drawn carts on the remaining bridge across the river Vuka gave way to the racket of tracked convoys of SFOR tanks and APCs, and the deep bass of the basement disco, turbofolk cassettes looping into my dreams.

The farm buildings at Ovcara were still smeared in charcoal with the Chetnik counter to the *sahovnica,* a cross with four *C*'s—Cyrillic *S*'s—for *Samo Sloga Sribina Spasava:* "Only Unity Will Save the Serbs." Below the site in a camp mess under blue tarp were coolers of *pivo*—beer—tables with bread, peppers, tomatoes, and bottles of *slivovica,* and a row of Porta Potties. Most days a suckling pig on a sharpened stake turned over oak coals on a motorized spit, a boom box played world music, and the scene felt more luau than funereal.

It got less luau as the work proceeded. Leitner and I observed in the shade of the sycamores and ventured into the dig as needed. The site being dug was forty by fifty meters bordered by pink tape. A string grid with cross trenches was staked out inside the tape. A backhoe gently scraped around the edges, but the main work was done by hand by three forensic anthropologists—taphonomists—whom I met for the first time on arriving at the site. Wylene from Athens, Georgia. Minouche, a Belgian. And exotic Quierin, half-Dutch, half Indonesian, the boss of the unit, whom I saw at once I had to get to know.

Disinterment is the most gentle of occupations. The beaten, shot, and bulldozed dead are treated with meticulous tenderness. The women dealt with the brutally slain with such precision and delicacy that a measure of dignity was restored. Minouche fitting pieces of flesh in place, Wylene easing limbs onto a stretcher, Quierin cradling a young man's skull—they seemed more acts of love than crime-scene investigation. The dead were honored so they might tell their tales.

The idea is to reverse-engineer a human life. Feel your way with probes and picks until you touch body parts. From the feet, carefully expose the corpse with rakes, trowels, and brushes. Record every finding by grid number on microcassette and continuous video. Zip the body and its clothes in a bag and stretcher it to the refrigerator truck for the morgue in Zagreb, where Leitner's pathologists would conduct the identifications.

We wound up with the best positive ID of any site in Bosnia and Croatia. Having the disappeareds' hospital records made it a relative piece of cake. Some even wore name bracelets. With

more than 95 percent certainty, 198 men and 2 women were identified by name and residence. All had been patients in Vukovar
Hospital. Most had gunshot wounds to the back of the head. The
manner of death of each was homicide.

The dig had been the hard part. As Quierin's team methodi-
cally worked their way through a huge pyramid of contorted
remains, it got increasingly grueling, especially in the heart of
the pile, where bodies had not yet decomposed and skele-
tonized.

Leitner and I helped around the edges when work bogged
down, pulling on rubber gloves and surgical masks, carting off
wheelbarrows of lime-caked earth. It took a few days to get past
what Leitner called the yuck factor. I never got used to the smell.

"Just don't smell it," Quierin suggested with a shrug.
"Taphonomist trick. Olfactory is trainable nerve."

Not mine. I hung back, playing Watson to Leitner's Holmes,
gauging his sense of the investigation's needs and venturing off
to explore them. In a corner of the pink-taped area was a low
point not yet dug though, covered only lightly. At one spot
methane gas bubbled in standing black water, signifying decom-
position. I parked a wheelbarrow and set in bailing with a
bucket. After a while a figure began vaguely taking shape in the
black pool, a skeleton with a belt and boots, like a Muslim
djinni—genie—the Bosnian spirit of the unquiet earth, approxi-
mating, for good or ill, a human form. Bearing for us a message.

Wylene called over, "Don't go chunking into those guys
yet." I waved an okay sign. I began carefully but blindly probing
the bubbling water around the corpse with a trowel. *"Hey."*
Leitner was at my arm. "Don't move," he said. I glanced back at
him. *"Don't move,"* he bellowed. "Everybody back away. Get
away from us—*now.*"

On hands and knees I saw then, ten inches from my nose, a
trip wire rising taut from the water I was probing through the
skeleton's rib cage to something in the chest cavity that was
round, green, and metallic. I'd gone through mine-awareness
training. I tried to remember what happened next. *"You* don't
move," I said to Leitner. "They could be anywhere."

"I am not so stupid."

"Then what are you doing here?"

It crossed my mind that neither of us would be there but for the other.

"Both of you, please shut up." Quierin whispering just behind us, inches away. "Listen. This is a PMA3," she said, antipersonnel, with a Cyrillic Serbian stencil for the FRY—the Federal Republic of Yugoslavia. There may be others in the shallow grave sites around the border. There could be dozens. "JNA," she added, "don't like you do your job."

Quierin would go out first, exactly as she'd come. She would red-flag each of her footsteps. We in turn had to mimic precisely her path of retreat. First, turn around inside your bootprint. Slowly follow the steps she'd marked. Step only inside a flagged bootprint. "*Go slow.* You have lots and lots of time. Once you make the perimeter, find the backhoe track. Go up the hill going *inside* the track."

"Can I breathe yet?" I wanted to know.

"Breathe," Quierin whispered. The moment—her hushed voice and closeness and perfumed smell, the stillness in which every minute movement mattered—bore a hypererotic charge.

"Colonel Leitner," Quierin continued. "Don't do anything until I am up the hill. Not you either, Elliot. I call the mine cell on the Motorola. Then when I say, Colonel Leitner starts up next. Elliot does not move even the pinkie until the colonel is all the way out and I say start. Who has a knife?"

I slipped out a UN "Peacekeeper" Victorinox and handed it back to her.

"This will be going slow," she said. "I have to probe every step. Be patient." She sighed and I heard the twisting of the sole of her boot, as measured as tai chi. "Greenhorns," she muttered. She stopped. Something else.

"If we have a casualty, don't help him, even if it's me. Leave us where we are, no matter how bad hurt. Comfort him with words and continue your exit. Someone will go back when a safe way is marked."

After hours, it seemed, she called to Leitner to come out. Each sucking step he took I expected a detonation. More seeming hours passed, paralyzed and cramping on all fours, staring through the rib cage of a murdered patient at a half-submerged green puck, obsessing on the questions the murdered man confronted us with.

"Elliot." Quierin's voice from above. "Now you."

By the time I'd minced up the red-flagged path, SFOR ops were on the scene—the Vukovar mine cell in flak jackets and mesh face masks, with muzzled dogs. I endured a condescending interrogation—lawyer in a war zone, cookie-pusher international getting in the way. And you watch your step too, Lieutenant, I said. Don't want you exploding my evidence.

That night, at a floating tavern moored to the Croat bank of the Danube, we mulled over the problem of evil, Quierin, Leitner, and I in a mixed crowd of local bourgeois and internationals. A table of French paratroopers in red berets, OSCE bureaucrats, and shitfaced NGO interns; dour, guarded Croats who'd suddenly erupt in brief bouts of pounding laughter; the tavern owner and his moll, a dramatic, flat-chested blonde, three diamonds on an ear, styled to a stiletto edge. An outer orbit of young women with the unanimated good looks of Marina Oswald sat listlessly here and there. Downriver, yellow rowboats trailed from painters in the current, and a silver pathway led to a sickle moon.

I poured shots of pear *rakija* to go with the *pivo* and *raznjici*—beer and pork kabobs—and toasted my companions: You saved my life; I owe you guys. I posed a question raised by the deadly dead man I'd cowered over. Act as you would have all others act, Kant demanded, but what can we do with those who murder hospitalized civilians then booby-trap their corpses? With crimes of terror Kant couldn't imagine.

Quierin shrugged. "They just trying to kill us. What they do." Quierin, at age thirty-four, seemed to bear the weary knowledge of all Europe's, all Asia's, aeons of calamities.

"Specifically—us?" I asked.

"Sure." Leitner considered the last chunk of spiced pork on his skewer. "We're here to imprison the people you indicted and they want to scare you away. Though trying to kill us and not each other is a little different."

The Exhumation Unit had had to deal with UXO—unexploded ordnance—dumped in grave sites, but until then, not trip-wire mines. Mass graves had been tampered with, but to remove bodies and thus evidence of crimes, not to commit new crimes and leave new bodies. Specifically—ours.

"Is good proof of JNA role." Quierin patted my hand and smiled. She thought me overwrought.

I nodded. I liked the hand pats. I was trying to come around to the exhumation attitude: nonchalance. We've seen it all. But this was my cherry grave site. Hell, this was the first time in a well-traveled life I'd been anywhere recently ravaged by war.

"What did you mean back there?" I asked nonchalantly. "'Greenhorns'?"

"Don't Mexicans call you that?"

Quierin wore a short muslin shift and a mock-leather bolero jacket, her going-out clothes for nights on the bombed-out town. Like other young Northern European women, her wardrobe ran to blacks. Becoming on Quierin, her home color, though she was not a classic beauty. Her features were too odd. Off-kilter. Glossy almond eyes that were a little walled. Frida Kahlo eyebrows. A slash of straight black hair chopped in a half-bang that shadowed the wandering eye. A star-shaped scar on a full right cheek. Full lips lightly parted in a Mona Lisa semismile that set off approach/avoidance shudders when they spoke in my direction. A loose intensity of features, an anything-goes look. Tough, blunt, leggy, funny, yet pensive, elusive, cloaked in darkness, Quierin combined Dutch candor and Asian mystery. A combination sexy as hell.

The broad, voiceless Danube swung around the Vukovar bend. Zephyrs of Gauloise and Shalimar drifted past as the river pulled. Quierin's ashtray overflowed.

I raised the Serb conundrum. *How can the good do evil?*

"Good guys do bad, bad guys do good," she said with a dubious look: provincial greenhorn. Innocent abroad. "Not who you are but the thing you do."

"It happens," said Leitner, "through the mediation of the superego. We rationalize. We dress acts of vengeance, domination, sadism in ideals like ethnic justice."

"Forget good bad people," said Quierin. "Just uncover truth. Exhume truth too."

Leitner swirled the liquid in his little glass. "I agree. Our job is to prove what happened every time it happens, in El Salvador, Rwanda, Chechnya, Boz." His military slang for *Bosnia*, which I would quickly adopt. "Prove it." He tossed off the glass. "Then tell the world."

"*Konobar*." Quierin hailed the waiter. Three fingers for a round of *pivo*. Leitner filled our brandy thimbles, then his.

I watched the lights in the river. Legions of the wrongfully dead seemed to rise, in my brandied imagination, from black water and demand their due—the children of El Mozote, Tutsis hacked to ribbons, Argentines thrown from airplanes, thousands shot kneeling in blindfolds on Srebenica soccer fields, Sarajevo market shoppers blown without warning to kingdom come.

The *konobar* stood with the tray of *pivos*, a tall, vain southern Slav in a Valentino pose, eyes all over Quierin.

"Away with this stuff," she said. "*Zdravo*." He stiffened, stacked his tray, and strutted off through the crowd.

"Boz," Leitner commented, "is the end point of history. The mass grave of ideologies and politics. Where dead mother empires gave stillbirth to doomed ethnic nation-states. Boz," he spoke toward the river, "is the hand from the crypt."

"The Balkans are the world," Quierin announced portentously.

I vigorously agreed, not sure what she meant about this place of the guilty aggrieved, where everyone had compelling stories, terrible secrets, unfathomable depths.

"America is not the world." Quierin finished her thought.

"Oh, yeah?"

"Greenhorns have no history."

Oh, sure. "Just the single longest-standing democracy ever on the planet is all." *Rakija* on the river after a brush with death in a grave brought forth forceful views.

"Hah," said Quierin.

"We are the world anyway," I added. "We're even the Balkans." Look at the blue jeans, lettered T-shirts, hamburgers, movies, rock music, basketball, footwear. "Europeans need to get over it." *It* meaning their history. History meaning us now.

I felt a foot traveling my shin.

"Poor America," Quierin said. "Awkward adolescent."

"Real great European role models. A hundred million cooked this century."

"Let's return," Leitner intervened paternally, "to your friend with the mine in his heart, what he tells us of their audacity. That they recruit their own murder victims and arm them to kill again."

But I'd concluded the skeleton djinni had a message for me personally. By a corpse with a bomb in his breast I'd faced the figure of death. It felt strangely liberating. Like Emerson, who couldn't leave for Europe after his young wife had died until he unscrewed her coffin and beheld what remained of his beloved.

The floating tavern strained and groaned on its guy lines, yearning to go with the river. Something in me strained to break loose too.

"Someday"—Quierin—Mona Lisa—smiled my way and I shuddered—"I like to see your cherishable America, home of the free."

Breathe, I remembered her voice and the heat of her breath on my neck. Again I felt the toe of her boot.

Leitner ceremoniously rationed out the last of the brandy. "To the wrongfully dead." He raised his tiny *rakija* glass. "The dead aren't dead. The master principle of forensic science: the dead speak volumes."

"*Zhivili*." We drank.

Quierin's black eyes glimmered and her black hair shone in the light of the Muslim moon.

The Jovanovic case didn't close until the month I left the tribunal. I'd been in trial on it off and on for over a year, in Vukovar three times trying to scare up witnesses, and in Bosnia on a half dozen other missions. Quierin stayed on the case, helping me put it together. She was back and forth between The Hague and the Balkans, but home most of the winter when the Bosnian earth was frozen. Taking off from the floating tavern, we got into an afterwork routine at Frederik Hendrik Laan pubs and Javastraat restaurants. I was probed for superpower bias and Puritan hang-ups. I was suspected of Yankee provincialism. I was found wanting in the tragic sensibility that comes naturally to Europeans. Ultimately I measured up.

Quierin was my not-Kathleen. Irish Kathleen, as I romanticized her, sang to me like a sea maiden, a kelpie, carried me off and kept the faithless world at bay. Quierin was of the world. She had a scientist's mastery of the concrete. At the same time, she improvised. She had a jazz sensibility, spontaneous, passionate, irreverent, and sometimes cynical. A difficult person, as I've said. She saw things as neither greater nor lesser than they were, and I relied on her sense of proportion. Nine years my junior, she steadied me. In my midlife naïveté I took refuge in her youthful worldliness.

Still our differences created imbalance. We tripped over misunderstandings. It kept me on my toes, never boring, but sometimes exhausting, stumbling along for miles.

Leitner spent a week at the tribunal testifying in the Jovanovic trial. He liked to eat so we'd prepare his testimony over dinner, usually at the Seinpost on a high dune above the beach at Scheveningen, west of the city. The Seinpost specialized in entrées that looked like flowered hats. Afterward came vertical desserts, aged genever, and Cuban cigars. One evening, Stillwell somehow came up. I told him what I'd heard Stillwell muttering from the bench by the probate window. Did Leitner think he was dangerous?

He hesitated. "What you overheard was not a threat but an outburst. Anger. Frustration. Like cursing when you bang your thumb with a hammer. Dale doesn't integrate well. Incoherence is expressed as rage. But he'd never act it out."

"You're sure?" It was a false moment of truth. "His wife's not at risk?"

Out a circular bank of windows the multicolored sky moved over the multicolored sea. Leitner paused, then shook his head, speaking with care. "I hope not. He's an injured, an afflicted soul. It's all quite sad. But Dale would not intentionally harm his wife."

With his relaxed physicality and resonant voice, Leitner had a Reaganesque air of comfort with himself. At times he might wax a bit expansive, play a bit for attention, or insist a little jealously on matters of reputation. Venial imperfections, I thought, that enhanced his credibility by humanizing him. In court he was professorial without condescension, schooling the panel of judges in the discriminate-function analysis of morgue data that ensured reliable identifications. He conveyed sagacity without pedantry, and a commitment to justice through reason. By and large, a dream expert witness—Dr. God, as Hancock had put it—but a model also for my wakening idealism. Hans Leitner, in my view, stood for the highest of medical values: a fierce concentration on physical truth in the cause of human rights.

As with any well-functioning team—bridge partners, lovers, ironworkers, friends—a rhythm developed between us, Leitner effortlessly taking off from my questions, which flowed effortlessly back to him. His testimony was followed by my evidence, explained by Quierin on the stand: the Serb army PMA3 mine from the bosom of the skeleton, tagged now with an exhibit marker, our only hard proof tying the JNA to the murders.

My lover was not only my workplace subordinate but my expert witness, testifying to the physical evidence that I—the lawyer examining her—had blundered onto in the field. Stateside, we'd be fair game for cross-examination. Here, love and justice could proceed as equals.

We concluded our case with a two-hour videotape of the Ovcara exhumation. I wondered how the accused could watch, seemingly mesmerized, as body after body was zipped up and borne away.

The accused was short, barrel-chested, gray-haired with a gray Slavic mustache, tidily dressed. Flanked by blue-uniformed UN guards, he passed time writing in a small black notebook with a blank or preoccupied expression. He projected neither the haunted look nor gangster swagger nor bitter nationalism of some fellow detainees. Incarcerated then for over three years, Mayor Jovanovic seemed resigned and vaguely disengaged, like a bureaucrat at his desk—one of Gogol's dead souls improbably thrust before the footlights to account for acts of horror.

The case against him was problematic, and unusually for the tribunal, the accused was well defended. Of the four Serbs indicted for the hospital massacre, three were JNA officers protected from arrest in the FRY. We'd found Jovanovic in Slovenia and nabbed him with a sealed indictment, but his was by far the weaker case. We knew he hadn't been at the Ovcara farm, but we claimed he had command responsibility for the murders, which could be a challenge to prove. Tantamount to showing civilian control of the military when the civilian was a small-city mayor and the military was Europe's fourth-largest army.

Dusan Kostenac, the mayor's lawyer, exploited my dilemma brilliantly. Witness after witness became a foil for his theme: In 1991, the JNA was in disarray, wasn't it? Little communication between units, no clear chain of command, desertion rate of 20

percent. Many soldiers didn't even know who their commanding officers were. Paramilitaries marauded at will, answering to
no one, least of all to civil authorities. Chaos, in a word. When
mob violence broke out, was this little gray mayor really pulling
the strings?

Kostenac is a huge, hairy Serb-American from Cicero who'd
sued and beat my railroad, though in Chicago days I knew him
only by reputation. Tough, profane, domineering, smart. His
poker face was one of smug command. All trial long he pretended indecision about whether he'd call his client. I knew he
wouldn't. The chaos defense was working too well. I was
wrong.

The mayor will testify, Kostenac told the panel late in the
trial, against his lawyer's advice. No poker face, Kostenac now
looked not anxious or fretful, but introspective. Troubled.

"Gospodin Jovanovic, *dobar dan"*—*good day,* Kostenac
said once the mayor was sworn. "What was being mayor of
Vukovar like? Describe the responsibilities."

Jovanovic did, dryly, tediously. They sounded at best cleri-
cal, at worst janitorial.

"Not like Mr. Mayor Daley? Or the lord mayor of London?"
Kostenac nodded to Judge Hamilton, president of the panel. "Or
the tough guy Giuliani?"

"Ko?"—*Who?*

"Mr. Big, calling shots."

"Ne, ne"—*No.*

"Does Vukovar mayor control police?"

"Malo"—*A little.*

"The army?"

"Ne." He shook his head briskly.

"The federal army of Yugoslavia? The JNA?"

"Ne, not a mayor. *Nikad"*—*Never.*

Could the mayor, by the authority of his office, tell the JNA
to fix the streets? Detain persons? Expel patients from the hospital? Kill them?

Ne, ne, ne, nikad.

"Who was running this railroad?"

"Ne razumijen"—*I don't understand.*

"Could even the JNA tell the JNA what to do?"

"Ponekad"—*Sometimes only.*

On it went, another set-piece Kostenac examination. I took a flier on mine.

"*Dobar dan,* Gospodin Jovanovic. Tell me, did you personally have any authority over the police?"

"*Ja?*"—I? "*Ne.* The mayor did not."

"You personally, not you the mayor."

"*Ne.*"

"Over the army?"

"As mayor, none."

"Not as mayor—but—" I stopped. "You did have dealings with the army, didn't you?"

"Objection. Asked and answered."

"Overruled."

"Didn't you?"

"*Da*"—Yes.

"You assisted the JNA?"

"*Da.*"

"The First Guards?"

"*Da.*"

"In some matters you could direct First Guard units also to assist you?"

"*Malo. Da.*" Flat affect, but his steady, sad gray gaze had depth. So steady it was almost soulful. I had the weird feeling he wanted to tell me something.

So I took another flier.

"Who in Vukovar after the siege had the authority to regulate the actions of the army within the city?" The, or one of the, $64,000 questions.

"Crisis Committee," he said. A glance at Kostenac.

"Who was on the Crisis Committee?"

"Police, military police, First Guard staff officer, civil official, and party leader. Serb ones."

"Including you?"

"*Da.*"

"Your position?"

Steady on me, he answered, "President."

There fell then a tribunal stillpoint, the sign in that hyper-technologized place of a moment of truth. Translators ceased translating, and keyboards ceased clicking. UN security froze.

Heads rose from monitors and turned in unison toward the enthroned witness.

"What," I said, sounding too loud and clear over my head-phones in the hushed, hermetic courtroom, "what actions of the JNA could the Crisis Committee direct?"

"Ista," he murmured. *Anything.* His gaze now dropped to his hands, where it stayed. "Distribute food, water, medicine. Secure suburbs. Enforce curfew and crowd assembling. Pacify. Escort journalists and ICRC"—the Red Cross.

"Pacify," I said. "Pacify Croat or Muslim neighborhoods?"

"Da."

"Did you issue such directions as Crisis Committee president?"

"Da."

"Did you order—" I paused. This wasn't my game anymore. It was all him. "Did you order the taking of lives?"

"Ne. Nikad."

"But you knew the consequences of your actions?"

He nodded. "Some lives were lost."

"You might tell an officer to search and secure a neighbor-hood?"

"Da."

"And you knew that meant civilians could be killed?"

He nodded. "Many lives were lost after the siege."

"Noncombatants were killed?"

"Of course."

"As a result of your orders?"

"I must say the likelihood is so."

"Hospital patients?"

"Ja?"—*I? "Ne.* But we learned what happened."

"Did the Crisis Committee give orders that caused it to hap-pen? The execution of patients?"

Downcast still, he said, *"Da.* I understand that it was so."

Another stillpoint. I hesitated in place a quarter minute more, then let the panel know I was done.

Kostenac rose, swelling massively in his robe, broadcast-ing a defiant, false grin. His eighteen months of chaos theory had just gone up in smoke, but his redirect was perfect, clean as the slice of an oar.

"Gospodin Jovanovic, did you authorize any action with respect to the hospital patients?"

"Ne."

"Were you aware such an atrocity was planned?"

"Ne."

"Where were you November 20 when the unfortunate patients were taken?"

"Borovo Naselje, with my mother."

"When did you first learn hospital patients had been taken and harmed?"

"Two days later, when I returned."

"Hvala"—Thank you.

To win a command-responsibility conviction I had to prove either the mayor ordered the hospital operation or knew about it beforehand and didn't stop it. Proof like that was hard to come by. The bad guys were good at making it disappear. If they tried to kill us as we were evidence gathering, consider the document destruction, the witness intimidation. An OTP axiom was, you'll never flip a Serb. With the mayor, something else had been going on, a truth unfolding then clamping shut. Whatever it was, was over now, or so I thought.

The three-judge panel retired for the week to deliberate. I could read in their faces that the mayor's admissions and Leitner's testimony were likely not enough. I steeled myself for a loss. It wasn't the end of the world. An acquittal would bolster in Serb eyes the fairness of the court they were convinced was out to frame them. It could lead to better cooperation in the Republika Srpska, and more arrests, and move us closer to the king-pins—Karadzic and Mladic; someday maybe even Milosevic.

And if we hadn't proved our case, maybe Jovanovic deserved to walk. Yeah, right. What prosecutor believes that?

Jovanovic was held in a UN-administered block of the Dutch military prison in Scheveningen. The night after his defense rested and the panel adjourned, when he was likely about to be released, he plunged a dinner fork with the inside tines bent back into an electrical outlet just outside his cell, shorting power in the cellblock and releasing his door. He fumbled to the laundry room in the dark and pulled an ironing board below the one high window. When power was restored guards found him hanging from the window clasp by the cord of an iron.

I had to ask whether I helped caused the death of a possibly innocent man. Accused him, retraumatized him, stigmatized him to the point that life was worthless. Or, in place of the crimson-robed panel that could soon set him free, did Jovanovic, independently of me, pass judgment on himself? Had the exhumation video been *his* moment of truth?

Unanswerable questions. A Serb conundrum. The only certainty was that the Serb mayor was haunted by the Serbs' victims. The skeleton djinni had risen from the black pool at Ovcara to exact revenge in the prison laundry.

Quierin, at the Goude Hooft, before things got heated, called it a European ending, not an American one with winners and losers, some phony victory or defeat.

For me it was worse than defeat. From the not unreasonable Serb point of view, we'd hounded a man to death. Leaving me now also haunted by a victim and taunted by the futility of ideals.

I was ready to turn in my prosecutor's ID. I wanted to go home, read briefs, write opinions. Be a judge.

CHAPTER 7

On September 11, June's roommate died. The day the Starr Report to Congress was published. It bothered me, her death, more than I'd expected.

The roommate had been such a pain. Midmornings the nurse, Rico, would come in booming—How my *girlfriens*? You gotta work *hard* today, you wanna be my girlfriens. Smile for Rico. That's a *good girl*—as though the way to reach the unconscious was with earsplitting baby talk. Yo, Watash—his name for me. You do June, okay? He'd gently collect the roommate from the bed and lay her gaunt limbs like those of a Raggedy Ann in the Quickie positioning chair, truss her in a Posey belt; bind her head, wedge cushions at her sides, and fit glasses behind her ears. I didn't understand the glasses. She never noticed anything, neither us nor the photographs that papered the wall, vacation scenes and family get-togethers; children, husband, parents, siblings—none of whom ever visited.

Before he left, Rico would swivel the cantilevered TV toward the roommate and turn it on. The Weather Channel. On his way out he'd say, Ciao, Watash, and holler *Bye-bye* from the hall. Then April or I would click the TV off or turn to the Discovery Channel. It was my conceit June liked animal shows, and I was paying the cable bill.

Colfax Rehab was an all-Medicaid hospital and it showed.

The staff wore an aggressive, veiled look, as if they knew things they were being paid not to reveal. Days were spent deferring calamities as much as addressing needs. The atmosphere was one of crisis management by people who could care less. I was never there at night when God knows what went on.

The hospital as a whole had a distinctive false smell. Minty clean. The common areas were all noise and confusion, sweltering in summer. Patients spent afternoons in the rec room strapped in their chairs, from elderly stroke victims to Colfax's heartbreaking kids: Johnny, a high-school-football casualty; Ricky, a twenty-year-old Pine Ridge Sioux air-ambulanced from Rapid City after a motorcycle accident; and Leah, clipped by a snowmobile when she was twelve. They sat parked every which way, like a parody of the deck class on an ocean cruise, ignored by the jokey, jivey staff, in a bedlam of radios, TVs, CD players, fans, bells and buzzers, and traffic noise from outside. The worst kind of sensory overload for brain-injured patients hypersensitive to stimuli.

The focal point was the big-screen TV. There you'd see Ron, who'd fallen thirty feet trying to scale his ex's apartment wall; Alfredo, who'd drunkenly leapt from a car going 75 mph; Lisa and Johnny and Ricky, young folks dealt raw deals; and sometimes June. A rail-thin audience staring rapt as Louis Rukeyser talked tech-stock jitters.

After April arrived, I cut back my Colfax visits to once every week or two. It was glorious running weather. The Flagstaff trail was my Colfax antidote; I took the straight-up route, trying to beat cyclists switchbacking on the road.

The hiring-partner lunches had been unproductive. Most of my inquiries were politely deflected. A lateral move by someone my age was—awkward. Upset a firm's dynamic symmetry of seniority and compensation. I'd be kept in mind, of course, when work was referred. Left unsaid was my shortcoming in bringing no clients in tow. My only former client, the railroad, still did everything in-house. The railroad wanted me back but I declined. I tried the law schools for faculty jobs. All they had was a one-semester legal-ethics gig for ten thousand bucks, not starting until February. I said I'd think about it.

Eventually a lunch paid off with one of the big insurance defense firms. I met the people who mattered, and in a round of

E-mails, we worked out the details, down to the wording on the notice:

> ### CATTO & CATTO, LLC
> *Is Pleased to Announce That*
> *Elliot Keane Stone*
> *Former Chief Deputy Prosecutor at*
> the International Criminal Tribunal for the Former Yugoslavia
> *and Former Regional General Counsel to the*
> Missouri and Santa Fe Railroad
> *Has Become of Counsel to the Firm.*
> *Mr. Stone's Civil Trial Practice Will Emphasize*
> *the Defense of Personal Injury Claims.*

Then I balked. With so many *former*'s it read like an obituary. And the firm's work seemed trivial, even mean-spirited, next to what I'd been doing. The mayor hanging above a kicked-over ironing board was still too raw an image. I wanted to do this next part right.

But another reason was June. I'd little heart for litigating against injured people for insurance companies, disparaging them, minimizing their losses, objectifying their suffering. I'd gotten too close to a person injured as badly as it is possible to be injured. Her disability didn't demean but purified her. Since those who cannot act also cannot transgress, the helpless are innocent as angels.

I called Henry Catto with my regrets. I stopped lunching with lawyers. I could afford to ride at anchor awhile. I passed time in the home office overworking my few referrals, reading the *Times,* checking the in box for messages from Europe.

Quierin hadn't followed the Catto deal. "Why go to court against accident victims?" With a fatalist's ease, she shrugged off my career dilemmas. "You have freedom. Do the thing you want inside. Follow your heart, or however you say it."

Electronic vocational counseling from a woman who dug up bodies for a living.

Quierin said she would be busy all fall with trials and a new grave site near Brcko in northeast Bosnia. At the tribunal, she wrote, "Kosovo has everybody buggy waiting for Milosevic to drop his shoe. Maybe next year is quiet. In the meanwhile I'm lonely for you."

We'd discussed marriage, but mine with Kathleen. Quierin was intrigued by the idea of a happy marriage the way scientists are drawn to unproven hypotheses. Quierin the anthropologist did not accept marriage as a natural or necessary condition. She was not a self-loathing single woman. She did not see herself as lacking. She was fatalistic about love affairs too. Ambiguous endings in love were also true to history, to the nature of things.

I missed her. I posted the sentiment without elaborating. Were I to elaborate, I'd first note her touch, of hand, breath, body, lips, lash; the feel of her sleeks and clefts. I'd add that I missed the quality of surprise, the teasing, the mercurial changes. That I missed how she inspired, with whispers, prods, and her own example.

I also missed the sense of proportion, the irony and nonchalance, that Quierin could bring to dire surroundings, mass graves or Medicaid rehab hospitals. The exhumation attitude.

When April and I arrived to find the roommate not there, the bed stripped and disinfected, the wall bare, and a sweet mint smell settling over a missing life, I felt uneasy, almost creepy, instead of relieved the suffering of a tortured soul was over. A spirit had fled the room. I could imagine the skeleton djinni from Ovcara following here, inhabiting June's roommate, and now departing with other plans.

April had no such illusions or regrets. "It's good for Mom." April's categorical imperative.

She'd decided to defer her junior year and was staying in west Denver with the parents of a classmate. On my Colfax days I'd give her a ride. Otherwise she drove June's Toyota pickup to Colfax or to pursue her "investigation." She was finding stuff. We were tightening the noose, she said. April was ready to stick it out—until June woke up or Stillwell was arrested. Do whatever it took.

Chow time! Rico wandered in and opened the cabinet. He pulled on some gloves, screwed the nozzle of the G-tube to the feeding pump, and rolled the IV pole next to June's chair. She was dressed in the daytime outfit I'd bought for her—sweats and running shoes, as though ready for a workout. A black eye patch for a roguish effect. The white running shoes were unsoiled, immaculate, because they'd never been walked in. The ends were cut out to make room for her knotted toes.

Rico flipped and caught a can of Nutren 1.5, poured it in and tripped the pump, tossed the can in the wastebasket, and wandered out again. Ciao, Watash. *Bye-bye.* The ten-second lunch: true fast food.

Following lunch and before the rigors of therapy, we socialized with June, one at a time so she could track.

"Man, are you good with her," April said. "I can't do it like you." She wore a Rolling Stones "Bridges to Babylon" tour T-shirt. Mick's huge lips and tongue. In matters of fashion April's taste ran to knockoffs of vintage concert attire. That the secretary of state kept company with seventies' rock stars spoke well of Madeleine's retro hipness.

"It's just talking," I said.

When June was alert, the way to engage her was to whisper softly and near her ear while closely watching her eye. She'd follow your look searchingly, until the effort exhausted and she nodded into sleep. I'd tell her what was happening in the world. Offer advice and praise. It would sound like a monologue, or a series of rhetorical questions, but it felt like a conversation. Like reading her mind through her one clear eye. That she worried about April and was glad she'd come. That she hated Colfax. She hated therapy. At Stillwell's name the mental message blurred.

I had a recurring fantasy of June one day blinking twice, sitting up, and telling everything that had happened. One night I dreamed she and I walked for hours in the mountains. Breaking barriers, June had written in her journal, was her job. It was our job now.

"She likes you," April said.

"What?" I pulled back from June's ear.

"I can tell she likes you, seeing her with you. More than likes."

"Watch out."

"She depends on you. She wants you to know that."

"I suppose."

"And she trusts you," April said. "Someone Mom can trust. That could be, like, a change for the better."

One day April staggered in with two bags of June's junk I'd

stored in the rental locker. A cuckoo clock from Garmisch. The case of horse-show ribbons and a framed photograph of June astride Yuma. Two of the Infants of Prague.

"You know why she likes this stuff?" April put the clock, flanked by the Infants, on the dresser. "She wants to go places. Like ride the trans-Siberian railroad. That is a dream of Mom's. Canadian Pacific. *Orient Express.* Mom says she chooses a career in transportation then never gets to go anywhere." April sighed with a quaver of distress. "All those places—Venice. Egypt. Bohemia, where Granddaddy came from. Now, you know—she can't even move."

"April." I inspected an Infant of Prague. "I'm sorry. It has to go back. It'll all be stolen by morning."

She replaced them with a series of three-dollar posters—Fly-Fishing the Pan, The Tundra in Bloom, Krummholz at Timber-line, Autumn Foliage on the Peak to Peak, The Big Horn Ram, The Bugling Elk. She brought in a replaceable boom box, June's Windham Hill CDs, and some of April's own.

Understandably, April had problems with Colfax, a for-profit hospital with no on-site MDs and a staff who looked drafted from the White Spot kitchen. Colfax was the only long-term brain-injury rehabilitation facility in the region that accepted patients on public assistance. It welcomed the wards of five states, each of whom was treated as a profit center backed by public funds.

With some difficulty I'd qualified June for SSI and Medic-aid. Her $100,000 settlement was long gone, and her pickup and half-interest in the house didn't count toward the $5,000 asset maximum for Medicaid eligibility. She had no health insurance and I persuaded the caseworker to skirt the issue of the value of her junk. Her husband would be wealthy over time, but personal-injury annuities weren't considered marital property, and Still-well couldn't afford a private hospital anyway, according to Hancock. Without public benefits he'd get socked with costs for June of two to three hundred grand a year, uninsured, and his annuities didn't hit that level for another eight years. Leaving June dependent on Colorado and Colfax to stay alive.

I thought Colfax staff had the hardest job in health care, help-ing those with the worst problems and the least resources, whip-sawed between tightfisted owners and paper-happy bureaucrats.

Colfax was owned by an obscure venture called the Queen City Trust, which appeared to act only through its attorneys, Whitelaw and Van Horn. My recruiting lunch with Arnold Whitelaw had been notably unproductive.

For-profit providers of taxpayer-funded care for the indigent to my mind combined the worst of the welfare and capitalist systems. One way to make money was by short-staffing. Colfax got eighty grand a year for June and every other ventilated, vegetative, or tube-fed patient—$216 a day, double the usual Medicaid rate since Colfax was a class-five facility for those with "special needs," in the circumspect official phrase. That came to $9 per hour per patient from which a profit had to be made. And that meant an underpaid, undertrained, overworked staff. It meant bedsores because patients weren't turned for days, infections because catheters overflowed and diapers weren't changed, call lights that went unanswered, and outbreaks of lice. It meant the overuse of unsafe disinfectants and the underuse of soap. Still, with a full house the Queen City Trust could gross $6.5 million annually from bed charges alone.

I was getting a reputation with the administration as someone to watch, but nothing like April's. April would yell. And even June could make her wishes known. She couldn't stand Jill, the speech therapist. Jill had a heavy-handed approach to sensory stimulation, ringing a bell in June's ear, pricking and pinching her arm, forcing a tongue depressor down her throat, passing a canister of noxious gas under her nose. June would shut her mouth and eye, clench her teeth on the tongue depressor, and grimace and freeze no matter how loudly the bell was rung or how painfully the arm was pinched. Jill would write her up as nonresponsive, Rancho Los Amigos level 1.5.

The part April didn't handle well was physical therapy. Its main objective was not therapeutic in the usual sense but prophylactic—to prevent contractures, the shortening of muscles and tendons that can permanently deform and cripple. The treatment consisted of range-of-motion procedures designed to pull incipient contractures apart. Every day June was taken to PT to be stretched on her back, then flipped and vaulted by the therapists onto a bolster on her stomach, and pulled hard in four directions. It was excruciating to watch, like seeing someone drawn and quartered. The soundless scream on June's face was more than a look of pain. It was a look of horror.

June was resting after PT in her chair in the room when Dr. Ivan Silverman made his first visit after the roommate's death. Dr. Silverman had up to eighty comatose patients to check on each time he came to Colfax. Neither the volume of his caseload nor the condition of his patients encouraged much of a bedside manner.

I introduced him to April.

"Silverman," April said. "What a pretty name."

"You like it?" First time I'd seen him smile. As June slept, he finished a three-minute physical exam and perusal of the chart.

"How's she look?" April asked.

"Looking better." He smiled a second time.

April said she attributed it to a quieter environment since the roommate was gone. No more mooing.

I attributed it to April.

"Family helps most." Dr. Silverman readied to move on.

"Hey, Doctor," I said, "what happened . . . ?" I gestured at the empty bed. The mint smell that had tolled the roommate's passing faintly lingered still.

"She died," he said, "of an infection."

"From what?"

"Spinal meningitis, I believe. Nosocomial in origin. It reached her brain, possibly through the shunt."

"Why wasn't she hospitalized?"

"Mr.—Stone, correct? This *is* a hospital. A rehabilitation hospital. These infections are difficult to diagnose. And intractable. Fatal, I should say, once they progress to the brain. They progress very quickly."

"Was she cultured?"

He stiffened. "I don't recall. I'm here only every two weeks."

"If she had a fever, she should have been cultured. Right?"

"Mr. Stone. You are a lawyer, I think? You should know your questions invade physician-patient confidences. I ask you to respect those confidences."

"Of course," I said. "I'm just concerned. Hygiene, precautions, procedures here at Colfax. On account of Ms. Stillwell."

He smiled a third, less pleasant smile. "I must go."

But April stood in his path. "Mom doing better," she said, "that's what rehabilitation is, right? Getting better?"

He nodded.

"Dying and rehabilitation are, like, mutually exclusive?"

He stared.

"It looks bad, dying instead of getting better."

"Dying is bad, yes. Of course."

"Just checking." April stepped aside and he struck off into the hall with such purpose he stumbled full into an unmanned biohazard cart piled with soiled linen and diapers and a rack of trembling bottles of antiseptics, disinfectants, and antimicrobial soaps.

June slept. It was a good time to leave. We'd learned to come and go without greetings or farewells, to drift in, to melt away, hoping she wouldn't notice. April put on a Cowboy Junkies CD.

It wasn't easy to leave June alone. I felt a need to bring her up to consciousness that leaving left unfilled. Leitner the shrink might call it the projection of a submerged desire to revive my dead wife. That I was drawn to June's bedside like a spiritualist to a séance. A smoky female voice drifted from the CD player. Looking at June's auburn hair unfurled like moss in a stream, her blossom-pale skin, her cool seclusion, I could kill the brute who had put her here.

I hadn't really gone to the tribunal from a commitment to justice but because I needed a change. My needs, not theirs, had got me there. I went not to strengthen the cause of justice but to be strengthened by it. Now I was thunderstruck by a thought. Justice for those unjustly harmed is a natural. What else is there? Why else be a lawyer?

Something *had* happened over there. Quierin had seen it way before I did. It took day after day with June for me to start to work it through.

I slipped out into the hall and April followed. At the door she glanced back and saw her mother watching. "Damn." She returned to kiss her cheek. "Bye, Mom."

As happened of late when June caught us sneaking out, her eye winced and flooded with tears. Without moving or making a sound, she sobbed, and we waited until it ended.

• • •

The drive from Boulder down the turnpike to Denver, south on I-25 and east on Sixth to the strip, past the sleaze shops and price-rite liquor stores, the rescue missions and cut-'em-up taverns to Colfax Center for Rehabilitation, was in most ways a descent, and the drive back in most ways uplifting. Compacted urban life thinned and flaked away on the grasslands like an ice floe breaking up in the sea. The prairie reached for the range, for rock and ice in a cobalt sky. Yet I went reluctantly, as when you've left something and forgotten what it was, and it's tugging you back. What it was, was June, my ward in the den of thieves, where patients die of infections for which a doctor isn't called.

"I'm going to start staying over," April said as we drove back after talking with Silverman. "In the roommate's bed."

"Hudnut won't let you." The administrator.

"They've got room. Two other empty beds." She plucked a coil of hair and released it. It sprang back in place. "She'll let me."

We said nothing. Hanging out with a coma patient, you appreciate the richness of silence. The first snow of fall rimed the ridgelines on the Continental Divide. As I drove west, I daydreamed east to Oxford, to the extravagant gardens of Corpus Christi College, and Goodbody's Pub, where Kathleen had made sandwiches and sang on a stool in the evening, red-brown hair spilling on a shoulder. Kathleen, from Galway, stood out in Oxford. Her west-Irish fire and feeling could strike the clever ironists dumb. After we married on the college green, my Hume/Kant abstractions felt less compelling. I got the idea, which Kathleen never fully shared, that I should become serious about making a living. Within a year we'd traded Corpus Christi's lush, poetic grounds for the grim stacks of Harvard.

"What if the DA just doesn't file?" April spoke from a reverie of her own. "Can *we* file something? I mean, like, a jury should see this stuff."

"Sure. You can sue Stillwell, civil suit for battery. One-year statute of limitations, so there's time. But . . ."

"Yeah?"

"Lots of problems with a civil suit." A probably insurmountable statutory obstacle, though I didn't say so. No PI lawyer in his right mind would represent her.

"Yeah?" April thought I meant the problems of proof—no weapon, no witnesses, and so on. "If Mom could talk," she said at length, "what do you think she'd tell us?"

I drove on. We passed the taxidermy in a cornfield with a giraffe on the roof. Halfway to Boulder.

"Do you think she'd tell us why he hit her? Or what he hit her with?"

"She won't remember," I said. "Retrograde amnesia. She was probably asleep anyway."

"Maybe she'd tell us what he'd been doing to her."

It was my recurring fantasy too, that June would tell everything. With Colfax receding, my empty house approaching, it seemed—absurd. If June could speak, wasn't she more likely to say, End this? Take this pillow and smother my damaged face. We should forget fantasies of June speaking.

But then, the next morning, she did.

Unusually, June was up and dressed and strapped in her chair. The TV was on—Rico. A band of rain approached the Ohio River valley. I clicked it off. Rico had remembered to brush her teeth. April sat on the edge of the bed to read June some stories from the *Post*. A videotape of the president's grand jury testimony might soon be released. June's eye met April's, their faces inches apart.

With a powerful exertion her eye slowly squeezed shut. Her lips faltered and shook, and she breathed, "Hello."

We were hunched together praising June and congratulating ourselves on a barrier broken when the Colfax receptionist looked in. She'd received a call so they'd gotten Mrs. Stillwell dressed. Mr. Stillwell was on his way.

CHAPTER 8

Hans Leitner stood at the door. He shrugged, as though to say, What are you and I doing here?

"Dale Stillwell is not coming in this room." April was moving toward Leitner like a boxer. "I swear he's not."

"Hold on, April." Of course Stillwell's lawyers would choose Leitner as the health-care provider to accompany Stillwell's visits, as Judge Otero had ordered. I introduced him to April and explained to her again what the judge had ruled. We were under his probate jurisdiction—I was, anyway—and could be held in contempt for keeping Stillwell out.

"Do I care?" she flashed.

"Hans," I said. "Help us out here."

"Just give him five minutes. He's in the car. He says he's worried about her. Just let him have a quick look, see for himself."

"He's not coming near her," April said.

"Sure. Fine. We'll put her over there. He stays over here."

April wasn't convinced.

"Look," Leitner said, "he listens to me." Hans turned in my direction. "Two weeks ago I testified he was competent—and he is. He's much better. He thinks he can manage on his own and he appreciated my telling the judge that. I think I can keep him in line. I expect the same of you, Elliot." He glanced April's way.

"You had the competency hearing already? And he's competent?"

"Cut his lawyers out of some work." Leitner chuckled and I smiled. April wasn't following. I'd explain later. This was very good news. I huddled with April, leaned on her to let the visit proceed. She rolled her mother to the roommate's bare wall and sat beside her, whispering that Stillwell was coming so June wouldn't be surprised. Leitner took off. More time elapsed than should have been needed to fetch his patient. Then there he was.

June looked pretty and proper in her best pressed blouse and pleated slacks, the snow-white Nikes with holes for her toes. Her glowing, uncut hair falling down an arm. She sat clutching the grips on her chair with the carved frown she used to greet the speech therapist. She observed the figure at the doorway with a steadiness that suggested patience as well as focus. She projected an almost regal air, granting a supplicant an audience.

Stillwell frowned too, but his eyes were drifting, to the floor, my face in a brief pass, his doctor's, a wall—an awkward parody of the Secret Service scanning a room while seeming to ignore its central occupant. He was superficially presentable in a denim shirt and cargo khakis, thick dark hair, and features that fell short of movie-star handsome mostly because of the conflict they expressed. His was the countenance of conflict, I thought. Of a man at war with himself. A human Yugoslavia.

The drifting eyes gave a sense of shame and volatility. Then they locked on April's.

"What's *she* d-doing here?" Stillwell demanded, balling and unballing a hand.

Immediately April lost it. She shot from the bed. "Take a look what you did to my mother." She wheeled the chair sharply around. "Look at her face. *You fucker.*"

"Wait just a minute." Leitner raised a hand. "Take it easy, Dale. Take five."

"Look at her," April said.

"I don't know—about that," Dale muttered at the floor.

"Then who does?"

"April," I said. "Don't go there."

"Who tried to kill my mother? Don't you want to know?"

Leitner slung an arm around Stillwell's shoulders, saying they should leave, try again another time. He was used to a measure of deference, to a calming effect, bringing order and understanding to contested questions.

"Not my job." Stillwell wriggled off and suddenly his wild look seized on his wife. "What're you doing to June? What've you done to her h-hair?"

"Jesus Christ." April was disgusted. "You need help."

"I don't need anybody h-helping me. You leave me be."

"You know," April said, her voice dropping, "I need a new place to stay. Wearing out my friends' welcome. Your house, that's half Mom's, right?"

"Leave me b-be."

"Maybe I could move in with you. Help you face up to things."

With that he started for her, eyes dancing. I caught and pinned an arm and Leitner and I wrestled him back.

"Out now," I told them. "Out. I'll call you, Hans."

June stared at the door after they'd left, with eye wide and, whether from the disorder of voices and bodies, or something else, the silent scream of horror when her contractures ripped.

Hans Leitner conducted his practice from Boulder in a bilevel, 1950s Bauhaus structure at the base of Flagstaff Mountain, landscaped with rock, pine, and aspen to simulate the wild. Inside were two workplaces: a writing office papered with diplomas and photographs, file cabinets, a disorderly desk, and a computer terminal with an infinity-sign screen saver. And a talking office for patient sessions, appointed with psychiatric clichés—cushiony furniture, a soothing blue-to-purple color scheme, Munch and Rothko reproductions, subdued recessed lighting. A sliding glass door opened onto a scene of tight ranks of spruce and fir marching up the north flank of the mountain I loved to run.

"We alone?" I called from the doorway. You could walk right in—just like Hans. "Patients? Helpers?"

"Alone we are." He appeared and waved me back. "I have a virtual staff. Bright young woman who works from home on the Hill."

"I've spoken with her."

"Three rings, Ellen picks up. She handles everything through my computer. I'd have forgotten what she looks like except she's such a knockout."

We repaired to the talking office. On the clichéd couch I talked. Stillwell's conduct was unacceptable. "It's obvious he assaulted his wife, but still he gets to visit? Then he takes a run at her daughter? He should be locked up."

Leitner neither argued nor agreed. He was listening as if it were therapy, poking through a dish of pistachios on the empty coffee-table top.

"Tell me he's not coming back."

"Elliot, she provoked him. Keep the daughter away and he'll behave."

"I don't want Stillwell near either one of them. I'll get a restraining order if I have to."

"Bad move. I'll have to tell the judge she provoked it. She's the next conservator if I understand correctly. I don't want to jeopardize that. Let's work something out."

"You have a dog in this fight?"

"Of course not, but he's my patient and my duty is to him. I want to make this work, Elliot."

"Your patient hurts people. He has a violent temper."

"I can't talk directly about that, Elliot."

"What's his goddamn problem?"

Leitner sighed. He let some time pass. He nudged the pistachios my way across the brecciated marble. "The organic residual is fairly minor. The treatment issues—I can't go into detail. A lot of it is reactive. His wife's in a coma, he's living alone, the police are asking questions. He has a significant adjustment disorder and I help with coping strategies. Being found competent builds him up a lot. But the disabling problem is PTSD. Fascinating case, but I really shouldn't say more. He's a pathetic figure, Elliot. Terrible things happened to him, and they're always in his mind."

"One tragedy to the next."

"At least June doesn't know what hit her."

"I'm not so sure."

"Really?" He touched a lip. "Look, I have no idea if he even wants to see her again, but if he does, he does, and the daughter should not be there. As I understand it, the judge said each of the rest of us has the right to be in the room. He said nothing about her."

"I'll think about it," I said. "We'll have to discuss it."

"She's a pistol." Leitner laughed off toward the mountain. "What's she want? Stillwell keeps telling me she poisoned her mother against him. Says she never visited."

"Not true. He wouldn't let her."

"Estranged, to hear him tell it. The mom and daughter. What is she looking for?"

"You mean—his money? Is that what you mean?"

"She has it in for him pretty fierce. Maybe she feels guilty herself in some way. About what happened."

Psychiatrists, I thought.

"Is she filing a civil suit? She seems like she might be a little sue-happy."

Forensic psychiatrists. "We've talked about it," I said vaguely. "There are some problems."

"Truth is, I can imagine how she feels. But Hancock told me Dale was protected by some statute. Can she get around it?"

"I don't think so," I admitted.

"Can she find a lawyer?"

I shook my head. "It's a goddamn outrage. So long as June's alive and healthy your patient's probably safe. He keeps all his money when his wife's like she is because of him and she has no legal recourse. She's *indigent*. You've been to Colfax."

"Yes, that place is more depressing than Ovcara. But you know, Elliot, she's better off not losing public assistance, shitty as it is. You have any idea how much private long-term rehab costs? He couldn't pay it. There's no alternative."

"June is starting to come out of it, Hans. It's an important time. If Stillwell pitched in, extraordinary measures now might help bring her back. If he *is* competent, he should do the right thing. I'd find some way to protect her benefits."

Hans studied me for an uncomfortable moment.

"June has started talking," I added, pushing the envelope.

He frowned.

"Her doctor says she's getting better. She may be on her way back."

"Who's her doctor?"

"Ivan Silverman."

Leitner rolled his eyes. "I'm sorry, Elliot, but it's wishful thinking. What I'm about to say is for your own good, as a friend. I've supervised hundreds of people in her condition. You have to be realistic. June Stillwell will not recover. Even if she fully emerges from coma, she'll never walk, talk, or speak except on a subhuman level. She'll never have a meaningful thought again. Her best prognosis is to gain some clumsy movement of her limbs, mumble disconnected phrases, and experience a few primitive limbic feelings like rage or despair without knowing why. She'll need round-the-clock care in everything she does for as long as she lives."

"The tissue damage was not extensive, Hans."

"I know."

"It's just—she's there. Inside. I can tell. I know she's not—subhuman."

Leitner was shaking his head. "It may be she's there, but I'm afraid it's where she'll stay." He stood and opened his palms, a classroom posture. "We spend on average a hundred and fifty thousand dollars a year on each of the ten thousand people in this country in irreversible comas, which I consider June's to be. One and a half billion every year for no reason other than to keep these hopeless cases alive. We prohibit doctors from withholding their treatment, while in the rest of America adequate services for the *treatable* mentally ill hardly even exist."

"I hear you. I can see how wrong Colfax is for most of its wretched inmates. I just sense that June is—different."

He kept shaking his head, sympathetic but firm. "June Stillwell has a lifetime claim on public funds of four or five million, maybe more. And there are, what, six dozen others like her just at Colfax?" He took a moment. "A commitment from society, just to Colfax's current patients, of over a half billion dollars. And to what end? In almost every case, to perpetuate suffering rather than relieve it."

"If you're right, Stillwell's done worse than murdered her. She's better off dead."

Leitner looked at me with feeling. "The greater tragedy, Elliot, would be if *you're* right. If she's imprisoned in her body, feeling pain, misery, claustrophobic panic—who knows? But helpless to change or end it."

He walked to the wide glass door. Aspen were turning color at the top of the view. "After Yugoslavia you come back here and you have to wonder about our priorities, don't you? How we allocate resources in this country. The medical costs for ten AIDS patients, all of whom will die, exceed the health-care budgets of entire poor nations with millions of sick people who could be made well with basic care. Ten victims of AIDS—a disease that can be avoided with a condom, distribution of which politicians oppose. The greatest physician who ever lived, Rudolf Virchow, the father of my field, pathology, said medicine is a social science. He said physicians are the natural attorneys of the poor. How our profession has foundered."

"Colfax patients are poor."

"The best treatment for most of them would be to withhold it," he said passionately. "Health-care policies that divert billions from the treatable poor to the irreversibly comatose are— evil. Think what a single Colfax patient's lifetime claim on public monies could do for the Vukovar Hospital victims, the widows and orphans and parents of the husbands and fathers and sons who were slaughtered at Ovcara. The world cares more about a president's blow jobs, or a society princess dying in a Paris car wreck, than the tens of thousands still rotting in mass graves like we exhumed. They're the true forgotten souls, the 'lost, and by the wind grieved, ghosts.'" He sighed and shook his head, fingers to his forehead. "I've gotten carried away. I apologize."

"I don't know, Hans." At Oxford I'd parsed flaws in utilitarian logic that subordinates individual interests to social needs, but this was real, not grad school; I was going on instinct. "I just feel—there's a value in doing right by June."

"Don't get me wrong. I went way overboard. I admire tremendously what you're doing." He turned before the glass. "I wish I could say or do something that would actually help. This torments you, obviously, a life passing but not passing, the helplessness you feel." He stood cross-armed in front of the mountain.

"I don't feel helplessness. I feel I *can* help."

He nodded approvingly. "I've learned a few things about you, Elliot. You've grown morally. You've come to understand moral purpose. The next level is understanding moral ambiguity. I think you know that too. I think you're ahead of me."

I knew moral ambiguity all right, after two years of prosecuting Darko Jovanovic.

"Doing what is right," Leitner said, "is more complicated than rules on stone tablets."

"Just what are you suggesting I do?"

"Step back. Be coldly realistic. It's for the best, believe me. Prepare the daughter every chance you have. False hope leads to disaster."

I shifted on the billowy cushions. My taste ran to brighter light and harder seating. Minimal ambiguity. I shook my head to clear it and changed the subject. "May I ask you some medical questions?"

"Sure."

"Is it possible, with traumatic brain injury, to lose the faculty of awareness of your acts?"

"To be amnestic? Of course."

"That's not what I mean. I mean do something but so convince yourself you didn't, you have no conscious awareness that it happened."

Leitner smiled and sat down. "That's not a feature of brain injury. It's more of a psychotic syndrome. Stillwell's not delusional, by the way. I wish I could tell you more but I can't. Remember that the key to Stillwell is post-traumatic stress. Think—you saw it in Vukovar and Bosnia. Boz is full of Dale Stillwells."

And Bosnia is full of war criminals. One Quierin E-mailed me about had a memory problem. Zaga, the Foca rapist, who had surrendered and pled guilty to a series of crimes he couldn't recall, pleas the tribunal rejected. He reminded Quierin of what you get when you cross Bill Clinton with a computer.

Which is? I replied.

A six-inch hard drive with no memory.

I stood to go. "One more thing." Leitner knew hospital risk assessment well. He'd chaired the peer-review panel at Platte Valley, the big public hospital downtown. I summarized what

had happened to June's roommate. "What do you make of that?"
What was the djinni trying to tell us this time?

"Well, it concerns me, frankly. There must have been signs
of meningitis charted in the nurses' notes—fever, other vitals.
How often are medical rounds?"

"Every two weeks."

"What day?"

"Friday. And she died on the Wednesday before."

"No, it's not good. No legal claim because you'd get next to
no damages for the wrongful death of someone in her condition.
And the problem really isn't Silverman. The problem's the public assistance system. In this country public assistance sucks, for
reasons we've been discussing. Silverman's seeing those people
at a sixty percent pay cut. He's doing what he can. It's not individual physicians, it's politics. It's good politics in this country
to cut health care to the poor. Virchow would call us to the barri-
cades."

"It's starting to worry me, Hans. The quality of care down
there."

"I'll talk with Silverman if you like."

"I'd appreciate it." As always, a good sounding board. We
fell easily into our accustomed roles of trial lawyer and consulting medical expert. Leitner loved riddles and the role of sage,
and he liked to lend a hand.

He opened the door to his sylvan entryway. "Colfax's protocols—those might be worth looking into," he said. "As an acad-
emic matter, probably not for a claim."

At my house on Mapleton Hill, Mahler blasted from a next-door
neighbor's open windows. The athletic couple on the opposite
side trotted off for an evening jog, matching reflector stripes
bouncing into the distance like foxfire in the growing dark.
Reluctant to go indoors, I brooded on the porch of my red-
shingled burgher's house, built in the twenties, where old Judge
Marler had lived and died.

Indian-summer evenings are lovely in Boulder. A lime
corona arced above the shoulders of the foothills. Venus burned
blue-white in the V of the canyon. Through the silver maple
overhead a frosty fall starscape was coming into focus. A chill
swept underfoot, an emphasis that autumn days were numbered.

I shivered and went inside, where there was little to savor except reheated satay from the Indo-Ceylon carryout. Quierin food. Quisine, I called it. She'd gotten me hooked.

After Kathleen's death I'd planned to clean house, trade Boston antiques for Ikea contemporary, paint the fleurette wallpaper white. I wound up only sending back to her family what would matter most to them: our Oxfordiana, the framed page from the Book of Kells, the view of Connemara, her grandmother's flatware and lace. Still on the kitchen wall was the fourth-graders' portrait of Kathleen in beans, a mosaic of glued, dried, and multicolored vegetable matter—pinto hair, split-pea eyes, a smile of limas. And the class of '91's "My Favorite Teacher" appliqué plate with a snapshot of Kathleen and her students as Dorothy among Munchkins. In the entry hall, a bust of Dante's Beatrice, the turn of whose delicate and almost beating ivory throat so eerily matched the old-fashioned, half-profile oval photograph of my wife I'd hung behind it: spectral sisters, pale but blood-struck, youth and beauty frozen in film and stone.

Idealization is a game grief plays. It was hard to recall anything wrong with Kathleen. I erased everything less than wonderful—how it got lonely with just us two; her occasional moods, homesick and distant, sometimes angry over nothing; her disinterest in the larger world. She was my crutch and I missed her support, but I willfully forgot how my dependence may have kept her from growing. The less-than-wonderful things became the attributes of someone else, the one who died. The one here haunting me was as perfect as Beatrice on her pedestal.

Kathleen's cassettes were still in the cabinet, from *Live at Goodbody's* to the one CD, *Kathleen Stone and Colcannon Live at Wandering Aengus*. I hadn't played any of them since she'd died, and I avoided others' versions of "Flower of Finae," "The Leaving of Liverpool," or "The Water Is Wide."

At least I'd overcome the semipsychotic need to ask the dead lover's permission for every new thing: "What would Kathleen want?" At a Javastraat pub with Quierin, I said it once. The topic had to do with re-upping for another tour at the tribunal's OTP. "Kathleen is dead," Quierin observed. "She doesn't want anything."

And Quierin knew a thing or two about the dead.

In the company of the bean mosaic and the appliqué plate, I nuked and consumed some Quisine. I did not play Kathleen's cassettes or CD. I watched an ignorant debate on CNBC about the Holbrooke mission to defuse Kosovo. I checked for Q-mail. None tonight. She might be deep in the E-free Bosnian boonies. Regardless, I sent a good-night message as breakfast greeting. I described Stillwell's conduct and what Leitner had said. "PTSD? You know sociopathology. What do you think?" I asked about Kosovo. "And what about you? What's going on?" I concluded it briskly, like an interoffice memo: "Q. Come see me."

I knew that was way peremptory as soon as it was sent. It lacked a rationale so I posted an amendment: "I miss your touch. I DREAM about it. I need your wacko Indo perspective. I need passion in my greenhorn life. Come dis America and walk with me in the mountains."

Thoughts of Quierin left me knocked back in my chair, throbbing like a rung bell. Her parting shots at the Goude Hooft were looking more perceptive. This is pretend, she'd said of us. The dead don't die like the colonel say. Go home and work it out with your wife. Bury her if you can.

I stared at the computer, conceiving a contest of ghost lovers, one from the present, one from the past, neither flesh and blood and here. Kathleen imagined up from the resonance of domestic objects. Quierin even more disembodied, our electronic dialogue like talking to the wind.

In an effort to spark a human connection, I called April at her friend's house. "All right," the friend's mother sighed. "April." The welcome did sound as if it was starting to wear.

"Yeah?" a familiar voice answered.

"It's just me, Elliot."

"Just me too. Just Ape, like everybody says. Not you."

"No."

"Think it, though."

"Don't either."

"Do too."

"April."

"Just jacking you up a crank. How come an old-timer like you's still awake? And make it fast. They want to hook up their modem deal."

I hit the highlights of what I'd learned from Leitner. The roommate's death was avoidable. It may have been negligent. We need to be careful. Stillwell's like a combat veteran who flips out when a car backfires. And it's great your mom is starting to speak but we have to be realistic. We can't get our hopes up yet.

"I'd of thought hope's the whole point," April said.

CHAPTER 9

"So you think him being competent is good?" April sipped a Pepsi. Led Zeppelin T-shirt, "Hammerwood Park." She took notes on a legal pad. Darla substituted coffee carafes behind the counter. She smoothed her candy-stripe jumper, keeping an eye with the hopeful curiosity of the under-stimulated.

The White Spot booth had become our war room. So long as I stayed committed to catching Stillwell, April would cooperate with me. Even to the point of isolating herself at the White Spot if Stillwell came back to visit. It was part of being a team.

"If I were Stillwell's lawyer, my defense to an assault charge is diminished capacity, not 'someone else did it,'" I said. "But with a judicial finding and his doctor's testimony that he's competent, there goes the brain-injured guy who couldn't know or control what he was up to."

"So why'd they give it up?"

"It's what Stillwell wanted—no more conservators running his life. It was against his lawyer's wishes, I'm sure, but Leitner is a straight shooter and he told it straight. The organic problems are apparently minimal at this point."

"We know he knew what he was doing."

"I guess."

"Now they'll charge him?"

"Russell Tucker will want his ducks lined up." The shade of Mayor Jovanovic crossed my mind. The indictment had been premature. There was pressure to grab the nearest Serb.

April had been making the rounds in her mother's pickup. She'd cozied up to Detective Roybal, talked to neighbors, and done her own weapons search along Stillwell's dog-walk route. She hadn't found the weapon yet, but she had some theories. "And," she said, "I located the milkman."

One of April's theories was—he used an Alpo can. "The scar is sort of like the bottom of the can, if it was bent just right. And the can is heavy. And afterward he feeds what's in it to Monty, then puts the can out with the curbside pickup. Perfect crime."

"Don't tell me it was Ecocycle day."

"It was Ecocycle day."

"Well—who knows? Run it by the medical examiner. What else?"

"The milkman."

"Tell me."

"Her name is Jessica Jones. Doesn't work for Horizon anymore; but I got lucky and found her in Lyons."

"How?"

"You know, friends and rumors. The former girl-milkman network. Cops thought, name like that—needle in a haystack. Cops around here are getting, like, demoralized."

She was right about that. In the days after June's assault the Boulder police did an indiscriminate sweep of the crime scene, tagging, photographing, and bagging everything in sight for the evidence locker, where it all remained, uninventoried, unanalyzed, waiting for a signal from Russell Tucker that he wanted it worked up for a charge. Instead he shut it down. Roybal was chapped. The prosecutors were pigeonholing the case as routine battering, run-of-the-mill spousal fisticuffs. Hubby's a head case. No minor children to intercede for. And, per the neighbors, the treaters, the shelter people, not a danger to the community. The DA wanted to send this one to anger therapy and community service.

Homicide and it might be different. Homicide was a touchy subject in Boulder, Colorado. The uncharged murder of the six-year-old daughter of parents of means had the tabloids and talk shows lashed to a lather. For the moment, Dale Stillwell was the unlikely beneficiary—Tucker had bigger fish to fry—but that could change in a flash.

"So what does Jessica the milkman add?" I asked.

"Only maybe the missing link." April edged closer, raised her eyes, and lowered her voice, as though Darla were listening in. "She'll testify, Elliot. We're tight. With my dad sort of in the dairy business, shipping end, she opened up."

"About what?"

"Okay," April whispered. "Pay attention. Mom was, like, this long-term customer. Jessica remembers her real well. Never met Mom, naturally, but milkmen get a feel for their customers from orders, houses, habits. Like they know the personality without having to meet the person. Milkmen get to sense, like, auras of the sleeping beings in all those darkened homes." April was working her hands for emphasis.

I frowned. "Jessica must be something. But I see evidentiary problems with this testimony."

"Here's the deal. Jessica Jones delivered milk to Mom's house every week for two and a half years and it was always the same. *Every single week.* Carport light is on by the milkbox. Milk order's always the same. One no-fat, one low-fat, and assorted minor dairy products. Always the same stuff."

"Except July fifteenth?"

"Carport light was *off*. First time ever. And there's a note changing the milk order. *For the first time ever.* Three low-fats, a half-pint whipping cream, and no cottage cheese."

I guess she expected me to whistle or something.

"The dairy still had the note. Jessica got it for me. *Stillwell* wrote it."

"Well?"

"Well, it spooked her. She had a premonition something bad had happened. *To Mom.* All dark and a note. Didn't make sense. To put out a note changing the order he ought to have the carport light on like always, instead of turning it off. What do you make of it?"

I shook my head. Clueless.

She drew back and appraised me skeptically. "You usually defend these cases, right, when someone's hurt? Except over in—Holland?"

"My defense days were another life. Days of the iron horse. I'm a different man."

"Wouldn't affect how you look at our case, being on the other side?"

"I hope not."

"Elliot." She leaned close across the Formica again. "Do you think I need a lawyer? You're great, but maybe I need my own lawyer. Or Mom does."

"I'm the stand-in for your mother. So I can't be your lawyer regardless, or your mother's."

"You said we could do a civil suit for battering."

"Battery."

"I want to."

"Not so fast, April. There's a problem."

"Who's the suit for," she asked, "if we file it?"

"Your mother is the plaintiff. She files through me as conservator, but the suit's for her."

April screwed up her mouth. "Basically you would, like, run her lawsuit?"

"Correct. I make the legal decisions for June."

"After my birthday, I'm the conservator?"

"Yeah. You file, not me. You call the shots."

"What can we sue for?"

"What you claim is the costs of all this"—I ran a hand across the view of Colfax—"for the rest of her life."

"Like many millions?"

"Yes, but that's not what you collect. That's the rub."

I explained the rub. Like other states, we had an exemption statute, a debtor-protection measure from Dust Bowl days that, except in cases of fraud or "felonious killing," safeguarded assets deemed essential necessities of life from execution to satisfy legal judgments. Because of the exemption statute, the bank couldn't take the dirt farmer's house to collect on a defaulted note, or his car, his schoolbooks, necessary wearing apparel, his burial plot, fuel on hand, or up to thirty head of poultry. Or "the proceeds of a personal injury settlement," which were deemed essential necessities since they compensated for the dirt farmer's disabilities.

Stillwell's considerable wealth was constituted entirely of the proceeds of a personal injury settlement. "Get a jury verdict for ten, hell, twenty million dollars, and he can thumb his nose and keep cashing those annuity checks, exempt under the statute. Your mom gets zip."

And no contingent-fee lawyer would want a case on which he can't collect a fee.

"Not fair," she said. "Got to be a way around it."

"No way I know of. Hypothetically, if Stillwell had killed your mother with the Alpo can, instead of just destroying her life, the felonious-killing exception would apply. Murderers can't use the exemption to shield their assets from their victims. Or we could try to show Stillwell came by his settlement fraudulently. If he's so damn competent after all, maybe he did. Of course, I blessed the settlement as proper. Sorry."

"Hypothetically," April said, "if we find a lawyer dumb enough to sue, and we don't care whether we can collect a judgment or not, what do we need to prove?"

"That your stepfather assaulted your mother with a blunt object on July fourteenth or fifteenth, 1998, injuring her severely."

"Like we're the DA?"

"We're both the cops and the DA but we have a lower standard of proof. Remember the Simpson civil case? The preponderance-of-the-evidence standard, not the reasonable-doubt standard."

"Getting Stillwell is like getting O.J.?"

"Yeah. Except for the exemption statute."

"Screw it. I'm in."

Darla stopped by to top off my mug. "I'm with you, honey," she said to April. "I think you should sue. Hells bells, he tried to kill your mom." She put mug, can, and glass aside, sponged up the rings, and padded back to her counter in sensible shoes.

"We still need a lawyer. Maybe I can talk somebody into it."

To my surprise eventually I did—the perfect lawyer for June. She played hardball, and she already knew the parties. She wasn't totally daunted by the collection problems. She was motivated by the glory of a giant judgment and the vindication that meant. Like April, what she really cared about was getting Stillwell.

Paige Jorritsma was stoked. As the Western Pacific's lawyer when Stillwell had sued the railroad, she'd been Stillwell's adversary for years. Now she could try to redeem the damage he'd done with the WP money he heisted and maybe get some back.

April talked her way into spending the night with June. In the morning when I got there, the Indigo Girls were singing "Southland in the Springtime." April finished clipping her mother's nails. She held June's hand in hers and leaned toward her face, eye to eye, mouth to ear. "If you can hear me, move." The thumb rose and fell. "If you know me, move." The thumb rose and sank again. "Talk to me, Mom."

"Hello," June said. She'd been saying it daily.

"Did Dale hurt you?" June's eye searched April's. Her breath labored from the effort to speak. "If Dale hurt you, move." The thumb rose and stayed.

April looked at me. Her eyes were shining. Something was wrong.

"She's telling us about it, Elliot. It's like the code we had for phone calls when Stillwell was there. Yes-or-no questions. How she talks about bad stuff."

"April?" There was heightened feeling in her voice.

"Mom's getting really better now. When I kiss her, she moves her lips like she's trying to kiss me back. I'm teaching her to swallow again. Cranberry juice in a dropper."

"Great, April. You're the one."

She looked at me wide-eyed, now pooling with tears. "You are a kind person, Elliot. I see that with you and Mom."

April had a way of throwing you off. Kind was not how I thought of myself. I thought I was analytical and aggressive enough to master the martial arts of trial work while keeping a judicious distance. Feelings did intrude, fear, desire. Was kindness, compassion part of the picture too?

She'd embarrassed me. I shook my head. "I found a lawyer for you. She's good and she's willing."

April blinked. She knuckled an eye. "She?"

"Very she. Four months pregnant."

"No way. What happens at trial? What if the baby's sick?"

"You don't know Paige. She'll focus, baby and all. Paige is tough as a four-bit steak."

April turned pensive, but the feeling remained in her look. "You know that administrator woman, Hudnut?" she said at length. "I think she'll let me stay here awhile. I said I wanted to be with Mom after what happened to her roommate. At first she's, like, that's not going to work. Then Ricky died yesterday and Hudnut backed down. 'You can have the empty bed,' she says, 'until patient availability improves.' Well, thanks, Hudnut. And when you move a new one in I'll get a cot."

Ricky died yesterday?

The kid from Pine Ridge Reservation—everybody's favorite. Ricky was quadriplegic, with a short life expectancy, but his coma was intermittent and light. He could hold his head up without support. He often recognized staff. He smiled. April liked to sit with him at social hour, asking yes-and-no questions as she did with June. He sat erect, handsome, draped with necklaces of feathers and beads and seeds and shells his father had brought from the medicine man.

June had fallen asleep, tired from conversing. It was wishful thinking, Hans Leitner said, to foster hope for the doomed inmates of Colfax. *You have to be realistic. False hope leads to disaster.* Could all of our care and effort and money and, indeed, compassion be going only to perpetuate suffering, as Leitner warned might be the case?

Now April caressed her sleeping mother's hair. I was struck by the blessing of mother and daughter living together after five years apart, though the worst of circumstances—violence, grief, guilt, hurt, fear—had reunited them. Maybe I was just relieved knowing that now, all through the Colfax night, June would not be alone. Someone who cared fiercely would be at her side in that precarious place.

Beyond Colfax and everywhere across infinity, planets raced in ceaseless flight. Everywhere except here, except for June, motionless, locked in time. Weighing hope for her against futility struck me as a spurious calculation of her needs and our imperatives. The responsibility of the able-bodied to the disabled may be a kind of absolute, like the responsibility of the able citizens of able nations to the beaten refugees of Yugoslavian wars. When are those who retain the strength to act, turn will to deed, create and change events, allowed to stop using their strength to keep the strengthless with us, to try to coax them back?

•   •   •

A few days later Hans Leitner returned my call.

I ran by what I'd learned of Ricky's death. The cause, according to the Colfax administration, was myocardial infarction. Ricky was ventilator dependent, unable to breathe unassisted. Jasmine, the OT, told April that when Ricky was found, the ventilator hose was detached. Could respiratory failure because of an unattached hose lead to cardiac arrest and death in a quadriplegic?

"Sure. Just because a heart attack killed him doesn't mean something else didn't bring it on. Who found him?"

"Nurse, on a routine four-hour check. What do you think?"

"First, sudden death from cardiac arrest in a twenty-year-old in his sleep would be suspicious in itself except he's a quad. So heart failure, if that's in fact what happened, is not per se a red flag. As I suspect you suspect, the red flag is the ventilator hose. When a ventilator hose detaches, an alarm bell sounds and all come running. If the bell failed or had been disabled, and no one came to assist, he could go into respiratory distress, failure, infarct and die in forty-five minutes, an hour."

"What do you mean, 'disabled'?"

"I see three possible explanations for the facts you gave me. Maybe four. One, the hose detached, the alarm sounded, but they were playing Hearts at the nurses' station and didn't hear it or ignored it. Two, the hose detached but the alarm failed so nobody knew. Three, someone disabled the alarm, then detached the hose."

"Intentionally?"

"Hypothetically intentionally. And four, he had a heart attack in his sleep and died like quads sometimes do and during resuscitation efforts the hose was innocently disconnected and the alarm ignored."

"What's your hunch?"

"I don't do hunches, Elliot. A hunch is wishful thinking. Leads to sloppiness, overconfidence, and error. Gather your evidence, analyze the data, and follow the data, not a hunch."

I knew Leitner well enough to take that with a grain of salt. Like many fine scientists Hans was not outwardly meticulous, and he had a short attention span. He followed data when it excited his interest, and I sensed he was curious about Ricky's death.

"How do I follow it here?"

"Not easy. Find the vent and test it. Was the alarm functional? Had it been disconnected? An autopsy would show any structural problems of the heart, any scarring, or coronary artery disease, or it might show a different cause of death or shed light on events that led to cardiac arrest. Check his chart. Did he actually infarct? Were there signs of underlying heart disease? What was his general state of health? Was there a history of detachments with this machine? None of which you're likely to get without filing suit, except autopsy."

"Autopsy's out. Ceremonial burial on the reservation."

"State should investigate. Probably won't. Do you have those Colfax protocols, by the way?"

"They just laughed when I asked."

"I'll get a set from the nurse administrator. She won't say no to a doc." He paused. "Say, Elliot. Stillwell does want to come again, if the pistol's not around."

"Tell me when. She won't be there."

"Thanks. And don't start getting paranoid. It's probably just cruddy equipment, Medicaid nickels and dimes, poor nursing at worse."

We got a half hour's notice from Hans Leitner, en route, that they were on their way. April earnestly coached her mother, then retired to the White Spot to keep an eye from the booth on June's uncurtained window. When doctor and patient arrived, I explained the ground rules—no approaching or disturbing June; no shouting. Behave yourself. I showed Stillwell his chair. He looked me up and down.

What did make him tick? Stillwell was physically, if not verbally, expressive, in the curve of a lip, the flicker of something shrewd. His hidden parts rose and disappeared like a branch rolling in a river. He turned from me to his wife and for a few seconds froze; his look intensified. Their withheld passion lent the illusion of erotic depth. Then his eyes raked the room. He went to the folding chair I'd positioned as far from June as possible.

For fifteen or twenty minutes Dale and June Stillwell faced each other across her room, mutually catatonic. Stillwell never said a word. June watched back, expressionless. After a while she dozed, then awoke, strengthened. Stillwell took on a hypnotized quality, transfixed like Mayor Jovanovic, mesmerized as the exhumation video played on. I felt apprehensive. Someone's privacy was being invaded, though how and whose were uncertain. Leitner motioned me into the hall to chat.

He told me he'd gotten through to Silverman, and Colfax had faxed him a set of staff protocols, which he'd have Ellen fax on to me. Silverman didn't know anything about the Indian boy on the vent, but he confirmed they'd charted signs of infection in June's roommate, low-grade fever, tachycardia, starting twelve days before she died. Under the protocols it didn't meet the criteria to ambulance her to the Platte Valley ER, and it fell within staff discretion to wait for Silverman's rounds. Twelve days is plenty of time for meningitis to hit brain fluid in a patient with a shunt. Leitner thought Silverman or an ambulance should have been called, but the real fault was with the referral criteria in the protocols. Grossly inadequate, but the care levels were set by the state, and bureaucrats get brownie points when they close a high-cost account like the roommate's. So sue the governor.

"Love to."

"And keep an eye on these jokers."

"April's sleeping here now. She's got everybody watching their backs."

"Good for her. Does she still want to sue my patient?"

I paused. "She'd like to, of course, if Stillwell's not prosecuted soon. She needs to see him held accountable."

"In her place I would too. But she's blocked by that statute, isn't she? She can't reach his annuities."

"That's right. We're looking at other options."

"*We?* April has a lawyer now?"

"Paige Jorritsma. You know her."

He whistled softly. "The Iron Maiden. That's bad news."

"The Iron Mama. She's pregnant."

Leitner laughed in his nose. "Say, Elliot, let's catch dinner someplace, John's or the Flagstaff House—Het Seinpost West."

"I'll check my calendar, see what I can fit in."

"Your practice up and running? I know some docs who could use a good lawyer."

"I don't work for insurance companies," I said, a little too pious.

"Just business organization stuff."

"Send 'em over." I lied that I was getting busy. I told him I had a court appearance coming up, my first since the Vukovar Hospital trial—which was true, except it wasn't until six weeks from Monday. Preliminary hearing in a white-collar case, trade-secret theft.

"In court," Leitner said, "there's nobody better."

I felt oddly touched. "At the moment I'm June's conservator, in charge of her finances. I wish Stillwell would help out. Maybe I can create a trust so she keeps her benefits. Since he's competent, he can go back to the railroad. Lay track or something."

"Elliot." Leitner lowered his voice. We stepped a ways down the hall. "I told you it was disabling, his PTSD. He can't work there."

"He seems pretty chill today. Weird but chill." I hoped to tease a little more out. PTSD was the key, Leitner had said.

"I'm talking out of school but—trains freak this guy."

"Trains and his stepdaughter."

"That's interesting," he said, "but the accident is key."

"June was hit mid-July, nowhere near the anniversary."

"True."

"So what happened?" Suddenly we reached the heart of the matter. "Did he see a movie about Jesse James? Did he hear a Johnny Cash song and jump the track?"

"Have a heart, Elliot." Leitner sighed and smiled. "You know I can't tell you anything he's told me."

From the direction of June's room came the sound of footsteps and a door banging a wall. I half-jogged down the empty hallway. In her room June looked okay, untouched, in place in her chair, her eye vacant. I approached, dropped my face to hers. Her breathing was rapid and shallow. No one else was there.

CHAPTER 10

The pursuit of truth is what philosophy is for, not law. Law is for regulating behavior and the orderly transfer of wealth, though truth is useful. Truth simplifies, in the words of Saint-Exupéry chosen for the motto of the war-crimes tribunal. It simplifies, but—the claims of forensic science and the New Testament notwithstanding—it rarely makes you free.

That law is used to transfer wealth, spreading the risk of loss, was something to which Paige Jorritsma remained unreconciled. Wealth, she seemed to feel, should stay put. Transfers of it through legal action upset a fearful equilibrium. What went around came around, and sooner or later, successful plaintiffs invariably got theirs.

Paige Jorritsma was a street fighter trapped against her will in the body of someone's attractive, thirtysomething, pregnant wife. She had shapely arms, a pleasingly spherical belly, short frosted hair, sharp features, and green eyes that were a little narrow, a little unhappy. She had a fixed, almost absentminded smile that could be mistaken for suggesting harmlessness when it actually expressed derision grown second nature. Paige cultivated a reputation with plaintiffs' counsel as a pathologically aggressive dominatrix who, when not stropping the blade, was reaching for the whip and chair. But I'd always enjoyed the pressured intensity of her professional company. Her story was simpler than her adversaries fancied. Her husband was a failed paving contractor and she overcompensated. She and April promised to make a pair.

Paige's defense-side cynicism put me to shame. Her railroad had paid a lot of money to a lot of folks, mostly over her objections. She could count on one hand the plaintiffs she thought a settlement had genuinely helped. Most were extortionists and con artists whom money just encouraged to continue malingering. Settlements broke up marriages, pitted children against parents, put simple people on the path to reckless ruin—quitting union sinecures and blowing it in Vegas or on a second-cousin dotcom entrepreneur.

"Never," she said at the war room White Spot booth, "have I seen a money settlement as evil as this." She relished the validation of her cynicism and the reversal of roles, the hypocrisy of Hancock for the defense.

"Paige, I've got kind of an agenda here." I was a little touchy about the Stillwell settlement; I wouldn't have been sitting in the White Spot if it weren't for Paige in 1996. There was a question or two about that I still wanted to ask.

April had an agenda too: get Stillwell. She reviewed for Paige what she'd seen from the booth window after Stillwell had slipped past Leitner and me, lunging cryptically in the parking lot, talking to himself. He whacked the roof of his doctor's car and head-bumped the doorframe. Local homies taunted and pointed. "You got to keep a better eye on him," April admonished me. "The man is very out there. Ask Darla."

On cue, Darla padded up with a fresh carafe. "I saw it all," she confirmed. Paige accepted a refill. "Long, black Lexus pulls in—you notice that. Out steps Dr. Frankenstein and the monster. I knew right off it was him. In a while he's back, alone this time. Banging his head? Lord have mercy." She let out a what's-the-world-coming-to humph and padded away. "If you won't lock him up, at least keep him out of here."

I pulled out two legal pads, penciled one To Do, the other Facts and Questions. "Let's talk about timing, the criminal case, damages, defenses, and facts. April's been digging up facts for liability. I've been probing his defenses."

The plan was to file claims in both negligence and battery and for punitive damages. When to file depended on the DA,

Paige thought. We should tailgate the criminal case so the cops and the DAs were working for us. Plus, we had to wait to depose Stillwell until after criminal charges were resolved.

"So he can't assert the Fifth?"

"Right," Paige said. "Problem is—Gutless Tucker."

"So long as Russell Tucker sits on his hands," I explained to April, "we can't examine Stillwell under oath. He won't answer any questions that might be self-incriminating."

"But if they convict him, he's fair game for us?"

"You bet. Plea bargain's okay too," Paige said. "After the deal, Stillwell loses the Fifth and we have at him."

April wrinkled her nose. She didn't like talk of deals, especially, she said, after what she'd been finding out.

"Let's discuss damages," I said. "Damages is an even bigger obstacle than having to depend on Tucker's office."

"Here we go," April muttered. She didn't like talk of obstacles either.

"Two problems. One has a solution, one may not. Let's say we win a megajudgment. Ten million."

"Fifteen," Paige said. "Her needs, we get there."

"Whoa, Paige. Got those plaintiff juices flowing?"

"Why not?" She smiled absently.

"Ten, fifteen, whatever, is immaterial," I continued. "If they're for ordinary damages, problem one is the man just files for bankruptcy. Annuities don't count in the bankruptcy estate and the judgment is discharged."

"Meaning?" April said.

"Poof, it's gone."

"Solution?"

"Malice." I tried to smile maliciously.

"Yeah?"

"Debts for damages for acts of malice can't be discharged in bankruptcy."

"Man's pure malice," April said, "but how do you tell it to a judge?"

"We call it intentional harm in the complaint. We sue for punitive damages."

"Make that thirty million." Paige smiled on.

"Get punitives and we've got malice and bankruptcy gets him nowhere. Problem one solved."

"What's the other one?"

"Collecting. Bankruptcy can't make Paige's thirty million go away, but Stillwell's twelve million of annuities still can't be touched because of the exemption statute. They're proceeds of a personal injury settlement with Western Pacific."

Paige made a face. "There are exceptions, though."

"Fraud and felonious killing. They don't apply."

"There has to be a loophole."

"What if we can't find one? April? Paige?"

Paige drummed a set of bitten nails. "Bottom line, once he pleads or gets convicted, that's collateral estoppel."

"Come again?" said April.

"Criminal guilt proves civil liability, is what it means here," Paige said. He pleads guilty, we don't even have to prove our case, except for how much he owes. And whether or not we ever collect, for a low-cost civil trial we still get to hold the batterer up to the world. I'd try that case."

Paige wasn't quite thinking like a plaintiff's lawyer yet. She measured the outcome of a PI claim not in bundles of dollars but ingots of shame.

"April? Your thoughts?"

She struck a surprisingly reasonable note. "I understand what you're saying about the exemption deal. Not fair, but nothing's to stop him, is what I hear you saying."

"I'll look at the law," Paige offered. "The exceptions. Other options." She eased out of the booth. "Second trimester, second cup takes you straight to the well." Standing next to the table, short dress drawn higher still by the globe of her abdomen, Paige looked mighty buff for a pregnant gal.

"You coming with?" Paige asked April. "I'll give you the dish on Elliot."

April bounced out of the booth and they huddled off toward the ladies' room, Darla tracking their passage. She twisted her head to shoot me a tsk-tsk look. She took her time coming over, pencil stabbed in frizzed brown hair. Stopped at my elbow and crossed her arms.

"Know what I think about the monster?" Darla asked rhetorically. "I don't think his brain even got hurt."

"Hard guy to figure," I said agreeably. I was ruminating on what had gone wrong in 1996.

"Russell Tucker," Darla continued in the familiar, judgmental tone of a talk show caller. "Got a big yellow stripe straight up his backside. Forget him. You gotta sue."

"Darla—" I began to complain, but her crossed arms unfolded and dropped to her hips in an even more opinionated posture.

"And you can't let Pepsi girl call the shots. Sorry, Gramps. You need to take the bull by the horns."

"Right, Darla. Thanks."

She took a step away, stopped, turned slowly back. "Alpo can'll never fly." She flashed me a tight, painted, personalized smile.

Paige beat April back, bumping her belly against the table edge as she scooted in across from me. "Stillwell," she said. "I don't get this guy. I know what April thinks, what do you think?"

"About what?"

"Who is he? Woman hater? Wild man? This a wife-killer plot for the money, or your act-of-passion jealous-rage scenario? Or a Tony Perkins psycho boy? Or some kind of Lennie-type *Mice and Men* simpleton thing? *Or what? What is the story,"* she demanded, *"with this man's brain?"*

"Darla thinks it's fine."

"Elliot."

"It doesn't matter who he is." He could be all or none of the above, and other things too. Stillwell was what we projected onto him. I even caught glimmers of a kindred spirit. A man who'd lost his wife and couldn't get past it.

"All we care about," I said, "is whether he did it, and did it knowingly."

"So catch me up on the brain."

"It's lots better, Leitner says."

"Leitner," she sniffed.

"Dr. God, Hancock calls him." I got in a dig.

"Please." Paige winced. She'd never forgiven Leitner, the defense doc who'd gone native—joined the plaintiff Stillwell and sabotaged her cross. Apostate, not God, and not to be trusted again.

"I know you don't like him, but he helps us here. He told me his patient's flipped out with PTSD but fully competent. He testified to that under oath. That seals it."

She nodded. "Okay. Competent and we should win. I guess we shouldn't care about his—hang-ups."

"No," I said slowly. "No, that gets us nowhere. But, Paige, how can you buy his being competent so easily when you thought the opposite in 1996?" This was the question I'd been chewing on. Just as well April wasn't back yet. "Was Stillwell competent or incompetent when you defended his claims?"

"It didn't come up till settlement. We assumed he could manage his affairs. That's how the case proceeded."

"The reason I ask"—I paused to check my rising feelings—"is you and Hancock *said* he was incompetent, and the judge *found* he was incompetent, and I got dragged in because you pressured me."

"There wasn't any medical testimony back then. The judge based his findings on . . . I don't know. Observation. Testimony now is, he's competent, so, hey. We're in good shape. He loses the defense."

"But the point is, how could you have brought me in before if Stillwell was not actually in need of a conservator?"

She nodded, getting it—a personal, not a tactical, matter. April appeared at the table. She edged in next to me. Paige gave me a questioning look. "Go ahead," I said.

"Because we had to, Elliot. Stillwell hated the 'w-weasel' Hancock. He wasn't going to do what Hancock said, so we had to find someone else. Otherwise there'd be no deal. You were perfect, Hancock's old adversary. That's how they sold it to Stillwell. I hear June Stillwell made the call. June wanted you. And it worked. We cut the deal."

"But look what that led to. Stillwell was forced to settle when he didn't want to." He knew his wife was behind it. *That's* why he was mumbling about killing her when I overheard him. "And then, even when he's not really incompetent, she controls his money—the person who caused his injuries."

Behind the counter Darla paused while filling in a check, brow furrowed in mock-concentration, pencil aloft.

I lowered my voice. "And so he clobbers her."

"Who knows why he did it," Paige protested. "It could have been—snoring. Bad breath. God knows. I sure don't. Anyway"—her unhappy green eyes narrowed further—"my responsibility was to my company. My company wanted out."

"But my responsibility was to him. We should have ascertained competency. The judge should at least have taken testimony from Leitner. We should have either offered it or let Stillwell control his own claim, even if it meant no settlement. We should have anticipated the marital conflict from handing June the keys to his money. I shouldn't have let her be substitute conservator."

"Nobody could have anticipated this."

"Oh, yeah? I felt it in my bones." I caught a breath, released it. April watched with concern. "My role in that settlement was wrong."

April touched my forearm. Metallic-blue fingernails sparkled. "Other things caused what happened to happen," she said. "You need to hear what I found out."

"Elliot." Paige touched my other arm. Her fixed smile faded to open and glum. "I was wrong too. Is that what you need to hear? But let's move past it."

There was a lot to move past. Not just how I'd been used by Paige and Hancock—and June—but a whole railroad career in which injured people were adversaries. I'd tricked and strong-armed plenty of hurt people out of plenty of money. Paige would say, shit happens, get on with your life, you're better off on your own. I lacked her easy answers. My rationalization for railroad work had been loyalty to my master—a principle in disrepute since the Nuremberg trials. Loyalty is the time-honored easy out from moral conflict. Serving a master well is so easy and mindless: defeat those who challenge him. The disabled brakeman. The kids at crossings who don't respect The Train.

"Don't forget what we do for a living," Henry Steele, my hard-ass predecessor, had said when I'd wondered about a nasty tactic. "We screw the little guy." Henry humor, as was the Smurf-like Devil's Advocate on the corner of my desk. It didn't bother me at the time. I compartmentalized, like the president. Work was work, life was life. Even when work entailed eliminating, with a statute-of-limitations defense, the claim of a paraplegic run over by a train, I had in Kathleen a refuge.

Having Kathleen, I'd begun to realize, had let me off the hook. Now not much remained from defense days except the minor virtue of skepticism. Suspend judgment, suspect dogma, doubt unverified propositions, and demand proof. Constructive skepticism, I was taught at Oxford, is the way to useful knowledge. And *Quantum Scimus Summus*—we are what we know.

"Yes"—I freed myself from the women touching my arms, intending to soothe—"let's move on."

"Okay. Where are we?" Paige asked. "We agree Stillwell's competent, now anyway, which means no mental-state defense. Without that, the only other potential defenses are, one, a third-party intruder did it, or two, June did it to herself."

"Correct."

"Any support for those?"

"No evidence of an intruder," I said, "but, with a maybe unlocked door, hard to prove there wasn't one either. She fell and hit her face goes nowhere. A laugher."

"If his lone defense is a mystery guest, I'm in. But how do we show Stillwell did it? How do we show it had to be him? April— what do we know so far?"

"What *don't* we know?" She turned up her palms.

Stillwell was the only person present when June was attacked in bed, but he said he had no idea how it happened. The CBI fiber analysis of the blankets had come back with June's hair and matches to their clothes and carpet—pointing inside the house, and back to Stillwell, not outside to a stranger. To nail it down it would be nice to know which of several potential motives had prompted the attack, and what had happened to the weapon.

"So I found out what happened to it." April tried for cool and coy, with a sideways smile, but tailed off in a giggle.

April's friend Detective Carlos Roybal wasn't happy with the DA's slow track. He had gotten her a set of crime-scene photographs and diagrams, the 911 tape, and had duped the answering-machine tape. "I'm on the machine, three calls hoping Mom's all right, which helps, but check this out."

She spread perhaps a hundred three-by-five glossy photos in an array. They'd taken pictures of next to everything in the house, no matter how innocent or mundane.

"I've already seen them," I observed.

"Look again. Charlie—Detective Roybal—thinks nobody,

not even you, Elliot, gave these a good, hard look till me. There's this tiny little detail I noticed the third time around." She shuffled through scenes of domestic objects, a cluttered desktop, figurines on the black marble mantel, bloodstained bedding and a mattress, hallways, bathrooms, the carport, details of a double-locked window sash, a kitchen series. She stopped.

"See this? See what I see?"

She tapped a nail against a photograph of a kitchen-sink cabinet, doors open, a trashcan inside full of what looked like discarded paper, a plumber's helper handle-up, cleansers, and a mixing bucket filled with tools.

"Well—no, I don't see."

"Look at the hammer." An aluminum claw hammer stood head-end-up in the bucket.

"Not the hammer," I said. "It would have made a completely different wound."

"No, this." April pointed with a blue nail tip at a tiny white glint on the peg end of the hammerhead.

"Reflection of the flash."

"That's what Charlie thought. What else could it be?"

Paige made a face. "It doesn't look like anything."

"I know," April said, "but I had a *feeling*. What if that wasn't light but—a *substance*?"

"Are you going to tell us the cops impounded the hammer?"

"They took *everything*. Sheets, bungee cords, dirty dishes, salad spinner. Everything but the sink. I don't know what he cooks with."

"Doubt he minds," Paige offered. "A carryout type."

And not alone, I reflected.

"Listen, guys," April said. "That hammer's with the other stuff in the bucket in a brown bag at the cop-shop evidence locker with dozens of other bags. Cops are out metal-detecting the rose beds and scampering on the roofs, but nobody's double-checking the bags."

"The hammer," I said, "did it have a—substance on it?"

April's smile waxed triumphant. "A little spot of white powder sort of caked right there. Dead center on the pounding part. Average person might not think twice about it till you work it out backward in your mind. Personally," she offered immodestly, "I'm attuned to powder. All those chem courses—substances, properties, unique compositions of stuff. How do you explain it, Elliot? What's a powder spot doing on a hammer-head?"

Hammers, it was true, ordinarily struck articles of metal or wood. The last thing this particular hammer had struck had to have been composed of something else, since the very next use would have knocked the powder off.

April hunched forward, gravely conspiratorial. "Mom's asleep. Stillwell decides on his evil thing. He picks up the ceramic object that's missing from the mantel, and he does it. He thinks Mom's gone and it sinks in how much trouble he's in. Now he's got to get rid of his weapon. He comes up with a plan. He writes a note for the milkman. He gets the hammer out and turns off the outside light so no neighbor could see him if they were looking. He steps out into the carport. He puts some newspaper down on the concrete slab and pounds up the ceramic object till it's nothing but powder. He leaves the note for the milkman to have an excuse for being out in the carport at midnight in case anybody *did* see him. Then he gets rid of the powder and the paper—outside, or maybe that's what was in the kitchen trash-can, or maybe he flushes it. He puts the hammer back. The only things he forgot were to wipe off the head of the hammer and turn the carport light back on."

Paige and I—a couple of skeptical, unimaginative defense lawyers—looked at each other and then at her.

"You go, girl," Paige said.

Sensing a moment, Darla stood at hand. She drew the pencil from her hair and moistened the point on her tongue. "The tab, big spender. For you and the harem." She smiled her just-for-me smile.

CHAPTER 11

At the tribunal I had decided that war criminals were different from common criminals. War criminals by
and large were ordinary folk—a neighbor, a coworker, bus driver or salesclerk, the director of Prijedor Hospital, the mayor of
Vukovar. This is why their failings were so moving, their conflicts so anguished, their acts so astonishing and disturbing.
They betrayed the capacity for savagery in us all.

I was starting to wonder whether common criminals weren't
mostly ordinary people too.

In November and December of 1998, Dale Stillwell
became a Colfax regular. He wanted to come twice a week. We
negotiated rules. No more than once a week, only on Sunday
(so it wouldn't interfere with therapy), and I had to be there
too. Still, every visit drove April deeper into a bitter fury.
Worse, June was no longer "doing better." She stopped speaking, she was less responsive, she slept more and more. I and
Leitner, and Silverman too, wondered about a fluid buildup in
the vesicles of her brain. A shunt might relieve pressure and
bring her back up. The first step was an MRI to verify the
problem. I applied for Medicaid approval and hounded the
caseworker to no avail. Few can match the institutional pes-
simism of Medicaid bureaucrats: MRIs won't help. Nothing
helps. No benefits are available.

"Hey, Dale," I remarked one Sunday as Stillwell was escorted in. "Why don't you pay for it? The MRI. Fifteen hundred bucks. A couple days' annuities, that's all it'd cost."

"Elliot." Leitner intervened in his calming way. "Not the time and place."

"But why not chip in?" I asked Stillwell anyway.

"I'll h-help." He looked to Leitner, unsure what to do. "I w-want to help."

"We'll talk about it," Leitner told me. "I'll let you know."

Stillwell's visits followed a pattern—the silent confrontation of husband and wife, April stewing at the White Spot, Leitner and I chewing the fat, Stillwell in the parking lot afterward jerking and jousting, lashing the air.

April suffered him more and more sullenly. She worried the DA would never act. That Paige would give up on the case. That other Colfax patients would die. That her mother would plummet past the point of no return.

Colfax was getting to April bad. She had bipolar mood swings—racing around on "the case" or moping in their room—all despair or all fantastic optimism. Colfax got to me too. It came to represent an oppressive, Kafkaesque edifice of medical and legal and governmental indifference, its false sweet-clean odor masking something wickedly wrong.

Quierin had responded to my abject message asking her to visit with a classic rag-out and abrupt volte-face: "You can't just whistle and hello I'm here. I know about your country. Yugoslavia next to you is a piece of pie. Home of the free? Home of the homeless. Putting girls in jail to have babies with handcuffs on? Or just zzzzt in Texas. Electrical chairs for girls! If mad cow don't get you first.

"Two people living in two worlds is the question first needing answers. Where are you? Who will you be? Who I am too."

Feeling her work pulling her away, sensing her receding, I considered letting Quierin win the tug-of-war and going back to Europe. Before I could cave, she receded entirely. Milosevic unexpectedly signed a cease-fire, letting Quierin's in-country work proceed. She hustled off to Bosnia before the ground froze in Brcko, a flash point in the pre-electronic Serb Republic. Immediately my Q-mail went dead.

I kept gnawing on the White Spot session with Paige, how

I'd been used two years before to neutralize Stillwell so his FELA case would settle. June's decline exacerbated such thoughts. I would not be used like that again.

Hearing nothing from Leitner, I prepaid June's MRI myself and put in calls to schedule the time and transportation. I vowed to get it back someday from Stillwell, with interest.

I stopped by Colfax one afternoon to find April sitting in June's wheelchair, frowning over the journal, wearing Iggy Pop, *The Idiot*. June lay on her side, relaxed almost to smiling from April's attentions, her long, charmed hair glamorously arranged.

April was reading aloud parts in the journal about the Therapeutics Riding Center. She'd gotten to Paul's breakthrough. "'He never walked once before,'" April read. "'He never even stood alone before and now he goes five steps in a row, not too wobbly. He tries to act cool but he can't stop grinning as if I could either. Sue says it's a miracle by me and Chaco, who's Paul's old dobbin, which truly walking is. But this is Paul, is what I tell him. It's all you, Paul.'"

"Let's take Mom around some horses!" April was suddenly eager and intense, mood-ring glowing. "Like the tack room or arena out there. Like, just to smell it and hear horses stamp and chuff and stuff. Just be there."

"Sure." Why not? "First let's see if the MRI shows something wrong. I'll call the riding center in the meantime."

"We can work on breakthroughs too!"

"Yeah, sure we can." I smiled. I went to paging through the week's entries in June's chart, which I'd checked out from the nurses' station on the way in.

"Surely sure," April murmured back. Soon she was lost in June's journal again. She flipped the fat manuscript upside down and turned back the final page. I knew what was coming. We'd been here before.

"The hexagram *K'un,*" she said. "Oppression. The lake is empty. Six in the third. He returns to his house and his wife is not there. Elliot—it's the last thing she wrote."

"I know."

"It's totally the worst you can throw. It means the hour of death draws near." April shuddered. *"Mom knew.* I can't stop thinking of him hurting her. I can't stop."

"April. This is morbid."

"Yeah? Yeah, fuck-all." She pressed her eyes.

"Why not put some music on or something? Be positive."

"Positive." She popped a rubber band around the journal and slid it in a drawer. "Sure deal. Surely positive." Her lips smiled but not her eyes. "*I* will be positive. I *will* be positive."

April fingered through her CD case and extracted the Cowboy Junkies. *Rarities, B-Sides, & Slow, Bad Waltzes.* At the second cut, from *The River Wild* sound track, I caught her wrist. The song was "The Water Is Wide." I reached across and hit Pause.

"Woo," she said. "Okay. Not music. Some other positive thing. How about—nice stories from the good old days? Feel-good stories to cheer us up? Or cheer up Mom?"

June lay in bed unchanged, pale, thin, and exquisitely posed, spellbound as a figure by Rossetti, gazing off at nothing of this world.

"Why not?" I said.

"You first."

"You."

"Bull. You. Something nice."

I thought a moment, looking down at the CD case I was thumbing in distraction. "Kathleen's voice," I said. I looked up. "You should have heard her." I could still summon it. A passage soft as fog, a held phrase like a rung bell. A voice as blended to Celtic song as wind in cottonwoods to water in a stream.

Kathleen believed in *song,* in the power of sung stories to delight and enlighten, purify and transport, to render sentiment into feeling. The power of voice to transform something as ordinary as speech, as maudlin as a lover's lament, as precious as a singer/songwriter's introspections, into soaring truths of the heart.

She sang all kinds, from "Paper Moon" to "You're the Reason God Made Oklahoma" to "A Whiter Shade of Pale," but she sang Celtic best. My good old days were listening to Kathleen—in Oxford, Galway, Cambridge, Boulder—as she sang on a stool, half-circled by the band, hands on her knees, knotting the cloth of her skirt, her soaring voice transforming.

"So then, what now?" April said. "You can't ever hear music again?"

I considered the kid with the bouncy hair in her mother's wheelchair. She had a point. I released the Pause button. Kathleen's song by someone else—I was floored by its beauty.

> Give me a boat that can carry two,
> And both shall row, my love and I.

I sang quietly along and rubbed my temples when it was over, and at exactly that instant I decided to return to Europe. I gave April an enigmatic smile. In a few weeks she would turn twenty-one, and I'd be free to go.

"You now," I said. "Your turn. Be positive. Something nice about you and June."

"Want to hear about my 4-H project?"

"Play fair, I was serious."

"Me too. My very last 4-H project. Remember, Mom?"

June's head rustled slightly though her eyes were closed.

"Mom remembers. 'Grasses of Wyoming: A Midsummer Survey.'"

The best thing about the country was grass, April thought. The endlessness of grass out on the Great Plains. Her other 4-H projects were gross—swine health tips, ditch maintenance techniques, modern methods of canning and preserving. But April was spoken to by grasses.

What made the project exceptional were the monsoon rains that year. Machines were converging on the Lander hayground from all over the state, windrowers, balers, loaders, stackers, hay-fork tractors. The windrows were high as houses where fields had been hayed. From a thirteen-year-old's perspective, in the unmowed fields of April's grandfather's ranch, all that stood above the rattling caress of grass were mountains, a horse, and her mother: the winds rising behind Yuma, and tall, capable, rodeo-capped June leading April through plush green curtains.

"When the time comes," April said, "I want to lie down and die in summer pasture."

June was making a soft smacking noise, involuntary chewing—enough of the here and now to remind us what industrial accident and domestic violence had done to April's pastoral.

"That's a nice Mom story, but what about Dad? Where's he in this picture? How about a nice story about him?"

April squinted toward the light. "Dad was gone of course. He's a trucker. He's always gone. Long hauls for the yogurt company. Yoplait. High-class, we were frequently reminded. So, in between, back home in Cheyenne it's just Mom 'n' me in our little world, and Yuma at the stable, and our pets, many dogs, Fidget the hamster, Roscoe the rat, Pretty the parakeet. Nice it actually was, it actually really totally was.

"When I was little, Mom would drive me down to the Denver zoo. She'd talk about places like Paris and Prague and Lander in the good days. We'd watch for hawks through the windshield.

"Mom likes animals." April's flowing speech braked and a hand moved in distress. Suddenly she was openly crying. She laughed and got the Kleenex. "Any stupid animal. You name it. *Chipmunks*." She blew her nose, then went to her mother. She sat at the edge of the bed and turned June and kneaded her winged shoulders as she slept.

"But you want to hear about Dad? Something, like, nice about Dad the truck driver? The driver of trucks?" She took a moment. "Every week or two Dad was home a day or so. He left this huge tractor trailer parked on the street in front of our itty-bitty house. No mistaking Dad's line of work. A man who moved large amounts of quality dairy product. When he left again, he'd run it a few hours first to refrigerate the trailer before they loaded. So the nice thing I remember about Dad is lying in bed at three and four in the morning listening to the rumble of this huge diesel engine idling in the street. Which is a dreamy, soothing sound, like all's well in the world. Because Dad's leaving.

"But the really nicest thing I remember is that what Mom kept saying she'd do, she in fact did. 'I'll show him,' Mom said. 'I'll drive trains.'"

The same day Paige called to say she could find no way around the exemption statute, June received a "Notice of Final Action" from the district attorney:

PEOPLE V. DALE WINSTON STILLWELL

Original Charges: Investigation of Assault in the First
                           Degree
                           Investigation of Assault in the Second
                           Degree

Case Disposition: District Attorney declined action.

After lengthy review, the District Attorney's office has
decided that there is insufficient evidence at this time to sus-
tain a filing of charges in the assault of June Mooney Stillwell. The District Attorney's office will review any
additional evidence as it is discovered to determine if a filing is appropriate at that point.

Physical Evidence Disposition: This evidence shall be
maintained in police custody.

The notice, which Russell Tucker had signed, was accompanied by an apologetic letter from his victim's advocate acknowledging what a difficult time this must be for Mrs. Stillwell and
her daughter, thanking them for their patience, commiserating
with them for their losses, and assuring them how seriously the
office regarded its commitment to prosecute crimes of domestic
violence.

The letter was addressed to June Stillwell in care of me, and
I drove down to Colfax rehearsing how to break double bad
news. Surrendering without a fight was a little lame even for
Tucker. We must be missing something. Without a criminal
prosecution to tailgate, and with the exemption statute certain
to shield Stillwell's annuities, Paige wasn't long for the case
unless we came up with a whole different angle.

June was alone in her room, April off in the pickup, nailing
down more facts against Stillwell, no doubt.

Late afternoon, April arrived in high spirits. She set on the
floor a Mole Hole tote bag with something inside it, turned a
three-sixty, and pumped both fists. "We've got it iced, Elliot. *I
found the weapon.*"

She cleared the night table and positioned on it a photocopy
of the police diagram tracing the outline in the dust of the
baseplate of the object missing from the Stillwells' mantel.

She'd taken the diagram to the Mole Hole to try to match it to a figurine base. An officer had already come around for the same reason. They'd looked for a couple hours but never finished. "There's thousands on all these shelves. 'You're welcome to try,' the lady says. So I make straight for the back wall. I have this feeling."

It took all day, trying one then another. The Farmer's Wife, The Dancing Girl, The Bishop, The Barrister, John Barleycorn, The Thatched Cottage, The Dutch Windmill, The Old Lady's Shoe. She'd already tried it on June's Infants of Prague. Thank God he hadn't used an Infant of Prague.

"What he did use, though, was this."

April extracted from the bag a figure wrapped in tissue paper, about nine inches high, three across, heavy for its size. She stood it on the windowsill and disrobed it of its tissue. Silhoutted before the Colfax parking lot stood a statuette of a little boy relieving himself in a Brussels street-corner fountain.

The Manikin Pis.

I hefted the Pis in my hand. He had a good, easy grip. The kid would pack a punch. His base was an irregular oval with a beveled edge that seemed to match June's injury. I stood the baseplate on the police diagram. They coincided perfectly.

"'It is enough that the arrow fits exactly the wound it has made.'"

"Yeah?"

"Kierkegaard," I said. "Good work."

"Now all Charlie needs is to have the CBI lab microanalyze the powder on the hammer to make sure it's the same composition as the Manikin Pis, and it all comes together. What the weapon was, why it can't be found, what he did with it, how he did it, and the evil genius has got to be him."

"This is—big," I had to admit. It didn't prove everything, but it was a giant step forward. Destroying it showed consciousness of guilt and a plan so sophisticated no one mentally impaired could have carried it out.

April wrapped and plunged the Pis back in the tote bag. "Can't let Stillwell see him," she whispered. Then she gave me a hug.

"We have found the Manikin Pis!"

• • •

The bad news of Tucker's "Notice of Final Action" was badly received, as expected.

"He gets totally *off?* He keeps all his money, when we proved the case? And he still keeps coming here and tormenting Mom and giving her the evil eye, making her worse?"

I suggested Tucker might change his mind if the chemical analysis of the powder confirmed what we thought it would. But Tucker's mind sounded made up.

"Oh, fuck-all."

April fell into a deeper gloom than I'd seen before. I tried to get an appointment with Millsap and Tucker. April seemed hardly interested. Paige let her know that unless we could somehow come up with a different defendant or claim, she was off the case. Stillwell's visits continued and April continued to glower. Her rage cooled to ice. She brooded at the White Spot alone.

I spent a Sunday afternoon, a Stillwell visiting day, in and around Colfax worrying over June, now sleeping all the time, it seemed, and looking less healthy. Stillwell's visits got longer every time. April was out, probably keeping her vigil at the booth. I had the feeling she would wait until I went home. I found football on a non-Monica network. First quarter of a dotcom bowl. April's birthday was approaching, when I was to hand over responsibility for her mother. A celebration of sorts would be in order. Something was needed to cheer things up.

"Chow time." Rico sauntered in. "Sing for ya supper." He flipped and caught a can of Nutren and popped it down the hatch. "Yo, Watash. TGIS, thank God it's Sunday." Rico had been working evening shift and a staggered week, Wednesday to Sunday. "I *love* stormy Monday, especially tonight." He did a boogie turn around June in bed. "Night shift," he sang. "It's a night thing. I be vanishing at the clock's twelfth stroke. Pumpkin in the night, soon's you get ya Sunday dinner"—the thousand-milliliter feedbag. "The midnight special."

Rico and I watched the ball game awhile. Neither of us knew any of the players. I asked about the Watash business. What's a Watash?

"African chief, man, what a Watash is." He laughed long and loud, got up and stretched, went back to work. A half hour later he returned. I'd moved on to the Discovery Channel. Creatures of the Kalahari. Meerkats weren't Rico's thing. He rolled the IV pole to the pump and rigged it for the feedbag later. He laid out a 60 cc G-tube syringe and specimen bottle—"Stillwell, J., 110A"—for the weekly analysis of stomach contents that followed Sunday dinner. Ciao, Watash, he said, and called from the hall, *Bye-bye*.

I had an idea. We could work up to horses. It was four-thirty. I silenced the tube, kissed June's forehead, and left to find a pet store before it closed.

The next morning I felt like an idiot—dressed for court like a railroad lawyer, swinging a birdcage instead of a trial bag. My prelim in the biotech trade-secret case was in the federal courthouse an hour later on the other side of Denver. Mrs. Hudnut eyed me warily as I passed her guardhouse. In the cage were two tiny birds, warbling silverbills, a little drab, but producers, I'd been promised, of continuous streams of song. They warbled sweetly indeed as I swung down the hall, cage in hand. Why hadn't I thought of this before?

"Hey, Jaz. Check the chirpers."

"Lovebirds, right?" Jasmine wiggled a finger through the wires. "Man, are they little."

"From Africa."

"African lovebirds. Jus' what we need."

In the room June faced the wall. April wasn't there. I cleared the night table and arranged the birdcage on it. A Rachmaninoff glissando bubbled from the birds. An agreeable fragrance was in the air, familiar and elusive. A new can of air freshener on the cabinet. Glade Mint Potpourri.

I touched June's cool brow and prepared to turn her. The skin around her eye was dusky almost to bruising. Her lips were purpled and partly agape. The beds of her new-clipped fingernails were blue as April's. A line of crusted fluid led from her mouth.

"*Jaz.*" I grabbed the alarm cord.

"Hey, *breathe*. You, *breathe.*"

Jasmine was there, parting June's eyelid. Nothing. She hollered for oxygen and an ambulance as she ran down the hall.

By the time I found April at the White Spot, nursing her tea, June was en route to the Platte Valley ER under full advanced life support and I was about to miss my prelim with a federal judge. I told April what had happened. She went straight to the hospital and I joined her after the hearing two hours later. April sat in the waiting room, her face in her hands. I couldn't get her to respond. With a shudder of post-traumatic stress, I entered the ICU.

It felt—the same. A place of preternatural brightness, multi-directional fluorescent light coursing through glass-walled rooms, nurses bustling in white smocks, orderlies bearing linens, here and there a doctor in a lab coat or surgical scrubs, each room as piled with pulsing electronics as a radio broadcast booth. For me, a place of bright, cold dread, of waking night-mares, the locus of loss.

June lay on her back, bleached in the blinding light. Spectral pale, as Kathleen had been, though at least June's face was free. And unlike Kathleen, June still had her long, red-brown hair. It lay spread across the pillow in all directions like Ophelia's waterborne tresses.

I made it to the armchair for loved ones' vigils. The glassed room was a hushed cell in a busy pod. A doctor and a nurse stood by, quietly watching not June but rows of glowing lines on a bank of monitors. A weak pulse signal stuttered and stopped. There was soon no flow on the arteriogram. The EKG tracing twitched and went flat.

In my months with June I had often tried to imagine her inner life. Mixed up with blackouts, delirium, hallucinations, the chaos and old night of the comatose, I imagined she would also dream, and also that she'd wake. That she had moments, and sometimes minutes, of such clarity that she not only knew who and where she was and what had happened, but why. That she knew why I was there better than I knew myself. That, mute and paralyzed, she might still brim with understanding and longing and hope.

I could recognize June's spells of lucidity by the fixity of her look and definition of her features, and how her face sagged and gaze dulled when the moment passed. She was like a swimmer in trouble, catching air. And I watching from the bank, helpless, unable to swim—

The water is wide, I can't cross o'er—

Unable to help. Yet I came to feel she not only knew me, and needed me, I needed her. It was not one-sided. It had become a relationship, of mutual helplessness, perhaps. I needed June. She needed me. And we both knew it.

And when she died, I lost someone I'd come in a way to love.

PART II

THE GRAND JURY
In re the death of June Stillwell
99CR1612-3

CHAPTER 1

Midnight, and the exhibitionist next door
paced the sidewalk in a velour robe, cursing a girlfriend on his
cell. The athletes on the other side discontinued their climbing
workout in a half-dead elm, grunting and cranking a jumar up a
rope. In Boulder, at my house anyway, a Chinook-warmed winter evening will bring the neighbors out in all their pathological
intensity. My pathologies were free-floating, soft as smoke.

Two miles east the Burlington Northern whistle blew at the
Baseline crossing. Stillwell would be able to hear it too, eleven
days before Christmas, his five-year anniversary. Not the old
Hank Williams quaver—*I'm so lonesome I could cry*—but a
four-part diesel blast rattling the bleak night air. Two longs, a
short, and a long for a city crossing. An arrogant, presuming
sound, scolding television watchers, disturbing children's
dreams. Trumpeting the primacy of trains.

I felt—after fifteen years—like a cigarette. I went inside
instead to check on April's funk. The police captain's call that
afternoon, his welcome news, had done little to brighten her
blues.

I stopped the CD player in the kitchen. Wordless synthetic
noise, far from the Cowboy Junkies. Something called house.

Not in mine.

"Yeah?" April commented.

"Let's talk."

She shook her head.

That morning at the hospital I'd invited April to stay downstairs until she knew what she was doing. On the ride back and in the hours since, she seemed deadened, lifeless. Deep grief—I'd been there, when you have to jot a note to remind yourself to eat. Sitting in the kitchen, she looked younger, like a baggy mall rat. She looked vulnerable, at sea.

The captain had been sorry to learn her mother had expired. That she had now succumbed to her injuries put the investigation on a different footing, he said. The department planned to send up a recommendation that Stillwell be charged with murder two. Thanks to April's help, and this tragic turn of events, it might get the DA's attention.

You will be contacted, he told her, by Homicide.

At April's request the death certificate signed by Silverman was faxed to my home office. It strongly supported the recommended charges: "(a) Immediate cause of death—cardiopulmonary arrest. (b) Due to, or as a consequence of—traumatic brain injury. (c) Due to, or as a consequence of—blunt force head trauma." The place of injury was "decedent's home." The manner of death was "homicide."

I checked in with Paige and brought her up to speed. She saw no reason now not to file a wrongful-death lawsuit. June's death changed everything. Allege and prove that Stillwell murdered June and we'd fall within the felonious-killing exception of the exemption statute. All of his assets would be subject to execution on a judgment if it was found he'd killed his wife. All the Western Pacific's millions.

Inspired as it was by June's death, Paige's heart for battle struck me as, if not unseemly, at least premature. It was the time for mourning, and I knew the drill. The ICU nightmares with fish-eyed faces in spotless smocks, death gadgets, incomprehensible explanations: The numbers are bad. The blood runs and runs.

Though, if less impulsive, I felt just as committed as Paige, and probably more angry, about lots of things, flaws of law, medicine, and institutions, human frailties and deceits. I wanted to read the Colfax and hospital records. I had to know what happened the night before June died. I'd defer Europe and see this through.

Which is what I needed to talk about with April.

"I am so not interested," was April's response.

Colfax Rehab was the last place on earth she wanted to see or talk about again. She put away her wretched CD and headed for the guest bedroom, pausing in the entry hall to pat the head of the Manikin Pis she'd put on the pedestal where my marble bust of Dante's Beatrice had formerly presided. The little urinating cherub unsettled me—malevolent in his mock-innocence, like the Devil's Advocate, but more sinister still. The Ovcara djinni's newest incarnation, which April rubbed to summon.

Overnight the temperature dropped thirty degrees and stayed there. I spent the morning muddling through a stock-purchase agreement for a neurology practice group, the new clients Hans Leitner had referred. The treble notes of warbling silverbills brightened my study with ironic, oblivious cheer. Nearly noon and still April slept. I made a sandwich, left her a note, and drove back down to Colfax.

The car radio burned with the fires of impeachment. Cupped in its basin, Denver lay beneath an inversion, steeping coldly in tea-colored smog. To the west an angry cloudbank foamed over the lip of the range.

Mrs. Hudnut was openly hostile. My ward's profit center had closed shop. "I believe you're trying to hurt this institution, Mr. Stone, and I'm not inclined to help you."

"Help" referred to complying with the authorization for release of records I'd signed and presented to her as conservator. I was prepared to pay for photocopying. I was prepared to make all the copies. I was prepared to wait until it was finished, as I had at Platte Valley Hospital, records from which I'd gathered en route and locked in the trunk. If she contested my immediate right to June's records, we could confer with the Department of Health. We could confer with them about other things too, like the deaths of neglected patients.

By the time I got to my car with the banker's box of records I'd taken two hours to copy on Colfax's antique, jam-prone Xerox, it was 7 P.M., seriously dark, and starting to snow. An upslope storm. Boulder would be buried. The turnpike would be backed up to Federal Boulevard. The thought was disheartening—captive in snowbound traffic to the airwaves' hypocrisy and bile. There had to be a better system. In Holland, for example, trains transported people from one city to another. Not our dark diesel monsters with blaring horns and twitching strobes, one-eyed cockatrices snaking across the countryside. But little all-electric trains, in blue and yellow toy colors with cabs at both ends like ferryboats. Nonthreatening. People-friendly.

Unlike here. Here, the unlighted parking lot crackled with street sounds—sirens, shouts, horns, a rap tattoo. The phrases and pulses of a Colfax nocturne. I'd never before stayed past sunset. It felt far colder than it should: I'd left my Boulder snow coat in the copier-room closet.

The front door was locked. I rang. I saw Mrs. Hudnut through the glass dissuading someone from answering it. She glanced at me with a head-nurse smile. I stepped outside the cone of sodium-vapor light and surveyed the place from its shadow. Behind the glass doors were a red pop machine and a blue newspaper box. Metal stairs with wire-reinforced windows. An orderly punched in a code to open a door and disappeared down an unseen hallway.

I jogged around the side of the building to the first-floor ward we'd watch from the White Spot. June's window was unlit. My teeth hurt. My nipples stung from the cold. Then there was Jasmine in someone's room, smiling and turning away. I caught up with her at a fire door and tapped comically at the pane. "What kind of fool—" She locked the door behind me and brushed some flakes from my hair and beard.

"What do you think, Jaz? This place jinxed?"

She sniffed. "More like cursed."

The copier room was dark except for a glowing green word: RESET. I grabbed my coat then stopped. Next to the closet door was another lettered LAB I hadn't noticed before. I have an aversion to labs but couldn't help pushing in the door and taking a look. Sleazy neon from outside gave the little room a lurid depth it didn't deserve. Shabby and underequipped, nothing like the glittering complexity of a high-tech hospital path department. One double sink and counter, one microscope and table, boxes, baskets, and carts, and a brace of oversized, avocado Frigidaires whining and shuddering from the effort to keep things cool.

What things?

I gently tugged a rubber-sealed door unstuck and the whine fell in pitch. A wedge of superwhitened light widened and engulfed me. My shadow leapt the wall.

The rubberized shelves were jammed with rows and rows of half-pint specimen jars. The stomach fluids of every tube-fed Colfax patient, not yet shipped for chemical analysis on the weekly Met-Path pickup, labeled and organized by room number and name. Between rooms 109 and 111 one was missing— 110: June's—like the gap on Stillwell's mantel.

A noise startled me and I eased the door to. A low, baying moan. From somewhere in the penetralia of the place a human voice was calling.

CHAPTER 2

The upslope dumped a foot on Boulder but spared the high country. The resorts would keep hurting. My neighbors to the west were waxing their cx skis. The exhibitionist to the east was housebound, sweeping past uncurtained windows in his bathrobe, the diesel in his Mercedes gelled. A good day to stay home, stoke a fire, open a file, post news to Quierin of June's death and the missing specimen, and log in summaries of eight hundred pages of June's medical records. Near the end of an increasingly puzzling exercise, the chime sounded with Quierin's reply, the first in a month. Six P.M. Mountain Standard Time; two A.M. in The Hague.

She was sad about the woman I visited. Did it mean I was "on the loose" again?

"Tied up now more than ever."

"I like to picture that."

I opened Instant Messenger and double-clicked the Q icon, the better to converse. "I mean I have to stay here and follow this out. I don't know what will happen. I spent all day with documents I don't understand. What about you? Three feet of frozen dirt in Boz, why not take Dutch leave?"

"What are you trying to say now?"

"Greenhorn figure of speech. But what can be happening in

the halls of international justice more important than you and me?"

"Oh, yeah. America is where all that matters is. Here is not mattering."

"What is mattering to you?"

"My hope is my work does something for the world."

"Tell me."

"In Brcko we get bad i.d. 24 of 80. They rebury bodies twice to mess us up. At Het Tribunal we get a little conviction for Celebici prison camp. Two little Muslims and one little Croat for twenty little years. Big Muslim Delalic walks out. Waarom? Better lawyer. OTP needs you, baby." The Office of the Prosecutor.

"And Kosovo?"

"This is when I am really worrying," she typed. "You know Slobo waits for spring offensive. Deterrence is our purpose, yes? Why do I do what I do but for never to do it again? No more new graves is no new work but I am glad with crime deterred. But if same criminals do same crimes in same places where five years we are prosecuting them, what has been deterred? Maybe then I agree I waste time here not with you."

"Maybe he'll pull back."

"Hah." Now she could type it. "Who stops Slobo? NATO? Monica man?"

"God, I've missed hearing from you."

"You go back to documents. I go back to bed."

"I like to picture that."

"Hah." Quierin signed off. "Not the only multicultural fox. What about Monica?"

"What about Monica?" I was obliged to ask.

"I hear she got a little Cuban in her."

When I'd asked April if she wanted to see her mother's charts, she made a face. "Later maybe." She layered up in woolens and down and was out the shoveled walk. She didn't want to do or say much of anything, though what kind of person willingly passes time pondering reams of medical records? Risk managers and QA reviewers, and legal geeks hoping to see something somewhere that didn't add up.

April could be a difficult houseguest. June was where we'd

intersected. Now it was hard to find common ground. Little engaged her except the cremation and service that Friday and the case against Stillwell.

Grief phase one is "alarm/shock." An emotional poleax. April was depressed, exhausted, angry, empty. And antisocial, I knew, because living people rebuke the dead simply by being alive. I tried to counsel her. She wasn't interested and you have to back off.

I began my summary of medical records with the last day of June Stillwell's life. The ambulance report rated her pulse and respiration each at zero. Skin cool and cyanotic. Eye fixed and dilated. No doll's eye reflex. No response to visual threat. No sign, in other words, of cerebral function. Breathing was "agonal"—a death's rattle, or very near it. And June was "asystolic." Her heart had stopped.

The EMTs bagged her with a valve mask resuscitator, opened an airway for intubation, and applied full cor—continuous cardiac massage and advanced life support—defibrillation, and an IV lifeline with atropine and dopamine drips. By the time she hit the ER, a weak sinus rhythm had been restored and a feeble Doppler pulse, but the diagnostics were grim. Generalized slowing on EEG consistent with massive, diffuse brain injury. The assessment was prolonged cardiopulmonary arrest with profound brain damage. The prognosis, if she managed to survive, was persistent vegetative state, a mock-existence as sunless and pointless as her roommate's.

After finishing the summary, I went back to nitpick for curious details. I found some parts to yellow-flag: At 9:15 a bloodwork order with "DS," or drug screen. A matching lab report listing only expected medications at appropriate levels. At 9:25 another order by the same doctor, A. Arcenault, reading "gas lau" or "lav." For laudanum? Blood gases? A corresponding nurse's note with the same six meaningless letters. Arterial pH 7.2. Hematocrit, 26. Platelets bottoming out. I needed a medical consultant to know what any of it meant.

Starting at 10:15, the phrases "no cor" and "DNR" showed up on every page.

No cor—no chest percussion, no defibrillation, no advanced coronary support; no vent, trach, surgery, or blood products.

DNR—a do-not-resuscitate order—but no signed forms or references to who authorized it.

By ten after eleven June was dead.

I left a message with Hans Leitner's assistant asking what *gas lav* or *gas lau* might mean, and I started in on the six-inch stack of Colfax records.

In June's five months at Colfax there were no reports of heart or breathing problems. An EKG in October was "unremarkable." Nothing suggested a predisposition to respiratory distress. On page after page of flow sheets and progress notes, her vitals and general health looked excellent, except for the last six weeks' drop in level of consciousness. Her lab screens showed healthy function except for a couple of abnormals starting mid-October, albumin and cholesterol, both low. More questions for a medical consultant. On paper June looked as healthy as I did. No warning sign anywhere she might suddenly stop breathing, arrest, and die.

Until that night. Rico, at the midnight meal and weekly sampling before his weekend began, charted nothing unexpected. His entry finished with "NRS," normal review of systems. But at the next four-hour check at 4 A.M., June was in trouble. "Shallow breathing, snoring, unable to rouse. Irregular pulse, some vomitus, twitching." *Unable to rouse* being less alarming in the comatose than in you and me. "P," at the end of the nurse's note, read, "Will call Dr. in A.M." Substandard, but within the do-nothing Colfax protocols that had permitted June's roommate's meningitis to infect her brain. There was no indication that either Rico or the 4 A.M. nurse had wakened April.

So it came on out of the blue. It began between midnight and 4 A.M. Sometime between 4 and 8 A.M. it progressed to respiratory failure.

"RICO?" I typed. I heard the front door open and heel-kick shut—*k-whack*—a trademark April arrival. I deleted the four letters and called April in. So not interested, but I still wanted to talk.

"You told them to take your mom off life support," I said.

"Yeah?"

"I wasn't aware you'd authorized that. It's in the hospital records."

"Take Mom off?" She shed an enormous, puffed-up, quilted

down coat, a walking air bag. It slipped off behind her like a second person taking a seat.

"Do not resuscitate."

"Absolutely," April said, shaking her springy hair. "Never resuscitate."

"I wasn't aware of that."

"Me either."

"What do you mean?"

She shrugged. "Somebody said stop trying to what? Like, bring back Mom to life?"

"Did you authorize them not to resuscitate your mother?"

"Huh-uh." She looked at me half-annoyed. "I don't know."

"April. It's important." I'd barely understood the DNR I signed for Kathleen, but I didn't care whether April understood it, only whether she'd done it.

"I remember somebody explaining something, like there's nothing more to do. She's not going to make it. Was it wrong?"

"No. Her brain was—"

"Yeah." April took a couple of steps, impatient, in oversize snowboarder pants and a sweater depicting a moose.

"So did you say, 'Okay. Pull the plug'?"

"No. Nothing like that."

"Like what then?"

"I might of. Said . . ."

"What?"

"Like, 'All right, I guess.'"

"Did you, April?"

"It's possible."

"What else?"

"Nothing else, Elliot."

"Nothing?"

"Huh-uh."

I must have looked put out.

"My mom died, you know, not yours." She threw a sudden look of contempt across my desk and screen. She was starting to come unglued. "She's my mom, get it? What do we have to do with you anyway?"

I took a breath.

"I mean thanks and all, but Jesus. Why do you care? My opinion—worry about yourself for a change."

"I care," I muttered. "I need to understand—"

"You need to understand." A singsong whisper. "Just the facts. Like some little Ken Starr guy wants to catch somebody by their thong panties."

The lowest blow. I'd prosecuted actual crimes. Crimes of actual war.

"April—"

"You need a life, Elliot. An observation."

I glanced at the records bristling with Post-its. Suddenly I was pissed. "Did you notice *anything* that night? And who told them to stop life support? Did you tell them? Yes or no."

She laughed: I was hopeless. She fixed me with a sarcastic smile, but her eyes were bright with pain. A very unhappy young woman, with reason. What a brute I was, cross-examining her two days after she'd watched her mother dying. It was best, I decided, declining to meet her shining gaze, her dare, to keep some things—the specimen missing from the Colfax lab—to myself.

"Forget it. It's just, I keep thinking about that place. How could you handle spending nights there?"

She looked at me.

"Spooky," I said.

"You get used."

"April—" I worked at a reasonable tone. "We need to try to think outside the box on this."

"Excuse me? The box?"

"We get a mind-set. It helps to go at it from a different angle."

Hopeless, I could see her thinking.

"If—if your mom didn't die from her head injury, but, say, somebody's negligence at Colfax, or something else, wouldn't you want to know? Don't we need to rule that out?"

"Something else—like somebody killed her, I guess?"

"I don't know."

April collected her air-bag coat by the collar, then turned and accosted me. "If it was something else, it's because you let him."

Now I got it, the hostile subtext. I'd let Stillwell visit June. I'd made April go along with it. I'd become careless of what went on while he was there. If something bad had happened,

Stillwell had done it, and I was complicit because I didn't prevent it.

"But what difference does it make?" She stamped, and her eyes started. "He hit her and she died. She died from when he hit her, or something he did later, or something else happened, but he's the one who made her life not worth it anyway. Or every week there he is again, staring her to death and she just gave up. One way or another he killed her, and I goddamn know he killed her."

She turned and left, air bag bumping behind her.

Paige more than shared April's convictions. "Get real," she said when I called. "We're the plaintiffs now. The idea isn't to kick holes in our own claims. This is straightforward wrongful death. Man batters wife, wife suffers, then dies. Let Stillwell's lawyers challenge causation. Why complicate my case?"

Because assuming June had died from Stillwell's assault might just have been wishful thinking. Because I'd promised myself I wouldn't be used by Paige when I sensed it was wrong. Because I had found June that morning and I needed to know. Because *quantum scimus summus*. We are what we know.

I scrolled through my summary of the records and tried to give it some systematic thought—assemble the evidence and analyze the data.

The day before June died, Stillwell was there, longer than usual. We knew he could formulate and carry out a complex plan. He'd been at Colfax often enough to learn the routines, the schedules, the layout. Had he figured out the weekly stomach-fluid specimens and how to slip into the lab unnoticed? April had shown he could commit a crime and destroy evidence of it afterward, just as he'd done with the figurine.

A question with Stillwell was motive. What did he gain from June's death? It increased his legal jeopardy. But the question with Stillwell was always motive. Why had he hit her with the Manikin Pis? Why had he come again and again to stare in silence at her battered face? What accounted for his incoherent anger afterward? He was cryptic to opacity.

Calculations of legal jeopardy were not what drove this man, though the elimination of those who knew his secrets might. Only June knew the truth of their interlocked lives. June was the only witness the night of his assault. She was waking from the coma, starting to speak. Had he compulsively come to fear what she'd say? Fixated, paranoid—or did he just want to finish what he'd begun? Did he sit staring in her room, working himself up, as he may have the night he crushed her face? Sitting, staring, obsessing on his grievances, rising—then walking toward June as she watched, immobilized, in wide-eyed terror—

While I chatted in the hallway or at the nurses' station. Complicit.

Whom was I investigating? Whose innocence was I trying to prove? My own? For that matter, whose death was I still trying to come to grips with?

To hell with it, I thought. Spinning my wheels. For the moment, facts mattered more than feelings. I opened a new file—"Manner and Cause of Death." I started a list, in a rough preliminary order of probability.

1. Complications of Head Injury—Stillwell. *Paige's, Silverman's, and the cops' explanation. End of discussion, but quite possibly correct. And the missing specimen jar might have an innocent explanation too: when she died, it was tossed because there wasn't any point in paying a lab to analyze it now.*

2. Negligence—Colfax. *There were daily examples of inadequate care. The house protocols crippled response to medical emergencies. There'd been a pattern of negligent deaths; Leitner as much as said so. And Colfax staff had plenty of opportunity both to alter the chart and toss the specimen jar to hide a screwup.*

3. Negligence—Silverman. *According to the records, June had a strong heart and no reason to suddenly stop breathing, but her coma was worsening for reasons Silverman didn't investigate. Did she have an underlying condition he negligently failed to diagnose and treat? This was the third death in four months of one of Silverman's comatose Colfax patients. The first two, and possibly June's, were preventable with better care. The pattern suggested medical incompetence. Silverman's attribution of June's death in the death certificate to head injury five months earlier*

> *had the effect of exculpating him, and Colfax. At best it*
> *was superficial. At worst, a cover-up.*
>
> 4. Homicide—Stillwell. *Finishing what he'd said he'd do*
>   *two years earlier in the courthouse.*
> 5. Homicide—Colfax. *How likely was that? But as Leitner*
>   *said, analysis must be ruthless. And it was clear that each*
>   *of the three deaths could have been intentional: a life-*
>   *threatening infection deliberately ignored. A ventilator*
>   *hose deliberately disabled. Respiratory failure deliber-*
>   *ately induced by medication or manually. A string of*
>   *deaths in a rehab hospital could lead the state to shut it*
>   *down or decertify it for public assistance. Suspects might*
>   *include disgruntled employees or a competitor who*
>   *wanted Colfax out of business. Who were the Colfax*
>   *investors, the Queen City Trust, and what were its objec-*
>   *tives? When I'd had lunch with its lawyer, Arnold*
>   *Whitelaw, I'd ventured some small talk about my conser-*
>   *vatorship, how I'd been spending my time. Why the*
>   *uncomfortable silence that had followed, the voice mail*
>   *that afternoon that Whitelaw and Van Horn would not be*
>   *hiring at this time?*

Suspects should include as well those with more unsavory intentions. A ghoul who got off on killing and justified it because the lives of the comatose are worthless anyway. Like the sociable psychopaths you run into in Bosnia, Slavic Tim McVeighs nursing *rakija*, nostalgic for the war. Rico again crossed my mind.

And those with misguided good intentions. A mercy killer, a Nurse Kevorkian, repulsed at seeing suffering prolonged in those whose lives consist of little but the experience of pain.

In the Netherlands it would almost be legal.

I warned myself not to stray too far out there. To follow the facts, as Leitner advised. It could be none of the five on my list, or it could be several acting independently. The specimen tossed to cover up negligence when someone else had killed by manual suffocation. I reread the list; it felt incomplete. I knew it was incomplete. Anyone who could demonstrably benefit from June's death ought, in the interest of honesty, to be included. Truth simplifies. Following biases and hunches instead of cold facts only led to error. Coldly, I outlined the case against number six on my list, whose name I thought better of typing.

April's material benefit from June's death was substantial. The civil case could now be filed because of the felonious-killing exception in the statute. She was free to go after Stillwell with a vengeance. The DA would be more inclined to prosecute a homicide. The injustice of Stillwell's going free and keeping his millions might be thwarted. Indeed, with no exemptions, April had a good shot at a judgment that could transfer those millions to her.

Alone, this was nowhere near enough to view her with suspicion. Children often benefit from parents' deaths but rarely kill them.

But I had to concede there was more. April had bullied Colfax into letting her room with June. She had unlimited opportunities to learn the ways of the hospital. If Stillwell was capable of a complicated plan, April, by figuring it out, had a superior capacity. April was a driven sleuth, and her recent lack of curiosity about what had happened was not in character. As I was learning, she was a serious sleeper, but could she really have slept through June's last night, then gone off unawares to breakfast at the White Spot? And, about the DNR order, April was not just incurious but possibly evasive.

Beyond advancing her goal of holding Stillwell to account, April may have wanted to end her mother's life for her mother's sake. Under living wills, many children have authorized the termination of the G-tube life support of parents no worse off than June was. And when June's coma stopped improving, April changed. She was down, often alone, brooding. The stress of the last weeks could have broken her.

To April, June was a heroic model. June had escaped a degrading, abusive marriage and come into her own in a man's world most men weren't up to. She was a Casey Jones. She drove trains. She enabled the disabled. She taught CP kids to walk. Determination, self-reliance, will, discipline, purpose in life, value to others: these are what Dale Stillwell had robbed June of when he smashed her face and rendered her helpless.

Prolonged and possibly permanent coma must have seemed to April the ultimate dishonor to the independent, courageous, generous, self-made woman who'd led April through the summer grasses. That prospect may have grown unendurable as April neared the time when she'd take over as conservator and assume lifetime responsibilities for her mother's ruined self.

I could almost conceive of it. The thought of forcibly ending June's suffering had crossed my mind too, driving back from Colfax with April the day before June spoke.

Every day June falls deeper into a living death and April grows more distraught. Hyperactive pursuit of Stillwell is the one thing keeping her going. Paige is doing nothing so long as June is alive. With the DA's "Notice of Final Action," April cracks. She's proved the case—Roybal says so—but Stillwell's getting off scot-free. Keeping all his money. And April, reinforced by me, has stopped kidding herself. The woman who was her mother is gone. She'll never return.

In a sleepless, midnight torment of fury and despair April rises to an elbow and contemplates the tortured form across the room. A clarity comes over her. She sits; she pulls back the covers. Her feet slip to the floor—

Of everyone, April had both the greatest range of reasons to hasten June's death and the best defense if caught: she had to stop her suffering.

And regardless of April's hand in the death, her continuing conviction about what had happened was still essentially right: her stepfather had brutally beaten her mother and put her in a coma, from which, after five months of misery, she died. He'd killed her, and merciful intervention by April wouldn't alter that.

That night, I woke in the middle of an REM interlude, thought awhile, got up, and E-mailed Quierin. I had some questions that were up her alley. "I'm thinking I'll come back," I added, "but not till this is over."

I opened the "Death" file and unhappily reviewed my list. Truehearted April couldn't belong there. But I'd learned from Mayor Jovanovic never to think you know someone's secrets, what someone, anyone, is capable of.

I needed to get to work. I needed to check out every medical question. I needed to prove myself wrong.

•   •   •

In the morning, unusually, April was up for breakfast. Chai and cantaloupe to my plain bagel and cuppa joe. Chinook, the snow-eater, chomped at the eaves. Mini-avalanches slid from the roof. A plow scraped the chip-and-seal on Fourth Street. The Mercedes next door strained and died.

Impossible, I thought, watching April split and score her orange globe.

I watched a little too closely.

"Yeah?" She looked up.

"Nothing."

"Hey, Elliot." She put down her spoon and leaned forward—a White Spot gesture. "Sorry about that crack."

"Crack?"

"That Ken Starr crack. That was pretty sick. I'm sorry." She returned to her melon. "And I almost never say that word. The *sorry* word."

I told her I'd forgotten.

"So look at me!" She sparkled. "Outside the box!"

Oh, yeah, the box. It gave me an opening. I asked April to consider postponing tomorrow's cremation service—

"Not on your life."

"Please think about it."

"Why?"

"There are questions we need to answer," I said, and the dead speak volumes.

The dead aren't dead.

CHAPTER 3

That did it. April blew up. I interfered with everything. Now I wanted to junk the service when it was totally pointless. She stormed off to her room before I could say anything. An hour later I tried the door to find her packing. From stuffing a duffel bag she looked up in tears.

"I totally admired you, you know. You were so there for Mom. You were so not the lawyer of the jokes."

Worse than a joke. A traitor.

"You were so how I envisioned a lawyer to be." She crammed clothes recklessly into the bag. "A fighter and a carer too."

"I'm in this with you, April."

She flinched at my presumption. She was done talking and by midmorning she was gone.

Paige's fax a few hours later sealed it:

Please be advised that I represent April Mooney regarding claims for the wrongful death of her mother. You must have no further contact with April except through me. Also be advised Ms. Stillwell's cremation and service will proceed as scheduled, and you are welcome to attend.

The informal version followed by voice mail: "Elliot, Paige. You know, Elliot, you were supposed to be a good guy for a change. Let's put the screws to the screwball. Call me. I can smooth this over. Let's put the man away."

Advice and threats began landing from every quarter. A certified letter that same day from Arnold Whitelaw, counsel for the Queen City Trust, with a please-be-advised salutation that he represented Colfax:

> Our office has learned that you made an unauthorized entry into our facility and may have unlawfully removed hospital property from the laboratory and perhaps elsewhere. This very serious matter is being investigated and, you may be assured, will be referred to appropriate authorities.
>
> Our office also understands you acquired hospital records under false pretenses. The death of June Stillwell revoked your authority as her guardian. You have no present standing to review her records or discuss her or other patients' care with any Colfax employee.
>
> You must immediately return all records improperly photocopied and all other hospital property in your possession, and have no further contact with hospital staff.

I sent the eight hundred pages to Whitelaw after copying a set for my bottom drawer. I left a message to call me for Colfax staffer Rico Tiradentes on his home answering machine.

It was starting to feel like a coordinated effort to get me off the case. I heard back from Quierin. She had some advice too.

"I do bones," Quierin wrote. "Tissue only if they make me. Tissue is yucky. For i.d. and manner of traumatic death bone's all you need. But with questions like you wrote me you better have tissue. All you got is bones if they burn somebody up. Talk to the Colonel."

I did. "I'd have to read the records to really advise you," Leitner said when his assistant finally tracked him down for me at the VA. "Listen, Elliot, I'm really sorry. You were that woman's champion. This must be hell, for the daughter especially, though, as believers say, it was a blessing."

"Tell April she's been blessed."

"I'd offer my sympathy except she'd take my head off. Tell her for me, Elliot."

"Can't talk with her. Sorry."

"What?"

"Some other time. As for reading all the records, I may ask you to do that. For now, can you give me your drive-by take?"

"Shoot."

I started with what I'd seen, the blue nail beds, dusky skin, purpled lips.

"Cyanotic," he said. "Oxygen deprivation. Ox sat in the ambulance?"

"Seventy or something." I found it in my summary. "Sixty-six percent."

"There you have it. Brain MRI?"

I flipped through the summary of the Platte Valley chart. "Massive, diffuse shearing injury to the cortex. Loss of the gray/white border."

"Anoxia. It all fits."

"But why? What stops oxygen from reaching the brain?"

"All kinds of things, starting with not breathing. Your differential would include PE—pulmonary embolism—myocardial infarction, maybe lung diseases, suffocation, not in these circumstances drug overdose, which is a common culprit. And there are a dozen less likely."

"They did a ventilation/perfusion scan and arteriogram. Normal."

"Means they suspected pulmonary embolism but ruled it out. Any chronic conditions that could lead to an arrest?"

"She was healthy. A couple of blips here and there."

"Blips, Elliot? You know better than that."

"As far as I see, she was fine, then boom."

"You aren't a doctor. How do you know she was fine? What labs were done?"

"The usual CBC and chem panels."

"And?"

"Almost totally normal." I hadn't even bothered to put them in the summary.

"Almost?"

"Low cholesterol, I think, which means healthy heart, right? And another one."

"I'll need that data, Elliot. Anything else?"

"Yeah. Let's see. DNR orders with no authorizations."

"You can call that a blip. Remember the crisis atmosphere. Not everything makes it to the chart."

When I'd gotten there, all was calm. A deathwatch.

"I don't have time for a full records review," he said, "but send me your summary. Hospital records aren't the focus anyway. Fait accompli by then. Colfax records, that's where you may pick up a scent. Send me her bloodwork."

"What are we looking for, Hans?"

"For why a healthy young woman suffered sudden death."

"Right. I'm with you. Now, tell me I don't have to be doing this."

"You have to. There's no one else, including me. We're all stuck on someone's side, except you. And, don't take this wrong, but—she died on your watch, in a way. You were her guardian. It's right for you to track down why."

"Right? A moral imperative?"

"Damn straight. And Elliot, something else you have to do. Autopsy."

"I knew you'd think so. Quierin said as much. But we've got a real problem. The cremation's tomorrow."

"You have to stop it. An autopsy's absolutely essential. You'll never know without one. Can't you force an autopsy as the guardian?"

"My authority vanished when she died."

"The daughter, then. April."

"I'll ask Paige, but it's not bloody likely."

"Cops?"

"They're sure they already know the cause of death. Stillwell hammering her with the—with an object."

"There has to be a way to force an autopsy."

"I can petition for it if everything we've been talking about adds up to a suspicious death under forensic standards. Does it?"

"Well—no. There has to be good cause to suspect death resulted from a crime."

We had questions, not good cause, even with the missing stomach specimen. I wasn't yet ready to get into that with him,

April, or Paige. Especially since Arnold Whitelaw was setting me up as the thief.

I had an idea. "Dead bodies are owned by the heirs, like any personal effect. Granddad's shotgun. Aunt Ellie's brooch. The heirs can dispose of it however they choose. Until Paige disinherits him, Stillwell's the principal heir. *He* can call for an autopsy."

"Until Paige what?"

"Murderers can't inherit from their victims. I'm sure she'll claim it."

He whistled. "Tough broad, though what's to inherit?"

"Hans, you know June's dying is bad news for your patient. Very bad news."

"I figured as much."

"Did you hear the DA decided not to charge him?"

"Yes, they had me in. Apparently that was helpful to them."

"Why?" Now he had me curious.

"Ask them, Elliot. It should come from them, not me."

"This may change things. June's death."

"I doubt it. Look, I'll try to talk Dale into calling for an autopsy. I'll do what I can before the cremation tomorrow. Send me that stuff. And let's have dinner sometime. Trade war stories about real wars."

The Hotel Boulderado is preferred for business breakfasts by local professionals. The lobby compassed with stained glass, strewn with figured rugs and period furniture; the cage elevator and oyster bar; the magnificent walnut double staircase with four staggered landings; and, at this season, a thirty-five-foot blue spruce opulently trimmed and lit—all call to mind a provincial Algonquin, a frontier adaptation of old New York. Teddy Roosevelt liked to stay here.

I also chose the Boulderado to meet with Paige the morning June was to be cremated for a minor personal reason. Its restaurant is called Q's.

"Cherchez la femme," I said, beholding Paige, a boss chick, in her final trimester. She shed a violet silk scarf and black wool coat, emerging in an olive pantsuit with a flexible waist. "When?"

"Ides of March, but I may keep growing for years."

Eggs Eisenhower for me; for Paige, granola and yogurt and an orange muffin. Coffee in a silver carafe.

"Strange times," Paige said.

"Passing strange." Clinton's approval ratings were soaring as the House managers sharpened their knives. "Bring me up to speed."

"We're filing right away. Wrongful death by felonious killing. I want you on board." She was dead serious, a green-eyed appeal. "I've done wrongful deaths, but homicides I have not done. You have and that's what this is. I want you to help me try this thing."

"I accept." I lay down the silverware. Eggs Eisenhower was not a sufficiently serious dish. "But Friday's too soon. We've got two years."

"Why not? We got ducks lined up, ready to quack."

"Not all the ducks."

"Elliot?" She looked a little aghast, as though afraid her water might be breaking.

"It's too early. It's—vibes." I threw out my hands.

"Vibes?" She now made a face that caused the waiter to start. An emergency? Or granola that offended? "Whose?"

"Different people, several. Colfax. Very weird vibes out of Colfax." Rico had returned my message. We were meeting that afternoon in the White Spot when he got off shift. "Stuff isn't adding up."

"Stuff?"

"Like the medical records. At least you ought to read them before you file half-cocked."

"What?" The green eyes blazed. "I mean, what is the issue here? What in the records shows you Stillwell's not our man?"

"There's nothing definitive."

"So?" Ominous drop in tone. "Elliot, we don't need to know exactly what happened the night June died. It's—irrelevant, except that she died. What he did to her finally did her in."

"Why the rush? Read the records."

"Are you," she said even softer, "going south on us?"

"Is that what April thinks?"

"No." She pushed her bowl aside. "Sad to say, April thinks you're it. World's gnarliest lawyer. I know you better, but April thinks you hung the goddamn moon, Elliot, no matter what I say. And"—falling cadence—"she feels betrayed. You, after her mother."

Paige was good at guilt, and at getting her way. She won juries by concentrated force of mind.

"You know how to defend a wrongful death," she said. "We've both defended dozens. Causation. Muddy the water. But we're *plaintiffs* now. Get it? Clear water. Simplify."

"This is about the cremation this afternoon," I said. "What you want me on board for."

"It's about you."

"It's just too soon to get on board." I wasn't going to accommodate anybody until we knew what happened. "I'd like you to get April to stop the cremation and ask for an autopsy."

"Absolutely not. And, Elliot, if you file a motion, it's Stillwell's Exhibit A. Conservator says death caused by unknown persons."

I thought about that. She was right. "I won't ask the court to override April's wishes. No motion, but please change her mind."

"You think I'm the kind of fool lawyer who creates evidence that could wreck her case? The other side doesn't care. Why the hell do you?"

"I'm not so sure they don't care." They certainly should. Stillwell's best defense to murder was to prove June died because of something other than sequelae of head injury. He'd hope an autopsy might show a failing heart, some other illness or intervention, or would at least confuse the cause of death. Under the "felonious killing" standard he could even admit the assault—the felony—but dispute the killing, and still protect his money with the exemptions statute.

"I understand why you oppose an autopsy," I said, facing her narrowing eyes. Many lawyers in her shoes would. "I might if I represented the plaintiff." I wondered if this first-time-pregnant plaintiff's lawyer had begun to smell a million-plus fee. "But it's important to answer your question," I said slowly. "Why the hell I care. I care about what we could learn from an autopsy because, after Mayor Jovanovic, I never again intend to prosecute murder if there is anything still to learn that could show innocence."

"Your friend Dr. Leitner," Paige said, conversational again, "does he think we should autopsy?"

"Won't know what happened without it, he thinks."

She smiled off at the art deco appointments of Q's. "A tool," she said airily. "Elliot, you are their willing fucking tool."

"Hans Leitner—"

"Is his patient's advocate. He knows courtrooms. He knows an autopsy might point away from his patient."

"If the facts support a case, I'd love to work it and try it with you. Right now I'm nobody's tool. I'm outside the adversarial orbit. The truth of June's death, that's all I want to know."

"April's going to be more bummed than she already is. She's leaving, you know. Back to California. I worry about her." Paige fished out a credit card, flashed it at the waiter. "Do not talk to her about this."

We didn't speak again except to say good-bye.

The cremation and service were that afternoon at two. Afterward, I'd meet Rico at the White Spot. In the meantime, a call for autopsy by either Stillwell or Paige and the cremation could still be canceled.

I saw it as a test of innocence, like a medieval ordeal. Trial by autopsy. Stillwell had tactical legal reasons to insist on an autopsy. April, if she really wanted to know how her mother died, would insist on one too. But if either had had a hand in June's sudden death, he or she would proceed with cremation, the cremation of evidence. Either could step forward, request an autopsy, and clear himself or herself of suspicion. Pass the test.

Hearing nothing from either Leitner or Paige, I ground through the snow to McConaty's Funeral Home east of town. A suitably grim, unlighted afternoon. Single-digit cold. A bald eagle in a dead box elder conning for carrion at the gravel pit. At McConaty's—"Caring. Dignity. Professionalism. Boulder's Only Observation Room"—a small crowd huddled in the chapel. I spotted Hans's mess of white hair, next to him Stillwell rolling his neck. Mourners were divided by the aisle into June and Dale camps. I headed up to Leitner's non-Stillwell side, eyed by Paige, and tapped his shoulder. We retired from the chapel to an anteroom with a display of urns, all, the price list assured, tasteful and environmentally sound.

"He still can stop this," I whispered.

"He's adamant," Leitner whispered back. "You know me, Elliot. I'm a pathologist. Postmortems are food for the soul. Give me a Stryker saw and step aside. I've eased a thousand minds about a thousand cuts, and I gave him every argument I had. Says he can't stand the thought of somebody slicing her up."

I must have made an ironic face.

"He knows the legal consequences, Elliot, especially now, but he still won't budge. He sees it as a—sacrilege, I guess. The dismemberment of the love of his life."

"Why 'especially now'?"

"You were right. A special grand jury's been empaneled."

A light flashed. The service was beginning. I found a place on June's side of the aisle. In the front pew were April, Paige, and a tough-looking cowhand type. Must be April's dad. Riding-center colleagues and some CP kids with braces in the aisle seats. Nobody from Colfax, not even Jasmine. Others I didn't know, maybe down from Wyoming. A few looked like railroaders from the Laramie yard.

Dale's side was mostly former caregivers. I recognized some. Brain unit or clinic treaters. Shelter staff. The rest probably neighbors. All there to help Stillwell make it through his latest tragic misfortune. Like ultranationalist Serbs, I thought uncharitably, who sentimentalize perps as victims.

I wasn't good at this kind of thing, because of Kathleen. A little post-traumatic tic. McConaty's mortuary was not a place I wanted to be.

April stood beside the altar and its lily sprays. Mall-rat no longer, in a black midcalf skirt and black cable turtleneck, she looked stylish, together. She commanded attention.

Her eulogy had parts of things we'd talked about: driving down to the Denver zoo, June winning her place as a crack engineer, dreams of travel to far-off lands, showing Yuma, wading through grasses. April wound up with "what Mom taught me." She bore in on two men, one on each side. Her father watched, transfixed, in tears. Stillwell looked as always. Roaming eyes, cryptic; whom the lightest touch could detonate.

What June taught April, April said, was that she mattered. She was someone. She could do what she set her mind to. She needn't live in fear. She could do big things if she had a big heart.

April told us what being a Casey Jones meant. How you can gain self-reliance and also selflessly give strength to others. How her mother gave the gift of strength to April herself, to her CP kids, to others disabled by injury. That she continued to give to others, even in death.

She surveyed Stillwell's gallery.

"Something else my mother taught." April turned and caught for an instant her father's eye, then mine. She looked back at Stillwell. "Don't back down from a fight. Mom did all she could to give me courage and purpose and strength, and I swear to God I will live up to her.

"Help me," she appealed. "Anyone who can."

From the front pew June's Colfax boom box played "Across the Great Divide."

> *The finest hour that I have seen*
> *Is the one that comes between*
> *The edge of night and the break of day*
> *When the darkness rolls away.*

I have to confess I lost it.

An awkward reception followed. Around a punch bowl with cookies and a hot-cider thermos, groups split into rival clutches. Stillwell was encircled by solicitous ex-caregivers. He looked unpredictable and dangerous as he tried to fend them off. A man with a trip-wire mine hidden in his heart.

Paige and April huddled with Buck Mooney, April's father, who looked ready to rip out Stillwell's trip-wired heart with his bare hands. April detached from their clutch and came my way with her father. "I get two more witnesses," she said. "Will you?" I glanced at Paige, who nodded her permission.

The three of us were guided to the crematory by an over-dressed and fair-haired boy with bad skin. Unfairly, I thought of those who staff the cineplex. We got to a door banked by blank black windows.

The cineplex usher cranked open the bank vault door and gestured behind him. Two more kids appeared with a cardboard

casket on a gurney, which they set on rails sloping into the
retort. They pushed the casket into the dark, closed and wheeled
the door shut, and disappeared.

Mooney and I sat against carpeted walls on velvet cushions.
April got a go-ahead. She hit a wall switch that cut the lights in
the observation room, except for two candles. Through the narrow floor-to-ceiling windows flanking the door, two even rows
of blue jets, like runway lights, flared from troughs in the fire-
brick. Soon the cardboard caught in a blossom of fire, which
died back to reveal a form inside. The casket crimped, then
seized and collapsed, unveiling through the flames a body swad-
dled in medical gauze, brass ID disk glinting on a bandaged
throat. It all then spectacularly ignited, gauze fluttering apart,
long hair aflame, fireworks colors, yellow, orange, green, purple, blue. The body quickly blackened, crackled, crazed, and
eventually contorted. Welted and misshapen, contracting
toward an obvious end: body falling to pieces; pieces to powder
and grit. June's remains.

A reverse exhumation. I wished Quierin were there.

"He'll pay," Mooney muttered at my side. He'd had enough.
April and I were alone. Duct fans whirred as June burned. April
hugged her knees and watched.

We sat in separate reveries, separate sacraments with separate meanings of loss and release. What June could have told us
in life, had she regained her voice, what her flesh could still
have told us now, gone. And what were April's thoughts?

A glare hit the glass windows; the door had opened behind
us. Stillwell blocked it, jaws working, eyes bugged, as June and
her secrets went up in smoke.

CHAPTER 4

"His wad of bucks." Darla wagged a finger. "Tucker still won't prosecute."

Light on diners, she sat with me at the war room booth. The cold spell held. Across iced-over asphalt, Colfax lay brooding and occult, with drapes drawn and viscid snow beading walls and window ledges like a substance extruded from within.

"Even now." She lifted her tea bag, inspected and submerged it again. "Now it's murder."

I hadn't figured Darla for a tea-sipper. "How'd you hear about June?"

"Pepsi girl."

"When?"

"You ran in Monday morning in your suit, ran out hysterical. Jailbait explains while she walks her check."

"I'll cover it."

"Big of you, Counsel. Eighty-five cents."

I gave her a dollar. "Keep the change."

Darla brought the tea bag slowly back to the surface. "Murder," she sighed, almost sensual. "No surprise there."

"How's that?"

"What else was he up to but knocking her off? She ain't going to put up a fight, and the monster has Colfax to blame."

"You know Rico Tiradentes? He's supposed to meet me here, ten minutes ago."

"Pigtail? Kind of loud, comes in with the road crew?"

"The who?"

"Trucker unit. When they load off the dock." She indicated. A royal-blue Falcon semi sat back-end to the steel-curtained bay. "That's the show. That's the action."

A subject to raise with Rico.

"Darla, you are an observant person." She smiled. A point of pride. "Were you working last Sunday?"

"I wasn't at church."

"You and April talk that afternoon?"

"Never came by. Not once, which was funny, it being a monster-visit day."

Hadn't April said otherwise? I made a note to ask if I got to talk with her again. I made a note to reconstruct everybody's whereabouts that day. "How was April when she was here the next morning?"

"Same as lately. Down in the dumps, chewing her bit. Kind of bratty. Not like back when she'd get—do I want to say *upbeat*? Pepsi girl. More lately in here she's all the time—introspective." Darla winked. Big word.

"Sure she wasn't here the day before?"

"For a fact. He was though."

"Who?"

"Him. The monster, first time ever. Standing right in that doorway glaring down my counter at your empty booth with that loco look. Like he was inside the outhouse when lightning hit."

I tried to picture it.

"'Where's he at?' monster says, like he's come to get you. I advise the monster the monster is not welcome in my establishment. I smack my chili spoon for emphasis. Monster mutters off about weasels and whatnot. Crazy as a bullbat."

"Thank you, Darla."

"Thank *you,* Elliot. If I may."

A couple of long-haulers in blue caps with gold emblems of talon-bared raptors had claimed stools at the counter and craned for Darla's attention. Road crew, but no Rico. Darla stopped on the way to the kitchen after taking their orders. "Say they ain't seen Pigtail all day long."

Outside it was getting dark fast. The last of the Colfax day shift disappeared from the vapor lamp into the wind-bitten night. I bought a *Post.* Congressman Hyde was urging Americans to catch the falling flag. A half hour more of nothing and I got ready to drive home.

"So long, sultan. Say hi to the harem."

"They dumped me, Darla. You're all I've got." It was true—bereft of women. Quierin in Europe, Paige and April now my adversaries, June and Kathleen dead.

"You know where you can park your camel."

I left a five for coffee.

This time a person picked up my cell-phone call. A female. Rico wasn't home and wasn't expected. "He's gone."

"Gone? Where?"

"Gone away. Who you?"

"Friend."

"Uh-haw."

"How can I reach him?"

"Kind of friend're you?"

"From Colfax."

Click.

The Colfax receptionist told me Rico Tiradentes no longer worked there. I asked for Jasmine Toombs. Ms. Toombs was with patients. Did I care to leave a message for her? No, I did not but I would like to know how Rico, Mr. Tiradentes, could be reached.

"Of course." A woman with the Hudnut manner. "And who are you, please?"

"Friend."

"Your name, please?"

"Junior." Ludicrous failure of imagination.

"Last name, please? And telephone number, and address, so we may contact you about Mr. Tiradentes?"

My turn to click.

Leitner's choice was 15°, known for nouvelle fusion and Blue Sapphire martinis with amusing names from the Starr Report. A poor choice it was for what I was hearing—that last fall June Stillwell was slowly being starved to death.

I finished a Vernon Jordan (the breakfast martini) and poked at some chanterelles and chèvre. Leitner ordered a second Dry Stain and another for me. Between Christmas and his East Coast travel it had taken close to two months to schedule dinner and a discussion of June's Colfax bloodwork. Leitner's wife, whom I didn't know, was to join us for dessert.

Nothing had broken on June's death until now. Still no Rico, still frozen out by Paige, and April was back in school in California. My solo practice was ready to take off, but I found I didn't really want it to. I was turning down clients and working instead pro bono at the Rocky Mountain Survivors' Center and an immigration law clinic helping refugees. Quierin and I continued the dance of the workplace. She was winning on points, though work wasn't what kept me now.

So tell me again, I said.

"The abnormal labs mean severe malnutrition. Albumin falling to .35, .3, .1. Cholesterol from 135 to 119 to 55. You don't see numbers like that except in nursing home patients shutting down or starvation victims."

June's labs began dropping in late October and steadily fell through November and December until she died. They roughly corresponded with her lapse back into deep coma and accounted for it in Leitner's view.

"She wasn't emaciated," I said. "A little thinner maybe." Spectral, I'd thought in the ICU.

"It wouldn't be striking," he said. "Over two months she'd be down maybe six pounds or so. Another eight, ten months she'd be in trouble and you'd know it."

"But how could this have happened? And why?" To weaken her? To shut her up?

"Substitute water or apple juice for liquid food, withhold protein supplements, or just chronic neglect, missing meals. That's how. Why? I don't know. Inattention?"

"April was there. She didn't miss meals."

"It could just be nobody watching her glide path on the labs. She needed nutrition boosts, but nobody realized it and she kept sinking. You didn't. 'Blips,' you thought." He offered a wry look. "Looking at her chem screens never occurred to me either.

I assumed nutrition was governed by Medicaid mandates. But I miss stuff like this all the time."

I lay the fork aside. I felt a little sick.

"By neglect or design," Leitner said, "someone let this happen to June. If you're looking for a wrongdoer, Elliot, the lab values may give you some straws in the wind. I'd take it seriously. Complain to HCFA or the state."

To hell with them. I had suspects on a list, about whom this bombshell said little. Except for the one in charge of June's nourishment, in charge of chow time, and of her stomach-fluid specimens too. Nobody else, including Stillwell, could have interfered with June's food levels day after day, week after week.

No wonder Rico didn't show at the White Spot and went into hiding. Was Colfax on to him? Was this what Whitelaw was worried about? Did it mean April was in the clear?

No. The labs began falling two weeks after she moved in.

"Hans, connect some dots for me." A Bela Fleck CD babbled from the wine bar. "Malnutrition to stopping breathing. What's the connection?"

"Medically, maybe none. Malnutrition explains deep coma, but not sudden death two months later. The dots may not connect."

"Two *independent* wrongs?"

"I didn't say that, but, as for why June suddenly died," he added softly, "you're out of dots, Elliot. No autopsy, no proof. Probably time to move on."

There was in his tone concern for me, the caring therapist coming through. I staunched a little suck of resignation. No autopsy, no April, no Rico. "There's got to be something," I said.

And wasn't there something? A thought, a phrase I couldn't quite come up with through the two-martini static. Except it might be important, might connect dots.

The waiter was at our elbows, rotundly declaiming specials. Leitner raised a palm. The recitation stopped. "I'll look at the nutrition charts," he told me. "Hell, send over the whole damn thing."

Appetite past help, I stood pat on my appetizer but ordered a third martini. A Tripple. Leitner countermanded the order.

"Petrus," he said. "On me. Monster merlot. Meal in itself." The young man took off happily calculating his 20 percent on the wine. Leitner kicked out and crossed his legs. "You wanted that judgeship," he observed, frowning.

"I did? I suppose." It seemed like another life.

"Elliot." He cleared his throat. "Hear me out. I think you're clinically depressed."

"Because I'm not hungry?"

He shook his big head gravely. "That's my assessment."

The boy was back, beaming and bearing a '95 Petrus like something to which his wife had given birth. Leitner brushed off the formalities. "Just pour."

We knocked glasses. *"Zhivili,"* he said, stirring memories. For a velvet instant swallowing the wine I thought I recollected what it was, the nagging, possibly important phrase, lost again in a flood of thought.

Hans gargled a swallow, nodded with pleasure. "Have you considered," he offered gingerly, "living and working alone may be—keeping you in a hole?"

"I prefer a hole. But it's not depression. It's post-Boz syndrome. Ask any OTP ex. You come home to this feeling of pointlessness."

"DSM-IV 309.28. Adjustment disorder with mixed disturbances of emotions and conduct, including work inhibition, social withdrawal, and your preoccupation with June Stillwell, a woman you hardly knew. The psychosocial stressor was returning to Kathleen's house, confronting unresolved bereavement. Are you dating?"

"An obsolete locution."

"So—not." He drew his feet under the chair and shifted forward. "I hate asking but, financially—you okay?"

"More than."

"Good. I can charge for the Colfax consultations."

"I'll pay whatever Stillwell's paying."

"He's pro bono. You're lucky. I raised my hourly." Leitner palmed his glass, made waves with the wine. "I broke the barrier, Elliot. A grand, for tier one. See, you didn't blink. No one has."

"Tier one is—"

"Corporate, like you were. Tier two is insurance companies.

They can have me for seven five. One and two subsidize tier three. Government, medical boards, prosecutions, humanitarian work."

I whistled. Heads moved at a table over. "Running with the big dogs. Won't they cross you for greed?"

"Plaintiffs' lawyers always try. Always backfires." He looked a little sly. "Americans venerate a top-dollar draw. Michael Jordan. That golfer, who is he? Juries get it. When insurance companies pop for a big witness, it funds his other stuff."

"Doctors for Human Rights."

"Precisely."

"And your practice."

"Excuse me?"

"Your patients. You don't charge patients a grand per talk session."

"Of course not."

I raised the purple glass. "To the monster."

"The monster."

"Stillwell, I mean."

"Now, Elliot."

"Darla thinks he is."

"Who?"

"The all-knowing Darla. The White Spot seer."

I kind of liked the wine and not caring about food. Watching Hans slip frilled paper socks from the stump ends of French-trimmed chops and saw up the rack like a professional. Hans had a way of seeming to frown and smile at the same time when something made him thoughtful. Entrées often made him thoughtful.

"Post-Boz syndrome," he said. "The prosecutor's malaise. Tell me about it."

"We went after bad guys. That's fun. This isn't." A careless gesture to indicate my practice.

"Spoken like a prosecutor. You need bad guys to battle. Monsters, in your terminology."

"Darla's terminology."

"I think you're more complicated, than other prosecutors, I mean."

"Who do you think was responsible"—for atrocities in the Balkans—"if not a short list of bad guys we're trying to arrest?"

"From a psychiatric perspective it was minor differences between proximate groups."

I'd heard this before, Freud's theory of the narcissism of minor differences. Trendy Balkan psychobabble, I thought. Our most violent hatreds are toward those only slightly different from ourselves. In Bosnia, ethnically indistinguishable groups exterminate each other because of allegiances to religions few of them observe. So it is with internecine conflict everywhere: Northern Ireland, Sri Lanka, Cyprus, northern and southern Californians, Longhorns and Aggies. Republicans hate Clinton because he's the Democrat most like them.

"The greatest threat is not the other"—Hans tapped it out on the tabletop—"but the almost-me. The almost-me drives me to desperate measures to mark off and defend my selfhood. Don't look like that."

A glassy look, lost in the middle distance. The middle distance was hung with pointillistic prints of fat people picnicking.

"I like almost-me people," I said.

Leitner made a noise and was off into superego theory and id aggression. He stopped, fingers splayed midair, seeing me struggle to track.

"I almost get it," I said. "Or, I get almost-it."

"Karadzic got it. He trained in this stuff." Dr. Radovan Karadzic, the Bosnian Serb president and a brother psychiatrist gone bad. Hans frowned with no trace of a smile.

"A bad guy," I said. "Let's arrest the fucker."

"Too simplistic. The problem will persist."

Woozily, I strove for complexity. The sconce flickered weakly through the old blood of Petrus held aloft. "Major kills over minor differences. A paradox. Paradoxes are cute."

"We're not exempt, Elliot. Prosecutors need bad guys, and that works. But what happens when the bad guy isn't a monster? What happens when the bad guy is a lot like you?"

I tried to imagine prosecuting myself.

"Tell me about your mayor."

"Jovanovic?" Instant detox at the name. "Presumed bad guy. They come in all sizes."

"A guy a lot like you."

"Oh, man." I feigned exasperation but the Devil's Advocate popped unbidden to mind: anything for the railroad, including screwing the little guy. Like the mayor pacifying his town.

"If the mayor was a monster," Leitner said, "who are we?"

Who are we? One of those bell-ringers shrinks use to stop you cold. Mind game, I thought without conviction. Then, what's his point? Then I remembered mine.

"My point, Hans, is this. Group pathologies I'm not buying. Not for the Balkans anyway. Collective responsibility, historical grievances, ancient ethnic hatreds, I don't buy any of it. It's good guys and bad guys. It's the dudes, like Ralph Waldo Emerson said. 'There is no history, only biography.' Yugos should read the man."

"He would make no sense to them. In the Balkans, there is no biography, only history. The dead rule and the living are ghosts."

"I don't buy that either," I said defiantly. The heads at the neighboring table looked again. "I don't buy the School of the Balkan Curse, blah, blah, the tragic land." I sent a forceful glance next door. "Being of the Great Man School of History. The Bad Man School of History, I should say."

"The Monster School."

"*Da.*"

"Not, then, ancient ethnic hatreds, but Milosevic the monster twisting minds?"

"*Da.* Among others. Many Balkan dirtbags. Put them"— *poot zem,* I was surprised to hear myself enunciate—"in ze Haag."

A college girl bused the table, short skirt, leatherette, a twice-unbuttoned blouse, the sweet, indulgent smile of a blonde with little to fear. Certainly not from us.

"Here's the problem with your great-man/bad-man theory, your monster school," Leitner said, "and with much of Western thought. Greatness is complex, paradoxical. And not cute."

His words seemed now to come from elsewhere, serious past seriousness. "We believe in ourselves as we do not believe in others." He spoke without moving a muscle.

"Tell me again."

"Your man said that also. Emerson. 'We permit all things to

ourselves, and that which we call sin in others is experiment for us.'"

"Wrongful killing we don't permit."

"What I mean is, greatness isn't easy or simple. It has nothing to do with noble sentiments. The great are good *and* bad. It's a psychoanalytic truth. The strongly good sometimes have to be strongly, courageously bad. Think de Gaulle, Oppenheimer, Jefferson. Even Virchow."

"They violate convention, you mean. Or they crack eggs to make omelettes."

"That is not what I mean."

"I think evil can't be indulged."

"Shall we arrest it and lock it up instead?"

"Good people need to fix individual responsibility when bad things happen. That is the highest calling of law in a free society. The tribunal mission, and I believe it now even more."

"Bad things? Like a mass grave? There's a mass grave in Arlington National Cemetery, Elliot. A bad thing in itself means nothing. Don't infer the work of monsters from something sad you don't understand."

"From June's death, you mean."

"Yes, I do mean that."

He remained spooky serious, but the thought of June got me going. "How about bad things like Racak?" Where forty-five Kosovar civilians had been massacred three weeks earlier. "And, since you've finished eating, tell me this. The Serb major at Srebrenica, gearing up for a three-day mass execution of seven thousand innocent civilians, who made a Bosniac watch his grandson's disembowelment, then forced him to eat the liver. Evil?"

"Horrifically so." Leitner folded his napkin on the table and turned his chair, preparing to stand, deeply serious still. "But the greatest evil, I believe, in the sense of greatness I used before, is not horrific. It is the evil that can pass for good."

A woman was standing beside us, hands clasped, with a mildly inquisitive look. Very blonde, blonde of lash. Wide shoulders and a small, ironic smile, lips just parted. Eyes so light and empty they almost seemed blind.

"Darling."

Leitner reached his feet. They touched cheeks. "Elliot Stone: Christina."

"I've so looked forward to meeting you," I said, also standing and overly decorous after the gin and grape.

"Yes? I am pleased." Her careful face turned from Hans to me and back. Her part, I thought, is to keep her husband's eccentricities in check. Theirs was not a glamorous relationship, I guessed. He got his glamour in court and committee rooms, and former war zones. She was no impediment, nor he to her.

"How do you know Hans?" The smile was a constant, resting mostly on him. Of all the attitudes her husband might inspire, subdued, affectionate amusement looked to be the norm.

"He helps me solve murders," I said. "In Europe and here too."

Leitner gave a big laugh and held a chair for his wife. He summarized the Vukovar case: "So far, we're batting oh for two, so solve is—"

"Wishful thinking," I interjected. "Hans also saved my life. Do you know the story?"

She didn't, and listened politely with the unwavering smile. "This Quierin," Leitner cut in. "Afterward, she and Elliot became, what were you? A number." About this, Christina seemed to have heard something.

I joined them in a round of Spanish cava.

"And how have you and Elliot been occupying yourselves, Hans?"

"War stories, chattering like sophomores. Elliot is a student of Western philosophy. Eighteenth century, I believe."

"Hume and Kant," I said. "Hume versus Kant."

"I read them once."

"Christina is an advanced nurse practitioner, OB ward at Flatirons. Trained in medicine but educated in the arts. She finds Western thinkers more interesting than do I."

"Then you may appreciate," I said, "that Hume was the better dinner companion. Kant had no sexual relations, rarely laughed, and never left the town of his birth. Hume loved talk, women, wine, and Scottish beef."

"This should trouble idealists," Leitner noted.

"Which roles are yours and Hans's?" Christina asked. "Who is Hume and who Kant?"

"We're working on that," Hans said. He passed his flute of cava before the oil lamp on our table, candling the effervescence. "The nearest thing to perfection is a bubble," he observed. "Perfect structure, perfect clarity, and perfectly impermanent. Perfection is attainable." He smiled. "But it never lasts. So—why not?"

He backhand-summoned the waiter and ordered Gregory Canyon chokecherry cobblers for the two of them.

"Christina," I said, "apart from your practice—"

"What do I do? I take care of Hans. He's hopeless, as you can see."

"Hopeless?"

"Capricious, I should say. I remind him to finish what he starts. I see that his socks match."

He laid a big hand on her sculpted knee. "Easily bored, it's true. Christina makes me pay attention. You'll be interested to learn"—Hans now put a confidential finger to his lips—"that Christina is a skilled matchmaker, and she knows a lot of nurses."

"Ahh—" I shook my head in the negative, understanding dawning.

Christina cocked hers, a touch coquettish. "You like Europeans, I believe?" Wan smile, transparent gaze.

"To a fault."

"I have a colleague at the hospital, also a Swede. I believe you would find her attractive, interesting."

I raised my hand in a little protest.

"Ingrid is a wonderful nurse. ICU, the tough stuff. And get this boys"—suddenly animated—"what an athlete. Very Boulder."

"Biathlete," Hans added. "Swedish national champion at nineteen."

"They're the ones who chase you through the woods shooting."

"I'd like you to meet her," Leitner said paternally.

"I'll think about it." Though, why not? Was it time to move on, as Hans had said back among the appetizers? "You guys are great." But I was shaking my head.

"It's his squeeze in Holland," Leitner said. "Still smitten."

We parted company on the icy sidewalk. I trudged east, ears

buzzing, watching my footing, then raised my head. There, cresting a roofline, the bruised moon in full eclipse. I glanced back at the Leitners, half a block away and headed west, and swung back to the livid moon. Natural wonder, stopping thought. In that thought-free moment, the nagging forgotten phrase rose, illuminated, moonlike. "Hans," I called, but they were gone.

CHAPTER 5

In the sublunar fog of the following morning I miked some Thai for breakfast and sat around waiting for Hans to return my call to his only-if-it's-an-emergency pager. On the street the next-door Mercedes was gelled again. In my house the little birds wouldn't stop chirping. I reflected on the headless pedestal in the entry hall that had borne Beatrice, then the Manikin Pis. I preferred Beatrice in bubble wrap in the basement. I no longer cared to be greeted at the door by Kathleen's ghost.

What was the matter with me? *A Swedish nurse.* Think of her, cool, competent, multitasking, taking a pulse, finding a vein, smocked and clogged. Short smock. Heeled clogs. Bending provocatively over prostrate patients. Defibrillating weak hearts like me. After long hours saving lives she works off the tension training. Shaking blonde bangs aside, laying cheekbone to stock, upper body taut and poised, squeezing off rounds. Thigh-grinding endurance work, then finally home, oiling rifles, packing powder, waxing skis, thinking of tomorrow. The injured and dying who awaited in the morning. Her quest to pierce the heart of the trackless forest.

Sometimes in the evening she may get lonely. She may want someone beside her.

In my morning-after fantasy Ingrid had perfect teeth. Perfect symmetry of face and figure. Eyes clear as glass, lively pink nipples, silky, flaxen fuzz. She moaned in Swedish.

Perfect as a bubble.

I wanted Quierin.

At the computer I told her so, and told her about June's labs. What if Quierin thought I should move on? Then I might. I asked whom she blamed for the wars, drunken Chetnik head-bangers or minor differences between proximate groups. "You're not almost-me," I wrote. "That's how come I like you."

Outside an engine wheezed, then a string of curses. None of my neighbors appeared to have jobs—somehow not required in late-century America. They probably thought I didn't either. I sank into a mood for no good reason except post-Boz, or post-Bombay malaise. What exactly was the point anymore?

Back when I had a railroad job, there didn't have to be a point, which, on reflection, was more unhealthy. I recalled with a shudder the Penaflor case. A double wrongful death. Father and teenage daughter wiped out at a country crossing in Weld County. Father had a 1.1 blood alcohol after a company ball game and barbecue. He sailed past the crossbucks into the path of my train. Both of them blown to bits, beyond recognition. The plaintiff's theory of liability was poor vegetation control, willow stands obstructing the sight triangle. But with a drunk driver in broad daylight I knew widow and lawyer might take any scrap I threw their way.

I'd poked through the wreckage with our accident recon-structionist, helping match a prong of angle iron on the engine to crush depth in the Penaflors' Voyager. The van was as crumpled as a ball of paper, the train majestically untouched, the armor-plated sovereign of the hinterlands. Its speed tapes were suspi-ciously missing, but my expert was able to back out from the wreckage that the train was going sixty though the limit was forty, while the van was only going ten. Not good for the robber barons. Plus, there'd been three hits and four near misses in the last eight years at that same unprotected crossing, which should long have been gated and belled.

At the prefiling settlement conference I'd suggested, the widow gratefully accepted $120,000, from which, after costs and fees, she'd net maybe $60,000 for the loss of her husband and only child. They never guessed I'd have paid $2 million more, with two deaths and a speeding train at a known hazardous crossing. Her lawyer had never questioned the missing speed tapes, never asked for FRA incident bulletins or the event-recorder printout, and ethically, I wasn't required to do his work for him. He thought he'd made out. He bounced through the door on the balls of his wing tips, swinging his briefcase, off to bank his $40,000 fee for a few hours' work.

Before she followed him out, the widow paused. She smiled, crying, and, regrettably, reached for my hand, mumbling affections for her husband and daughter. I actually recoiled from her touch before falling back into role. Years later I squirm with shame at the memory of Amelia Penaflor's earnest and needy grip. After they left, the ex-judge mediator gave me a wink. Another couple million saved by the railroad. Another little guy screwed.

My mentor, Henry Steele, wouldn't have been bothered, but his values were keyed to another time. He put loyalty to the railroad before country and God. Afterward, in the unleashed, deconstructed, home-office nineties, an age of unapologetic disloyalty, my friend Moss had called me a glorified Pinkerton guard.

Not long after the Penaflor settlement I sat conflicted in my office. Part was Kathleen's death throwing my aspirations in relief. Part was the sheer humorlessness of grief, how irony is overwhelmed by feeling.

Grief blows irony's socks off. The grieving choke on the very truths the ironic are fending off. Grim with truth, I fixed on the Devil's Advocate—the red, rubberized figure with horns squatting where he always had, at the southeast corner of Henry's glassed-topped Duncan Phyfe desk. Bearing my name, mocking me. When you're wasted with grief, little ironic touches can piss you off. The real message, I realized, was not ironic but literally true: Elliot Stone, Advocate for the Fiend.

I snatched Henry's stupid little action hero and dropped him in the trash.

The phone rang. "Have you changed your mind?" Hans asked. "Shall I tell Christina?"

"No, no. *G-a-s-l-a-v* is written in June's chart. Means what?"

"Gastric lavage, probably. Didn't we talk about this? Have you gotten the fluid?"

"What? We never talked about it. I forgot about it until last night."

"You didn't say anything."

"I forgot, okay? What's gastric lavage?"

"Irrigation of the stomach. Stomach pumping to you. Probably used her stoma, for the feeding tube. That would be handy."

"It says 'gas lav' under doctor's orders."

"Well?"

"Why pump June's stomach?"

"It can be a pre-op procedure. Maybe for something they ended up not doing. It's also done for poisoning. That could have been suspected."

"Why suspect poisoning?" I bit my tongue about the missing specimen bottle.

"As a precaution. She comes in corked out and no one's sure why. Just in case, they run a lavage, like they run a V/Q for pulmonary embolism. There's a stoma, so it's easy to do."

"But there aren't any results."

"The results are that her stomach was pumped but she died anyway, so maybe poison didn't kill her."

"Don't they analyze the fluid?"

"Sometimes. In June's case, why bother? She died."

"I think the doctors thought June was poisoned."

He said nothing, which I took to mean: Elliot, time to move on.

"Look," I continued, "you said you'd read all the records. I'm bringing them over. No more amateur hour. I need a full-bore, grand-an-hour medical analysis for free. I realize I owe you for this, and for mentioning the mine in the guy's chest cavity back in Vukovar. And that wine last night. It was really good."

"I'll take you up on it sometime."

We met for lunch ten days later at Triana, a tapas bar. The long, strange winter was starting to break. John Elway got his repeat in the Super Bowl, but a cold fog shut Denver down and the streets were reveler-free. Clinton won his trial in the Senate on a split decision. Nor was that an occasion for public celebration. Revelry didn't suit the times. Public life was too embarrassing—Cokie Roberts asking Clinton's lawyer if his own wife thought oral sex was sex. Focus on the personal. Mountain bluebirds were back in Boulder County. The Flagstaff trail was clear of ice.

Hans Leitner focused on the tapas. His appetite ran to marine invertebrates. Scampi, octopus, calamari, and clams. He lay at my feet the twelve-pound sack of paper. "With one exception, nothing unexpected."

"The gastric lavage."

"No, that was more or less expected."

"But we don't know what it means."

"So find out," he said. "Have the fluids analyzed."

"You're joking. They keep what they pump out?"

"Usually. There should be a protocol."

"I'm calling them now."

"No one will tell you on the phone. Go in person. Play lawyer."

"Yeah," I said. "I know how to do that."

"I wasted a lot of time on this." He kicked at the sack of records.

"What do the hospital labs mean?"

"She was thrombocytopenic. Low hematocrit. If they'd been able to stabilize her, a transfusion was coming next. It never got that far. Listen, Elliot, it's not the hospital labs, it's the Colfax labs. The malnourishment." He gave the sack another kick. "In all of this, know what smells? The Colfax nutrition charts. They don't add up."

"Take me through it."

"The scrips are fine. The right food in the right amounts." He unfolded a note of jottings from his shirt pocket. "Fifteen hundred calories daily, sixty grams protein, one hundred seventy grams cholesterol, seventy grams fat, one hundred twenty percent vitamins and minerals, the right balance of free water. All good products; actually, the best. Pricey stuff. So how does that square with albumin heading south? How does she get malnourished? You sure you sent me everything?"

"Copied it myself."

"We've got no dietitian consults, no weight-tracking forms, no enteral feeding records, nutrition assessment sheets, or progress notes. Just the care plans and feeding orders, but nothing showing what she actually got or how she was doing."

"So?"

"It smells."

"It could mean—"

He waved me off. "That's your job."

"A tilt from neglect to deliberate?"

"A tilt. But, please, Elliot, keep alert for the innocent explanation."

"Why? I'm a lawyer."

No smile. He tidied his place and beckoned for the bill.

"Paid," I said. "On me."

He frowned in his thoughtful way. "I like lawyer jokes, Elliot, but that one had a sting. We look at proof very differently, lawyers and doctors, like highly evolved expressions of the half-full/half-empty glass. You're half-full—"

"If not completely full of it."

"And we—medical scientists, I mean—analyze what's missing. As a scientist, I try to prove my own theories wrong. Test them. Exhaust the contrary data before ever entertaining a hypothesis as correct."

"You mean you don't do hunches."

"The lawyer's objective isn't truth, but persuasion." He'd given this some thought, it appeared. "Getting others to believe your proof, not demonstrating the validity of the proof itself."

"I'm an advocate, yes, but not—entirely. I believe in the criterion of truth." I'd thought about this too. Truth simplifies.

"Your man Kant thought perception was reality, right? There were many truths."

"No. He thought truth could be reached through intuition. So do I."

"It seems there really is a difference between us."

I thought I heard a tiny cluck of self-righteousness in this pronouncement. If he cared more than I did about the truth, let him show it.

"How's your patient doing? Dale?"

"Adjusting. His wife died less than three months ago. You should appreciate what that's like."

"Hans, I'm going to ask you a question you can't answer. Don't answer it, but give me an honest response. I think Dale

Stillwell exploded with rage at his wife as the cause of his deficits. He almost killed her with—a heavy, edged object. He thought he *had* killed her, and he's been covering up the crime from that night right on through the present. I think that's the truth. Am I right?"

He worked the knuckles of a hand. He seemed to be deliberating whether to speak. "To a point you understand Dale Stillwell, but there's a piece you're missing. You won't have the truth without the missing piece."

I fell back in the chair shaking my head. "You're playing with me."

"I gave an honest response. I can't go further. I probably went too far."

"Okay," I said, "but now I won't sleep."

He peaked his bristly gray brows.

"Until I find the missing piece."

I assembled my letters of credence. Authorization for the Release of Gastric Lavage Fluids, conservatorship papers signed by the judge and stamped by the clerk, a durable power of attorney recorded with Flatirons County, and highlighted excerpts from the Probate Code and Medical Records Act. At my front door I was met by a deputy sheriff with papers of his own—a summons and subpoena to appear and testify before the grand jury empaneled to investigate the death of June Stillwell.

After swinging by the bank for a notary's jurat, I hit the turnpike for Denver. En route I called for Rico again. I'd been calling once or twice a week. They knew and hung up at my voice. I called the doctor, A. Arcenault, who had ordered the gastric lavage. Not available. I left my cell-phone number.

Platte Valley Hospital, like other hospitals, has low-ceilinged mazes to puzzle through and disorienting signs: IMAGING, BRAIN, PAIN, TUMOR, TRAUMA—instead of nice words with felicitous attributes—Hope, Strength, Sorrow, Courage, Love. Pathology was called Lab. Medical Records was called Legal.

The desk clerk at Legal looked promising. Magenta spiked hair, death rouge, Monica gloss. A single bottle-green gem on a nostril stud. No Swedish nurse, but she might bend some rules.

"Wait." I studied her from two angles. Her tag read Silbi. "Show me your palm. I'm good at this."

She made a we-get-all-kinds face but held out her hand. Magenta nails.

"I say—Silbi was born in August."

"Yeah. Okay. What year?"

"After Elvis died."

"He didn't, ain't ya heard? How'd you know August?"

I touched my nose. "Peridot. My wife's birthstone."

"What day's she?"

"Twenty-fifth."

"I'm thirtieth. So whatcha here for?"

Now playing lawyer, I elaborated my official documents.

"On my way." She smiled. No questions asked. Twenty minutes later, she was back empty-handed. "Can't help you— sorry."

"What happened?"

"It's, like, not there. Gone."

"But—what happened to it? There has to be a record."

"We have procedures that we follow."

Tranquil and opaque when challenged, a good choice for Legal.

"Listen, Silbi." I glanced behind me, then edged her way. "That fluid may hold the secret of whether someone was murdered. I've taken a vow to get to the bottom of it. I have to find that fluid."

Purpled eyebrows rose. Silbi was getting interested. Copying medical records for Legal got mighty dull. She smacked her gloss, shook her head, gave me an empathetic look. "Problem is, her bottle ain't there."

"I'm going in."

"I'll show ya." She came around the counter and led me left down a hall past oncoming traffic—doctors in lab coats, techs with trays of trembling glass containers, all of them wearing laminated photo ID cards around the neck. I felt naked.

"I don't much like labs," I confided. "Kind of squeamish."

Inside a double swinging door all manner of organic material lined a wall of shelves. Tupperware containers with organs suspended in formalin: breasts, colons, livers, hearts. A side door marked TUMOR BANK. Slide-making apparatuses and paraffin-block machines. Busy workers in white outfits at chopping-block counters and sinks. It's nothing, I told myself. It's like a big restaurant kitchen without any appetizing smells.

Silbi approached a woman for a key. She led me to a locked mini-freezer labeled GASTRIC LAVAGE. A clipboard hung from a handle on a chain. "See." Silbi traced back two pages to December 14, 1998, where "Stillwell, J." was checked in both the received and discarded columns. The discard date was February 8, 1999. She unlocked and opened the freezer, packed with barcoded blue bottles. "I went through 'em one by one with the scanner. None of 'em popped up Stillwell or Mooney."

"May I see the procedures book?"

"Off-limits." But she winked. I followed her to a bookcase. She pulled a fat, black loose-leaf notebook, thumbed through, and opened it to Gastric Lavage Protocol.

It looked pretty simple. All you needed was a 36-French tube, irrigating syringe, and four liters of half-saline solution. Two steps—aspirate stomach contents and save for chemical analysis, then wash out the stomach with saline solution ten to twelve times until the returns are clear.

"See this here?" A magenta nail pointed to "Retention Policy: freeze eight weeks then discard." "Like the log says was done, strictly per procedures."

It had been eleven weeks since June's death.

"And discard means—" Though I knew.

"Biohazard disposal. Chuck it out, burn it up."

"If I'd come three weeks ago—"

"Yeah. That sucks." She hefted the notebook back on the shelf. "How about this place?" Her eyes swept the lab. "Come back at night, you see all kinds of stuff. There's thirty thousand tumors in that vault."

"Let's get out of here."

Silbi led me up the hall again to Legal. "So, let's think about what you can do. What was the plan, why were you looking for her bottle?"

"A hunch, intuition. There might be poison."

"What'd the report say?"

"No report."

"Has to be. Procedures."

"What do you mean?"

"We don't do tox here per the chemical-analysis protocol.

You need a special gizmo. They draw a dropper from the bottle and send it out. Got to be one of those Front Range Poison Center forms in the chart."

"Nope. Nothing."

"I'm gonna see." She slipped into the *S–Z* aisle behind her and returned with June's original hospital chart.

"Wow, you didn't tell me she died *here.*"

"Maybe that's why there's no report."

"Nope. Got to be." She flipped pages like a cardsharp, stopped suddenly, whispered, "Somebody murdered her?"

I nodded.

"You don't think—like a nurse or some fellow employee of this place?"

"Oh, no. Hospital's in the clear."

"Oh, okay." Silbi resumed flipping, commenting as she flipped. "Technically, her being dead, you should have brought the okay from the PR of the estate, which you didn't, but never mind now." Thirty more pages flipped. "Why'm I thinking I know this chart?" she asked rhetorically. "Something, young woman dying out like that? Something. Well." She reached the end. "It ain't here. You're right."

"Meaning nothing was sent to the poison center?"

"Evidently, or the report never got back. Which does represent a failure to follow procedures. Somebody'd get a hand slap on a random chart audit. Maybe that's how I saw it? But there's no checkout record. Pulled it for the cops?"

"Not the cops."

She smacked her gloss. Pensive. "So—this is pretty important?"

"It really is."

"So—" She blew her lips.

"Thanks for trying."

"I wanna help ya."

"Maybe next time."

"Next time."

I wrote my cell number on my pathetic home-office card and skipped it to her across the counter.

"Hey," she called as I was walking out. "About Elvis. I go all the way back to 'Burning Love.'" She waved. "Tell your wife hi from a fellow Virgal."

I resisted the impulse to return and give Silbi the whole sad story.

Hospitals . . .

Like a golf course designed by a great pro, the Flagstaff Mountain trail feels like a runner's work of genius, though it isn't. The Civilian Conservation Corps laid it out in the thirties. Nine miles round-trip from my house, fifteen-hundred-foot elevation gain, little loose rock, and stunning vistas and terrains that proceed like a narrative.

I leave from home, cross Boulder Creek at Eben Fine Park, then switchback up the north flank of the mountain above Hans Leitner's office. Arid, yucca terraces give way to ponderosa woods. Then you pitch out onto a bluestem meadow, wind through thickets of Indian plum, circle monoliths of Dakota sandstone, rim canyon lookouts on cliff ledge routes, climb through chokecherry and pump across the summit to the crag, the turn-around, from which, in one direction, the suburb-scabbed plains stretch like battlefields toward Chicago, and in the other, fold on fold of pine-fir foothills mount to the Indian Peaks Wilderness, the not-won West. It's aesthetically compelling, a story with beginning, middle, end, edgy with the chance of bear or lion; also an interior journey shaped by reflections on accomplishment, memory, mortality. Like all good narratives, an ordering experience. Afterward, tranquilized by exercise hypoxia, you feel the big mountain has put the little hassles in their place.

So it was early March 1999, the first Flagstaff run of the year the odometer would turn. I tried to tie together the latest loose ends. After leaving the hospital I'd stopped by the poison center. No record there a sample had been received or analyzed. Dr. Arcenault's office called back. They'd been advised not to speak with me. By whom? "An attorney." Dr. Arcenault's attorney? His insurer? Whitelaw, the Colfax lawyer? "Who the hell is keeping the patient's conservator from talking with the patient's doctor?" On hold, two, three minutes. "Hello, sir. This happens to be a deceased patient and it was the attorney for her estate."

I rammed the phone against the dashboard. Hassles. I checked it, operational; the dashboard's padded. Irresponsibly—a cell-phone call to Europe, 2 A.M. in The Hague—I called

Quierin. Not there. So where was *she*? I left a priority message.
I drove back in the dark stewing over what I'd have to tell the
grand jury when they put me under oath. The next day Quierin
called.

From a Flagstaff perspective the loose ends looked like this:
After possibly systematically starving June for several months,
Rico disappears just as he's to meet with me. Two of June's
stomach-fluid specimens disappear, from two different hospitals, and a sample to be analyzed never reaches the poison center lab. Possibly the specimens were discarded under hospital
retention policies. But low odds the disappearances of both plus
the interception of the poison center sample were all innocent
coincidences. Assuming, Hans's warning aside, a noninnocent
explanation, high odds whoever ditched the Colfax specimen
did the same at Platte Valley Hospital. Did that clear Stillwell
and Rico, since neither had been at Platte Valley as far as I
knew? Why had Stillwell come after *me* in the White Spot the
afternoon before? April *had* been at Platte Valley. Where was
she the afternoon before? Like Rico, now April was also gone,
somewhere in California. Both April and Stillwell had failed
trial-by-autopsy. Why did both prevent the procedure that may
have put all these questions to rest?

Physical evidence had disappeared. People were disappearing. And what was the piece Leitner said was missing? A
spaghetti of loose ends.

There's a chalky stretch of the Flagstaff trail against which
footfalls make a hollow sound, a resonance that almost echoes.
You imagine someone closing on your heels, and I can never
keep from snatching a look behind me there. Just a towhee in the
currant scrub. A ponderosa hulaing on the breeze that feathered
hair at my neck.

Quierin had sounded as if she were in the next room. "I get
weird"—wee-urd—"vibing from your messages," she said. No
doubt in our weekly chats I'd been sounding despondent, in the
dead of winter, at a dead end in June's case. I told her I wanted to
talk about poison.

"Just like I tell you. Weird. I hate poison anyway. Bullet hole
in skull I like. Speaks for itself. But poison can be anything and
all you got with this woman is a little bone. Only poison reaches

bone is metallic toxin like arsenic, mercury, lead. That's a big goose egg. To find poison, don't look for poison."

A haunting thought among the hollow footfalls.

"Smart poisoner won't use poisons people think of. This guy smart?"

"Maybe not."

"Smartest is nontoxic chemical that makes toxic metabolite. Even better is toxic interaction between nontoxic chemicals. Next best is something ordinary like paint, turpentine, Drano, antifreezes. Also clever is expected drug in unexpected quantity, like aspirin or Valium OD. Reason is routine tox screen only catches what you say to look for, so for smart poisoner forget routine and go for the whole hog. I don't know how you look for not-smart poisoner."

April, I remembered, majored in biochemistry. "Could be either kind," I said.

"Not matters anyway since you don't have tissue. You're out of shit luck. Best now is analyze medical course. What substance causes that? Get the colonel's help."

"Hans thinks I'm jumping the gun. He thinks poison is a stretch. I should look for an innocent explanation. But, since I haven't told him about the missing specimens, no wonder he thinks I'm losing my grip. He's pretty sure someone was starving June. There's proof of that, he thinks."

"Could be both. Why not tell him?"

"He's Stillwell's doctor. Stillwell could use this information. April's lawyer would kill me if I passed it on to Stillwell's team. I may have to talk about it soon anyway."

"Tricky business."

"Awkward as hell. Come over and help me."

"Yeah, I want to meet the Great Satan, but work is first. Crazy time here. Bad guys on the move, Operation Horseshoe. Forty thousand VJ army, SJP cop militia, make ring around Kosovo. Arkan's down there with Tigers, White Eagles, half our whole indictment list. Whole OTP is hypered and rattling."

"Where were you last night at two in the morning?"

"Sleeping in bed."

"Wish I was there."

"Me too, baby. But I can't help you with this woman. I need

a dead body. What's a taphonomist without a dead person to work on?"

"Like a baker without dough. A sculptor without clay. A lawyer without clients. Me without you."

"I'm nobody without dead people."

"You think I should give this up? Move on?"

"Hell no, you should not."

"Why not?"

"You can't let bad guys get away with it. Cross fingers not in Kosovo either."

"I love you. You agree with me."

"I *inspire* you, greenhorn. You hear Clinton"—*clean tone*—"got rid of his cat? Bad time to be saying, 'Come, Spot.' *Dui,* baby."

Pounding down the homestretch switchbacks, I could see Hans Leitner's office below. The glass of the slider caught the sun as it opened. Moving beneath pine boughs, his patch of white hair, then his face turning up, appraising the mountain. "Who are we?" he'd said at dinner, and I wasn't sure.

I waved—he couldn't know me from this height—and ran on. He continued staring up, hands on hips, like a climber deciding on a route.

CHAPTER 6

Hospitals . . .

Rose Memorial this time, maternity ward, where Paige, when I called, insisted I come, she had nothing better to do, it would help pass the time, and she wanted to know.

What was it with these *fin de siècle* females, putting work before babies and beaux?

Connor Jorritsma, only six pounds ten, looked pretty feisty compared with his nursery mates. "Takes after Mom?" I asked Jack, the dad, giving me the obligatory incubator tour. But Jack, a muscular guy in sweatshirt and jeans, was lost in wonder at the glass wall, eyes watering at the sight of his son. Back at the ward room he left me and Paige to our business.

"Don't think you can take advantage of my confinement," Paige said from her bed.

"Stay away from April, you mean?"

"The whole bit."

"May I congratulate you?" I put the blue irises I'd brought on her window shelf. "Good-looking guy. Bald is back."

"Acknowledged. How's your practice?" Paige making small talk.

"Pits."

"Sorry."

"Beats working."

"Doubtful."

Paige in bed in a light blue gown, jade eyes glazed from sedatives, lips just parted in a looser version of her aggressive smile, looked, well, great.

"How's April?" I sat in an electric recliner.

"She calls. Flunking two classes. Shacked up with some numbnuts surfer. Refuses to get Prozac at mental health."

"She seemed so together at the service."

"She does that. Comes together, comes apart. It sunk in, her mother. Plus, you know, now I'm it. Her one and only it. She calls me, like a mother substitute. I'm not up"—she laughed lightly; it became a cough—"to being anybody's mother."

"You'll feel better when the drugs wear off."

"Case is what keeps April going. She'll be together for trial."

"And the case?"

"Chugging along fine on my own. Pop out a baby now and then, then back to chasing the boys. I scared Hancock so bad he brought in ringers so three suits can soak the poor fuck. Kevin Kirwan and Bernie Edson, no less."

"I wish I were helping. I really do."

"Not even sure I need you anymore. I'm kicking ass, Elliot. Murder's fun when you hold all the cards, and the defendant's a fruitloop, and there's a lower standard of proof, and no damages caps. It's a great case. You're missing out."

"Where are you?" I asked.

"Deposing cops and fact witnesses."

"They holding up?"

"Like a brick shithouse. I disclosed the milkmaid and the Mole Hole woman, which has 'em scratching their heads."

"They won't know what to ask."

"Not till after expert disclosures. The blood spatterist and the chemist on the powder residues."

"So keep on running them around the barn."

"Until I get my claws in Stillwell." Her loose smile tightened. "I want to put him under oath first, then Leitner, then whatever experts they scrape together, but the DA's holding that up. Stillwell's taking the Fifth. And trial's set for June seventh. We're on Otero's rocket docket."

"Otero *again*?"

"Best draw possible. Judge knows Mr. Stillwell well." Paige

pushed over onto one side. The effort showed in her face. "Now tell me what brings you."

"To do you a favor but you won't take it that way."

"Continue."

"I'm sitting on some facts you don't know about." I tilted back ten degrees in the recliner. "I haven't told anybody except Quierin, but, speaking of the DA, I'm under subpoena to testify tomorrow. I thought you ought to hear it first."

"Why tell me a thing?"

"I think of us as on the same side, Paige. These facts aren't going to help your case. But I have to answer under oath, and you need to be ready for it."

She half-shut the glazed eyes. "Elliot, don't be a cheese-dick."

I stiffened. "I'm going to tell it straight, Paige."

"No, I know that. I mean, don't apologize, for Christ's sake, and cut the whiny self-justifications. Hand me the legal pad."

"If I've got any of it wrong, tell me, so I get it right tomorrow."

"Go."

I went.

It turns out, I said, the reason June Stillwell began sinking into deep coma in October was severe malnourishment. Her lab values were consistent with those of someone who was being slowly starved. She was ordered all the right food, but she wasn't getting it. The records that would confirm that are missing from the Colfax chart, suggesting the malnourishment was covered up. The night before she died, she was under the care of the same Colfax employee, Rico Tiradentes, who had been responsible for feeding her. That week Rico left Colfax and apparently disappeared.

At Platte Valley Hospital someone authorized do-not-resuscitate orders. April was there but claims not to remember. Gastric lavage, which is done when poisoning is suspected, was ordered at the hospital, and the night before, June's stomach fluids were drawn for routine weekly lab analysis. Both the Colfax and the gastric lavage specimens should have been chemically analyzed for what June had ingested. Someone or something kept that from happening.

At this Paige groaned. "Making it up."

"I wish," I said. "The two specimens and the poison center

draw have all disappeared without being analyzed and without explanation, as I can personally attest."

"Personally attest? *You* discovered them missing?"

"Yes." I explained that hospital personnel had shown me the specimen was gone and had shown me the protocol. The poison center had told me they never got the sample. And the day after June died, I'd let myself into the Colfax lab and seen that June's stomach specimen was the only one missing. Colfax was accusing *me* of stealing it. "The only other physical evidence of why she died was her body," I said. "You know what happened to it."

"Leaving the cause of death—"

"Not presently knowable. Just as or more likely than head trauma are starvation and poisoning by persons unknown, all potential proof positive having suspiciously disappeared."

I was done. I fiddled with the recline button. The chair tilted back and forth. "That's it. I think it's all true."

"Except the inferences."

"I'll keep it factual, but the grand jury will draw the same inferences."

"Where—" Paige sat upright. Her fist tightened and the veins in her forearm swelled. "Where do you get off? Sneaking into hospitals with no legal authority?"

"I won't volunteer any of it, but if I'm asked, I have to answer."

"It's time to go, Elliot."

"You'd be blindsided if I didn't tell you."

"Go." She smiled fixedly. "And good-bye."

But I wasn't asked and I didn't volunteer. I couldn't have been more relieved after catching the drift of my interrogation.

Inside the guarded door lettered GRAND JURY, DA Russell Tucker sat by himself at a carved oak desk inlaid with leather, while the rest of us—twelve jurors, Deputy DA Millsap and two colleagues, the court reporter, and I—sat in auditorium folding chairs around folding tables that had been pulled together. The reasons Tucker attended weren't clear since Millsap asked all the questions.

At his special desk, Tucker showed himself capable of two attitudes—frowning like a Lawman or reflective like a Lawyer. Either impassive and ice-eyed, the embodiment of Justice. Or meticulously penning a note, then pensively gazing off, stroking his chin, the embodiment of Law.

Poses, I realized, were all Tucker had left. With his lock on the nomination, he'd learned he could do nothing at all but look good and still get reelected. The bad press being generated by the media camped outside, agitating for another grand jury in the child murder case, must have pained him to no end after all the years of image work.

The jurors looked basic Boulder, monocultural, a few professionals, some graduate degrees, a free spirit or two, a couple of Afro-Americans. The foreman, a League of Women Voters matron, swore me in, and Deputy Millsap took over. The jurors seemed interested in the background stuff, railroads and war crimes. Millsap led me next into what conservatorships were. He skipped over the central points of this topic: Stillwell's accident and June's role in it, the settlement money and June's eventual control. These were at the heart of the case against Stillwell; they went to motive. Maybe they'd heard it already from other witnesses. I suppressed the urge to bring it up.

I was a partisan, I realized. Not good, though it might gladden Paige. I'd advised hundreds of deponents never to volunteer anything when questioned under oath. Never to speculate. Don't just start talking. Give narrow, factual answers that respond only to what is asked. Not so easy to do when you have a hidden partisanship and your interrogator is a nice, boyish guy like Millsap lobbing open-ended questions on mushy, general topics.

"While you were domiciled in Holland two years, what connection did you have with the Stillwells?"

He'd said "connection," not "contact," not "communication." Pretty broad, so I volunteered, mostly to clear my conscience.

"Connection? Only that I made in my mind. I kept wondering if I should have told authorities about Mr. Stillwell's talking about killing his wife, which I overheard in 1996." I described it. Jurors took notes. "I did discuss that statement once in The Hague with Dr. Leitner."

Boyish Millsap had a bland poker countenance. "The jurors may want to follow up on that." Tucker was embodying Law at the moment, poising his ballpoint midair, looking away with a thoughtful brow. Not even listening, I figured.

"Let's turn to"—Millsap checked off the questions on his topmost yellow sheet and flipped it underneath—"Mrs. Stillwell's affairs and belongings." How he'd subheaded the next inquiry. "Your job included apprising yourself of Mrs. Stillwell's effects?" We slogged through them for half an hour.

"Were you able to communicate with your ward, Mrs. Stillwell?"

"I thought I could. She indicated—" I stopped, not to volunteer. Tucker gave me an icy Lawman look, arms folded, frowning. I waited for Millsap to ask if June communicated who may have hurt her, but, instead, he moved on. He'd expected me to say, "No, she couldn't communicate," I realized. What was going on?

"Now—April Mooney." Millsap read from the subhead on his pad. Here the pace accelerated.

When did she insist on staying in the hospital in her mother's room? Do you know why? Why did you permit that? Did you begin to observe changes in Ms. Mooney's mood? When did she first mention her intention to sue Mr. Stillwell? Did she seem fixated on that?

"Did Ms. Mooney tell you why she and her mother became estranged?"

"They weren't estranged. Far from it."

"Isn't it true the daughter never visited in the Stillwells' home?"

"I heard that but—"

"Mother and daughter hadn't seen each other for, what? Over a year?"

"I think so—"

Do you know Ms. Mooney's whereabouts the day before her mother's death? What about that night? She said she was with her mother all that night. The next morning when you found Ms. Stillwell, where was April Mooney?

"Mr. Stone," Millsap said. "June Stillwell was helpless, wasn't she?"

"Yes."

"Anyone wanting to do her harm, or even end her life, could have readily done so, without resistance."

"What are you implying?"

"Did April Mooney cause a scene once when her stepfather came to visit?"

"*He* did. He tried to attack her."

"Did Ms. Mooney provoke him?"

"His being there was the provocation. This was the man who'd tried to kill April's mother."

"Mr. Stone. Listen to my question." Now all I wanted to do was volunteer. "When Mr. Stillwell came to visit his wife, did April Mooney call him a quote fucker unquote?"

I threw out my hands. "Maybe. I guess so. But—" I panned the jurors for signs of dismay. Most were diligently scribbling notes. I looked at Tucker. He'd phased back to Lawman again.

"Are you in contact with April Mooney?"

"Not presently."

"Why is that? Did you have a falling-out?"

"I suppose—"

"Over what?"

In tight-lipped, don't-volunteer mode, I said, truthfully, I wasn't entirely sure.

"You thought there should be an autopsy."

"That—was suggested. Yes."

"Why did you think an autopsy of your ward, June Stillwell, was necessary?"

I tried a waffle. "I'm not qualified to say whether it was necessary or not."

"You asked for an autopsy."

"I talked about it. With Dr. Leitner. And with Ms. Mooney's lawyer."

"To determine the cause of death?"

"I suppose."

"Did Ms. Mooney oppose an autopsy?"

"I did not discuss it with her directly."

"Did you learn she was opposed from any source?"

"I was told that. I was told Mr. Stillwell opposed an autopsy too."

"So—what happened?"

"Well, there wasn't an autopsy. The family preferred cremation."

"Mr. Stone, you lived in Holland. Did you discuss your time in Holland with April Mooney?"

"Of course."

"Did you and she talk about mercy killing? Euthanasia?"

I had no idea. "I don't know. I don't remember that."

"Thank you, Mr. Stone."

"I want to say, about April Mooney—"

"Thank you, I'm done. The jurors may have some questions. Perhaps Mr. Tucker."

Tucker, in high frown, heard his name. "Nothing," he said. And not a juror said a word.

I mustered a nod and smile and headed for the door posted by deputies. Terrible preparation, lame performance. Why hadn't I taken these pissants seriously and had counsel present? Fool for a lawyer. I had to talk to Paige. This thing was greased.

Kevin Kirwan and Bernie Edson, Hancock's ringers, sat on a bench against the wall of the reception area, matching black brief-cases between their legs. Hancock stood next to them playing with keys in his pocket and going on about something. Kirwan and Edson didn't look interested. Edson acknowledged me with a tuck of his bald head. "D-D-D-Dale—" I heard Hancock chuckling.

Four or five reporters and a TV crew lounged on another set of benches. All at once they sat up straight and began kicking out tripods, unsnapping lens caps, smoothing hair and straightening ties.

A little hubbub gathered behind me. The jurors recessing, strolling out single file. Educated, white, upper-middle-class sheep, I thought uncharitably, led by the nose.

There stood Tucker. He went two paces past the door and no farther. He beckoned softly with both hands and the clump of media came forward. He flashed his fingers and they stopped at just the right spot for the camera angle to include over his left shoulder the white-lettered words GRAND JURY.

The only reason he'd sat through my testimony was to set up the photo op afterward. I barely throttled the impulse to grab a boom mike and whack him.

What was happening to me? As a railroad lawyer I'd been as genteely self-contained as any garden-party host. Afterward, I was a prosecutor like these guys—sort of. I understood the bureaucratic exigencies of the job and observed the courtesies, uncomfortably. But here I was about to flip. Tucker throwing April to the dogs, then going out to his favored press, seriously turned my stomach. Way close to losing my cool, I reached deep for a reason to behave myself.

In his limited way, I reached deep to think, Tucker was good, a master of illusions. I could already hear the intro on the evening news: "After an afternoon leading a grand jury investigation in an unrelated homocide, Boulder District Attorney Russell Tucker briefly answered questions about the murder that has the nation mesmerized and in mourning more than two years after a pretty six-year-old was found beaten and strangled in her Boulder home—"

Tucker's press conference was over in three minutes that included one sound bite and both trademark poses. The thoughtful Lawyer explained how seriously his office continued to treat the matter. The tough Lawman got the sound bite: "I have one thing to say to the killer of this little girl. We *will* find you and you *will* pay for your heinous acts. You can run, but you can't hide."

He begged off a clamor of questions and strode out of camera view with the look of a dedicated public servant too busy with the people's business to spare a moment more. Three minutes for local TV was enough of a comment to excuse not talking to the bloodthirsty national media camped outside the courthouse.

"Russell." I caught his elbow. "What's going on here?"

"Here?"

"The June Stillwell case."

The politician's arm swung up and settled on my shoulder. "What a tough one, hey?"

"First you say you won't file charges."

"There's no statute of limitations on murder, my friend. You get a murder and you get new evidence, I'll always reconsider."

"New evidence?"

He laughed heartily, nodded to a passing cop. "The thing is, in Colorado a DA's hands are tied. No subpoena power except through a grand jury. Hell of an investigation tool. Where this one's going—" He shook his head. I saw the Lawman coming. "I will promise this to you as a man who I believe sincerely cared about this woman. Whoever took her life, however that was done, we will find out. Believe me."

"You mean, he can run but he can't hide?"

"Excuse me?" Tucker's PR guy now had his ear and they were off to the more serious work of feeding and fending off the tabloids.

Then something actually alarming: Chief Deputy Pissant Millsap huddled with Hancock, Kirwan, and Edson. "Mr. Millsap," I said. "Come here please." A test of his neutrality.

Millsap extricated himself, leaving Hancock with a doofus look, and quick fury from Kevin Kirwan, a control freak who detested interruptions. Evenhanded and faux innocent, Millsap smiled and huddled now with me.

How commonly, I wondered, do witnesses develop homicidal designs on their cross-examiners?

"I get the broader context," I said, smiling benignly in our huddle. "You have the garroting of a mini–beauty queen, rich, beautiful-people parents, you screw up the case, and it's the post-O.J. dry spell. Reasonable facsimile of juicy celebrity murder and the talk-radio Savanarolas are demanding the head of Russell the Smooth."

Millsap kept smiling.

"Inevitably, your office's pathetic record prosecuting violent crimes catches press attention. Along comes June Stillwell, brutally beaten in her home and no evidence of an intruder. A no-brainer circumstantial case, but your jerkwater office won't charge anybody since you'd face a defendant with money, and money buys legal talent."

Millsap started to say something.

"*Let me finish.* Tucker's afraid of good lawyers because he's afraid of losing. Because losing looks bad in the paper, and looks matter to Russell Tucker. Mexican with a PD, whole different story than a wealthy wife beater."

Millsap had stopped smiling. "*Wait,*" I said when he opened his mouth. "I'm trying to understand something here. I'm trying to understand whether, when the national press started to wonder about a pattern of prosecutorial timidity, *you put on this farce designed to obscure why June Stillwell died purely to cover Tucker's candy ass?*"

Now Millsap was laughing soundlessly. He looked happy but his eyes roamed the reception room.

"And he papers over his cowardice as some compassionate,

high-minded liberal social policy of rehabilitation rather than retribution. Poor Dale Stillwell, a brain-injured homeless-shelter volunteer. He doesn't deserve prison, no matter what he did."

"I'm sorry I rubbed you the wrong way."

"Your grand jury isn't serious, is it? It's a ploy so you can pretend to the inquisitorial press you take murder by rich people seriously. So you can lay off the preposterous failure to charge Dale Stillwell on a secret decision of citizen jurors."

"This jury is serious indeed."

"It's a cover for Tucker. How can you work for that fraud?"

"Whose side are you on, Mr. Stone?" Millsap asked blandly. "And, by the way, what did you think you were doing in 1996 when you became the Stillwells' fiduciary then immediately left the country? Or in 1998 when you became the wife's fiduciary *against* the husband, who'd been your ward? Or now? It seems to me you may be withholding evidence. You may be defaming and threatening our prosecution in order to protect someone. With all of your conflicts of interest, who's the someone? Whose side are you on? I'm curious."

And then, seeing me at a sudden loss, boyish smile on high beam: "What kind of lawyer are you these days?"

"You little fascist whiffet," I muttered, and one or the other of us spun on his heel.

Hancock stood across the room bouncing in place with his strong-arms, Kirwan and Edson, and at their center, a fawned-on Russell Tucker.

I approached Hancock. "How's your wife?" I said for no reason at all. Hancock fingered his ring.

"Do you know my wife?"

"Jackie." Summoned from somewhere.

"Jackie's fine. Why do you ask?"

Though not by nature a sly person, I smiled slyly.

Kirwan, Edson, and Tucker stared. The idea of a loose cannon on deck got around the room.

"Russell," I said. "You told me whatever, whoever killed June Stillwell, you will find out."

"Absolutely." Frowning Lawman.

"Even if it's Kevin Kirwan's client?"

"Of course."

"Even if it's—Kevin Kirwan?"

Much insincere hilarity, except from Kirwan. What they were up to was now clear. I knew, but they didn't, that I held the keys to the strategy.

"Heinous times," I said. I took my leave.

Outside the Flatirons County Courthouse cops patrolled two perimeters. One, the hysterical line of demonstrators at the cordon with signs demanding justice for the murdered child—WHY NO GRAND JURY?—another the media anthill of bored techs, engineers, cameramen, anchors testing poses in front of Flagstaff Mountain, aerials, generators, boosters, satellite relays and transmitters, pickup units, video and sound trucks and trailers. At a trailer door now and then, a celebrity mediaperson showed his or her face. One figure brooded conspicuously alone. In faded dungarees, battered tennis shoes, a hooded gray sweatshirt over a bearded, sunglassed face. Geraldo, undercover as the Unibomber, gunning for Russell Tucker.

My house was a quick walk from court. Halfway home I phoned Paige's room at Rose Memorial. Jack answered. "She's sleeping." I have to talk to her, I said. "You upset her. Leave her be." Tell Paige to call me, it's really bad.

Before I hit the front porch, the cell phone rang. Paige. "You fuck up, amigo?"

"It's reality time. You, me, and April need to face some facts. It's worse than you ever imagined."

"Short version. Five words or less."

"April is a target."

CHAPTER 7

This time Jack stayed in the room, maybe to
keep an eye on me. With Jack watching TV, Paige nursing Connor in the recliner, me on a stool from the nurses' station, April,
fresh from Santa Cruz, sitting on the bed, swinging her legs, and
Detective Roybal taking his leave, we resembled a family
tableau of dysfunctional crackers in a tar-paper shack.

Jack watched CNN on closed caption and shot looks at his son
and wife, sometimes at me. The look I got was more suspicious
than circumstances warranted. It wasn't just me, I thought, but
what I embodied—law and lawyering, which he thought Paige
preferred to him.

"Actually," Paige said when I finished summarizing the
afternoon, "I don't think you fucked up too bad." My testimony
was secret, but I could give them the flavor of Millsap's questions and what he didn't ask.

"You didn't reveal our evidence," she said. "You didn't
reveal *your* evidence. They'd have had a field day."

When Paige had called April with my bad news about the
grand jury gearing toward April, she'd almost welcomed it,
she told us. It gave her something to fight, to pull together for.
She took incompletes, left without prejudice, and caught the
next Denver flight out of San Jose. For the first time she admit-

ted to herself she wasn't ready for school yet, or much of anything, and wouldn't be until "Mom's case" came to a close.

"And what you're saying, Elliot—I mean, God. Mom was starving? And you think—"

"Maybe."

"Poison? God."

"Possibly." I gave April a careful once-over. White Wrangler jeans, moss-colored fleece over a white Bee Gees "All for One" T-shirt, an apricot scarf knitted by her mother that hung knotted from her hand. Without makeup and rings she looked less Latin. Black Irish maybe, with dark, unruly hair and glittering blue eyes. She seemed older, though only three months had passed, and chastened, in a way. My heart went out to her and I reeled it back.

"Possibly poison, but the evidence was cremated."

"I can't believe you broke into Colfax," April said.

"Nice to get a little credit."

"Showed balls, Elliot."

At this I softened. Who wouldn't? "You guys are awfully understanding. But where I fucked up was losing it with Millsap and Tucker."

"Lost cause," Paige said.

"You should hear what Charlie says." Detective Carlos Roybal. "Milksop and Mother Tucker. What did you call Millsap?"

"Whiffet," I said. "A small dog."

"A pup. I'm telling Charlie. He nearly quit over this."

"So what I'm telling you isn't a total surprise?"

"Looking for a way to let Stillwell off is no surprise," Paige said. "Roybal's been banging his head bloody on that one. Picking April as the way is a surprise."

"They'll never actually do it," I said. Chary of going after a head-injured guy who could pay for lawyers, they wouldn't prosecute his stepdaughter for the mercy killing of her comatose mother while letting the dirtball who caused it walk. Especially with Paige representing her. April was Tucker's straw target, a false lead to distract from his real work, which was to chalk up June's as an unexplained death.

"I agree," Paige said. "Mercy killing is Tucker's out."

"But—" April looked not worried, but concerned in a way I hadn't seen before. "What's this exactly mean for me?"

"Want to take it?" Paige asked.

I nodded. "There'll be impacts on each proceeding, the criminal one and your civil wrongful-death case. With the grand jury hearing testimony skewed to implicate you, you have to take it seriously. Millsap sort of hinted you should. It has to be posturing, but the stakes are so high we have to plan for the worst case."

"And what about Mom's case, the second part?"

"I've got to think this has serious implications for suing Stillwell." I glanced at Paige. She agreed.

April's calves stopped swinging and her color rose. We'd reached a subject of much importance.

"Now we know Stillwell's defense," I said. "He didn't even have one before."

"Yeah?"

Paige broke in. "Elliot's saying, and I agree, that when the wrongful-death case comes to court, they'll put *you* on trial. It's something we defense lawyers do all the time, I'm sorry to say. Attack the plaintiff as the true guilty party."

"Paige is actually very good at this."

"Forgive me, I have sinned."

"But"—April was incredulous—"that's just crap."

"The defendant doesn't have the burden of proof," I said. "These dicks can say anything, so we need to overprove the case against Stillwell. We need overwhelming proof. All the facts." The first-person plural was back.

"But Stillwell's lawyers don't know about the grand jury testimony," April said. "Tucker can't tell them, can he?"

"Kirwan may be feeding Millsap the questions," Paige said.

Jack stood; the TV ran on. He touched a big hand to his son's flossy, sleeping head. "Going for a Coke. Anybody?"

Paige shook her head.

"Tell me how we deal with it," April said.

"Two fronts," Paige said. "At trial we lead with you. You're your own best witness. Kirwan jumps down your throat right out of the chute as the grasping estranged child who'd do anything to get her disabled stepfather's annuities, jury won't forgive him."

"He's too smart for that," I said. "They can't just attack. He'll soft-pedal it, plant seeds, raise questions."

"That's the second front," Paige added slowly, finally getting it. "We have to have answers to all these questions."

"It's like we have to not just convict Stillwell but prove your innocence."

"So." Paige exhaled. "Elliot turns out to be right. We have to explain exactly how your mother died. Don't gloat, Elliot."

Jack returned. "I'll hold him." He reached down.

"Example," I said. "We have to prove it wasn't you who took the stomach-fluid specimens."

"So we have to find out who did." Paige buttoned her blouse and went to the bed. She put her arm around April.

"Well, how?" The color hung in April's cheeks.

"Who might help the most," I said, "is Rico. Second best, Jasmine."

"My buddy Rico," April said.

"Who just might be the *real* bad guy."

"But—" April held her fists together, then knocked them on her forehead. "I can do it, all this, sure. But—"

The concern—fear?—was back. Something not easy to talk about.

"What, April?"

"I wonder, what if he believes all this?"

"Who?"

"Dale."

It hit Paige and me simultaneously, the thought of Stillwell, convinced by his shysters that April had murdered his wife, coming after her. A thought that, like April's fear itself, presupposed Stillwell *wasn't* the murderer, which is what hit me next.

"I'm, like, wondering," April said, Paige's hand over hers. April didn't enjoy admitting being afraid. "I maybe should be careful."

"You're right. We have to assume—"

"April is in danger," Paige finished my sentence. "We know what this guy's like. Roybal and his cops can help."

"Count me in." It was Jack. "From now on you stay with us," he said to April. "That bastard comes around, I'll brain him another one."

The sense of a joint mission, of April surrounded by friends, filled the little room, but almost immediately doubts crept back to mind. I watched April smiling and thanking Jack. Who was she really? What had she done?

"Look at that," Paige said. "Jack, turn it up."

A scene on the cantilevered television of a train jackknifed and derailed, cars torn open, a vast wreckage of twisted metal and iron rebar like Pick Up Sticks, railroad medics laying blankets over those in shock. Bougainville, Illinois, according to the announcer. The train called the *City of New Orleans,* full of students, having struck a tractor-trailer at a gated crossing.

It wasn't just professional interest that caught Paige's atten-·
tion. "Anything could make him snap," she said. "You keep your guard up."

My attention was caught by something else. *Blankets . . .*

"Jack, hold it." He'd remuted the news. "Leave it on."

Now Clinton stood next to a map of the FRY, Kosovo in yellow, Serbia in red. He explained that, while the KLA had accepted the terms of Rambouillet, Serbia would not. The Serb encirclement of Kosovo was tightening. In a final effort to avoid war, Clinton was dispatching special envoy Richard Holbrooke to meet with Milosevic March 22. If that meeting failed, NATO forces, under Supreme Allied Commander Wesley Clark, stood ready to launch massive airstrikes. All international agencies, including the United Nations, had ordered personnel evacuated from Serbia, Kosovo, and Bosnia.

The ICTY was a UN agency. Its exhumation teams would be on the evacuation list.

The clip jarred me back to the criminal case. "April," I said. "The grand jury. You need a lawyer. Paige?"

"No way." Connor was crying, thin, racking wails, catching for breath. "I know less about grand juries than babies, but I'll get her fixed up."

"There's a lot to do," I noted.

"You're accepting my standing offer to co-counsel?"

"If April wants me."

"Always have," she said.

As I headed back to Boulder, squirting through the mid-March slush, it felt like a start toward clarity, though the unsettling implications of the grand jury still hung in the air like smog. I drove first to Hans Leitner's wooded office on lower Flagstaff.

No one answered my ring, so I jotted a note and looked for a mail slot. At the slider that gave on the patio the catch was bent and the glass rattled in its frame. A typical Hans oversight. Intellectual rigor, practical disarray. Absorbed in the preoccupation of the moment but slipshod to the point of courting danger.

I could possibly pry the slider open but thought better of it. I found a black-lidded mailbox hidden in ivy and left the note there: "You disclosed information I told you in confidence. Call me. Elliot."

I wandered past his patio furniture into the pines and clearing I'd seen him in from the trail. I looked up in the direction he'd been looking, at the ragged north face of the mountain, gobbed with spring snow.

A footstep inches away, then a hand on my shoulder.

"You've been running up my mountain again." Hans smiled. "I think of it as mine since I gaze upon it every day. You probably think of it as yours."

"I left a note for you."

"I heard the ring, then the little door bang, which made me wonder. I'm just finishing up with a patient."

That came, oddly, as a surprise—that the doctor would be with a patient.

"I went before the grand jury today."

"Not fun, is it? I did my turn a while back. Listen, I've still got that patient." Hans gestured. "Let's meet for lunch? Or double-date. Remember Ingrid? Dead-eye Ingrid?"

"Hans"—I frowned—"the DA knew things he probably learned from you that I'm surprised you disclosed. When April called Stillwell a 'fucker.' How she wanted to file suit. That she and I had a falling-out. That she insisted on cremation."

"You aren't serious." He looked hurt. "'Fucker' April did in fact say. I heard it. I didn't learn it from you. And the rest—it's nothing. And nothing they didn't already know. If you're asked, you have to answer. You know that."

He made a circle in the clearing. "You need to hear about the confidences I've *kept*. The DA does *not* know about Colfax's neglect. About June's albumin and cholesterol. About the woman dying of untreated meningitis. About the kid who bought it when the ventilator detached. Not from me anyway. They don't know for two reasons. Because they didn't ask, and because I do consider that that information all came from you in confidence. So I didn't bring it up, even though it's helpful to my patient."

He gave me that concerned, caring look again, the one that meant I needed medication.

"I don't know," I said. "I hate what that office is doing. Or not doing." A young woman was briefly at the curtain by the patio slider below. "You need to get back."

"I do. But let's have that lunch. If not Ingrid, we can talk about Kosovo. DHR"—Doctors for Human Rights—"wants me to be ready to push off over there. This has implications for our dialogue, Prosecutor. Your monsters are at it again."

"It bolsters my case, unfortunately. Let the dialogue resume."

I followed in his big splayed footprints. The phone was ringing in my car.

"Hi, hello. It's me from Legal. I remembered where I saw that woman's chart, who was murdered?"

"Is this Silbi?"

"You *are* good with names. Like my birthstone, eye for detail. You need that for homicides. Me, I'm good with faces. Wanta know?"

"Sure."

"QA was looking at it. I got the chart out again to look for, like, clues, I guess. And it comes back to me."

"QA? Quality Assurance?" I backed around in Leitner's drive and turned onto Arapahoe.

"Yeah. Do the peer review. There was this mix-up I remembered. ICU nurse runs into Legal saying Dr. A.'s pissed, we got a misplaced chart, you file it here?"

"Dr. Arcenault?"

"Correct. So I look under the name and it's not there. I help look in ICU. Fifteen, twenty minutes later a guy finds me, says don't worry. It's back. It went up to QA by mistake or some reason. Then in a couple days, along comes the murdered woman's chart for me to file in regular records. Of course QA and she's a fatal, so I'm curious and read it but nothing jumped out."

"This mean what to you, Silbi, as someone in Legal?"

"I figure, has to be an explanation it went to QA. Possible medical error is all I can think. The *M*-word, to you. QA might do this when somebody reports an incident. QA can pull a chart even from a nurses' station."

"What do you think made this chart—wander?" I was then walking up my steps, stopping at the door. The next-door exhibitionist stood, robe flared, at an uncurtained window. He waved. I waved.

"Raises questions," she said in a singsong. "Raises questions. Who made a report and why, if there was. And the timing. Might be serious to pull a chart from ICU and Dr. A. doesn't know about it. But it was only gone a few minutes. Normally, Morbidity and Mortality will look at such a chart 'cause it's a fatal, but that's always weeks after. So you're not the only curious one. Call me when you find him."

"Who?"

"The killer. And come back for evening shift. Confront your fear. I'll take you on a tour."

I thanked her, opened my door, and hit a switch, illuminating the headless pedestal. As I faced another night alone, Silbi's tumor tour sounded pretty good. I sat down and flicked on the news for a Kosovo update, flicked it off, picked up a pad, and jotted some to-dos:

 1. *Briefing from P.*
 2. *Enter my appearance.*
 3. *Meet with Arcenault—me or P?*
 4. *Sue Colfax as Co-D? One way to learn truth.*
 5. *Lunch with Hans:*
     a. *QA procedures and incident reports.*
     b. *Exactly what DA knows from him.*
     c. *Confidentiality.*
 6. *A's criminal lawyer—who?*
 7. *Have a come-to-Jesus w/ A?*
 8. *PRIORITY: Meet w/ Jaz. Jaz help find Rico.*
 9. *PRIORITY: Find Rico.*
 10. *PRIORITY: What's the missing piece?*

It helped to be litigating again, in gear, rolling down the track. Mind off vaults of tumors and the empty house. The place could use some spring cleaning. Redecorating maybe. A woman's touch. The touch of a woman other than hopeless Liz Jones, my elderly retainer, once-a-week charity-case house-keeper who didn't mind dirt so much. A woman like—Ingrid? Silbi? Paige? April? Like—Darla?

Only Quierin would do. I went to the computer and told her so. I asked about the evacuation, what it meant for her digs, for us.

I opened a beer and played Kathleen's CD, so not a problem now that I sentimentalized Quierin in the lyrics' terms. The Atlantic as the water that's wide, that I can't cross o'er. Liverpool as The Hague—

> *It's not the leaving of Liverpool that's grieving me,*
> *but the pretty girl I'm bound to leave behind.*

I opened another beer. A Grolsch. The telephone. April.

"God, I don't deserve you guys," she said. "Can you believe Jack?"

"Not really."

"New baby, their first, and he's got me too?"

"What's up?"

"I wanted to say—sorry." The *sorry* word—for the second time. Like fear, it wasn't an easy admission. "I'm dumb. I get ahead of myself."

"You're young, my dear. You have much to learn."

She wasn't buying that, quite. "I'm so right, you know. You will. But the other stuff—I get it. It's relevant. So, sorry."

"Thanks, April. Where are you tonight, by the way?"

"Their house. Family of four. I'm gonna help out Paige with Connor, like a whatsit."

"Au pair."

"Elliot. I called for another—thing."

"Okay."

"I decided—I want you. I always knew you were number one."

"April—" I was stunned, baffled. "Me?"

"Will you? I have to defer payment until I can pay, but I want to. In full."

"Why do you want me, April?"

"Didn't I say you are my hero lawyer? How you cared about Mom? You put yourself last. You're there."

"You mean, your grand jury lawyer?"

"It's not that you're this supersmart, crafty person, okay? But if someone's out to nail me, I know you're my guy. Please. I mean, I hope."

"Not—supersmart?"

"Super, I don't think. Pretty smart, though."

"I have no experience in U.S. criminal courts. I got blown up today. I've got these conflicts." According to the whiffet. "I had duties to Dale, then your mom. Now you?"

"Duty follows strange paths. Duty, if it's pure, leads to justice."

This kid could close a deal. Still, I wondered about ulterior motives. If she told me as her lawyer about the night before her mother died, it would be privileged. I couldn't reveal it, even to a grand jury.

"I'll do it." I wanted to know, regardless. I also wanted to help her. "Deferred payment, sure, don't worry about that."

Now, when she was feeling grateful, and sounding open and honest, and a little voluble, and everything we said would be privileged, could be the perfect time for the come-to-Jesus talk. The one-on-one when the client comes to Jesus with all that burdens the soul.

The truth about June was a ghost many wanted to see. Paige and April now seemed to. I did, Hans Leitner did, and who knew who else. Our adversaries, Millsap, even Stillwell had to want glimpses of the ghost, parts of the truth. They might also may be frustrated by the reticence and refusals to speak, disappearing evidence and witnesses, mandarin rules and loyalties that sealed lips, the feints and dances and deceptions.

Now could be the time to call up the ghost. Just ask.

"You will?" April said. "Be my lawyer? My hero lawyer?"

"Not hero. Functionary, flack man, water boy. This isn't about me."

"It's about Mom."

"No, it's about you."

Most criminal defense lawyers don't want to know. The guilty also deserve their lawyer's best, and a lawyer who knows his client's guilt can rarely give it. Why did I have to know? Because of the conflicts, the shade of June, even Stillwell, in the background?

I had to know because my duties, which ran to my client, should also, my client told me, lead to justice.

I would ask April about the night before her mother died some other time, I decided, when I could read her face. I would ask her then if she'd ended her mother's life.

But the answer to that question arrived in the next day's mail.

CHAPTER 8

In Kirwan and Edson, Hancock had recruited cutthroat insurance, defense mercenaries, Colorado's finest. They had firepower, finesse, great backup, and, in Kirwan's case, it must be said, a freakish kind of charisma.

Kevin Kirwan struck me as a guy with a morbid inner life, but in front of juries he shone. He projected a zest unusual in our line of work. A jug-eared, sparkle-eyed, epicene boyishness on which nature had played a cruel trick. In his mid-fifties, Kirwan had the puckered skin of a senior citizen with a three-pack-a-day habit. Still he acted the courtroom showboat, strutting, joking, constantly scribbling in bright colors on butcher-paper charts, turning to curtsy to judge or jury, both ingratiating and domineering. Premature aging gave this a tragic look, like a child with progeria syndrome. His partner, Bernie Edson, was Kirwan's dark side, a smirking, bald, pompous, by-the-book prick, rigid as a soldier at dress drill. But especially in combination, juries loved them. Bernie's incomprehensible Latinisms fit dull folks' idea of legal professionalism, while Kirwan's dance of the fairies was so seductive opposing counsel forgot to object.

And they always won. Kirwan discreetly circulated his stats, his last jury loss in 1977. They tried a lot of cases, not that often as a team, joining forces only for donnybrooks that threatened to end the string. Like ours.

Paige knew these hard-liners. Every case was war. They rarely settled; they took no prisoners. They didn't just beat a plaintiff at trial, they hounded her for costs afterward, drove her into bankruptcy, then sued her in bankruptcy court. We needed not only facts, skill, smarts, and conviction. We needed luck.

We started getting some.

In my noon mail drop was a thank-you card for April. Apparently, she'd given my address as hers the few days she stayed with me in December. The card said her donation was much appreciated. It would go toward filling the desperate needs of deserving individuals and to assisting crucial medical research. The card was from the Rocky Mountain Transplant Bank.

When I called, Jack answered. April was out strolling Connor. I reached Paige at her railroad office and told her. Then April returned my call.

"Of course I did," she said. "It's right there on Mom's driver's license. You're one, aren't you? A donor?"

"You had June harvested for organ donation?"

"The day she died, they picked her up, and they brought her on Friday to the funeral home. Which organs, I don't know. What happened with them either."

Something April had said at the service came back: giving strength to others, even in death. I hadn't understood it then.

"Why didn't you tell me?"

"Why should I?"

"You don't know how happy this makes me."

"Get a grip, Elliot."

"You weren't destroying evidence."

"Excuse me?"

"If you'd cremated your mother to stop an autopsy, you would have cremated all of her."

"You lost me. What's the point of an autopsy if her organs aren't there?"

"Exactly!" April didn't delay the cremation for an autopsy because that would be, like, duh, as she'd say, if organs weren't there to examine. Or, as I'd say, trial-by-autopsy and April won. "Did Stillwell know about it?"

"Hell no."

And Stillwell lost. "April, do you think any—organs might still be kept?"

"Don't they have to put 'em in fresh? Rush 'em over on ice in a little box?" The scene in *Sleeper* with the nose.

About organs April was right. Very short shelf life. But some tissue can be banked, the allograft tech at the transplant bank told me when I called. Skin, the long veins, cardiovascular muscle, some tendons and ligaments, pulmonary and aortic valves. Cartilage keeps for years. She'd see what was done with the June Stillwell donation and call back.

"If you've got anything," I said, "put a hold on it."

I left a message for Fox, my other client, a cellular biologist. I'd done great work for the guy. Trade-secret-theft charges dropped. The next message was for Hans Leitner, the Great Helmsman of Forensic Pathology. Paige would pitch a hissy fit at the idea of working with Hans. The transplant bank was the first to call back.

"Our records show a limited harvest with this particular donation, with residual returned for cremation service. No harvest of bones, for example. We salvaged kidneys, liver, lungs, and corneas."

"Were they used, if that's the word?"

"All delivered within the week. Corneas after ten days."

"Were they rejected, accepted?"

"That I don't know. I could track that down if you need it. Regardless, you can feel very good about the decision to donate. Lives may well have been saved. Blindness prevented."

"Anything salvaged but not used?"

"The saphenous veins. That's a very long, lower-extremity vein, ankle to hip. They're used in cardiac bypass. One of Mrs. Stillwell's went out just two weeks ago. Another life possibly saved. One's still here."

"Any skin?"

"We harvested a little epidermis and some thick skin for dermal grafts. Passed that on to UH Burn Unit per usual, and don't know the status. Otherwise—patellar tendons, broad sheath tendons from the side of a thigh. And her heart. Those are all still in the bank."

"Her heart? That's impossible." Who would want a transplanted heart that hadn't beaten for three months?

"Not for organ transplant, of course. We salvage heart valves and we keep cardiovascular tissue in the ultrafreezer up to a year, if there's room, as appears was done in this case."

"This is wonderful news. Thank God for you people."

"It's important work. But I take it you're not interested in medical use of what remains banked?"

I said I represented the daughter. We had concerns about the manner of death.

"Does this involve the police?"

"Private. I'll have Mrs. Stillwell's daughter call or see you. You won't let these—" What? Pieces of June?

"Nothing's walking away."

I took a turn in my backyard to digest it. I got the birdseed sack from the shed to top off the feeders and took up a post on the bench above the fishpond to check the action. Nothing dramatic. Juncos and chipping sparrows, and two white-crowneds, new arrivals, on the ground below the big Droll Yankee catching scraps from the table. At the thistle feeder two chickadees, blackcaps, two goldfinch. Whup of wing, flash of color—sulfur-yellow evening grosbeak, the first of the year, going for sunflower seeds. Then all fled to the skies as one, two, three magpies sailed in. The neighborhood rogues. I once watched a fox bask on the same bench where I then sat until a magpie finally drove him off, pecking his plushy tail.

I should hold off working with Hans. I didn't need a fight with Paige just after we'd made up. Questionable whether he'd feel comfortable overseeing a tissue assay. And could I really be certain the results wouldn't wind up in others' hands? His conflicts, in such a role, put mine to shame.

We needed an expert but we should stay in-house for now. A White House basement operation. What we needed was an expert in the analysis of biological remains. A taphonomist.

A magpie swooped onto the bench arm four feet away, iridescence glittering. Black-and-white evening dress and a streaming, gleaming tail. A handsome rogue, and fearless, and smart as a whip.

Only Quierin would do.

That weekend it was warm enough to convene the war room outdoors. Halfway up Mapleton Hill, my yard enjoyed a view of Flagstaff Mountain and the Flatirons, a row of red slabs five hundred feet tall, like stelae plunged in the earth, at their base a skirt of pine-fir forest that steroid home developments were nibbling away.

Paige had met with Dr. Arcenault. Hell of a nice guy. He'd told her about his daughter, brain-injured in a car wreck, and their eventual decision to let her go. So June's case especially moved him. As a doctor as well as a parent, he'd never been able to fully reconcile what he'd done, stopping fighting for her life. He remembered April and personally shared her anguish. He vaguely remembered Silbi's story about the chart being briefly missing and said it was no big deal. Bungling.

"Why did he order a gastric lavage?" I asked.

"It's what you thought," Paige said. "Because it may have been a poisoning. When an otherwise healthy young person has sudden respiratory failure and cardiopulmonary arrest, you cover the bases. Pulmonary embolism, myocardial infarction, OD, poison. And get this. There also was a smell. Her stomach smelled. Not an unusual or unpleasant smell—"

"Like air freshener."

"That's what he said. A little sweet. He talked about etiology, what caused it. He eliminated MI and PE, and the drug screen didn't suggest a drug overdose. The bloodwork showed she was hemorrhaging somewhere, but he never sorted it out. To this day he can't say there wasn't something she ingested that set this off. The poison center never returned a report. For which he has no explanation."

"Because they never got the sample."

"He says he drew it and it was put in the refrigerated pickup for the courier. But differential diagnosis got beside the point. It was all he could do just to keep her afloat. He knows nothing about the DNR."

"Did he want to autopsy? Did he ask anyone?"

"Platte Valley won't do autopsies anymore. He didn't bring it up. Did you reach Dr. Fox?"

Fox, my other client, the genetic-blueprint thief. I told Paige and April I had and that he thought he could help. I'd talked with Leitner too and put him off. Temporized about lunch and imminent war. I nixed Ingrid. He suggested his knockout virtual assistant, Ellen Vesco, newly boyfriend-free. "Quierin and I are still a thing," I told him. "A number, you called it." In my mind, anyway.

I needed to talk with Millsap—was or wasn't April a target? If so, or potentially so, April needed to think about the Fifth when the inevitable subpoena arrived. No target freely testifies to a grand jury.

"Except President Clinton," April correctly pointed out. Wearing a long-sleeved, yellow Meat Loaf "Live at Wembley."

"Special case. Different considerations."

"Different," she said, "but parallel." She'd been thinking about this already.

"Here are the pros and cons. The big con of course is the risk of prosecution. A cross-examination by Millsap designed to incriminate you, set you up. No lawyer who wants to keep his license would let you give unprotected GJ testimony."

"Tell me pros." April looked undaunted.

"There is a reason not to take the Fifth. In Colorado, if you take it in a criminal proceeding, that can be brought out in a subsequent civil proceeding regarding the same subject matter."

"'Brought out' means—"

"Kirwan can ask at trial whether, when questioned under oath about your role in the death of your mother, you refused to answer because it could possibly incriminate you. I'm sure Kirwan's doing all he can to get them to send you a letter."

"Your recommendation?"

"Take the Fifth, of course. Just like who's-it, David Kendall, must have said to Clinton."

"I can't wait to talk about it."

"First, let's see if you're a target."

I surveyed my yard: plum, cherry, apple, peach, and Kathleen's bulbs bolting to flower; the lime cast of cottonwoods and peach-leaf willows budding to the north; to the south Flagstaff and the Flatirons, summits wreathed in cloud.

"I have," I said, "a couple of other questions." The modified, anticlimactic come-to-Jesus. Get it over. "Paige?" Just in case.

Paige nodded and went inside.

"Now I need to be insufferably stupid." I leaned April's way. "You need to be ruthlessly honest. Ordinarily, I wouldn't ask questions like these, but this is different. You taught me that. We're looking for truth and justice, right?"

"Is that one of the stupid questions?"

"Pardon the ponderous lead-up. I do have to say this. Everything you say now in response to my questions is privileged. No one else will know. No one can make me tell."

"Don't care."

"April," I sighed. "Confidentially, client to lawyer, tell me what you did the night before June's death."

"Went to bed ten or eleven. Everything's fine. Slept all night."

"Nothing disturbed you? People coming and going? Your mother?"

"People came and went every four hours every damn night. Nothing ever disturbed me. I sleep." She shrugged. "Sound, I guess. Something about me."

"In the morning?"

"Mornings, what I want is my cup of tea. What I *want* is chai, but forget it. All Colfax has is burnt coffee in the nurses' urn."

"So, to the White Spot?"

"Like, every day. I wish I'd checked Mom, but I didn't. I normally didn't. I get up, get dressed, wash up, stagger over and ask that nasty know-it-all to please fix me some tea."

Sweet Darla?

"I didn't think once about how Mom was and I'm really sorry."

The *sorry* word.

"Look at her? Anything?"

"Just up and went. What else?"

"The DNR?"

"I've thought about that. I didn't tell anybody not to resuscitate her."

"You're sure?"

"Dead sure."

I searched her face. Nothing contradicted what she said.

"What else?"

"Where were you the afternoon and evening before?" I asked.

"You're sure it's privileged?"

"Yeah."

"With Charlie. Carlos."

"Detective Roybal?"

"I don't want to complicate the, uh, pending whatever. Separation or something." She rolled her eyes. "Other questions?"

"Only whether you did anything to hasten your mother's death."

"Huh-uh."

"No?"

"No, is right. Of course not, you whiffet."

"You donated your mother's organs and tissue to the transplant bank."

"Yes."

"If you were trying to destroy evidence of poisoning, that would have been stupid."

"I guess."

"No point to an autopsy since the organs are already gone."

"Yeah."

"And you hire me, me, and when everything we say is privileged and any awful secret can be revealed, there aren't any. You're clean."

"Clean?"

"Pure as baby's breath. Plus, you're not the kind of person to do a bad thing."

"I don't know about that."

"You're not a bad person."

"No."

"I believe, a hundred percent. We need to make a jury believe too."

DIA is twenty minutes farther than Stapleton, and everything else takes longer too. Parking, bag check, the train, the walk to the gate. Fares jumped the day it opened. Services shut down at 11 P.M. and are pathetic to start with. Bush-eague food, books, and Bronco and Rockies memorabilia. A $5 billion–plus replacement of a perfectly serviceable airport. Monument to the egos of politicians already mostly forgotten. Like Ozymandias' colossal wreck on the lone and level sands.

Were the casually attired arrivers and departers rolling their bags across gleaming floors under the canopied vault ranting in private the way I did every time I came to DIA? Probably not, so I ranted in private about them for a while. Casual attire was too kind. Some of them were slobs. A few, in sleeveless T-shirts, shorts, sweats, yelling into cell phones, would have drawn looks at a Little League picnic. Bring back the grace and courtesy, I silently ranted, of the days when flight was sacramental—a rapture from the earth—and we dressed as though for church. What would the saints of aviation—Lindbergh, Earhart, Saint-Exupéry—think of the death of the glamour and romance of travel by air?

And what will *she* be wearing? A T-shirt, it turned out.

I was at DIA on March 26, 1999, because two days earlier marked perhaps the most heroic moment in the history of international human rights, Supreme Allied Commander Wesley Clark's announcement of the air campaign to halt Yugoslavia's forcible expulsion beyond its borders of more than a million citizens and the brutal cleansing of an entire semiautonomous province. For the first time ever, full-scale war by a multinational force was begun in the cause of human rights. Quierin's work for the tribunal was suspended for the duration of the war. There would be much for her to do when it ended.

On the driverless train the recorded voice of a onetime S&L TV pitchman belabored the obvious: "This train is going to Concourses A, B, and C." This train don't carry no gamblers, I thought, observing the travelers in shorts. No crapshooters, no midnight ramblers. Rant warming to song.

We shot down a subway buzzing with thousands of blue pinwheel wall ornaments excited by the crush of train-driven air. From the platform I escalated to the gates and the mediocre concessions of Concourse A. A quick stop at the best of them, Rocky Mountain Chocolates, and I was loping up the moving sidewalk to A26. British Airways 1443 was just then easing to the gate. An attendant released a door and fastened it open. Nobody in the pipeline. Then a few first-class types, well-heeled midnight ramblers. And soon enough, my girl, three guys trying to keep up with her in the Jetway.

We met, embraced, kissed as a stream of plane mates parted around us. A thirties-movie moment, modernity momentarily swept away in a cloud of Shalimar.

Quierin's friends shook my hand, waved, hit the trail for baggage claim. She stepped theatrically back, smiling broadly, and threw out her arms. *"I love America.* I love Madeleine! I love Wesley Clark! And look at this—airport! *I love this airport!"*

How could Ingrid have ever crossed my mind?

Quierin was wearing signature black: black jeans, black leather jacket. She spread both arms as far they went, index fingers pointing. A singular and commanding stance, enough so the stream of plane mates slowed and several stopped. Silently, she freed her jacket from one shoulder, then the other, black eyes locked on mine like a stripper, Mona Lisa smile curling. She slipped out one arm, another, let the jacket fall to the buffed floor, then drove her fists ceilingward in triumph, slowly turning a full circle before the audience she'd sensed had assembled, T-shirt drawing a smattering of applause.

Across its plain white front was a bold black Nike swoosh that, on second look, was seen to be tipped with an F117A Nighthawk fighter, converting the swoosh to an airstrike trajectory. On the back it was lettered:

NATO
Just Do It

As we rattled back to the terminal, I murmured in her ear, "This train is bound for glory." She had the goofy, quizzical look of a Euro-traveler after a fifteen-hour passage to the New World, and something else distinctly hers.

"You love Wesley Clark?" I asked politely.

"Of course. He is my supreme commander. I love America to produce such a man. I love my greenhorn lover to come from such a place that produces such a man."

"Quierin, I'm honored."

"I see you in him. Men both of thought and action. Men of ideals. Elliot, that is who you are."

Supreme commander? I could live with that.

"And what a magnificent airport!"

"Don't go overboard."

"I love going overboard. I love going heads on top of heels!"

We reached Boulder at twilight, 1 A.M. on Quierin's clock. Places like Colorado impress the Dutch. Like Scotland, Switzerland, Tibet, Peru, Bosnia. Places that aren't flat. As we crested the overlook above the city, she went overboard again.

At the house Quierin plopped her handbag on top of the headless pedestal. I showed her around. "The house of Kathleen," she observed. She poked a finger in the silverbills' cage. A weightless fluff ball clasped it like an outlandish feathered ring.

"Not Kathleen's anymore." I opened two beers and warmed the meal I'd prepared, a meal of actually cooked food. I presented my chocolates. She trumped them with Leonidas Belgian bonbons for me. We talked, less overboard as time passed, jet-lag dreamy. "The virtual life isn't worth living," I said.

"Dead lovers aren't worth loving."

"Live bodies make better lovers." A taphonomist's bumper sticker?

We came to a not exactly awkward moment, a pause—what next? I went to where she sat and kissed the top of her Indo hair. She nosed her face into my shirt. I felt her fingers at the small of my back work their way around my hips to unbutton my shirt, unhook my belt and fly. Kissing my stomach, she slowly came to her feet.

In the bedroom I undressed her and was allowed a look before she switched off the light. Curtains drawn, we were blind, haptic, feeling our way. Perfume pervaded the darkness. Quierinworld. We held on in bed as if to ensure we would never be separate again. She breathed the way she had at Ovcara. I touched her neck and back. I ran my fingers everywhere, rediscovering her buttocks, calves, thighs, stomach, breasts, nipples. Her eyelids, scarred cheek, Mona Lisa lips. Finding her asymmetries. Kissing her face to thigh. Breathing her in. Murmuring, she explored me with her magic touch, the heat of her mouth. And when she finally clutched so deep and strong that my spine seemed to stretch, the surges poured ecstasy but also reconciliation and release. Absolution, for leaving, for staying. Afterward, slack and damp, fingers clasped, I thought, this is the single thing worth living for. Not sex but this. Quierin's touch. Then I said it out loud. Then I thought it again.

After a time in bed in silence, Quierin went to the window and drew the curtains apart. She stood fringed in moonlight, turned, came back to bed, and we held each other again.

"I saw something today," Quierin said, all time sense lost to lag. She rolled to her back, the wandering black eye catching moonlight. "The airplane is over the Arctic. First you see icebergs. Then ice stars underwater. Then colors change with ice underneath. Then layers and layers of ice, transparent, translucent, solid. Blue, green, white. Then endless white floes forever, from seven miles high. The pure beauty of the earth.

"Idealism," she said, "is true to the earth."

CHAPTER 9

"How better way to wait out a war than with you winning a case?" Quierin asked rhetorically.

We began the day with scones at Spruce Street Confections, a bakery on the European model, planning next to walk up Anemone Hill and get back in time for Jamie Shea's daily briefing from Brussels. Quierin told me that, out of respect for the role of commander in chief, she was swearing off Clinton jokes for the duration of the war.

I briefed her on the claims and the players in the case, June's heart tissue ultrafrozen in liquid nitrogen at minus one hundred degrees. "Next step?"

She sipped a double espresso, straight up. "Do screens. That's brainless."

"What's involved?"

"Lacking kidney, which is rum organ, you have heart, and heart's not shabby. Little bits is all you need, plus good lab, top equipment."

Choice of lab was the dilemma. The day before, a registered letter had arrived from the DA for April: April was, officially now, a target. Kirwan had won out. The last thing I wanted was to turn over June's ultrafrozen tissue to Russell Tucker and the Colorado Bureau of Investigation. How could we prevent a superficial evaluation that missed what was there? How could we prevent positive results from being withheld or misused against April?

Dr. Fox, my other client, knew labs. Any hospital lab, biological lab, forensic lab, poison center—any lab equipped to do this—he told me, would want to know how we got human tissue, whose it was, and what were our purposes. They'd check it out and learn June Stillwell's death was under grand jury investigation. Then they'd call the cops. "But I have a friend," Fox said. Music to a lawyer's ears.

"So we're off the shelf," I said. "Under the radar. What do we do?"

Quierin explained tissue assay for poison, a stepwise process with an ever-wider sweep as you work from the usual suspects through the universe of chemical compounds. She fired a post-scone Gauloise. Alarm registered around us.

"Let's walk," I said. "Basically, here, no indoor smoking. Don't say anything. No one would understand."

The staircased trail up Anemone Hill began six blocks west. "Shall we go with Fox's friend?" I asked.

"Start somewhere." I followed her black bicycle shorts and baggy sweater up the winding sandstone route, Boulder Creek foaming six hundred feet below, Quierin's bottom weaving before me. "Work your way up."

Saturday, a week later, the war room reconvened at my place. Thick, wet snow had us indoors. Lots of get-acquainted probing and girl talk among April, Paige, and Quierin.

"How's my man Connor?" I asked.

"Weight gain hitting sixtieth percentile. No smile. No hair. Broader perspective on the world. Not yet angry and appalled."

"You want to go with this?"

"I bow to your thinking."

"I'll take the fall if we get in trouble."

"I'll keep out of your way as you're falling."

April said she'd had tea with Jasmine.

"White Spot?"

"Yeah. Really disappointing. Totally weird. She, like, was only listening. Kept checking around for the snoop—"

"Darla."

"She was, like, saying everything not to help. Don't know nothing. Nothing about Rico. Nothing about Colfax."

Paige suggested she might in fact know nothing.

"Why change from being my friend?"

"Any sign of Stillwell?" I asked. April wore a Grateful Dead tee, elastic skull in a swirl of curving color. SOUND CREW, STEAL YOUR FRACTAL.

"Just in nightmares," she said.

Quierin lit a Gauloise, knowing smoking was prohibited inside. She strolled to the kitchen door and out upon the flagged patio, requiring us to follow. There we stood stamping our feet in the snow for the duration.

She exhaled through the flakes at the Flatirons, then turned with a coy half smile. April and Paige began batting snow off each other's heads of contrasting hair—big, black, and curly, frosted and short. Soon they were giggling. Never before had I belonged to a team of all good-looking women. Charlie and the Angels.

"Next item," I said, businesslike, "is April. What is your decision? You know my advice, especially with a tissue assay for poison coming up. You can't subject yourself to these shithooks that have it in for you. You can't talk to that jury when they've told you, by this target letter, they're thinking of indicting you for murder."

The mood sank. Paige turned her back, a wounded posture, but she didn't argue. April nodded. "Okay," she said softly. Chapfallen. Quierin either didn't care or wasn't following. She squinted west to discern ridgelines through the snow.

I drafted a notice of intent to take the Fifth asserting April's innocence but vulnerability to prosecution by this DA. I enclosed a copy with a letter to Chief Deputy Pissant Millsap acknowledging his target letter and informing him Ms. Mooney would avail herself fully of her constitutional rights in any appearance before his jury. I suggested we meet to work out a way for her to cooperate. In conclusion, I reemphasized that I now represented April Mooney. To clarify Millsap's doubts about which side I was on.

First we had to convince the transplant bank. June's tissue was donated. It didn't belong to her daughter. Playing a hunch—these were people of compassion—I had April tell the whole story, Stillwell's assault, her mother's coma and death, suspicions now ginned up against April by Stillwell's lawyers, her need to know the truth. The allograft tech, Gillian, the same one I'd spoken to, was with us as long as the transplant bank was protected. I gave her the release of liability and indemnity agreement I'd drafted.

"We use as little as possible," Quierin explained. "Most all your tissue stays. Results can be reproduced later by any law enforcement agency. We come back if we need more."

Quierin and Gillian took off for the ultrafreezer in latex gloves. They returned with a bag of ice and a stoppered test tube with two little pieces of June Stillwell's heart.

That night Fox waited for us with a security guard at his company gate. He and metaGen, his present employer, were grateful enough he was off the hook for trade-secret theft that they loaned us a lab after hours.

Nine P.M. on Thirtieth Street, uncomfortably close to the Boulder cop shop. A low-slung, white sign: METAGEN. A white iron framework like a railroad gantry rattled into its housing and the guard waved us in. Fox got in the front seat and directed me through the austere, arc-lit, functionalist campus. Guards swept the recesses with Maglite beams. Here and there a bank of windows blazed where men in shirtsleeves worked. The center green was white. Its spotlit fountain formed the shape of a datura flower. The spray had burned a black hole in the snow.

Our mission was starting to feel fundamentally irrational, like a prison break-in. Fox seemed a little tense. "I don't know tox from shoe leather. I don't want any more trouble."

"Who can read the machines?" Quierin asked.

"Vince. MD/PhD, had his own lab. The MD he doesn't have anymore." Vince had been defrocked after police samples he analyzed kept coming back missing more than they should have. "Occupational hazard," Fox said. "Some toxicos end up with their noses in it."

"What's he do now?" I asked. "Cook methamphetamine?"

Fox waggled his hand ambiguously. "He wants to be paid up front. Three hundred bucks. He's in there waiting for us, adjusting the equipment."

"All we need's a tech," April said. "We don't need some— tweaker."

Fox twisted in the seat and checked April out. "You need a man with a plan." He pointed to a parking space, a guarded door.

"Foxie." Vince grabbed his elbow once we were inside. He turned to me expectantly. Bug-eyed, chewing a lip. I handed him three Ben Franklins and got a friendly chuckle for thanks. He gave the women a salacious up-and-down.

The lab looked pretty good to me, except it was a lab. I hugged myself, the better to avoid brushing up against something. Vince reinforced my view. Bad things happen to people in labs.

There were two brilliantly lit central counters with rows of stereomicroscopes, a stool for each. The usual sinks and cabinets and a half dozen expensive-looking machines with computer keyboards, cranks, and dials and a couple of bubbling tubes. Quierin made the rounds. "Where's the GC/MS?" Gas chromatograph/mass spectrograph, she explained. The gold standard.

"He's got AA—atomic absorption—thin-layer chromatography, liquid chromatography, and immunoassay," Vince said. "Gas chromatograph he's too cheap to have." He laughed, a startling sound. Shrill honking, high in the nose.

"What do you do now, Vince?" I wondered.

"What tox I can find. BAs and pee screens to monitor drunks and abuser docs on probation like me." A quick peal of laughter. "Anywhere I don't have to testify. Forensic's out because of the cross. Isn't it true, Doctor, you pled guilty to three felonies?" The full-nosed version. "Isn't it true, Doctor, the BME yanked your license on account of theft of, destruction of, inhalation, ingestion, and injection of evidence in criminal cases?" The bug eyes, then the laugh, a double.

I glanced at Fox. He made the ambiguous hand waggle.

"Let's get this show going on the road," Quierin said.

Vince made a serious face. "We're going to perform what is known as a full tox screen. If you ordered a full tox screen in a legit tox lab, you would get the screen for which you have paid tonight."

He went to the sink where the test tube lay in ice, opened it, and held it to the light, separated its contents in a dish, three two-gram fragments of heart tissue, and went to work. He inserted a sample in what looked like a firebrick-lined microwave. "AA is a simple heat process." He spoke pedantically. "It finds metals. Mercury, lead, zinc, copper, arsenic."

"Yah. Yah," Quierin said. "I do hundreds. Waste of time. He won't use heavy metal."

"Do you want a full tox?" Vince asked. "Or would you prefer to skip a screen that just might find what you're looking for?"

"Arsenic is only candidate. Where he gets arsenic?"

"A sloppy toxicologist would think just that. A clever poisoner knows arsenic may be overlooked and finds it in pesticides in abandoned sheds." He snuffled righteously.

After a bit the furnace was finished and Vince read the results.

"No arsenic," Quierin said.

"No."

"Any metals?"

"No, there aren't."

The huddle proceeded to the immunoassay station. It didn't take long. "Bingo!" Vince shouted. "Positives!"

Fox and I joined the huddle. Two hits. Ritalin and nonspecific barbiturate.

"Don't get too excited," April told Vince. "Mom's not like some street user who OD'd. She was in a coma. Ritalin's standard for cortical stimulation." She explained June's circumstances.

"Please." Vince made a noiseless laugh. The sarcastic version. "I know pharmacology. I know the indications for Ritalin. The barbiturate, however, needs to be explored." His wobbly head frowned down at April.

"What're the concentrations?"

"We don't get concentrations on immunoassay," Vince said. "We get matches."

"So let's explore." April shook her hair and turned.

The next step was TLC, thin-layer-chromatography screen, a serious step up in sensitivity. "Bingo!" Vince got positives. On a computer printout, Ritalin again. An asterisk, for a spike that didn't match any screenable substance. Possibly an artifact. And the barbiturate was identified. Phenobarbital.

We'd found the culprit, Vince declared. Phenobarbital is a sedative, easily obtained from the Colfax dispensary. Crush and mix large amounts with feeding liquid, and you get CNS—central nervous system depression, respiratory failure, and death.

"Except," April said, "Mom was given phenobarbital every day as a seizure prophylactic. She had a head injury." She thumped her own to clarify the point.

"Smart poisoner," Quierin said, "could OD victim on drug she takes every day, hoping drug screen misses levels. What is concentration? Therapeutic or overdose?"

Vince drew the printout through his fingers, inspecting it. His nose tracked the tracing. "The peaks are not real impressive actually. Concentrations I can't do with this."

Quierin huffed. "It's just her daily med. Anyway, phenobarbital won't leave nice, fresh smell. Right, Dr. Vince?"

His shoulders shuddered. "Sure."

"So," April said, "that's—all? That's a full tox screen?"

"Yes, it is."

"I want to know about the asterisk," Quierin said. "I play my money on it."

"How many compounds," April asked, "can these two screens identify?"

"Ninety," Vince said. He rolled his neck and it cracked. "The ninety top offenders in ODs and poisonings."

"Useless," said Quierin.

"Ninety?" April said. "Out of potentially, what? How many hundred thousand compounds?"

Vince became histrionic. He seized his big socketed head with both bony hands. Punctuating syllables with half flaps of his elbows, he said, "There-is-nothing-more-I-can-do."

"GC/MS," Quierin replied.

"We don't have one. Denver General Hospital has one. The Denver police lab has one. Some industrial labs"—Vince looked accusingly at Fox—"have one. Forensic labs have them. They cost a lot of money, and they do not have one here." The straightened face returned. "We have done our best."

"April and I are taking over this operation," Quierin announced. "We're gonna run this dogtown ponyshow. Give us money back."

The laugh in full salute. Fox slowly backing off.

"You received a full tox screen," Vince spat. "That was the deal. You'll never find a GC/MS lab that will do a secret assay."

"Yes, we will," Quierin said, "and I know how."

Now he approached, glowering. He wanted to hear. "How?"

"Put it in dirt."

Vince stared at Quierin, frozen for several seconds. "You're right! That's brilliant."

Fox was relieved at the lift of mood. He touched my elbow. "I think you've got some talent here."

"Forgive us, Mom." April helped Quierin mince new cuts of cardiovascular tissue. I'd picked up a bag of potting soil at McGuckin's. Has to be clean, Quierin said. No fertilizers, weed killers, whatnot.

Quierin reported, after a telephone survey, that five Denver environmental labs had gas chromatograph/mass spectrograph for analyzing soil, water, and hazardous waste for toxins, pesticides, herbicides, PCBs, and metals. We could mince and mix heart tissue in potting dirt, ask for a GC/MS soil analysis, and no one would think twice.

The asterisk is not an artifact, Quierin assured me. We will find it.

eTs—enviroTox services of America—though indulging in the eFad for midname capitals, was a less grand operation than metaGen, but it had a desktop Hewlett-Packard GC/MS. Quierin and April had mixed up paired sets of samples, two with June's tissue, two of clean soil. I followed the women in, Vince no longer in the picture.

"I like your lab, Andy," I said. "It isn't creepy."

Andy appreciated the compliment. His name appeared in green cursive within a green oval above the pocket of his white, short-sleeved eTs shirt. The building decor kept to health and nature themes in a green-and-white color scheme. The *T* in the eTs logo was an evergreen tree. The slogan in the glossy literature I feigned an interest in read, "Dedicated to a Cleaner Healthier Colorado." I detected no unwholesome smells. Nothing that might explode, catch on fire, or eat your skin.

"How can I help you folks?" Andy said. Maybe thirty, clean-cut, no-nonsense, clear-plastic-framed glasses. Cheerful, genuine.

"We've got some dirt we'd like you to look at."

Quierin intervened. She'd been to Internet EPA sites investi-

gating protocols. "We need two GC/MS screens," she said.
"Two samples each. Volatiles, then semivolatiles, prepped with
EPA prep method 35–50, analysis method 82–40 for volatiles,
82–70 for semivolatiles." Andy jotted notes. "You got that software?"

"You bet. Use it every day."

"Cost us what?"

"That'd be ninety bucks a pop. One eighty."

She looked at me, eyebrow hitched: Vince ripped us off.
"Okay, let's get rolling dice, see what they say." She gave
Andy the four plastic Baggies, two clean, two with an ounce of
soil mixed with a gram of tissue. "Do in order numbered," she
told him. "We can watch?"

No one else was there. "Why not?" Andy smiled.

He spilled each Baggie's contents into a separate tray and
tagged the trays with numbers, V-1 and 2, and SV-1 and 2. "Hey,
they look pretty clean to me," he said. "Let's make sure."

While Andy prepped the samples for GC/MS, Quierin took
us aside. Volatile compounds vaporize at low temperatures, she
said. Won't persist in free state in tissue, but with tissue frozen
in liquid nitrogen, who knows?

"Volatiles would be like solvents, gasoline?" April asked.

"Yah. Ammonia, chlorine, some pesticides, cyanide. Plenty
nasty volatiles."

Andy prepared, homogenized, and incubated the soil mixture in liquid form. The analyte, he called it. He drained it into
an injector at one end of the machine and the 82–40 V-1 run
was under way.

"So," I said as to a car salesman, "what's this baby do?" I
rapped the hood with a knuckle.

"Two machines in one," Andy said. "GC and MS. Gas chromatograph is your classic column analytical tool. After the analyte is injected, it's superheated, pressurized with helium gas,
and forced through a capillary column—"

"Wait a minute—"

"Coiled tubing with a very fine bore. Like a still," he said,
"packed with resinous beads."

I liked Andy, though he looked like Millsap a little. "What's
that do?"

"It separates our mixture into its chemical compounds," April offered.

"Exactly," said Andy. "What comes out the end of the column are separate molecules in sequence. Readouts show peaks for what all compounds are there, but not so's we can identify what they are."

"Mass spectrograph does that," April said.

"You got it. GC separates, MS identifies." Andy went to the other end of the table. "Here's how. The separated molecules stream into the MS inlet. That sound"—a shrill whine—"is a high-speed pump maintaining a vacuum. In the vacuum each molecule is ionized and"—dramatic pause and finger burst—"boom. Blasted to bits. The shreds of molecules of a particular compound fly apart in a unique sequence and pattern the software can interpret. Like reading a fingerprint except we get peaks, not whorls. Extremely powerful device."

GC/MS was used, Andy told us, to identify steroids in athletes, dioxin in dust, genetically modified corn in cereal, the composition of interplanetary particles picked up by the *Voyager* probe, and a whole lot more.

"Some peaks I can identify by sight," he said. "Others the microprocessor in here can match to CAS numbers, Chemical Abstract Services. If we have to, we can do a spectral search on the NIST computer library program."

I asked Quierin if I'd heard that right. *Spectral search.*

A green light went off. The V-1 analyte had finished the run and Andy studied the readouts. Nothing. Just low levels of background soil, expected since it was pure McGuckin's. V-2 finished twenty-five minutes later. The same except for one weak peak. The computer made a poor match. Andy looked up the CAS number. Toluene, a volatile hydrocarbon, but only a 40 percent correspondence. Nonspecific.

"The asterisk?" I wondered.

Quierin hunched her shoulders. "Keep looking. Cross all your fingers for semivolatiles."

Andy injected the SV-1 analyte in the GC and we waited. Quierin left for a smoke. April jiggled a leg. Andy collected the readout. Like the others. Low-level soil pattern. No semivolatile chemical compounds. He injected the solution with the last sample, SV-2, to be superheated, vaporized, and fired into the coiled column of beads.

Quierin strolled back into the lab. "Nothing in SV-1," I told her.

"Duh, like your client tells you. It was dirt."

"Like what I'm seeing so far," Andy told us. "Three clean samples of very healthy soil. I think you're in business."

We killed twenty more minutes. The green light blinked off on the final sample. The printer set up—*ch-tit-chit.* Paper began to peel into the tray. Andy picked up the sheets when they finished, turned them over. Looked at each in turn.

"Okay. Okay, okay, okay," he commented as he went. "Okay, whoa. Not okay. What the hell? *Look at that spike!*"

He handed the graph to Quierin, flipped through the sheets, and then went back from the beginning. "This is wild. This one wild peak and two more sort of similar, metabolites, no doubt."

"What is it?" Spoken by all three of us.

"New to me." He worked the keyboard. "New to the hard drive." He looked up excitedly. "It's time for a spectral search. First, we need resolution enhancement, best readouts we can get."

A new set of tracings of peaks peeled off. He loaded a CD-ROM.

"How many compounds in this NIST library?" April asked.

"Most of the simple semivolatiles."

"How many's that?"

"Sixty thousand or so."

Andy entered a series of searches. "Why that one wild peak?" he mumbled to himself. "Okay. There's the toluene CAS number like before. Poor match like before. Not toluene. Benzene, only a little better. Which means, however, it's got to be a benzene ring hydrocarbon. Okay, there we go. CAS number 108–95–2, ninety-eight percent match. That's it for dead certain."

Andy got out the fat notebok that cross-indexed numbers to compounds and split it open in his lap. He found the page of 108s, ran a finger down to 108–95–2, then across.

"Jesus." He scanned us with concern. "I can't believe this—" He shook his head to clear it. "Phenol," he said quietly. "That's what this is telling us."

Quierin caught a sudden breath. "That's terrible." She looked away. Her eyes started.

Andy lifted off his clunky glasses and blinked. "You don't get phenol in soil. It's gone in a couple days. Hazardous waste site, only time I ever saw it. Huge spill. EPA enforcement branch came down like a SWAT team."

He fitted his glasses back and double-checked the CAS index.

"Look," he said, "you folks have got a problem here. Where's your property at?"

CHAPTER 10

After a few days on databases—ToxNet, RIRS, HCDB—and at the chem department library with April, Quierin got us together at my house to explain June Stillwell's death.

Quierin knew phenol, mostly from Bosnia. The local crews always wanted to use it at grave sites, and Quierin kept having to confiscate the stuff. It didn't surprise her that maybe 90 percent of the database case reports were from former Soviet and East European states. In the West, straight phenol was obsolete except at "antiquated" hospitals, as one of the articles put it.

Chemically, phenol is a hydrocarbon in the benzene series. A clear fluid that could be mistaken for water or denatured alcohol except for its characteristic smell, sweet and slightly minty. At hospitals that still have it, phenol is used to sterilize gowns, linens, mattresses, and in solution, to wash down premises. I remembered the biohazard cart, the bottles of colorless liquid, the familiar smell.

Phenol is also a terribly toxic, caustic poison sometimes known as carbolic acid. It destroys tissue on contact. Breathing fumes or skin contact can be fatal. Lysol and some paints contain small though potentially fatal amounts. But we were dealing with straight phenol. Andy called back with a concentration of 170 parts per million free phenol—250 times his machine's detection threshold for phenol in soil—a little less for the metabolites, the two weaker spikes. Which meant, Quierin thought, roughly an ounce of free phenol was used, several times a fatal dose.

As in the leading article, from the *Journal of Forensic Science,* describing the death of a grad student who'd been drinking with colleagues. After the bars closed they went back to the lab intending to sample ethanol they knew was in a beaker on a lab table. The grad student's companions thought better of the plan and went home, leaving him. The tech who opened up the next morning saw him dead on the floor. Next to the beaker of ethanol was an identical beaker containing phenol, from which the decedent had taken a sip by mistake. The autopsy found tissue ravaged throughout the alimentary canal. GC/MS identified free phenol in all tissue sampled in concentrations a little less than June's.

Confirming entirely my view on labs.

Phenol causes both severe burns and systemic toxicity, Quierin continued. She stopped and considered April. "You should be here for this? I'm Dutch direct."

"I know it already." April sat straight at my kitchen table in the moose sweater, palms down, ringless. "I read the reports. I'm fine."

"Later I get to a part," Quierin said. "For that part you have to get out of here."

"We'll see."

Quierin told us what phenol does. All tissue it contacts burns, separates, sloughs. The stomach is fried. Probable GI bleed. Systemic effects follow—CNS depression, lethargy, shock, weakness, collapse, sometimes convulsions, arrhythmia or irregular heartbeat, and breathing stops. Phenol is highly lipiphilic: it has an affinity for tissue fats, which takes it to organs and blood. If we checked, we'd find out kidney and liver didn't work for transplant. Maybe lungs too.

"So picture fits. Cause of death, cardiopulmonary arrest from sudden acute respiratory failure associated with cardiac arrhythmia. Classic phenol hit."

"Arcenault was on the right track," Paige said.

"He had bits of the pieces. Labs show hematocrit, platelets down, which equal GI bleed. He has mystery of stopping breathing but no way can Arcenault know why without GC/MS. He

sends sample but it doesn't get there. He does everything right,"
Quierin said to April. "Was past hope already."

Now—what did phenol say about the poisoner? Anyone at
Colfax could have picked up a bottle and poured some in a coma
patient's food. Could have been Stillwell, Rico, or anybody
there. We knew June was deliberately undernourished. Someone at Colfax had done that. Why, Quierin couldn't figure—to
starve, then to poison. But it was evidence of intent to harm June
in that place. Malice in that place.

The choice of phenol was either random, just grabbing a bottle with a skull and crossbones on it, or deliberate. Whether by
chance or design, it was a smart choice. Metallic poison sur-
vives even cremation. Too durable. Volatiles have the opposite
problem. Mostly gone before midnight. Unless there's an
autopsy, semivolatile phenol works and escapes detection if the
poisoner can get rid of both specimens and the poison center
sample. "This happened by chance?" Quierin said. "I don't
think so."

"How would he have known," Paige asked, "there'd be a
gastric lavage? Or that Platte Valley didn't have a GC/MS and
used the poison center instead? And if he knew that, why didn't
he also know the stomach fluid would be stored two months and
take that too?"

"Why you think?"

"I think," said Paige, "Stillwell popped his cork, impulsively
grabbed a bottle and poured it in, and the rest is all coincidence."

"I don't think—impulsively," said Quierin.

"He or she entered the room not just with phenol," I added,
"but also a can of Glade, mint flavor, to throw off whoever
found June. Me."

"Coincidence again. Glade happened to be there."

"Maybe." April touched her fingers together. "It was part
deliberate, part chance. Like life."

"Say all is maybe coincidence except just one thing,"
Quierin said. "Choice of phenol. Glade shows me poisoner
knows about phenol. If he knew phenol and chose it, we know
one other thing about him. Very important thing." She regarded
April. "Time to go, girl. I tell you later."

"Fat chance, Quierin." April had readied for this moment,
her face a picture of resolve.

Quierin looked my way. I nodded, and Quierin began describing how June Stillwell died.

Sometime between when I left at four-thirty and midnight, somebody poured a little pure phenol, say an ounce, into the thousand-milliliter clear plastic bag hanging from an IV pole in June's room. At midnight Rico gives June the big meal of the day, comes back, and draws the weekly sample from the mix of liquid food, water, bile, and phenol that is in June's stomach.

When it hits tissue, phenol has a temporary anesthetic effect. It burns and destroys the stomach wall, but for a while June can't feel it. When the anesthesia wears off, June is ripped with unimaginable pain. She retches and vomits, ineffectually, with no conscious control. The phenol is driven by peristaltic waves into her small intestine and starts to gut it too. The systemic effects set in. By the 4 A.M. check she's in CNS depression, breathing shallow, unresponsive, twitching, probably seizing, with a weak, irregular pulse. Arrhythmia. All of which the nurse records. Signs of impending death, but the nurse writes, "Call doctor in A.M."

"You were next person to see her," Quierin said to me. "By then June's not breathing and rest is history. But what I say about poisoner has to do with the eight hours before. April, I'm really sorry. Now I go back to that again."

April nodded. She bit a lip.

A conscious person who ingested phenol would be screaming and struggling from pain as soon as the temporary anesthesia faded. She'd be stomach-pumped, charcoaled, and narcotized. She might die, but not with agony like this. This pain was *vreselijk*—dreadful. Severest burn, which no pain can match, from inside out. June can do nothing. She suffers hours like grad student locked in lab. She has to suffer fires of hell inside her with no way to call for help and her daughter just across the room.

April had turned toward the window. She raised a hand to her forehead and shut her eyes, but they creased and tears began to come.

Quierin's point, I saw, was this was not a mercy killing. The administration of phenol to the feeding tube of a comatose woman sensitive to pain was an inconceivably vicious act, though possibly not primarily sadistic. There were other reasons to choose it—sure to work, hard to detect, anybody could have done it. Cruelty may have been a downside to the poison of convenience. Regardless, June was grotesquely tortured before she was killed, burned to death from inside out. Her inability to speak or move was exploited to protract her suffering.

"Giving phenol in feeding tube to coma patient who feels pain—" Quierin muttered a Dutch imprecation. "I think of nothing worse. And I think of lots of really bad things. This thing was atrocity. This was diabolical." To April she added, "I can't believe your mom lived so long."

"He is a monster," I muttered.

"It's not Dale," April whispered.

Paige leaned forward. "But think about the hammer. He can be crafty."

"He isn't this—kind of person." April shuddered. *"Why,"* she cried, *"did someone do this to Mom?"* Abruptly she was shaking. Quierin knelt beside her.

"What if"—Paige's green eyes drew to slits—"Stillwell is actually *really* smart? What if he used phenol *expecting* it to be found, by autopsy, however, one way or another. And look—we've found it, haven't we?"

Quierin was confused. "Why?"

"So the cause of death isn't his assault. It's poison by someone unknown, anybody."

"Take it another step," I said. "He wasn't setting up someone unknown. He was setting up April, whom he's always hated. *And he still is.* And it's going on right now in that grand jury room."

"Then why no autopsy?" Quierin said. "And who steals specimens?"

The questions hung there. I kept a thought to myself, too farfetched to voice: Has someone else been covering Stillwell's tracks?

April stood and turned into Quierin's arms. "Your mom was a hero," Quierin said. "She fought eleven hours."

If so, June's death answered a question I'd pondered the months she lay in a coma. She didn't want to die.

Over the next weeks the case powered toward trial through depositions and motions, tactical sorties with few new breaks and still no exit strategy. Late May, Quierin and I watched a *Washington Week* feature on the war. Henry Kissinger thought it a very bad idea. Jesse Jackson and Kofi Annan wanted to appease Milosevic. The House Armed Services Committee treasonously voted to cut off funds for combat midwar. Apache attack helicopters were crashing on takeoff. There was tragic collateral damage to trains, bridges, hospitals. The Chinese weren't too pleased about their Belgrade embassy. Quierin, I, Tony Blair, and John McCain wanted to invade.

The phone rang. I got it in my study.

"Yo, Watash. Rico here. Hey, man. I think I need a lawyer."

PART III

WRONGFUL DEATH
Mooney v. Stillwell
98CV0012-5

CHAPTER 1

Paige was refining her opening statement and questions for voir dire. With trial less than two weeks off, she couldn't be bothered that, for the first time in history, a sitting head of state, Slobodan Milosevic, had been indicted by an international tribunal for crimes against humanity. Or that this was not the work just of the NATO allies who'd gone to war for human rights two months earlier, but of the United Nations. The world. Could the Federation of Planets be very far off?

Paige had asked me to critique her jury selection outline. It was textbook voir dire. Searching, revealing questions on themes of battering, an indoctrination on the horrors of domestic abuse, targeted to women, wives, mothers of daughters. Oprah could have used it.

Quierin and I took a day off after the Milosevic indictment to celebrate. We hiked to Lost Lake and drank snowbank-chilled champagne as cinnamon teal and goldeneye circled within a ring of late-spring ice.

Our trial plan was to revert to Case A—the claims against Stillwell for assault resulting in death—but prepare a fallback Case B for the final phase of trial, rebuttal. Quierin was organizing Case B testimony. The handy thing about rebuttal evidence is not having to disclose it to the other side. The risk is the judge may disallow it unless it truly rebuts something first raised by the defense.

My jobs would be second-chairing Paige in our case in chief, cross-examining defense experts, notably Hans Leitner, and taking care of the loose ends—dealing with the DA, talking with Rico, finding the poisoner. Fast. April was now under grand jury subpoena to testify on the third day of our trial. Rico was supposed to call back with a safe place to meet. A week passed and I thought I'd lost him. Then a message: "212 Albion, 9 P.M., next Friday, park up the street."

Neither Stillwell nor April had been deposed. Since both were targets, both were taking the Fifth. In any other case we'd get a continuance of the wrongful-death trial until after the grand jury was done, but neither side wanted that. Kirwan wanted to force trial now so he could parade what he'd engineered before the jury: April as a grand jury target. We wanted to try it now since we thought we knew things the other side still didn't.

As expected, the defense won a motion *in limine* to exclude Stillwell's medical records. They weren't raising a defense of impaired capacity since Stillwell had been adjudicated competent. His medical care therefore remained privileged. Paige deposed Hans Leitner, but nothing much came of it. The *in limine* ruling prevented him from talking about Stillwell's mental and emotional conditions and treatment, and from producing his records. Paige thought that helped more than hurt. Leitner could testify about what he saw at Colfax, and about June, but not about his own patient—a big relief to Paige. She finished the deposition not worried about Leitner, but I still was. Always a dangerous witness. There had to be an angle we weren't thinking of.

The pressing question had to do with April's testimony. Kirwan wasn't calling Stillwell as a witness for the defense, but we could call him and force him to refuse to answer questions that might be incriminating. Which would look bad. April could look better by testifying freely, answering every question asked. That meant she'd have to waive the Fifth and allow the defense to take a pretrial deposition. A waiver in this lawsuit would be a waiver to the world. Millsap could have her in and set her up.

"I want to do it," April said. "To hell with the whiffet."

I called Millsap to propose a deal. "You wrapping things up? Indictment likely?"

"You know I can't discuss that." Peremptory tone; wanted me off the line.

"You'd like April to testify?"

"That's why I served the subpoena."

"She'd like to talk."

"Bring her down."

"I have a proposal." I tried to sound coy.

"I see no reason not to enforce the subpoena."

"You want to know what happened?"

"Of course."

"You think it's Stillwell or April?"

"They are the targets, as you know," he said dryly.

"What if I were to say you are utterly clueless about the cause of June Stillwell's death."

"I hear it every day."

"You won't believe what I've found out."

"So tell me."

"It'll knock you asshole over teakettle."

A gap in the conversation.

"Mr. Millsap, the proposal is this. April Mooney waives the Fifth and testifies in her trial. A waiver there is a waiver for you. But she needs immunity."

"Out of the question."

"Pocket immunity."

"Out of the question."

"A sweetener. I'll retestify if you want, and you will. Others too, people you never heard of whom you'll want to hear from. All of this will leave you speechless, because when we've finished, you will finally understand how wrong you got it."

"Are you done?"

"Would you like a proffer of what she'll say?"

"No. I'm under instructions, Mr. Stone, that this investigation may receive no immunized testimony. I can't even pretend I can negotiate with you."

Unexpectedly ethical; lots of lawyers would pretend just that to see the proffer.

"Will you do this—extend April's subpoena until after the civil trial, to the week of June twenty-eighth? If you agree to that she'll waive. You can have at her, no immunity."

"That's the deal?"

"If you reject it, she won't waive and won't testify for us and you'll never get to ask her anything."

"We'll need to kick it around."

"I appreciate your indulgence, Mr. Millsap, and the bond of your word."

"We'll consider it."

"I have to hear from you by end of day Friday."

I didn't. The pissant played it out, waiting to see if April would waive and testify in her trial anyway, correctly concluding she'd have to, as the plaintiff, to win.

At four-thirty Friday afternoon, a few hours before my rendezvous with Rico, I left Millsap a message. A bluff: Deal's off. She's not testifying at her trial or to your jury. Ever.

He called back at four-forty. "I need a sign of good faith. Give me a reason it's worth my while."

"Okay. June Stillwell was poisoned. How's that?"

Another gap.

"She was poisoned. There's irrefutable physical evidence. This civil trial is the way to the poisoner, but I need your help."

After a while Millsap spoke. "I'll withdraw the subpoena but I have to know more."

"I'll touch base next week," I said. I called Kirwan to offer April for deposition. I now had to find *all* the answers before April ever sat across from a Russell Tucker grand jury. Conjure up June's ghost and behold the truth whole.

In that part of Homestead on Friday night, with my white face in a new white Subaru, I felt more than conspicuous. I felt showcased, like a casserole turning in a microwave.

It had at one time been a neighborhood of starter homes. Now maybe half were ender homes, overgrown and graffitied, boarded up or burned out. Trikes in yards, junkers at curbs, random piles of trash and busted furniture. Here and there just a concrete pad remained of a place torched by arsonists or razed by the city. Here and there was a tidy brick bungalow with garden art and trimmed grass, a steel front door and burglar bars.

I can do this, I thought, as I began a hapless shuffle from a block away. A front door opened. A figure watched. A raked Grand Am rolled past, drive-by style, Dr. Dre on deep bass. The door slammed. I readied to pivot and push on the ball of a foot.

Of course I could do this. I'd walked the *korso* full of young Serbs, ex-soldiers, war criminals certainly among them, all of whom knew I was a prosecutor from The Hague. I went alone at 2 A.M. into gutted public housing looking for witnesses to testify against their countrymen. I had a Motorola handset then and the Czech HQ of NATO SFOR six miles away, motor pool full of tanks. Now I had a cell phone. I could call 911 and the Denver PD. I preferred SFOR tanks.

Though partly boarded up, 212 Albion looked possibly inhabited, a faint glow at one uncurtained window. I knocked, turned the knob, and stepped into what may have been intended, in starter days, as a living room. I found the light and spoke Rico's name. I thought I heard movement.

Nothing on the walls but large Roman numerals, XIV, VIII, in black spray paint. No furniture except a Salvation Army veneer coffee table, a metal chair, and two low-slung loungers. A rabbit-eared TV on the floor. Soil, excrement, something smeared in the starter carpet. A litter of clothes and odds and ends. A frying pan with old food in it sitting on the carpet. A half-gone bag of Doritos spilling out. On the coffee table two ashtrays brimming with ashes, but not a single butt. Dozens of charred wooden matches. Occluded, asthmatic air, heavy with ammonia, though everything was filthy. A bedroom door ajar, from which the faint glow and sound of movement had come.

And now a guy at the bedroom door. Not Rico. Way not Rico.

A jolt of panic—I'd walked into the wrong house—but I froze, running muscles paralyzed.

The guy was NFL lineman size, wobbly, muttering something. He came my way then turned, careened in a slow motion, swaying stagger, Rockies cap sideways on his head. He turned back again and retraced the same staggering arc, back and forth, muttering over and over, shoulders rolling, and chopping air with the blade of a hand:

> *Never believe dat cliché*
> *Dat crime don pay*
> *I's bon dis way*

He didn't register me at all. It occurred that I could just leave. I looked at my feet, New Balance–clad, rather than at the lineman a few feet away. Took a breath. Raised my eyes to his chest level.

"Rico around?" I said.

His head snapped. "Siddown."

I chose the metal chair by the front door. I sat with right leg back and cocked.

The rap and stagger resumed. Maybe it was dancing. Same lines again and again. *I's bon dis way—*

Now a second bedroom door cracked. A half face. New beard. No pigtail. "Watash." We knocked knuckles, exchanged greetings. The rap kept coming around.

"Tha's Bow Wow," Rico said. "He's my brother."

"He doesn't look like your brother."

I's bon dis way—

"Comrade in arms, is what I'm saying. Desert Storm. He got the syndrome."

"He smoke the crack," I whispered.

"Tha's mostly an act."

"Mostly?"

"He's my eyes and ears," Rico said, settling in a lounger. "Trouble come round, he's on it like a duck on a bug."

I nodded. "That's—good. We can talk?" I indicated the lineman.

"Don' mind Bow Wow."

"Why'd you call me?"

"I need an esquire. I'm tired of hiding, man. I can't live this safe-house life no more."

Safe house? Crack house.

"Look at this," Rico said, whipping out an arm. "Think about here, man. Here, there. One place, 'nother place. *I am trained in hygiene, man.* I am sick of this shit."

"Why me?"

"I want—what's that whistle? Blow that whistle, but I need protection. And I want to sue."

"Who do you need protection from?"

"Colfax."

"Who do you want to sue?"

"Colfax."

"Let's talk about it."

"First I want to know your rates. Also, you handle many of these kind of cases?"

"What kind?"

"Employment discrimination, wrongful termination. Like that. You won't believe what they done to me. I think I got a real good case."

"Rico." I relaxed my getaway posture, extended my leg, popped the knee. "I have some very important questions I have to have answered before I could begin to think about being your lawyer."

"Shoot 'em to me, Watash."

"Did you poison June Stillwell?"

He spit out air, jiggered his head. "You in the crack?"

"Somebody poisoned her." I told him about it.

"Why they want to burn her?"

"They? Who is they?"

"Colfax. I mean, they capable, but why?"

"What happened after I left the afternoon before she died?"

Bow Wow reeled back into his doorway. The door shut behind him.

"Nothing. I mean, I don't know. I don't think I saw her again till the midnight feed. Then I's gone."

"Someone put phenol in the feedbag."

"*Phenol?* Man, is that cold—" Rico stopped. "You lookin' at me, Watash?" He held his fingers to his sternum.

"You had the opportunity. So did others."

"Like you too. Jaz tol' me you come poking around."

"Like me, correct. But what do *you* remember about that night? Did you see Stillwell go in the room? Another staffer? April? Anyone?"

Rico worked his mouth. "Not a blessed soul. But I wouldn't, would I? I was around her room those eight hours maybe twenty minutes total."

"You did the midnight feed?"

"Yeah."

"Anything else?" An important question. If Rico had been the poisoner, he wouldn't have drawn a specimen, accounting for the gap on the refrigerator shelf.

"Nah, just went in 'bout eleven-thirty, started the feedbag, cleaned up when it's done. After a while come round again and took the specimen, brung it to the lab."

"Bag on the IV pole, how'd it look?"

"Like it look, man. Tha's all."

"Just you doing this. Nobody else?"

"Ain't a two-man job."

"Tell me about drawing the specimen."

He was nodding and pulling his chin. "That was something funny."

"Did you notice a smell?"

"My *hand* smelled, man. Then it burned like hell. Burned holes." He held out his right hand, three white blotches, pencil-eraser size. When he'd drawn June's specimen with the 60 cc syringe, there was a back-charge from the stoma. Something that had never happened before. A few drops hit his hand.

"The stoma squirted. That was truly weird."

He'd washed at the basin, stopped by the lab, and took off for his weekend. A half hour later his hand started burning. "Like somebody held cigarettes to it. I washed and washed it but it kept on burning. That smell stayed too. Yeah, it did."

"How did it smell?"

"Kinda like how they say, Irish Spring, fresh and clean. I thought it was her soap, but not how it lingered."

"Why did you put a can of Glade in her room?"

"A what?"

"Glade. Air freshener."

"Air freshener—nah, why?"

"Why didn't you report your hand burns to Colfax?"

"I was off at midnight and I was gone, man. Into the night. I thought that shit'd go away, but it didn't. It halfway ruined my weekend, like my hand was grilled, man. I was gonna tell 'em, but they fired my ass."

Rico got a call on Wednesday from administrator Hudnut not to report that afternoon. He was terminated. She wouldn't explain, but she was adamant. "Like, never show your face in here again. Bitch she was, but thinking about it, maybe Hudnut has a heart. 'You need to disappear,' she says. 'Now.'"

"That's why you didn't show at the White Spot?"

"Things got spooky and I was gone. Want to hear?"

"Not yet. One other important question I need to have answered."

"I'm here."

"Over the months you cared for June, you were intentionally starving her, weren't you? Rico?"

"Yeah. Correct."

Now I got up and careened around the room. "Rico! What the hell was going on?"

"I was just a boot, Watash. Doing my job."

"Starving June Stillwell?"

"Yeah. Yeah, I was. I didn't know it till down the road some. But, yeah, tha's right, that was exactly the idea."

I glanced at Bow Wow's room. No light under the door. Just us now. "Rico, I have to know about this."

"This," he said intently, "is why I called you up, man. This my question for you. Can I sue? They been trying to kill me."

"Bow Wow's my cover. We got points up and down the block. They call Bow Wow with a suspicious like you. He check 'em out. But I'm ready for what it is, witness protection. Ready to sing."

"Sing to me, Rico. Client to lawyer."

Rico worked his shoulders; he'd been waiting for this. "Nutrition and supplies, that was the burn. Come down to this: pimping the comas.

"It *costs* to feed a coma. I could dine at the Brown Palace for what them little cans cost." Not to mention, he continued, the supplements, minor meds, ointments, collars, cushions, pumps, poles, tubes, caths, diapers. *"Diapers,* man. We push twenty thousand diapers a year to Falcon. Leave a diaper on a coma four, five days, coma don't care."

"Half it," was the standing dietitian order. Everything was prescribed. Just give half the scrip across the board. The staff was told the dietitian's reason was inactivity. "Say comas get sick and fat on a whole scrip. Made sense at first. What we do with the half that's left is load it at the bay. To so-called *return* the so-called *unnecessary* supplies."

Falcon was the fence. Its blue trucks were bound for the warehouses of Falcon Medical and Pharmacy Supply in Encino, California. Falcon took expenses, plus an honest ten. QCT—the

Queen City Trust—kept the net on one-half of eighty coma patients' taxpayer-funded food, supplies, and routine medications.

"Know how much an articulated, pneumatic Quickie wheelchair sells for?" Rico said. "Four thousand bucks. Suction machine? Fifteen grand. Know how much twenty thousand bootleg adult diapers bring in California? Fourteen thousand bucks. Little can of Nutren 1.5 is five dollars ten cents. We was running sixty thousand cans a year to the coast. That's three hundred–plus thousand bucks just on Nutren. Made just as much on feedbags. Made more on meds. Add in supplies, little stuff, tongue depressors, cotton swabs, shit. QCT's clearing two million pure profit a year, on top of six million in Medicaid bed payments."

"Where do you get these figures?"

"We started tracking, me and a couple drivers."

"You wanted a cut. You threatened to go to the U.S. Attorney unless they cut you in. A mistake, Rico."

He locked his hands behind his head, closed his eyes. "Not—quite." He sighed. "By a while I wised up to the hose. Ain't no dietitian. Just short-weight the comas, they won't complain. Go down too fast, give 'em boosters. Keeps 'em going a year or two, sometimes."

"But—eventually—"

"Yeah, Watash. A year or so that way, something's gonna get 'em."

"Starvation rations."

"Tha's the rag."

"A skim-and-fence operation, and they counted on a homey staff who wouldn't get it. Or care."

"QCT ain't stupid. On paper, they clean. The way HCFA do an audit, inspector matches scrips against benefits paid, and Colfax is golden. But this homey got it. Did I want a cut? Yeah, I let it be known. But the threat part, huh-uh. I thought it was you who ratted me."

"Jesus, Rico. You wanted in on *this?*" The enormity, the perversity, of it was sinking in. "Colfax is a for-profit death camp, man. A slow-kill Auschwitz." Starving inmates ignored by the world, helpless even to beg for help, caged in a black, protracted decline. And as soon as the hearse pulls away, an ambulance arrives with the replacement.

It was the ghastly reverse image of a hospital. Like Vukovar Hospital, where patients were murdered, not treated. Because of greed, not politics, and therefore even worse. It qualified as evil, on my or Leitner's or anybody's terms.

I stared at him.

"You get in, you can't get out. They like some kind of Mafia. They send these guys. Mean white dudes with no hair."

I stared.

"I'm not proud about it, Watash."

"Why'd you think I was the rat?"

"Jaz told me 'bout you mooking around, and I know you on your high horse. Listen to you now."

Up the chain they must have freaked when they heard I took June's records. They thought I'd cop to the scam and did an in-house investigation to see how exposed they were. They fired and threatened Rico—tipped off or maybe just because he was too close to me and April, and he knew too much.

"What did Jaz say about—me mooking?"

"All kind of people got the third degree. Something was missing from the lab. Jaz let it out, how she snuck you in and the lab door was open after."

I stood at the XIV wall, trying to make sense of it. A grotesque criminal enterprise, starving eighty people and reselling the food. How was it served by phenol?

"Silverman has to know," I said.

Rico shrugged. "That guy, your buddy did."

"What buddy?"

"Big guy, white hair, come with the meatball."

"Hans Leitner?"

"Tha's him. He remarks, you give her half the scrip? Half the protein, half the k-cal, half the vitamins, all that. I say, yessir. Dietitian guidelines."

"And?"

"And nothing."

I worried my lower lip. Window glass reflected the wall behind me, spray paint reading "VIX." A hall of broken mirrors.

"You're in danger," I said.

"They let me know what they'd do to me, to my mom too. Then they try to do it anyway."

"Are others in danger? Jasmine?"

"I fear for Jaz."

"Me?"

"Tha's why I wind up calling you. Rat or not, you're with me. Colfax don't like you either."

"Who is 'they'? Who is the Queen City Trust?"

"I never know. Just the two dudes who don't talk. Hudnut, who I mentioned the cut to. Couple times I hear about 'Doc.'"

"What? Loading dock?"

"'Doc' Doc, like a medico, is how I take it."

"Who is Doc?"

Rico shook his head.

"Shit." I sat back down and shut my eyes and pressed my fingers to my temples. No good. The gears kept slipping.

"Yo, Watash. They think I'm gonna blow the whistle so they fire me. What is that?"

"Retaliation, among other things. A basis to sue, but others are better."

"Hah." He slapped a knee. "I thought so."

"Rico, I'd say you've got a pretty good case. Better than you ever dreamed."

CHAPTER 2

Ellen Vesco answered my call in the morning.
"Please find Hans if you can," I said. "Interrupt him if necessary." Ellen has a pleasant, mellow voice, a friendly efficiency.
We were getting to be pals. She'd do her best. Then I drove to
the capital, the secretary of state's office. The Queen City Trust,
a for-profit Colorado corporation in good standing, was empowered by its articles to operate a long-term rehabilitation hospital
for the indigent and "for any other lawful purpose." The corporate instruments were unrevealing boilerplate. A change of
name in 1996 from Colfax Community Healthcare to Queen
City Trust, Inc., probably coincident with the hospital's sale.
The names of the original 1977 incorporators and officers were
on file, but not those of the new owners. With the 1996 sale, the
registered agent changed to Arnold Whitelaw. All subsequent
filings were made by him alone. The only address ever given
was that of Whitelaw and Van Horn, LLC. No way to identify
his clients from the official records. Driving back, I called Beckwith, an ex–railroad claims agent turned private eye. I asked
him to find out what he could unofficially.

The phone in the dashboard rang. "Hello, Elliot?" Ellen's
mellow voice through the white noise of the turnpike. "Hans is
waiting for you in Boulder."

In Leitner's office glade a western tanager made Tinker Bell

loops. Above the trees the Flatirons rose bright pink against a
blue Rockies morning. The office door was slightly ajar. Inside,
a breeze from the open slider mingled and stirred, but it was dim
and warm as a womb.

"In here," he called. The working office.

"Hey, Doc."

Hans looked over his half-rims, then removed them.
"Elliot?" He sat in shirtsleeves at his desk, working at a computer. I took a leather armchair opposite. I tried to imagine him
capable of crimes against humanity. Since the essence of the
offense is criminal acts against unarmed noncombatants, the
more defenseless the victims, the more aggravated the wrong.
Killing children, for example, or hospital patients. By that standard killing the comatose may be the worst crime against
humanity of all.

Behind him was a bookcase of heavy volumes. Beside it, two
six-drawer cabinets of honeyed Scandinavian wood. A narrow,
glassed view of pinewoods where a Steller's jay twitched on a
bough.

To my right was the wall of respect. The glory wall. I'd
never before studied its licenses and diplomas from elite places
of learning. Its commendations and awards, from the Sisters of
Mercy to B'nai B'rith. The military honors and the many photographs. Queen Beatrice pinning a medal, Bill Clinton grip-
ping an elbow and shaking a hand, Hans escorted by a
thoughtful Colin Powell, a portrait signed by Sandra Day
O'Connor, Hans in Wellingtons knee-deep in bodies, Hans with
a troupe of Bosnian children, a troupe of Salvadoran children,
and in Eritrea before a derelict clinic. A *Good Housekeeping*
plaque honored Hans as one of the Best Doctors in America.
There were grateful letters from important people—a senator,
the surgeon general, the president of Guatemala, Bernhard
Kouchner of Médecins Sans Frontières, the International Rescue Committee. But not a trace of Christina.

A shrine of self-regard, I thought. Hans Leitner leveraged his
war-crimes work spectacularly well. Compared with me.

If he thought me acting strangely, he didn't say. He was all
bonhomie.

"Quierin's in Boulder, I hear. I never thought I'd see it, hon-
estly. Let's go out, relive old times. What in Boulder approxi-

mates a floating tavern with skewered spiced pork and a bottle of *rakija?* Not the Dushanbe Teahouse. Taverna Terzakis? What do you say?"

"I'm interrupting your work, Hans, but you must be bored."

"Bored?" He laughed. "Putting together a team for Kosovo is not boring, I assure you."

"But what a tired routine you have." I bent the end of a paper clip and twirled it. "A whacked-out patient now and then. One more inept deposition by one more lightweight lawyer. With your taste for adventure, why not strike out for something more exciting? You enjoy dangerous enterprises, don't you?"

"Elliot?" He watched me cautiously, half-rims back at their post.

"I changed careers in 1996," I said, skimming back over the glory wall. "So did you."

"Well, no." He smiled almost happily. "But it is true of you. You changed careers, then two years later you changed careers again. You came back here, and, Elliott—I raised this once politely. Something happened. I worry about you a little."

Bonhomie deliquescing to heartfelt concern. Concern congealing to counsel.

"Know what I think?" he said, hands folding in front of him. "I think you've decided against career in favor of calling. That's what you're searching for."

Not a bad point. "You nailed it, Doc. You're absolutely right."

"Unfortunately, that doesn't work. Want to know why?"

"No." I was catching on. He knew how to rouse my curiosity toward a topic he'd control. "Our work in Europe opened my eyes. Now I have to bring it home, live it from the inside out. And it will work."

"You're headed for a fall if you intend to change the world."

"You are the change you wish in the world."

"Kant to Gandhi? Oh my. Is this about justice? You should remember that justice cannot be 'done.' It's a process, not a deed. As a man of career, not calling, you know the process of justice. Elliot, I'm speaking as a friend. Return to your career."

I watched him.

"There. I said it."

"A step away from injustice qualifies as justice. A lie dispelled qualifies as truth."

"This morbid obsession—"

I shook my head, eyes closed. "Stop. You knew they were starving her."

He stared.

"And all the others. You knew it since you were behind it."

"What—"

"How could you work Vukovar Hospital there and Colfax Hospital here? Is *that* the paradox of the man who is both greatly good and greatly evil? The great compartmentalization, is that it?"

"Are you saying—"

"Do you deny involvement and probably a controlling interest in the Queen City Trust?" I was close to coming unglued, index finger at the point.

"What the hell are you talking about?"

"Tell me this, Hans. Did you know, way before the blood work, the albumin and all, back last fall, that June was only receiving half of her prescribed nutrition? Tell me you didn't know."

Leitner offered a blank look, inner software, I suspected, in search mode. It was a yes-or-no question.

"Why do you think that?"

"Did you know?"

"Don't cross-examine me."

"Oh, I will, in a week or two." I let it sink in. His mouth turned a little down. "But now I'm asking you as a friend and admirer and because I have to have an answer. No wires."

He snorted.

"Check me over if you want. Did you know?"

"Who's saying this? Your friend Rico?"

I prickled with duck bumps. Rico should be warned. "No. Nobody even knows where he is."

"I ask because the answer is yes. I ask because it's too soon to break this. I want to know who's talking."

"You did know?"

"Yes."

"It was your scam, wasn't it, Doc?"

"Mine? Let me show you something, Elliot." He opened a

file drawer and pulled a folder labeled HHS. "I do a lot of QA consulting for hospitals and the government. I even have a card." He produced a battered wallet and showed me: *HCFA Senior Medical Investigator.*

"Look at this letter." He found it in the folder. It asked him to organize the evaluation of rehabilitation hospitals in Colorado for compliance with state and federal law. It contained a grant of authority signed by Nancy Ann Min DeParle, Administrator, Health Care Financing Administration.

"So, yes, I know. But this is extremely serious. It's not what half-cocked amateurs should go sticking their noses in. Nobody should be talking about it yet. I led you there, but only to June. I see I shouldn't have."

"I don't believe you. I think you run Queen City Trust."

"I don't know what that is."

I told him.

"Elliot, listen very closely. We're going to take down Colfax. I'm using some of your information, the kid on the vent, the infection protocols. I'd cite June Stillwell, if we could ever learn how she really died, and there's more you don't know. One thing I know is, whoever owns that hospital is both smart and not very nice. Don't fuck this up. You and I could be in personal jeopardy."

"I still don't believe you."

"This would be funny except for what it says about your mental state."

"Prove it."

"I just did." He thumped the folder. "And if I'm some two-bit Medicaid grifter," he added sarcastically, "why would I have clued you into my racket when we talked about the blips on June Stillwell's labs? Do I really have to prove myself to you?"

"Yes. It can happen when people have callings."

"There are physicians who make a living by Medicaid fraud. True medical racketeers. Am I that kind of doctor?"

I said nothing.

"All right." He hit a key to bring up his calendar. "Tomorrow morning everything I've got can be rescheduled by Ellen. If he can fit us in, I'll meet you at nine at Roy Wellman's office, the head of the Colorado Health Facilities Division, in charge of hospital enforcement. Shall I call him now? Tomorrow I'll tell him what I've learned about Colfax, and to keep it under wraps. You can add whatever you want. And you will then observe that I am not informing on myself."

I didn't want the state involved. Too much to learn, too little time. So he caught me out, just when I thought the ghost was emerging from the shadows. A morbidly obsessed man on a mission, gunning for a calling with a loose cannon.

"No. Maybe—later." But not too much later, with eighty patients on half rations. Two weeks max. I got up and went to the door, drew it open, winced in the flood of light. "Hans—I—" The apology died in my throat. Why so quick to accuse him? Because he was almost-me? But he'd misled me, elaborately.

"Elliot, your friendship means a lot. Let me help you solve this."

"I'm obliged." I gave a neutral farewell wave and turned into the dubious promise of the luminous day.

As the bombs stopped and Serb convoys started north and 1.4 million refugees headed home with NATO escorts, the trial in *Mooney v. Stillwell* began. Milosevic had capitulated. Unconditional surrender, which didn't quite register on the dyspeptic, postimpeachment media, so cross-eyed by scandal they'd see total victory as a wag-the-dog trick. No ticker tape, and Wesley Clark did not ascend to the cult-commander status of a Schwarzkopf, except to Quierin, who went overboard about the triumph of action in the service of ideals.

The Serb surrender had implications for us, and it threw the trial's hazards into relief. By the end of the month Quierin would be needed at Kosovo's dozens of fresh mass graves—a taphonomist's dream. The digging would start once grave sites were located and secured. Hans Leitner was going about the same time for Doctors for Human Rights. An Article III Geneva Investigation for violations of medical neutrality. In other words, more Vukovars. Quierin and Hans had been talking Croatian Airlines versus Swiss Air, the Sarajevo versus the Skopje route, whether Albos should man the crews. Quierin might have to ship out on two days' notice.

The hazards of trial, I mentioned as the two of us rumbled toward court the next day, sardined into Paige's 4Runner among exhibits, banker's boxes of Redweld files, trial bags, and demonstrative aids and equipment, were not a little daunting. We needed to prove what happened the night June was assaulted, to find out who poisoned her five months later, to identify the Colfax kingpin, and to discover how all that intersected. A Chinese puzzle.

"Your area, I believe," Paige said, cutting off a bobtail van. She drove as aggressively as she cross-examined. "Per the division of labor."

I protested. "I've narrowed it down. April didn't do it."

"Yeah?"

"I don't think Rico either, and Hans isn't Queen City Trust. Leaving Stillwell or whoever QCT is."

Rico thought the Colfax Mafia capable of a rub out. Hans was closing in on their fraud. Rico was a big worry to Colfax, and so were April and I, with our snooping and complaints. June was where the four of us converged. She was why, for separate reasons, we all kept coming back. Each visit by any one of us carried risk to the QCT. Taking out everybody was obviously out of the question. What about a single, indirect hit? Eliminate the reason we came. The problem patient, who had a lawyer hanging around, and a nosy daughter living with her at Colfax day and night.

The Colfax kingpins would have in-house knowledge of how to do it and how to cover it up, and the hospital-to-hospital connections to interfere at Platte Valley. And they had a patsy. If phenol was discovered, Rico could take the rap: He administered the poison, then was never seen again. Plus, the plan worked. Neither Hans, Rico, April, nor I had set foot in Colfax since the week June died.

"Your area," Paige said. "But step on it." She demonstrated, downshifting to pass a microbus on a double-yellow uphill curve.

"Forget us, Paige. But you have a child to think about."

We topped the overlook and beheld our destination, ever a conversation stopper. The round green architectural error on a height above the river, Flatirons County Courthouse, like a giant op-art tin of Skoal. The wheel of justice.

"I still have time," I said. For Case B, the rebuttal testimony proving starvation and phenol poisoning and nailing it on QCT, Stillwell, somebody. "How's little Connor?"

"You have one week. Ten days max." Then Paige added, "Jack's a help. Kid won't sleep."

District Judge Raphael Otero's courtroom had begun to fill with the muster for trial—the bailiff, a deputy sheriff; Hancock and Edson with two paralegals, setting up an ELMO overhead projector and Kirwan's butcher-paper easel; a trickle of minor media; the customary courthouse flaneurs and voyeurs turned on by wrongful-death litigation. A tan, lithe law clerk sat with a spacey smile. She was elsewhere—exams or a wedding or climbing the Bastille in Eldorado Canyon. Paige was cloistered with Kirwan and the judge in his chambers, arguing pretrial motions.

Judge Otero was mild-tempered, precise, and reasonably bright, eight years on the bench after a decade with the attorney general. He was inclined more to equitable than technical jurisprudence, but had the reputation of being reversal-shy. Decisive but a little timid, a problematic combination. Instead of working his way from A to B, he might too readily conclude, "I can't go there." Like most trial judges he placed too high a value on efficiency. He had a soft spot for the humans involved that was a challenge for a lawyer to touch.

To the right of his bench hung an oil of Judge Horace Marler, who'd built and lived and died in my red-shingled house. White-haired, spectacled, cerebral and solemn, in the frowning manner of judicial portraiture. Does my aimless home practice bring honor to your house, Judge? He didn't appear to think so.

I reflected on Otero's empty dais and my own past ambitions for the robe. It's a hard job, judging, living up to the impossible standard of wisdom, the concord of head and heart, counterweights that mutually constrain. For me, it had been a bad idea that came from the wrong place. Too much from the head.

Quierin and I flanked April at the plaintiff's counsel table, the one nearest the jury. Moral support supernumeraries. April seemed to need it, jaws tight with exaggerated attitude, eyes restless with suppressed alarm.

"When we get a panel of jurors to select from, look sweet but serious," I said. "Catch their eyes when they talk so they know what they say means a lot to you. Stillwell will avoid their eyes. We want the contrast."

Quierin squeezed April's hand and got up to go. She had witnesses to work. The court reporter appeared from the door behind the bench and primly settled in at her machine. The hearing in chambers was over. Next came poker-faced Paige, then Kirwan beaming, but he always beamed in court.

I sensed someone behind me—like footfalls on the Flagstaff trail—and turned, elbow behind chair back. A tall chief-executive type, gray pinstripe, Zegna or better, silver hair swept stylishly back, tangly gray eyebrows, frown lines so set he looked tragic. Our eyes met, his as empty as sockets, and I remembered. Arnold Whitelaw. I felt color rising.

Paige was tugging. I leaned to her whisper. "Chickenshit may let Kirwan do it."

"The Fifth?"

She nodded.

Hancock had been standing, then sitting and playing with a pencil, standing again, then searching the room and biting a cheek. Now he sallied out the aisle and into the hall. A minute later the jury commissioner opened and braced the double doors to let in seventy-five citizens. They spread out, picking seats like a cineplex crowd. The mechanized air hummed with anticipation. It couldn't have been lost on the citizens that one of the parties was missing. But soon there came Hancock, demoted from trial lawyer to bag handler and usher, escorting his man, bad timing intact.

None of us had seen Stillwell for six months. We were as curious as everybody else. How would the monster keep it lidded when accused of murder in a court of law?

In a herringbone-tweed sport coat with a regimental tie, a short, sprayed haircut, khaki Dockers, and spit-shined Tony Lamas. "What a joke," April whispered as he entered the well, Hancock holding the gate. I patted her arm. Both parties needed to keep it lidded.

Stillwell looked pulled tight as a wet glove. April kept staring at him. He stared only at his own clenched hands. Hancock rubbed a tweed-draped shoulder and Stillwell flinched from the weasel's touch. He spread and inspected his fingers and ran a thumbnail back and forth along a palm.

I wrote on a Post-it, "They have problems of their own," and stuck it in front of Paige.

Judge Otero was announced and the assembly came to its

feet. The judge took his place of command, shook out his robe, donned glasses, opened a laptop, and called fourteen citizens to the box.

Paige and Kirwan were each highly accomplished jury-selection stylists with vastly different styles. One was Oprah, the other Hans Christian Andersen. Paige projected deeply serious concern. Voir dire noir. The panel opened up to her, bonded, soon volunteering inner feelings on domestic violence, offering their own moving stories, of a friend who had barely escaped June's fate, a relative in a coma.

Kirwan followed. His message seemed to be, let's have fun, implicitly trivializing the plaintiff's oh-so-serious claims. He knew all fourteen potential jurors' names without referring to his list. His first objective was to demonstrate that feat by stepping away from his notes and saying a little something to each by name. He wanted them to know this was a performance. *His* performance, mnemonic tricks and fairy tales, and little else. Not crime and justice, surely.

Next, the jaunty man with the wrinkled face danced to his easel and began a weird, complicated tale, illustrated by pages of sweeping Magic Marker drawings, supposedly about the etymology of the term *red herring*. An English fox-hunting ploy of some kind, with a signpost of a dangling fish, and elaborate cross routes through the woods that he mapped on butcher paper for the curious venire. Throughout, he was hyperanimated, arms spread in elaboration, finger thrust here and there, spinning on toe and heel. At the easel, pages filled and flipped. Cartoons appeared of foxes, dogs, horses, and fish, a Mr. Rogers show-and-tell. When he wasn't drawing in flourishes, he was prancing, parading almost girlishly before them. It was his stage, not the judge's, certainly not ours.

Kirwan finished and we broke for ten before choosing eight of the fourteen. April went for the ladies'.

"Jesus, Paige." I'd not seen a Kirwan voir dire before. "He didn't ask questions. I couldn't follow what the hell his idiotic story meant. He didn't learn anything about any of them. He's—nuts?"

"It's intentional," she said. "Kirwan has this idea you never learn who'll go your way by getting a panel to talk. 'I pick buttercups,' he says." The children's game of holding flowers to chins to find out who likes you.

"Kirwan is interested in just one thing, jurors who are captivated by him. He tells an incomprehensible story in voir dire with the same mannerisms he'll use with witnesses. Swooping around, making his loops. He doesn't ask questions, but he constantly watches their eyes. He looks for a particular sparkle. Those he knows he can engage and distract throughout trial, who'll come each morning looking forward not to evidence but to Kirwan performances, and who'll do what he tells them at the end.

"He's picked hundreds of juries. He can spot his sparklers, and, you know, he never loses."

"So I hear."

"You watch," Paige said. "He'll do all he can to make jurors focus on him so either they don't notice or they actually enjoy his high-spirited trashing of April."

"The greatest evil," I quoted Hans, "is the evil that can pass for good."

"He does want jurors to feel comfortable denying victims' claims. To have fun as he takes them there."

Less Hans Christian Andersen beguiling the children than the Pied Piper leading them away.

What the hell, we stuck to our plan. Back and forth, one by one, we and the defense eliminated prospects. We eliminated Stillwell types, blue-collar guys and caregivers, hoping to wind up with empathetic women. Kirwan eliminated the dull-eyed, the poor sparklers, regardless of who they were.

We were zeroing in on the same people, I realized with alarm. And that's whom we wound up with, eight empathetic mothers of daughters who'd chuckled at the shaggy-fox story. Who reflected a butter-yellow glow.

CHAPTER 3

After a final hour woodshedding April—keep your game face no matter how Otero rules—at the lunch dive down the street known to courthouse regulars as La Placenta, then Paige's brilliant opening statement and Bernie Edson's sodden rejoinder, April took a breath, shook her hair, smiled, and stepped to the box to be sworn. Eight mothers were all ears.

Paige had told a quiet and moving story, keyed to a Power-Point photo series—June with Yuma, June the Casey Jones, June with Danny the Down's kid, the oblong bloodstain in June's mattress, her gruesomely battered eye, the mug shot of Stillwell, the hammer in the bucket, the milkbox note, the gap in the row of figurines on the mantel, the CBI powder report.

At counsel table Paige had unwrapped the Manikin Pis. She walked him slowly past the women, cradled like Connor. The judge had to tell Hancock to stop making tabletop noise. Rattling his Luden's. Stillwell seemed to appreciate the intervention.

"A bitter man was brutally injured in a railyard accident for which someone would have to pay," Paige summed up. "The woman who nursed him back to life, but who controlled his wealth, became the focus of his rage. He blamed her for the accident, his disability, for everything he wasn't. He brutally beat her as she lay in bed, then meticulously hid the evidence of his crime. And after five months of helpless agony June Stillwell finally died."

The last PowerPoint image filled the monitors, June's death certificate with orange Hi-liter: death a consequence of *traumatic brain injury* from blunt-force head trauma *in decedent's home*. Manner of death: *homicide*.

"You," Paige addressed her audience of eight, "will be April Mooney's one chance to right her mother's savagely wrongful death."

In the quiet that followed, there had come the sounds of a person behind us shuffling along a bench, receding footsteps, a door creaking and clicking shut. I checked. Whitelaw was gone. He'd come only to hear what was said about Colfax.

"All this," bald Bernie Edson wound up next, opening a palm toward Paige, knee hammering behind the podium, "is a *red herring* to distract you from the real cause of June Stillwell's death. Euthanasia. Mercy killing." He pointed, accusing April. "A daughter unable to bear the burden of her mother's hopeless coma, ending her suffering, taking her life." The accusing finger dropped to his side. The stare lingered.

I'd stolen then a glance at Stillwell. He sat swollen and bug-eyed. He glared at his hands. Enigma, or the next incarnation of the skeleton djinni, malevolent messenger from some place of torment?

April, both plaintiff and accused, now promised from the witness box to tell the whole truth. She looked at Paige, her examiner, and then at the jury, with fragile blue eyes.

"Tell us about your mom, April. Where was she from?"

April talked about Lander, the ranch, the Wind Rivers. She told of the troubled first marriage June left because of physical abuse—Paige's trial theme. But her mother remade herself, April explained, the top engineer in Laramie, a prizewinning show rider, world's best mom. Photographs were introduced and passed to the jury. June was on top of her little world until that terrible Christmas Day when Dale got hurt and she committed the rest of her life to healing him.

April told about the kind of person June was, her gift for helping others, the riding therapy with CP kids, how she gave up everything for Dale. April quickly hit her stride, the poised young woman of the memorial service. Otero was rapt. She addressed the hostility between herself and Stillwell. That he wouldn't let her in the house. The code she and her mother had cooked up when she called and Stillwell was present. She said June, always an optimist about Dale's progress, had sounded down and defeated for six or eight months.

"Did there come time when you feared for your mother's safety?"

"Yeah." April nodded earnestly. "Mom'd been abused before. I knew how it made her afraid, and afraid to leave too. I could hear it in her voice, that fear."

Kirwan popped up. "Objection. Hearsay."

Not offered for the truth of what June said, Paige responded, but to explain April's concern and subsequent actions. With a limiting instruction to the jury, Otero let her continue.

April called the night before the attack. She asked if Stillwell was treating June okay. June said yes, but it wasn't convincing. Something was wrong. Stillwell was worse, June said through their code. June admitted to being worried and afraid.

"I asked if it was worse than it was with my dad and she said it was. Different but worse." April had to stop. "My dad broke Mom's arm and tore her spleen, so I knew—" April was weeping. Eyes started in the jury box. The court reporter angrily hammered her keys. "Mom said she had to hang up. So next night I called I'm so afraid for her." Swiping at the tears with the back of her hand. "I called and called but she didn't pick up."

The answering machine tape was played to a silent courtroom. April's voice high and tremulous. "Mom, answer if you're there. Mom, *please* answer. *Please, Mom*—"

"And the next thing I heard—"

It was too much. Judge Otero called a compassionate recess.

The rest of the direct examination was equally moving. June's prostration, her evident suffering, her faltering efforts to communicate, her decline and death. Stillwell's first visit when he came after April. How April and June learned to communicate again by code. That raising a thumb meant yes.

"I said, 'If Dale hurt you, move.'"

"And what did she do, April?"

Kirwan made another hearsay objection. Otero again let us go.

"Mom," April said, "raised her thumb like this"—painfully laborious but finally and decisively erect.

Then June stopped talking. She got worse and worse, until she gave out. April told the ICU like it was, the bright white light, the helplessness. The high-tech place of terror and loss.

When Kevin Kirwan's turn came he went not to the podium but center stage. He smiled kindly toward April, with a minute bow. "Ms. Mooney, forgive the few questions I'm obliged to put to you." Next to the easel with a quick step, almost a skip.

"Fucking pantywaist," Paige muttered to me.

"Where were you"—Kirwan smiled—"the night before your mother's death?"

"In bed."

Kirwan drew it. "Where was the bed?"

"In Colfax hospital."

"In your mother's room? Next to your mother's bed? Maybe six feet away?"

"Objection. Compound." Paige hoping to clutter the performance.

"Sustained. Break it down, Mr. Kirwan."

He smiled apologetically at the jury, mini-bowed to the judge, asked the same questions one at a time as he drew a second bed with the number six between them, circling them in red and writing December 13 at the top, hands expressive as hula as he went between April and the easel.

"What happened that night?" Kirwan asked.

April hesitated in a way likely to be misinterpreted, then replied, "I'm not sure."

"What do you think happened?"

"Objection. Calls for speculation."

"Sustained." We won but it looked like we wanted something kept from the jury.

"You notice anything?"

"No."

"Why?"

"I was asleep, Mr. Kirwan."

"*Sleeping?*" He wrote in blue under the circle. "All night?"

"Yeah."

"And the next morning, how was your mom the next morning?"

"I don't know."

"Well, was she in bed?" He made an *X* on the bed drawing.

"Yeah." Sounding a little sullen.

"She was in a bad way, wasn't she?"

"I guess."

He wrote *Guess?* under *Sleeping?* "A terrible way?"

"Yeah."

"What did you do?"

"Got up and went over for some tea."

"But what about your mom, April?"

"I didn't know." He wrote: *Didn't know?*

"How long were you over having tea?"

"I don't know."

He did a three-sixty, opened his hands. "Until after the ambulance left?"

"Yeah."

Teacup and ambulance cartoons, and a bold double line between them.

Kirwan went next to DNR and *no cor,* flashing the records on the projector, looping each entry in orange, softly incredulous at April's denials.

Now, April, he said. You dropped out of college to be with your mom. You moved in with her at the hospital. Spent every day and night with your mom her last two months. Saw every detail of her daily routine.

Your mother was your hero, wasn't she? Strong, independent, courageous. She helped others, and now she was helpless. Now weak and dependent. She was not the same person. She was never coming back. Hers wasn't a life. It was a living torture. Paige objecting to stop the flow, but Kirwan hurtling forward, overwhelming April's resistance. She tearfully agreed to most of what he said.

A picture of a young woman burdened with an unbearable tragedy was emerging. Kirwan's strategy was becoming clear. The more sympathetic April seemed, the more profoundly she cared for June, and the more distraught she was at her suffering, the more credible his euthanasia defense. So Kirwan forwent the customary ridicule of the plaintiff. He treated April paternally, almost as *his* client, almost as his daughter, wanting these eight mothers to feel for her, to see her as having done what they might want done in such straits. Having a loving daughter's courage to let her mother go.

A jury of mothers, then, might serve Kirwan's plan. Jurors who could believe April ended June's suffering and could forgive her for it. And, Kirwan hoped, lose sight of Stillwell in the process.

"Ms. Mooney," Kirwan said in a concerned way, "who is Elliot Stone?"

"You know, he's my lawyer here." The jury had yet to hear from me.

"Point him out if you would."

She did.

"Elliot Stone." He gave my name an Englishman's lilt. "Elliot Stone was also your mother's court-appointed conservator and guardian? Guardian of her welfare?" He wrote it at the easel.

"Yeah."

Elliot Stone had been a lawyer in Holland, Kirwan said. What did April know about euthanasia in Holland? Mercy killing? He circled it.

April didn't know much.

"After your mother's death, her guardian, Elliot Stone, asked you to authorize an autopsy, didn't he?"

"Not—really."

"He wanted the cremation stopped."

"Yeah."

"You did not want the cremation stopped so an autopsy could be conducted."

"No. We wanted—a service."

"Cremation?"

"Yeah."

"And no autopsy to find the cause of death?"

She could have spelled out, here, or on redirect, that she thought an autopsy would be pointless after organ harvest, but we'd told her not to play that card until rebuttal. Questionable counsel, I wondered now.

Kirwan next stopped in pretended disarray. He put a finger to his lips, shuffled through some papers, conferred with Hancock and a paralegal, eventually produced a document,

Defendant's Exhibit A, which he handed to April. He put a transparency on the ELMO projector.

"Objection," Paige said sourly. "Request for sidebar outside the jury's presence." The curious mothers were escorted out. Paige, Kirwan, and I went and hung on the bench.

"Your Honor," Paige said, *"Dunbar versus Burkhardt* allows evidence of having invoked the Fifth Amendment only when that in fact was done. Ms. Mooney never formally invoked the privilege. Unlike the defendant, she waived the privilege, on the record in deposition. An earlier intention to do otherwise doesn't come close to meeting the *Dunbar* standard. This evidence is far more prejudicial than probative under Rule 403."

"Ms. Jorritsma," Kirwan argued next, "wants to have her cake and eat it. She wants unilateral prejudice, just against us. She intends to cross-examine my client about his taking the Fifth but shield her client from a like cross-examination when both maintained exactly the same position before the district attorney, and both benefited. The grand jury has heard from neither one. This document speaks for itself as the jury will understand."

The issue had been earlier raised in chambers but deferred to now. Otero looked pained, his soft spot showing. "I know that however I rule, the other side will appeal. I appreciate Ms. Mooney's courage in waiving and testifying, but you can bring that out, Ms. Jorritsma."

He was a father too, I thought. He saw the equities were all with April. He thought we were going to win so he was going to rule against us. To deny Stillwell an appeal point; to protect us, and him, from a reversal. Chickenshit, as Paige had put it.

"Objection overruled. Defendant's Exhibit A will be admitted. Bring in the jury."

Kirwan's cross ended with an ELMO projection of the notice of intent I'd filed.

"When the grand jury investigating your mother's death wanted to question you about it, you had Elliot Stone send this notice."

"Yeah."

"You intended not to answer questions about June Stillwell's death?"

"Yeah, I guess. Then."

"Because"—now Kirwan's voice dropped to intimate, hardly audible decibels—"because your testimony may tend—to incriminate you?"

He wrote it diagonally across a fresh sheet of paper—*INCRIM-INATE*—and circled the word in red, concentric loops.

"Yeah, but it wouldn't have, but I guess I had to. Elliot—"

"Objection," Paige said. "Privileged."

"Sustained."

"This Elliot was . . ." Kirwan began. I braced for the theatrical use of my name. "Elliot Stone, correct?"

"Yeah." April sighed. "Correct."

"How bad was it?" April wondered, arriving back at my place. The Pis had been restored to his sentry, a yellow Exhibit 17 marker on his butt. The silverbills were silenced for the night by the blanket over their cage.

We convened a tactics session around my patio table. The long June gloaming would last until nine. Bats schooled and shoaled for insects rising from the weedy stream and fishpond. In the dream-blue air above them, nighthawks did the same. Phlox blossoms floated and waved like fireflies in the shadows. From next door came the sweet strains of Mahler's *Song of the Earth.*

"You were wonderful," Paige said heartily.

"Otero thinks we're going to win," I emphasized.

"That's why he screwed us," added Paige.

On redirect Paige cleaned April up pretty well, pointing out the protests of innocence in the notice, that, with the target letter, April had no choice, and that she'd waived Fifth Amendment protections nonetheless. Still, it was a cynical postimpeachment world. What did the mothers think of the daughter plaintiff now that she'd been branded with *incriminate*?

Quierin stood apart, kicking at the unmown grass like a bull. "There's too many trees in the forest," she said. "April is not what we need to be worrying about."

"One thing anyway," I said. "We get rebuttal." The defense had put cause of death in play. After we finished our case in chief, and the defense presented theirs, the judge should allow us to rebut any evidence they'd introduced of a mercy killing. "Once the jury hears Gillian"—Gillian Maclean, the allograft tech at the transplant bank—"they'll know April wasn't covering anything up."

"Some rebuttal." Paige sighed. "Poison rebuts our case too."

"This," Quierin said, "is the big fish in the frying pan I'm talking about."

"I don't think they know about the bad stuff." How we would refer to phenol, the missing specimens, starvation rations. "Not any of it. And I don't think they have any direct evidence on April, or we'd have heard about it. It's all circumstantial."

"You mean, like our case against Stillwell?" Paige gave me a constricted smile.

I took her point. Kirwan's tactic was to play our game, mimic us. Every time we talked about July 1998, when June was bludgeoned while Stillwell was there all night long, he'd talk about December 1998, when June succumbed while April was there all night long. Discrediting the defense's circumstantial proof implicitly discredited our own. The jury might split the difference and say nobody had proved anything.

"Sandbag Kirwan on rebuttal with June's poisoning," Paige said, "where does that take us?"

"If it's Queen City Trust, it takes us to a mistrial, then retrial against Stillwell and Colfax as codefendants. Not so bad."

"If?" Paige rolled her eyes. "We need to *know.*"

"So—all in all"—April looked at us in turn—"pretty bad?"

I suggested a round of O'Doul's.

"Stop doodling, Elliot." Quierin ceased stamping and banged into the kitchen, emerging with a bottle of kosher pear brandy instead, closest rotgut she'd found to *rakija.* She took a slug off the top and passed it to me. "You need action now, man."

The brandy made it around.

"I visit Jasmine today. I let her in on phenol. Know what she is saying? Not April. Not Colfax either. Nobody at Colfax. Know why?" Querin issued a challenging look. No takers. "Anybody at Colfax waits one day so stomach fluid isn't sampled. Has to be somebody outside who was there just that day and has to do it then."

"Yes," Paige said, thinking of her favorite defendant.

"Or else," I said, "Colfax can't wait even one more day."

"Hah." Quierin handed me the bottle. "Just playing guesses is spinning our tires."

"Who the—" April scooted back, half standing. Above the wooden gate behind me, a face, not Stillwell's. Rising licks of thin blond hair: my neighbor to the east. I opened the gate, revealing him in a velour robe, ungirdled, black Slim Boy briefs cinching a pink paunch, a glass of Scotch in hand.

"Yes?"

"I knocked," he said defensively, ambling in. "No one came."

"What is it?"

"I heard the ladies," he whispered to me. "You should know—I'm here. Just in case."

"Why," I whispered back, "should I know that?"

"Reports. Around the neighborhood. A peeper apparently."

Was he talking about himself? "I see." I led him out by the elbow. April was jumpy enough as it was. I pointed him toward his house.

He sighed, hand on hip, thumb in thong. "Perverts. Everywhere you go. Republicans are the worst."

"Thanks, buddy. Keep an eye out." Exhibitionists make good sentinels. They know how to see and be seen.

"That's what neighbors are for, man."

Back in the yard, Paige and April had gone indoors. Quierin lay spread-eagle on her back in the grass, watching bats and nighthawks execute maneuvers, two planet pinholes in the canopy. "The wild blue yonder," she said. "I love that word. The *yonder.*"

I lay beside her and watched the bats and birds. "Sky over Kosovo."

"No more off the radar, Elliot. We're about to lose. We have to take it to them."

"Take what to whom?"

She pitched to an elbow and seized my hand. "You have to talk the talk, Elliot. Walk it. Now is the moment."

"You mean follow my calling. I love you."

"Elliot, you donkey. There isn't time."

"I've been wondering about that." I rolled back to watch the aerial array. "I can't jump down Whitelaw's throat unless Hans gives me the go-ahead. When he does, I'm taking Bow Wow."

"Ask him."

"Hans says he wants to help solve it."

"Yah. He twice says to me that. So let's do it."

"What about you? What are you up to?"

"I think, attack from the rear. Don't get naughty ideas."

She slid a long Indo-Dutch leg across my lap and planted a knee on the other side. She pressed my shoulders down in the quilt of grass, the yielding earth, and found my lips. She eclipsed the spectacle of the sky.

CHAPTER 4

Next morning, same drill. Lawyer setup, par-
ties to the tables, staff on the bridge, captain to the poop deck—
black-robed Otero gravely assuming the bench, opening his
black laptop. Unusually for a trial judge, Otero didn't horse
around. He resisted Kirwan's banter. He looked preoccupied,
maybe a little depressed.

The jurors had conferred on matters of fashion. It was dress-
down Tuesday—cotton slacks and some denim, bright blouses,
two knit T's. They were rolling up their sleeves.

April, in a flowered blouse and black linen jacket, looked
resilient and unimpeached. Quierin was out somewhere
attacking from the rear. Paige and I planned to alternate witnesses and finish up our liability proof on Wednesday afternoon with Stillwell, a surprise call to maximize jitters, throw
him off his script and maybe provoke rash behavior. We would
underscore the contrast between his still hiding behind the
Fifth and April's waiving it before trial began. Crossing fingers, he might win it for us with ten seconds of rage. Blurt out
the djinni's message.

I took the first two witnesses, an EMT, then Officer McNally.
I introduced the 911 tape with Stillwell's flat affect—"My wife
is bleeding. I think she fell." Next, the ambulance report: severe
traumatic eye and head injury, 3 on the Glasgow Coma Scale.

The blood-matted blankets Stillwell had covered her with. Police photos of blood collected like a Rorschach at the depression in the bedding, of the bucket of tools under the sink, the gap in the figurines on the black marble mantel, close-ups of the pattern of dust.

McNally was an entirely plausible cop. No doughnut pusher, he took pride in appearance—buffed up in a tight blue uniform, a modified mullet he ran his fingers through at breaks in the action. He detailed the crime-scene investigation. No blood found except on the bedding and blankets. No sign of a break-in. Nothing missing but the one figurine. He described taking dimensions by caliper and transposing them to grid paper to create the diagram of the figurine's base. He recounted what Stillwell said, that they'd watched TV, slept together. An ordinary night. Nothing unusual in the morning.

Bernie Edson cross-examined. Kirwan scribbled questions on Post-its and passed them up to his partner. Unlike Kirwan, Edson never left the podium, though it seemed a spot he didn't much like, like a mutt chained to his house. He gripped and rocked it, jiggled a leg, hiked one foot to the bar, then the other, declaiming questions in compound clauses. Bernie has a quirky, twitchy smile, not pleasant. More like a subdued snarl, flashed teeth, then quickly drawn lips to pass it off as smiling. Twitching exaggerated the skinhead effect. I imagined a rubber face pulled over the creature or workings inside.

The EMT agreed with him that June was stable when he arrived. No immediate life threat. That the front door was unlocked when he got there. McNally conceded he couldn't find a "weapon." He detailed their exhaustive search. Bernie then asked about Stillwell's mental deficits.

"Objection." I stood. "Irrelevant under the *in limine* ruling."

"Goes to the reliability of statements to the police."

"Overruled," Otero said. Another one for the defense. Another sign he thought we'd win.

"No harm done," Paige concluded over lunch at La Placenta.

Back in court she announced Doreen Ray, the probate clerk, who testified to what we both had overheard three years earlier, Stillwell's mutterings about killing June. Kirwan didn't bother to cross. Jessica Jones came next. Two and a half years of milk drops and for the first time the carport light was off and a note left changing the order. The note was introduced. Fifteen-minute witness. Short and sweet.

"How did you first hear about June Stillwell?" Kirwan asked her, dancing to his easel. "The police?"

"It was April told me about her mom."

"April? Rather than the police? April Mooney—the plaintiff?" He circled the name.

"Right."

"She told you, didn't she, that her mother's husband beat her."

"Right."

"April Mooney tracked you down to tell you Dale Stillwell beat his wife."

"Objection."

"Sustained. Move on, Mr. Kirwan."

"I'm done, Your Honor." He beamed.

The Mole Hole proprietor went over well. The Pis was admitted as a trial exhibit. The cross-examination was roughly the same, *April*s decorating the butcher paper.

The portly blood-spatter expert was our pro. His testimony began Tuesday and went all Wednesday morning. On Power-Point he illustrated the dynamics of blunt-force trauma. With simulations of June's face he drove home the bell-shaped wound, the appearance of a beveled edge, the angle of impact. The crusting and viscosity of blood showed hours had passed before the EMTs arrived. The pooling of blood to the depression under June's head and the absence of blood elsewhere proved she had been struck in bed and didn't move afterward, and that no one else was in the bed from that point forward. The force of the blow was such it likely came overhand, from a standing position. Like swinging an ax.

The base of the Exhibit 17 Pis was shown a perfect match for the Exhibit 11 diagram of the base of the missing figurine, as well as the configuration of June's wound. All three Power-Point images merged into one irregular oval, outlined in high-visibility orange. The Pis, or one just like it, was, in the expert opinion of our blood-spatter man, the object used in the attack.

Edson began his cross: "What is a red herring, Professor? What does whatever happened July 15 have to do with the chain of events on December 13 that took June Stillwell's life?"

Pro though he was, our man couldn't say.

Detective Carlos Roybal, Charlie, the next scheduled witness, joined us at La Placenta. We debated dropping him. Too close to April. Kirwan could make it look as if she were influencing the police. Paige wound up calling him just for the hammer and the chain of custody of the point of white powder. Predictably, on cross Kirwan went straight to April.

"Beyond the scope of direct," Paige objected.

"Overruled." Another defense tilt. The next hour was all April, in Roybal's patrol car, at the evidence locker, at lunch, then a dinner at the Greenbrier, a snowboarding weekend in Steamboat.

The late break came, and Paige, April, and I exchanged glances. It was time for Stillwell. April nodded affirmatively and took a bladder break. Stillwell was acting pretty strung out, never meeting April's glare, running for Cokes whenever he could. Hancock stopped trying to be his buddy. Kirwan and Edson left him alone. At lunch I'd seen him pacing the reception area, popping a pill, chugging his pop.

At the back of the courtroom April now returned with Quierin. They whispered at the far bench. Quierin left again and April came to us. "Put Stillwell on hold. Put on the chemist instead." The powder analyst from the Colorado Bureau of Investigation, cooling his heels in the hall. "Quierin's on to something."

The chemist made sense here to bring the story full circle. I put him through his qualifications, his thousands of cases, how the microanalysis was done, the minute error rate. I held the hammer in my right hand, the Pis in my left. "Assume someone pounded this figurine into smithereens with this hammer." I acted it out. "Would that be consistent with your findings?"

He turned to the jury and explained in detail how his powder analyses could lead to no other reasonable conclusion. The mothers were enthralled. They saw this witness as climactic, the missing weapon fully explained. It was a good call, ditching

Stillwell for now, avoiding his unpredictability, but my thoughts were elsewhere. Quierin was on to something. It had to be good.

"'Bout time we caught a break," I said after Otero adjourned us.

Paige and April gave me the look—hopeless retro-chauvinist shoat.

"Surfers catch breaks," April informed me. "The Q creates them."

The homeless shelter staff had begged off talking with April or me the year before. Stillwell allies. Quierin, April said at the Wednesday tactics session, tracked down shelter board members on the Internet and started calling. One, a schoolteacher, agreed to meet. She'd often helped hash and hand out blankets while Stillwell was there. He'd been a model volunteer, but more important, he connected with those guys. They'd all had raw runs of luck like him. Some had the same kinds of problems, mental, emotional. Some were in and out of the post–traumatic stress ward at the Denver VA, and Stillwell related.

Then maybe fall 1997, the teacher started seeing a different Dale Stillwell. Sometimes he was normal. Sometimes he didn't know where he was. He might not hear when you spoke to him. He might be jumpy, panicky. He had a hair-trigger.

That year at Christmas, the anniversary of the accident, at the holiday fund-raiser, a $500 dinner of chicken soup, broccoli, and a roll, Stillwell just—checked out. No one knew why. He just walked off from the steam table and out the door. The teacher asked Stillwell's pal Darwin to stop him, but Stillwell kept walking. Left his car behind. The last time the teacher ever saw Dale Stillwell, he was headed down Broadway on a bitter night with a ladle in his hand.

"Where Quierin is now," April told us in my backyard, "is looking for Darwin. What do you think?"

"More bad evidence," Paige said. "You guys have a talent for it."

"This could be the guy we've wanted," I said. "Someone who knows about the missing year."

"Where's Quierin looking?"

"She thought she'd try first along the creek."

The bats had long dispersed. Robins sounded the colors from treetops and chimneys, and the air was still and chill. The neighborhood-watch naturist patrolled the perimeter. Quierin shouldn't have gone alone.

Paige and I worked up the next day's examination outlines. Except for Stillwell and a cameo turn by Darla, we were through with liability and about to head into the other two components of a wrongful-death trial—damages and cause of death. The medical witnesses were the tricky part. We agreed to drop Arcenault. "Too risky," Paige said. "He might say something unexplained happened to end June's life." We decided to prove up June's day of death just through the hospital chart authenticated by a Platte Valley records custodian and deny Kirwan his Arcenault cross.

"Kirwan's making me nervous," I said. "He may be pulling a Willy Mays." Say Hey Willy sometimes deliberately struck out early in a game to draw the same pitches at a later at-bat, having fooled the pitcher into thinking he couldn't hit them.

"You mean Kirwan's pretending not to know about the bad stuff?"

"Possible. So we get careless, open up the bad stuff with the medical witnesses, and he blasts it out of the park. 'What is phenol, Dr. Silverman? Where at Colfax is it kept? Would April Mooney have access?'"

"Paranoia."

"With Kirwan it pays."

The sky cooled to navy, pinholes everywhere. The temperature hit light-fleece level. No Quierin. Inside, the phone rang. Hans, returning the message I had left yesterday with his assistant. "I want to confront Whitelaw," I said, "but I don't want to blow your cover."

"Don't do it, Elliot, but not on account of me. As I said, these are not nice people."

From my study I then saw the front doorknob turning, the door swinging in. A bearish figure in a blue-jean vest, Charlie Manson hair and beard, a taut rope in a meaty hand.

"Hans, I have your permission?"

"Yes, but—"

I rang off. At the end of the rope was a small dog. A pug, like Stillwell's.

"Elliot." Quierin now tucked inside the door. "Meet Darwin."

Before court Thursday morning I left a message for Rico with his mom: loan me Bow Wow this weekend. I put Millsap off again till Monday. We deferred calling Stillwell until after the weekend and led with our damages witnesses.

With a familiar fascination I watched Dale Stillwell as court was declared in session. The unconvincing composure, the cosmic distrust, the defiance and resignation that warred in his eyes, all of it called to mind proud, young Yugoslavs who'd done awful things for inexplicable reasons. Many of our detainees possessed heroic qualities—physical courage, loyalty, love of family, ardor, self-sacrifice. Yielding a point to Leitner, most weren't monsters. Some were almost like us.

Stillwell possessed such qualities too. Darwin had told us Stillwell was the reason he was still alive.

Thursday's testimony began with Jasmine Toombs, our only Colfax witness. I conned the gallery for Whitelaw. Not yet. Jaz explained her training and certificate, what Colfax was, what occupational therapists do.

"Not to be confused with vocational counseling?" Paige asked.

"At Colfax our average Rancho is under two. We ain't sending out any résumés."

Paige handed Jasmine a copy of June's Colfax chart. Jaz authenticated it and it was received in evidence. Referring to chart entries, she explained June's levels of consciousness, the baby steps by which she'd improved, her learning to speak, her hand signals, the torture of physical therapy, the tears when April departed.

Everything was double-edged. As June was shown to be emerging from coma, euthanasia would seem less likely, and pain and suffering damages went up with consciousness. But head injury would look more remote as the cause of death. Jasmine ended with the crisis that morning, my yelling for her. Jaz calling the ambulance.

Bernie Edson cross-examined. If he knew any bad stuff, it could come out now. But Bernie stuck to his head-bobbing knee hammer, his April refrain. For which Jaz was ready.

"Yes, Mr.—what's your name? Edsel? April was there most of the time, that's correct. It was April taught June to talk. Taught her to swallow. It was April bringing June back. Never seen such in a Colfax relative, how bad that girl wanted her mama to get up and walk on away."

"April was saddened by her mother's condition?" Bernie twitched—the snarly smile.

"Excited by her progress, Mr. Edsel. Full of hope she was."

The other damages witnesses went just as well. The Western Pacific yardmaster on the accident and June's skills and pay grade. The director of the riding center. Special Olympian Anna, weaving on braces to the witness box, with whom the jury fell in love.

Anna declined the bailiff's offer of help. She settled in the chair, clacked and stowed the braces, and smiled with candle-power that lit up the room. I handed her a display case of her show ribbons. She proudly held it overhead. She unstrung her gold medal and gave it to me for the jury to feel and see. She attributed everything to June.

"June taught me to believe in myself. I can be a winner, June kept saying. I can do anything in life." Haltingly spoken, moth-ers in tears. "June was the best coach in the whole world."

But even Anna was double-edged. The more compelling June's loss, the more understandable ending her suffering.

We kicked the economist over to the second week and went home to work on Friday's tricky medical testimony. Quierin debriefed Darwin over *tjap tjoy*—Indo-Dutch chop suey—and fried bananas, *pisang goreng;* soup bones for the pug. He's a pug, Darwin said, but I call him the beagle. It looked like I'd acquired houseguests.

Darwin had been pinned in a foxhole for a month thirty years earlier at the siege of Con Thien. A marine rifleman in a line unit, raked with artillery, rockets, mortar, hundreds of rounds a day, no sleep, no one to shoot back at, glued in his hole waist-high in brown water reddening from emersion foot. Half the battalion was already shell-shocked by the con-stant NVA incoming, when a twelve-foot rocket hit next to

Darwin's hole. He crawled out and staggered off bleeding at the ears and mouth. Medevacked to base and never again the same.

In Boulder nobody knew combat PTSD like Dale. Dale showed Darwin you could live with it. "Keep your mind in your head." Then Dale went off. "Survival of the fittest," Darwin said. Mirthless chuckle. Bitter old joke.

CHAPTER 5

Trials can have moments of truth and *Mooney v. Stillwell* was no exception. As foretold, the moment came unwarned and unbidden, at the close of the last day of the first week, a name called from a dream.

Each day the jurors looked increasingly relaxed. By Friday they were citizens on routine assignment and ready for weekend liberty, presuming they'd mastered the issues, blind to the bafflement and dissension that roiled the plaintiff's ranks. They'd bonded to Anna, connected to our case. I ventured the speculation we'd convinced them of Stillwell's culpability. Paige agreed. But this case will turn on causation, she reminded me. Like many wrongful deaths, only more so. Today's a tightrope walk, though we're sure to draw out the defense.

Dr. Richard Longacre, our nontreating brain-injury expert, made a practiced line for the gate and box and affirmed the oath with suitable sobriety. He had a marathoner's gait and build and rock-steady carriage in the chair. I asked if he was prepared to describe for the jurors the mechanisms and sequelae of traumatic brain injury, and I inquired into his qualifications to do so: one Cornell and two Harvards, a five-year residency at Duke, NIH fellowship, president of the Colorado Head Injury Foundation, adviser to the James and Sarah Brady Institute for Traumatic Brain Injury, twenty-year medical director of Craigmile

Rehabilitation Hospital, lead editor of the treatise *Organic Brain Syndromes*. A quasi–Dr. God. I'd let his fingers inside my brainpan.

"What is coma, Dr. Longacre?"

"Unconsciousness," he said, "that persists. In Greek, *koma* means 'deep sleep.' A sleep from which one does not waken."

"What is it that regulates consciousness, that lets us waken from sleep?"

"May I?" Dr. Longacre pointed to Kirwan's easel.

"Please."

With a blue Kirwan marker he drew a crude brain inside a skull and a red spot at the brain stem he marked RAF, for the reticular activating formation. "The light switch that turns consciousness on and off," he said. "The brain stem is fixed at the base of the skull, but the rest of the brain can shift inside the skull and partly rotate. A sudden, violent blow to the head can twist the brain stem like a washcloth, which is what happened to Ms. Stillwell. The only injury was to the RAF. Her cortex was left fully functional but unable to function because the switch turned off."

"Fully functional? Not a vegetable, then?"

"Not at all. Coma does not mean brain death. In coma the ability to respond and function is profoundly impaired, but some level of awareness often persists. Sometimes a fairly high level. Some of the comatose are acutely aware of their misfortune, their surroundings, the grim events of their daily lives. Helpless is a better way to see them."

June, he went on, had suffered a small, focal brain-stem injury leaving her unable to rouse, but to some extent sentient, and for a while increasingly so. The injury was not operable, but she was far from a hopeless case. Indeed, she was gradually emerging as the injury healed and the benefits of daily stimulation accumulated. The most useful stimulation, Dr. Longacre thought, was not June's routine therapy, but persistent positive interaction with her daughter.

This kind of progress, however, is always halting and fraught with risk. June took a turn for the worse and suffered respiratory arrest, a complication that can sometimes happen.

"Even in the best hospitals?"

"Even in Craigmile. Sudden death is a painful fact of long-term care in the brain-injury ward."

"Summarize, if you would, Dr. Longacre, June Stillwell's injury and subsequent course."

"She took a vicious blow to the head, suffered five months, and eventually died. Throughout those months, more probably than not, she underwent physical agony and emotional torment, longing to respond to loved ones, but unable."

"No more questions. Thank you."

Longacre's fluid assurance sounded great, but I knew Hans Leitner could pick apart testimony like this with an arm behind his back. If he was helping the defense, we were in next for a rough go.

I checked the gallery. Sure enough, Leitner sat in an open white dress shirt rolled to the elbows, way over on Stillwell's side, excepted from the sequestration order as Stillwell's doctor. Was he moral and medical support for the defendant, or a member of the defense litigation team? His first visit to the proceedings, as far as I knew. Not, I hoped, for the purpose of destroying our causation case.

Leitner saw me, flicked a two-finger wave. I nodded in reply.

Kevin Kirwan strutted into the well of the court as if he owned it, matador in the *plaza de toros*. Hancock and a paralegal managed an oversize X-ray lightbox through the gate and set it up three feet from the jury. Kirwan invited Longacre down and handed him a laser pointer. He offered his trademark executive smile: Not to worry. I'm in control.

Otero and I circled behind the jurors to watch. The bailiff cut the lights.

"The first injury, Doctor, in July. Show us where it was on MRI."

Longacre pulled films from an envelope, skipped through and found one, snapped it under the lightbox frame and turned on the light. The dancing red point of the laser circled around a small, white oval. "Right there, at the RAF."

"And describe the appearance of the rest of the brain on these images." He did. Healthy tissue.

"Now, Doctor, look at these films from *December*, five months later. Show us the areas of injury."

The red laser danced here then there. "The injuries are massive and diffuse—everywhere." Spreading white tracts of damaged tissue all of us could see.

"A terrible change, was there not, from July to December?"

"Yes."

"An entirely new brain injury."

"Yes."

"Much worse than the first."

"Obviously."

"Something awful happened to cause this different massive injury."

"Anoxia caused it. Oxygen was cut off to the brain due to respiratory arrest. Stopping breathing."

"The *July* injury, that one little spot, that wasn't severe enough to kill, was it?"

"Objection. Misleading."

"Overruled."

"No."

"Nor to cause sudden death, stopping breathing, five months later."

"By itself, no, the injury didn't produce delayed respiratory arrest."

"Thank you, Doctor. Return to your seat."

Longacre mounted the witness box, sat, and rebuttoned his jacket. Hancock and the paralegal carted the lightbox off and Kirwan skipped to his easel. A couple of juror buttercups began to flicker.

"Now, Doctor, let's be clear. June Stillwell was not your patient."

"No."

"You never treated her."

"No."

"You've never even seen her." Kirwan wrote it. *Never seen her.*

"No."

"You would defer to the superior knowledge of a physician who actually observed Ms. Stillwell's condition over several months."

"In some matters, yes."

"She was a patient at Colfax hospital?"

"Yes."

"Colfax and Craigmile hospitals are very different places, aren't they?"

"Certainly."

"Craigmile is the premier brain-injury unit in twelve states."

"It has a good reputation."

"Unlike Colfax."

"I don't know."

"Where anything can happen."

"Anything can happen anywhere."

Kirwan wrote it—ANYTHING CAN HAPPEN ANY-WHERE—and circled it in red.

On redirect I asked Longacre to explain how the two injuries could relate. Traumatic brain injury producing coma, he said, puts a patient at risk for a host of complications such as infection, pneumonia, aspiration, ARDS, which can progress to respiratory arrest, anoxia, massive brain damage, and death.

Kirwan got a last shot, recross. He paced in a measured arc, a dead-serious stare-down of the cornered witness. He stopped short and smiled—the flare and flourish of a cape. He formulated a word—"What"—shaping it with scoops of his hands. "What—" His sword thrust. "*What* was the complication, Doctor? *What was it?*"

Kirwan then drifted to rest, stock-still at the easel, marker held at the ready, waiting.

Longacre watched him. "We don't know."

"You don't know, you mean."

"No I don't. That's right."

At lunch April wondered again: How bad?

"No home run," Paige said.

"Texas leaguer, but he's safe at first."

As happened at trial eateries, I'd found and stuck with a reliable dish, La Placenta veggie burrito. Fewer mystery meats, less postprandial distress. "More interesting is what Kirwan didn't ask."

"I caught one of them smiling on cross," Paige said. "The big gal in orange pants."

"Ms. Mullen? Morton?" We still didn't know their names.

"Not good when they find your guru amusing."

"Did you see Bernie's tie?" April asked.

"Yeah." Black with bright yellow oblongs.

"They're Tweety Birds."

"That's disgusting." Paige referred to her tamale.

"Flaming coot thinks he's cool," I observed.

"Kirwan's buzz cut," April said. "Take a good look. I think he rubs a little henna in."

"God," Paige said, "I'd like to ram it up those boys."

"They may be better trial lawyers," I said, "but we have more hair."

"We have great hair," Paige agreed. "Look at April. Look at Otero. For a judge, he's pretty hairy. We're going to win this thing."

April pulled and released her coils. "Who's next?" she wondered. She set a partial plate of taco salad on a neighboring table.

"The anti-Longacre." Paige sighed. "Silverman. An unfortunate juxtaposition." And a witness Paige could have to herself. "I'm hoping for a bunt."

We entered the courtroom just in front of Ivan Silverman and Arnold Whitelaw. They took a seat together at Whitelaw's usual perch directly behind me, a study in contrasts: short versus tall; rumpled secondhand brown versus sleek Zegna gray; receding gray stubble versus swooping waves of silver locks. I could feel Whitelaw's sunken eyes at the back of my neck.

When he reached the gate, the witness didn't know where to go. Judge Otero pointed to the box. Silverman clumsily climbed in and was sworn.

My Post-it read, "Make it fast." Paige did.

Silverman's qualifications included med school in Leningrad, as it was then known, emigration with the Soviet collapse, the license-reciprocity process, his solo internal-medicine practice, Colfax.

"Why, Dr. Silverman, is medical care for the poor important to you professionally?"

A softball. Silverman missed.

"I'm not so busy. I can come to Colfax when maybe others can't." As he spoke, he watched his scuffed brogans.

"Describe June Stillwell's course at Colfax Rehab."

He consulted Exhibit 24, the chart. "She was getting better, seemed healthy. Then the coma went deep again. That happens with comas, up and down. Then, unfortunately, she died. Comas are at high risk for complications." A small, inappropriate smile.

Paige handed him Exhibit 29, the death certificate, and projected the transparency on the screen.

"What did you determine was the cause of your patient's death?"

"Cardiopulmonary arrest was the immediate cause. The underlying cause was blunt-force head trauma producing severe brain injury."

"What did you determine was the manner of death?"

"Homicide."

"Where was the place of injury, the act of homicide?"

"At Mrs. Stillwell's home."

"And when?"

"July fifteenth, 1998."

"Five months before she finally died?"

"Yes. Roughly five months earlier."

Bernie Edson crossed. I couldn't stop looking at the Tweety Birds.

"Complications? You said something about complications."

"Yes."

"Did complications of her coma cause cardiopulmonary arrest?"

"Yes."

"What complications?"

"It could be—"

"You don't know?"

"There are many. The comatose are prone to infection, pneumonia, heart disease. Some have respiratory illnesses, some DVT, some aspirate and choke since they cannot swallow." Again, a shallow smile.

"I'm not asking about the comatose, Doctor, but June Stillwell. What caused *her* to suddenly die?"

"Maybe aspirated vomitus. Gastric contents."

"Maybe? You don't know?"

"Not definitively." He sagged in the chair.

"So you're guessing."

"Aspiration, I think."

"You think, but you don't know."

"Yes." The sag became a droop. "I think."

"You were her doctor."

"Yes."

"But you don't know her cause of death."

"I—no, as I say. We specifically don't."

"And this"—Edson waved the death certificate—"is what you thought. What you guessed. But you don't know."

He shrugged. "No."

Edson tossed it. It fluttered to our tabletop.

"Do you remember April Mooney? This young lady here?"

"Yes."

"Family members can be helpful to you?"

"Yes."

"And they can get in the way of good medical care."

"Sometimes."

"How was April?"

He shrugged again.

"Did she interfere, Dr. Silverman, with your medical care and treatment of her mother?"

He hitched a shoulder. "Not always."

Edson left it there. No redirect by Paige. Get Dr. Quackov the hell out of here. I composed another Post-it: "We got sandpapered but Hans isn't helping them." Nothing on the labs, albumin and cholesterol, malnutrition. Nothing on the other suspicious deaths. Silverman was their last chance to get such evidence in. So they didn't know about the bad stuff. Sometimes Willy Mays struck out because he actually missed the ball.

We were out of witnesses except for the records custodian from Platte Valley sitting in the front-row bench. Silbi Randall. I called her name and she stood and turned, one profile then the other. Spikes worked to fine points, deep violet swags below startling penciled eyes, an olive military jacket and suede half-boots. UGGs. She slow-marched to the witness box, spikes vibrating, bearing the hospital chart like the Book of Books, possibly overimpressed with her role. I asked just four questions—who she was, where she worked, what her responsibilities were, and whether Exhibit 30 was a complete and accurate copy of the original hospital chart. There was no cross-examination.

Midway through her answers Silbi had tapped on her peridot nose-stud and smiled strangely. I tried to act as though nothing had happened, but the strange smile persisted, coquettish and girlish, like a suppressed giggle. Another witness to get the hell off the stand. Afterward, she was excused by the judge, but chose to stay in the courtroom and watch. I glanced behind to see if Whitelaw was still with us. He was. Silbi caught my eye again, stranger yet, rolling her head and pumping her fists as though they held maracas. I realized she wanted to speak with me.

The judge excused the jury to go over housekeeping matters with the lawyers, confirming which exhibits had been admitted. That done, he called the late-afternoon break. Paige smiled absently at Edson. "Lose the tie, Bernie." I ambled back to Silbi.

"Don't think I ever had a witness start tapping her nose-stud while testifying under oath."

"Nose for detail," she said. "Nose for trouble. Told you I'm good with faces. Names, forget it."

Faces? Names? "Tell me, Silbi."

We huddled head-to-head. "That guy in court?" She dropped an octave. "He was there that morning."

"Where?"

"Platte Valley when she died."

"Let's go outside."

We went to the far end of the courthouse lawn under a cottonwood snowing seeds, though it was eerily still. An enchanted June day.

"What guy was there? Stillwell? The defendant?"

"No, the tall, white-haired guy. I saw him head-on once I sat down in the testimony chair. He's in the crowd on a bench. That face, I say to myself, I know that face. He's a doctor, right?"

"No. He's a lawyer."

"I'm sure this guy's a doctor. I can see him like it's yesterday. Surgical scrubs, ID around his neck, but not regular staff. That face. I never saw it but that one morning."

In the unearthly stillness a gong struck. The breathless air wavered and the name rose from the dream. The track kept filling with muddy water, the lion just ahead.

"You're talking about the big man sitting over on the left. Thick white hair. White shirt, no tie."

"That's him."

I whispered it now. *"Leitner."*

"Whoever. Names, I'm lousy at."

"He is a doctor. You're right." A shade, a semblance was taking form, a shadowy outline of possible truth.

"You remember with the chart mix-up?" Silbi asked. "We were, like, running around looking, remember? I notice this doctor I've never seen in the small conference room. In greens, reading by himself. It was him."

"Reading?"

"Chart, I thought. And I thought, who's the new doc on the block? I see him again a few minutes after from my counter in Legal. Headed down the hall, same, exact guy."

"Which hall is that, Silbi?"

"The one to the lab I showed you down."

"How do you get to the drop-off for outside pickup?"

"That hall."

The air was ringing, a symphony of Leitners. "Silbi, I'm—blown away."

"The nose knows." She tapped it.

CHAPTER 6

Inside, we passed Leitner and Stillwell slow-walking the hall.

"Elliot—"

"Later." I touched my watch. In the courtroom I gave Paige a sixty-second thumbnail. April and I had to cut out. Paige would stay to handle the end-of-the-week jury-instruction conference. I thanked Silbi abjectly and asked if she'd help some more. Thrilled, she said, and she looked it.

I drove April and Silbi to Paige's. They took off in the pickup with the original chart and I went home. Quierin opened the door.

"Big day," I said. "Where've you been?"

"Out in the yonder." She gave me a welcome-back smooch and butt grab. "I'm learning a lot from Darwin, but he needs a bath." She trailed me into the bedroom, talking as I changed. "He likes my cooking. I like the beagle. I say they can stay awhile."

I suited up in shorts and a race shirt. Den Haag CPC Half Marathon '98.

"Where are you going, Elliot? You have the look."

"Going for a run."

"Doing something stupid."

"Not necessarily." I gave her a thirty-second thumbnail. "April can fill you in."

"I don't hear from you in two hours, I'm coming after. Where I should look for the body?"

For deep cover, running togs can't be beat, especially in Boulder. Runners go anywhere and no one thinks twice. To clear my head, put things in perspective, I trotted across the creek, through Eben Fine Park, and onto the Flagstaff trail.

There were hours of light left this ninth-longest day of the year. Lots of time to try to unvex the question of motive.

Mountain bluebirds sailed from my path like flying fish. Yucca spikes hedged the trail. A bull snake vanished in the buffalo grass. I stood aside for a coed in coordinated spandex, hurtling downhill, ponytail tossing, a husky panting behind her. A senior rested on a hump of granite, walking sticks x'ed at his feet. The tallgrass meadow was shoulder high. Boulderers free-climbed Monkey Crag. Wild iris speckled the chokecherry flat. From the summit the city could be seen entire, cupped in open space like the green hands of God.

As I ordered and reordered the facts, they made more and more sense, except for why. I retraced the route down the mountain, kicked left at an overlook, and shaped a way through the woods. An easy bushwhack on the needled floor, ducking boughs, until the glass slider winked through the trees. I listened. Nothing but the chitter of a squirrel. Creeping now around the perimeter, I saw movement and shrank down. A tuft of needles swaying in the foreground had made the background seem to jump. No cars, no light from inside. Seven-thirty on Friday evening. A golden opportunity to risk my law license in the hunt for motive.

The slider lock looked just as frail, the fishhook clasp in the door barely grabbing the bent staple catch in the frame. The door had a quarter inch of play. I wiggled it violently to rattle off the clasp. It held. I cocked the heel of my hand on the handle and put my shoulder into it. The door went nowhere. I pried up a two-foot flag of thin sandstone from the walk and wedged it between the frame and the handle. I gave the flag a full-body, two-handed sumo shove. The clasp pinged and the door popped open, shivering in its tracks. I jumped inside and drew the curtain to.

Such a forbidden enterprise, how could I possibly defend it?
I drifted through the gloomy talking office without conscious
intention. A period still life in Rothko purples and Munch blues.
I had no idea what I'd do when I got to where I was afraid to
think I was going. I murmured to myself words of explanation.
It's not to win the case. There were others to protect. As though
some moral oversoul demanded answers: What the hell are you
doing in here? Uncontrollable curiosity is all. Being nosy. Following my nose. The nose knows. The nose gets it. Right on the
nose.

Right under my nose.

Each step I worried less about the laws I was violating. I
became a more committed criminal.

In the shrine of self-regard his screen saver was off. Computer shut down for the weekend. A comforting sign. He had a
three-in-one fax, photocopier, printer. I idly raised the cover.
Empty glass. I sat in his high-backed chair, swiveled among
his trophies and testimonials, tried to imagine myself him.
Look through his eyes. The bookcase had some provocative
titles. *The Disposition of Toxic Chemicals in Man.* But he was
a forensic scientist, founder of the academy, and the title
belonged. Forget the computer; I wouldn't know the pass-
word. The beautiful blond cabinets beckoned. Twelve deep,
sliding drawers.

I stood and tested a pull—unlocked. I ran it out and scanned
the neat headings in a hand not his. Ellen's or Christina's. Four
inches of HHS that might include his Colfax inquiry. FDA.
VA. Clippings, which I skimmed, with subfiles labeled DHR,
Kosovo, Bosnia, Malpractice, Tort Reform. I slid another
drawer out. Journal articles, all of it, as well as two others. Two
or three feet of Pathology. The same of Forensic Medicine.
Then Organic, Psychotic, Personality. A half foot of PTSD,
another of Psycho-Pharmacology. Three drawers of patient
charts in alphabetical order. Near the back of the last, under *S,*
was Stillwell, Dale. Two drawers of Legal. Criminal was
divided into Domestic and International. Civil contained
Depositions and Case Reviews, organized by law firm. A
drawer of Research. A drawer of Committees and DHR. A
drawer of financial papers, taxes, billings, collections, invest-
ments, insurance.

I sat back down with the unhelpful thought of how outraged I'd be if someone did this to me. Then hairs began to prickle. I could care less. I weighed his mouse in my palm like a relic. I spread fingertips above the desktop as though to attract an electrostatic pulse of insight, a gathering imagined glow of almost biblical enlightenment—

Thou preparest a table before me in the presence of mine enemies—

In that instant every detail fell into place like a kaleidoscope twist that sorted scrambled fragments into the jeweled geometry of motive. I felt simultaneously stupid and brilliant, for not seeing and then for seeing it. I felt as if I'd awakened, both woozy and refreshed, from a long, confused sleep, a coma of misunderstanding.

I didn't even need to read it. I knew what was there, four feet away. Other sensations intruded. A car engine rumbling. Rumbling stopping. The melodramatic sound of a car door closing. The *fump* of an expensive sedan.

I fancied I could hear his footsteps. I considered changing seats. I stayed in his.

"Hans, hello. It's time to come to Jesus."

"I'm calling the police."

"I'll give you two reasons not to."

"Get up. Get out from behind my desk."

I'd never seen him like this, purple with agitation. I shook my head no. He turned away to gather himself. The trick now would be to make sure what I knew was four feet away didn't wind up gone.

"Want to hear the reasons?"

He swiveled back to me, level and calm. "Elliot, you've snapped. You cannot behave this way to a friend. This is— criminal trespass, breaking and entering. Burglary?" He glanced pointedly at the cabinets. One drawer—the correct one—was an inch ajar. The copier hood was still up. Inadvertent cunning.

Hans paced in front of his glory wall, hugging his elbows. "I worry so little I hardly lock the place. Damn stupid but I never expected—*this*. And *you,* of all people."

"You'll find everything where you left it." I too cast a conspicuous glance at the partly opened drawer.

"I hope I don't have to press charges. I sure as hell want an explanation."

"You won't press charges."

"Why shouldn't I?"

"Thought you'd never ask. The reasons are, one, the dead aren't dead. Two, I know the missing piece."

"Now I'm supposed to ask what the hell that means."

"Exactly."

"Tell me what the hell it means."

"June Stillwell's tissue was harvested before she was cremated. Through it, June's ghost can speak still. Like the ghost who spoke to Hamlet, who told a tale of a vial of poison, a tale that would harrow your soul. And the ghost said, Revenge me. Revenge my foul and most unnatural murder. Murder most foul."

Leitner watched me, agape.

"'Adieu, adieu! Remember me.' I'm Hamlet, Hans, and I've sworn it. A ghost has said, *Remember me.*"

I hadn't expected to see him pale, as though he too had seen the ghost of June. But I did. He sat in his visitor's armchair fingering a row of upholstery studs.

"And the missing piece? What is the missing piece? You, Hans. The missing piece is *you.*"

He made an implausibly confused face, then waved a hand to clear the air. "I wanted to talk with you this afternoon. You remember I tried to stop you at the courthouse."

"You'd decided to come to Jesus on your own? Now is a better time. You won't leave anything out since you know I know you're the missing piece. And have witnesses to prove it."

"How did it come to this, Elliot?" He rubbed the bridge between his eyes. "Trying to find evidence against *me,* for Christ's sake."

"So you want to know what the evidence is? Okay. Shortly after June was taken by ambulance to Platte Valley Hospital, you went there too. You changed into surgical greens. You wore your ID badge. You exercised your authority as a sitting member of the hospital quality-assurance committee to quickly review the chart alone in the small conference room.

You saw a sample had been drawn for analysis at Front Range Poison Center. You hotfooted it to the courier pickup and pocketed the poison center sample. Plus one last visit to Colfax to snatch the stomach-fluid specimen there. You didn't think you were seen at either place except as a doctor making the rounds."

I had his attention. He wasn't disagreeing. I pushed my luck.

"But you *were* seen. At each place people saw what you were doing and will testify about it."

"Elliot—" He had a pleading look, both worried and calculating. "Which people are you talking about?"

"There's more. The gastric lavage fluid. You hadn't been able to grab it too because the lab freezer was locked and you didn't want to ask for a key. But you knew the retention protocols. Your QA committee wrote them. I called you about *gas lav* the week June died. You never returned the call. You made sure we didn't talk until after eight weeks had passed, when you knew it had been destroyed because of the protocols your committee wrote.

"You controlled Stillwell. You made sure he didn't ask for an autopsy. You knew Silverman would never look into it. You spent months coaxing information out of me and heading me in wrong directions. Telling me I should move on.

"You got into it. You went out and stared up at the mountain and now I know why. You were thinking through a mental chess game—covering up a poisoning. With June cremated and all the stomach samples destroyed, Silverman looking the other away, Arcenault stymied, me neutralized, Paige and April caring only about Stillwell's assault, you thought you had it made. You didn't count on the transplant bank."

And to keep him off balance I added, "Or Quierin."

"It is really very remarkable." He glowered now, hurt turning to pique, since hurt wasn't working. "First you come here to accuse me of starving hospital patients to scam Medicaid funds. Now you break in with this wild story about destroying evidence, covering up murder."

"I was wrong. You're not a Medicaid scammer. I apologize."

"If this were true about some poisoning, what could possibly be my motive?"

The kaleidoscope twist. The partly open drawer.

"We know it was phenol, Hans. GC/MS ninety-eight percent match. High concentrations."

His shoulder slipped. He saw I wasn't bluffing. I skipped a beat then asked, "Everything I said is true, isn't it?"

Finally he heaved a breath—literally deflated. Diminished. His eyes rose from the floor. "Yes. But you're wrong about why."

"Why?"

"I didn't want him to hang."

"Go on."

"He told me that morning. He'd been calling all night. Filled the tape with urgent messages. I didn't want to deal with it. I put it off until the morning, and I blame myself for that. He was always getting half crazed, but I should have talked with him when he first called."

"What did he tell you?"

Leitner studied a thumb. "He was a mess. It's hard to say what he was after. Second thoughts? I wasn't hearing that. Mainly he wanted to know if it would do her in. Phenol, he didn't know the first thing about it. He told me he found a bottle somewhere in that god-awful place and put some in her feeding bag. I said she probably wouldn't make it. I knew she wouldn't. When I called Colfax, she was already in the ambulance. I tried to calm Dale down, then drove straight to Platte Valley. It was obvious she was done for."

"Was he trying to kill her? Was that his intent?"

Leitner groaned. "He knew it was some kind of poison. Turns out he told me thinking it was privileged, physician/patient, and it isn't."

"Crime-fraud exception. You have a different rule."

"Right. They can make physicians tattle if it's not strictly for treatment, and it wasn't. He wanted to know if it would work. Without the privilege, what Dale told me I can tell you, or testify to if ordered. Dale is a pretty smart guy, you know. One twenty-eight IQ. But he thinks things halfway through. He didn't care if the poison was found. I think he assumed it would be and that suspicion would fall on someone else."

"April."

"Possibly, but that's not why he did it. He couldn't take June's coma. It tortured him."

"Because he put her there."

"Well—yes, but it's more complex." He frowned and smiled. "He had to stop that Colfax nightmare. It was ending the suffering he'd created. Ending his suffering too. In his mind it freed both of them. You wouldn't believe the rationalizations that attend such acts."

"He did it to save his ass. To shift the blame to someone else."

"Dale isn't that—linear. He's an interesting man."

"Hans, what about you? What in God's name were you doing?"

"I knew phenol would be found and that even Tucker would prosecute a phenol poisoning. If it was blamed on someone else—that's worst of all."

"You're not telling me you covered up the poisoning to shield April?"

"No. Self-interest was part of it. If someone else was charged, April, Colfax, June's nurse, that guy Rico, whoever—think of the bind I'm in. Dale had confessed to me. I'd have to turn him in. I can't feature doing that to a patient of mine, especially Dale, though I may have to now, I suppose. Now that you know." He puffed, fluttered his lips, wagged his shaggy head.

"Phenol is a horrific way to die."

"I couldn't believe this couple had come to such a tragic end. Her dying that way, his being the cause—"

"So you tried to make sure no one ever found out."

Leitner just sat there with a helpless look. So not Dr. God. I didn't like him as Dr. Helpless.

"I'm in trouble, I know. What should I do, Elliot? Can you refer me to whatever kind of lawyer I need? I don't want to lose—all this."

"What will you say under oath next week?"

"I'll tell the truth. I respect the oath. If you ask, I'll repeat what Dale told me because of the exception to the privilege, but, please, Elliot, don't ask what I did. Don't ask about the specimens. Your case doesn't require you to end my career."

Leitner begging—not pretty.

"Kirwan knows nothing about the phenol," he said quietly.

"I figured. Or about the Colfax scam or the other deaths.

Your investigation. You haven't told them anything, which I appreciate."

"You owe me one," he said. "You said so once."

"But, Hans, don't you remember? I bought lunch. We're even."

CHAPTER 7

"Dui, Colonel." Quierin waved gaily, a Gau-loise in her fingers, from the wheel of my car parked next to the Lexus in Leitner's office lot. In the doorway he stared. He acknowledged her with a slight lift of his head, then shut the door. I trotted over and got in on the passenger side. "Let's haul ass."

"Yah, boy. I am one ass-hauler." She left rubber on Leitner's drive.

"This is so cool," I said. "I have an accomplice."

"Hah."

"I mean, Hans thinks I have an accomplice. He checked me out when I left. It's hard to sneak out documents when you're in a running outfit. I could see he was relieved. But now he'll won-der whether I somehow passed you something before he got there." More inadvertent cunning.

"You okay?"

"We can slow down, Quierin."

"Five minutes and I was going in."

"I'm fine." I laughed. Nervous chuckle. *"It was fucking nerve-racking."* Almost screaming. "Now I'm better." I squeezed her bare knee. Short, black Levi's cutoffs, gringo sum-mer garb. One of my T-shirts, a Bolder Boulder.

"You going to tell me?"

• "Leitner admitted June was poisoned and he stole all the samples. He'd rather we not bring the samples up at trial."

Quierin squeezed me back. "You are on the roll. You are smoking, baby."

"We've got plenty big problems still. He's a cagey son of a bitch. We need to understand Stillwell, truly understand him. I need to talk with you about Darwin."

"There he is." In front of our house, in our friendly little neighborhood, Darwin was walking the beagle. He waved. The exhibitionist, topless on his front porch, yelling at someone on a cell phone, waved as well. The athletes on the other side, returning from a run, were too self-absorbed to wave. They'd make lousy sentinels.

Quierin cut the ignition, handed me the keys. "I want war stories from the mountain man," she said, and kissed me. "I never thought life in America would be sexy. I am so good influence on you."

In the morning we met indoors to foil surveillance. April, in a Beach Boys T-shirt—*Spirit of America*—was fresh from a session with Silbi and Moschetti, a documents examiner. I'd rummaged through my desk and found a handwritten letter I'd kept from Hans. April and Silbi picked it up on the way to Moschetti's.

All the Platte Valley doctor's orders on December 14 appeared to have been written in the same black ink, April told us. But with infrared magnification, Moschetti found two black-ink entries in a different pen from those in which all the other orders were written: *DNR* and *no cor.* Preliminary ID: Bic rather than Uni-ball. And the hand and slant were also different, Uni-ball italic versus Bic vertical. The words *Doctors for Human Rights* in my correspondence from Hans reproduced every letter in *DNR* and *no cor,* except *N.* Comparing it all, in Moschetti's opinion the two Bic entries in the chart were in Hans Leitner's open, upright hand. His lowercase *o*'s that didn't close; his lowercase *r*'s that looked like *v*'s; and his *D*'s and *R*'s with characteristic gaps.

"Confucius say doctor alters chart gets in deep kimchee," Paige observed. "This complicates things. Otherwise, where do we stand?"

I'd pitched them the overview, but we needed to play it all

the way out for April. Quierin lay on the floor propped on an elbow. Tigress at rest, to my mind. April intently took notes. The silverbills played counterpoint.

"Here's the deal," I said. "Hans Leitner is Shoeless Joe Jackson. The star of the team who throws the game."

"Shoeless?" Quierin asked. "Without shoes?"

"Cultural reference. Never mind."

Quierin tapped her temple and spun a finger, a judgment on the culture.

"What he gives us is this. Stillwell confessed to his doctor. Doctor ran around destroying the evidence to protect him, but he missed some. I ask the doctor what Stillwell confessed to when I get him on the stand. Doctor says Stillwell poured this grotesque poison into the liquid food of the woman whom we all know he battered into a coma."

Paige jumped in. "Kirwan and Edson know nothing, right? They're beautifully sandbagged. Their defense, that head injury wasn't the cause of death, is turned against them. They're right. It wasn't. They have no way out, no possible rehabilitation of Stillwell, no countervailing evidence."

"And Stillwell can't deny it," I said, "because he'd waive the Fifth and he can't since now he's looking capital charges in the eye."

"And Kirwan can't discredit Leitner. This isn't some jailhouse confession. This is a confession to the murderer's own doctor. And what a doctor. They've been building up Hans Leitner from opening statement forward as the oracle of Delphi. On direct Kirwan spends probably a half hour buffing his shining accomplishments, then gets bushwhacked with this on cross."

"Kirwan tries anyway," I said. "He makes it worse. Declares Leitner a hostile witness. Looks terrible. Tries to say it could have been April—but Stillwell confessed. Tries to say there's no proof of poisoning by phenol, Stillwell's a head case, fantasizing or something, distraught by June's death. Which goes against every insinuation he's made all trial long that something like poisoning is exactly what happened."

"And then they get coldcocked by the second sandbag."

Paige meant our proof in the rebuttal case, which catches the defense double-blind. Stillwell's confession is borne out by irrefutable physical evidence. Gillian, the transplant bank tech;

Andy, the eTs lab tech; the GC/MS readouts. Quierin the wrap-up witness, with her tribunal credentials, pulling the phenol evidence together and telling the jury what she'd told us.

"Jury will be horrified. Outraged. Devastated," Paige said. "Stillwell's bad as Ted Bundy. Crushed his wife's face and finished her off with a ghastly poison, then got his lawyers to blame his victim's daughter. We win."

"Kirwan loses. First time since the Ford administration."

"Early Carter actually," Paige said.

"And we don't just win, we win big. Kirwan loses big. With uncapped punitive damages—"

"Friends," Paige said somberly, "we are looking at one of the largest fucking verdicts in the entire fucking history of the fucking planet Earth."

"April, what do you say?"

"Well—" She laughed, briefly. She tossed her hair across her face, then shook it clear. "It sounds—like, great, duh, of course." She ran both hands through the black coils, raising and letting them fall, then let go a rapid run of words. "He did a terrible thing to Mom, and no amount of money's too much for him to pay, biggest fucking verdict, whatever, you bet. But—" Another quick laugh, sign of an internal debate.

In full-blown déjà vu, I was jolted back to sitting around the jury room table three years earlier with Hancock, Dale, and June, giving them half-assed settlement counsel.

"Money isn't the whole point, is it?" As her mother had, April appealed to me. "And what about the quid pro quo thing he wants? And what if he's not telling it straight? If it's not true, well—God."

"You don't like Hans asking us to steer clear of his mischief with the evidence?" I said. "We could ask about it anyway, after the confession comes in. I made no promises."

"I guess I don't trust him, like, totally."

"Look what he's offering in return." Authentic devil's advocacy was now required. "Certain victory. Huge verdict. Stillwell nailed, sure to be prosecuted, everything you've always wanted."

"Not—necessarily."

"It is impossible," Paige weighed in, "to walk away from this. This civil judgment will make the twenty-eight mil against

O.J. look like small-claims court. And twelve million of it is fully collectable annuities."

"And of course that's what Leitner's counting on," I said. "That we cannot walk away from this. That when all's said and done, we're the doctor stereotypes of tassle-toed lawyers and greedy plaintiffs." It was a personal send-up too, a rebuke to my moral superiority about justice and truth and calling. A dare.

"Elliot," April said with a burdened look, "what do we do?"

Hers was a variation on the only question, according to the Stoics, that matters: how to lead one's life. The answer was easy, I thought. So did Quierin, I could tell from her composure, the enameled clarity of her gaze. First, no more baseball metaphors. We were playing chess, though the occasional boxing simile would be accepted. Second, we do what I'd sworn. What June's ghost demanded of us: *Revenge my foul and unnatural murder. Remember me.*

Kevin Kirwan met us on the slab piazza of his Tech Center highrise, a stick figure among monumental art in brute concrete—a toppled obelisk, a staircase to nothing. He waved an electronic weekend key at a touch pad by the Palladian entryway. Another touch brought and opened a brushed-aluminum elevator that took us quickly to the penthouse suite. He held open the koa door of Kirwan Varney & Edson for Stone Quierin & Darwin. And the beagle.

We followed Kirwan's familiar strut through the reception atrium down a hall of glass-walled offices to the library and a vast malachite conference table ringed by floor-to-ceiling windows with views from prairie to range. To the south a towering iron-gray anvil of lightning-netted cloud projected a fifty-mile shadow from Castle Rock to Golden.

"Looks like rain," Darwin observed. The beagle sprang to his lap.

Paige had stayed behind with the yeoman scut work of witness prep and outlines for the rest of our case-in-chief, and notes for a closing she might never give. I'd peeled off some time on Saturday to draft a *qui tam* complaint under the federal False Claims Act. The act allows a "relator," in our case Rico, to sue Colfax on behalf of the United States for public moneys fraudulently taken. The relator gets a quarter or more of whatever is recovered in the case. The first person to file is the only relator entitled to pursue the claims. I left a message for Rico saying we had to move fast before someone else did and asking for his go-ahead. Come Monday morning, he and Bow Wow should be on high alert. I also left a message for Arnold Whitelaw wondering if he'd accept service of process on behalf of his clients. One of those voice mails you delete with a vengeance. Then you burrow your face in your hands.

The scale of his digs didn't work for Kirwan, nor the Empire furniture, the parget ceiling, the parquet floors of gleaming cork. On his feet the smallish Kirwan filled a courtroom. He sustained the illusion of youth. Sitting dwarfed at his green stone table reduced him to wizened mortality. This was his lair, his advantage, but it felt the other way around.

Quierin declined a seat just yet. She strolled the bow of windows, touching them now and then with the ball of a finger, a skywalk above the earth. She tested the charmed glass.

We loitered briefly in awkward small talk. Kirwan, to assert control, launched a reasonably funny story about his partner Bernie. Something about federal judge Nottingham hailing him back from a third honeymoon.

"I always thought of you as a couple," I said, earning a three-second stare. Kirwan's jocularity was part of the problem. Nothing between us was funny, especially not now.

"This is truly a first," Kirwan broke stare to observe. He was acknowledging it was time to talk, though his tone was that of a junior high principal: I'll hear you out, but you won't change my mind.

Looking at him, I thought, henna. At a certain cut of light, Kevin Kirwan is exposed. Unnatural qualities come to the surface. It was time to shake it up.

"Kevin, let's get this on the table. You're pretty good at manipulating juries, but this time we're going to drop-kick your butt to the Western Slope." I jerked my head toward the bank of windows.

"Maybe this was a bad idea. I'll show you out."

"Quierin—am I bullshitting Mr. Kirwan?"

"Bullshit you not." A pause in her window dance. "I hear you the never-lose guy," she said, approaching. "That's history now, you don't help out. You're toasted. Burnt."

"It pains me to say it," I interjected, "but we have some goals in common, Kevin. If you don't want your string to end, you better do as asked."

I explained what was going to happen, what Leitner's testimony would be, our proof of phenol, what I planned.

"There's nothing you can do about it now. You don't call the defendant's doctor, we will, and we'll ram your defense right up your bottom. You set yourself up. You massaged these jurors beautifully. They are so ready to hear traumatic brain injury didn't kill June Stillwell. You're looking at a death sentence, Kevin, for your own superlawyer rep, and a real one for your client."

"Horseshit," he said slowly and sour. "I'm calling your bluff. I'm calling Leitner now."

"Do that, the deal's off and your guy fries. I'm hoping that happens because I'd love to beat you bloody."

He tossed it around in his mind. "What is—the deal?"

"We sit down with Stillwell, the three of us. Darwin here's Stillwell's buddy. Right, Darwin?"

"Rog."

"Stillwell trusts Darwin, Darwin trusts Quierin, Quierin trusts me. It's a chain of trust, Kevin. We tell Stillwell all about it, how his doctor's going to send him down the river. We hear his side."

"If he admits what Leitner said he said—"

"He fries."

"Even if this was a good idea, he obviously has to have counsel present."

"Fine, but only by telephone. You can listen but you can't talk, and it can't be Hancock."

"You're asking me to allow opposing counsel midtrial to meet with my client, the defendant, to discuss the critical facts of his defense against the claims you are prosecuting against him? Which happened to be for murder?"

"Exactly."

"I can't permit that. It would violate every ethical duty I have. Plus, I don't trust you, Stone. You're a turncoat. You're weird."

"Okay," Quierin said. "Go down flaming."

I stood. "Paige will be pleased. She likes to horsewhip

opposing counsel, but she loves castration best. She steams up at the thought."

"You need to leave now. Don't forget the fucking dog."

Darwin's eyes narrowed.

"Think it over. You're screwed. This is your only hope. Run it by your client. Change your mind, you've got my number, but there's not much time. Call Leitner and we never talk again."

"Plaintiff's next witness is Darla Carlson," I said once judge and retinue had settled into session Monday morning. Stillwell wasn't there. Nor Whitelaw, nor Leitner. Kirwan sat alone at counsel table. I hadn't heard from him since leaving his law palace to wicked sheets of cold June rain. The turnpike was flooded and closed at Federal. Boulder took two hours. The only call was Rico. "Do it, Watash."

Darla looked her best, prim, home-permed, and loaded for bear. I asked her place of work, position, hours. Where was the White Spot diner in relation to Colfax Center for Rehabilitation?

"Right across their lot. Anybody come in or out the door, I can see 'em from my counter."

"What opportunity have you had to observe visitors of Colfax patients?"

"What visitors those poor souls get, which is only a few, I see 'em coming and going like I say. There's a pattern to it, Mr. Stone. Once a week, then once a month, then once a year, then never again. It's hopelessness setting in."

"Ms. Carlson, please just address the question at hand."

"Excuse me, Mr. Stone." She smiled her best.

I'd planned to ask Darla to identify Stillwell, but he wasn't at the table.

"Are you familiar with the man who visited at Colfax named Dale Stillwell?"

"Familiar? I guess not. But I know who he is."

"Mr. Stillwell is the defendant in this case. Did you ever see him arrive at Colfax to visit a patient?"

"Durn near every time he came, I expect."

"Describe what you saw."

"Doc's driving his long, black Lexus. Stillwell's sitting shotgun. Park and go in together. Always together, him and the doc."

"Describe the doctor."

"Big, white-headed, do I want to say 'authority figure'?" She had an astigmatic squint when thinking. "One of those I-am-the-man type men."

Kirwan took notes, declining to object.

"Describe Mr. Stillwell."

"Black-headed pretty boy, is how I'd put it. It's not his looks but his actions."

"His actions? Did you have an opportunity to observe Mr. Stillwell when his visits were over?"

"Oh, yes. Most likely every time."

"How did he look? How did he act?"

"Wild man, really, on several occasions. Whamming the hood of the car, one time with his head. Head-butts an expensive automobile?" She caught a snicker. "Might pump a fist, go in circles. I mean, this was a fellow with his tail up. This was a man enraged."

"Objection." Kirwan beamed. "Speculation. Impermissible opinion testimony."

"Observations of anger," I said, "are proper lay opinion."

"Overruled. Continue, Mr. Stone."

"Enraged? Did he appear violently enraged?"

"Heck yeah, and it wasn't 'cause something's wrong with him."

"Objection."

"Sustained. The jury will disregard the witness's last remark. Ms. Carlson—"

"Yes, Your Honor?" A pretty look for the judge.

"You must answer only the question asked. You must refrain from telling us why you think a person did something or acted a certain way. Only your observations, please."

"I'm sorry, Your Honor."

"Now," I said, "Ms. Carlson—"

"There he is," Darla shrieked. She pointed at the far doors as though she'd seen a ghost. Everybody in the courtroom, bailiff, clerk, reporter, all of us at counsel tables, even Kirwan, the whole gallery, craned around in unison to see Dale Stillwell with Bernie behind him, and to watch Stillwell march angrily up the aisle.

"Oh, Lord." Darla touched her throat. She thought he was coming for her.

The judge's gavel sounded. "Ms. Carlson. Please."

"Yes, Ms. Carlson," I said. "You recognize the defendant, I take it?"

"The same." She kept a wary eye on Stillwell as he took his place.

"Was Dale Stillwell ever present inside the White Spot diner?"

"Just one time, the day before she died."

"You're referring to the death of June Stillwell, his wife?"

"Her death, poor soul." Her hand started toward her heart. "Afternoon before. He was visiting her, like, every Sunday. Long time. Hours. Then all of the sudden there he is in my shop acting crazy as Larrabee's calf. 'Where is he?' he hollers. He's looking for you, Mr. Stone, is how I took it, and I was concerned."

"What did you do?"

"Run him out with my long spoon."

Titters from the mothers.

"Was he alone?"

"Just him. Lots of times he come out alone, do his rage thing in the lot. Doc'd join him by and by and off in the Lexus they go."

Kirwan's halfhearted cross-exam hit on April themes. All her time in the booth. There again the morning her mother died. The judge called the morning break. The eight mothers filed out to the jury room. Kirwan palavered with Edson, nodded, looked at Stillwell, who also nodded. Kirwan caught my eye, pointed to an empty corner of the gallery. I joined him.

"He wants to do it."

"I knew he would."

"He'll sit down with you if his buddy's there, the dog guy. Strange thing is, he seems to like you, Stone. He doesn't care for me or Bernie. Hates Hancock. Bernie or I will listen in on speaker. We won't say anything."

Back at the table I popped my co-counsel on the shoulder. "Sorry, Paige. Kirwan caved."

"Damn."

"I'm taking off to pick up Quierin and Darwin, then to Stillwell's town house. I've got the release. I'll need a notary. I'll brief Millsap, get some cop backup for tomorrow. What else?"

"Nothing, Elliot. I'll just hang around here and wind up my beautiful case-in-chief with our economist talking about all those big, beautiful dollars the jury won't be giving us."

"Longing and regret look good on you, Paige." Green-eyed lady, ocean lady. Born to melancholy.

"You and Dale have fun."

CHAPTER 8

Mooney v. Stillwell was a dream case for a trial judge. It had the weighty subject of murder. It had big money, emotional traction, the family drama of daughter versus stepfather. More and more media drifting in, bored with the Tucker-watch in the child-murder case. Legal talent, including Kirwan's twenty-two-year string, and a classic, symmetrical, counterpunch structure. Powerful claims of wrongful death by felonious killing boldly met with the defense that the plaintiff herself was the murderer. A double feature—the trial of Stillwell, then the trial of April.

I never know what judges are thinking, especially cautious types like Rafe Otero, but it had to be looking good for us. The defense had insinuations but no hard evidence implicating April or any third party. At the close of testimony Monday, Paige informed Otero the plaintiff rested her case. Knee-hammer Bernie Edson made the obligatory motion to dismiss our claims for want of proof. Paige cataloged what the proof had been. Without catching a breath the judge ruled our evidence far more than sufficient to make out a prima facie case of wrongful death by felonious killing, denying the motion. We'd win, in other words, if the case stopped there. Time for the defense movie.

Their lead witness was a criminalist willing to go out on every limb Bernie Edson had paid him to. Professor Craver offered himself first as an expert in domestic violence. He explained that the attack on June did not fit battering profiles—quarrels that get out of hand, escalating rage, mindless beatings with multiple blows. Instead, June was struck but a single time lying on her back in bed, perhaps asleep. Unheard of as an instance of domestic violence. Nor had a history of spousal abuse been discovered, and there always is a history. The husband should be low on the list of suspects, or not a suspect at all.

Next Craver analyzed photographs of the Stillwells the morning of the attack. He'd blown up a magnified view of the red spot on Stillwell's forehead in his mug shot. Once the bump filled a four-by-four poster, it resembled the planet Mars as the *Explorer* drew near. The professor also was an expert in head-butt wounds. They do more damage than you'd think.

Finally, Professor Craver knew a lot about sleep violence. Over Paige's objection he was allowed to speculate that, as a known sufferer of post–traumatic stress disorder—notorious for reexperiencing nightmares—Stillwell may have head-butted June in a flailing dream of an oncoming locomotive.

Paige cut him off at the knees on cross. Craver skulked away, credentials in tatters, with cross-examination nightmares to look forward to. But he was just the warm-up for Hans Leitner. The main event.

Tuesday morning Kirwan called Leitner to the stand. The air of hushed expectation, arrested tension, that Leitner often generated was amplified by his place in the trial, clearly the rock against which the gathered swells of April's case would break and either fly into spray and foam or engulf the defense.

Leitner straightened a blue blazer so navy it made his white shirt and hair seem to glow. He adjusted the knot of his tie, forest green, figured with waterfowl. Kirwan asked him to state his name and professional address. The familiar baritone filled the quiet room.

"What is your relationship to Dale Stillwell, Dr. Leitner?"

"I am his physician. Mr. Stillwell has been under my care and treatment for close to four years."

Kirwan's exam had to toe a fine line. Because of the *in limine* ruling our side could not inquire into Stillwell's psych history, and their side could not offer it in mitigation. Stillwell's medical and psychiatric records likewise remained confidential. Leitner was forbidden to disclose anything about his treatment. He could, however, discuss his role at Colfax, his observations there of Stillwell, April, and June, and offer opinions about June's condition and death.

Kirwan ventured next to the Emerald City of Hans's career and credentials. There he dwelled, as predicted, a half hour before reaching the Colfax visits.

"Dr. Leitner, did your assistance to Dale Stillwell include accompanying him on regular visits to his wife, June, at Colfax rehabilitation hospital?"

"It did indeed." Leitner explained the court order and his limited role.

"An imposition on your busy schedule—"

"Which I was happy to accommodate, Mr. Kirwan."

Kirwan was examining out of role, tethered as Bernie to the podium. He wanted all attention on the big man in the box.

"What ground rules were you able to work out for these visits?"

"Mr. Stone and I"—Hans smiled my way—"had a kind of little negotiation. Dale could come once a week, on Sundays. Ms. Mooney"—he nodded at April—"agreed not to be present."

"What led to the need for ground rules?"

He pulled on his chin. "An altercation between them."

"Provoked by—"

"April Mooney opposed Dale's visiting. We explained the judge's order, which she"—he searched for a word—"grudgingly accepted. The two of them together just didn't work. No love lost, on either side, and never has been, I understand. Ms. Mooney used some provocative language. Accused him of harming his wife."

"And?"

"It was very tense. She was very protective of her mother."

Paige passed a Post-it. "Not too bad."

"After that, did you see April Mooney during the weekly visits?"

"I believe not. She was actually living right in the room soon after, but would leave the premises whenever Dale visited June."

"On every visit Dale came with you and left with you?"

"Every one."

"Every one. And you were with him and could observe his interaction with his wife?"

"Well, frequently, yes. But, also frequently, I was not physically present when Dale was with June." He was going off the script he and Kirwan had worked out before trial. A signal to me: green light.

"Describe Dale's and June's interaction."

"June, of course, had minimal ability to interact. Dale seemed troubled, profoundly so, by the tragedy of her circumstances. He'd sit and stare fixedly at her until it was uncomfortable for me to remain in the room." Green light flashing.

"Did you ever observe Dale Stillwell say or do anything directed at his wife that could be called hostile?"

"Hostile? Not in my view." Hans turned to the jury to elaborate. "It was more complex than simple hostility. It was more than mixed feelings of love and hate. Dale was devastated by the loss of June, both his loss of her and her loss to the world, to life as we know it. It tortured him and was fed by feelings of guilt."

"Dr. Leitner," Kirwan interrupted. "Stay with the question, please. Your Honor, I move to strike as unresponsive and violative of your *in limine* ruling."

"Granted. The jury will disregard the witness's opinions about the psychological impact on Mr. Stillwell of his wife's injuries."

"Dr. Leitner, did you ever observe Mr. Stillwell acting in a hostile manner toward his wife?"

"Mr. Kirwan, I must say, the fixity of Dale's stare, especially in hindsight, bespoke a kind of ill will."

If Kirwan had doubted me before, he didn't now. His witness was flipping before his eyes. Beaming hypocritically, he leapt to the topic of June.

"Dr. Leitner, you have a great deal of clinical and research experience in traumatic brain injury?"

"A fair amount, yes." He gave it a recap, at the VA, the Armed Forces Institute of Pathology, microautopsies of brains, administration of brain-injury units.

"You had weekly opportunities to observe June Stillwell's course."

He did and he summarized it. He added that he'd reviewed Ms. Stillwell's medical records "at Mr. Stone's request."

"Mr. Stone? Elliot Stone?" Kirwan did a faux double take. "I'll want to come back to that. First, though, do you know Dr. Richard Longacre?"

"We all know Dick. He's a wonderful clinician at a top facility, Craigmile, and a famously defiant optimist, I might add."

"Dr. Longacre testified here without the benefit of having ever observed Ms. Stillwell. You personally observed June Stillwell's progress week in and week out," Kirwan said. "I wonder if you take issue with some of his opinions."

Leitner did and elaborated their differences. June's coma was irreversible, in his view, and in fact worsening, though, assuming adequate nutrition and nursing care, she had a close-to-normal life expectancy. "Medically, she was as healthy as any one of us. Healthier in some ways, since we aren't safeguarded by round-the-clock nursing."

"She wasn't going to be hit by a bus crossing the street?" Kirwan asked.

"Or pick up a viral infection in a movie theater, no. Her risk of sudden death was actually lower than ours."

"Her life—" Kirwan fingered his tie. "What kind of life was it?"

"No one really knows except that it probably consisted primarily of unrelieved physical suffering. Not a life in any meaningful sense. Or an existence anyone should be forced to endure." Sensing the lack of objections, he added, "As I believe her loved ones came to appreciate." The jurors sent consoling looks April's way.

"Now"—Kirwan snapped to—"back to Elliot *Stone.*" He loved announcing my name with an anapestic trill of villainy—El-li-ot *STONE.* Like La-dy Mac-*BETH.*

"Elliot Stone asked you to read June Stillwell's medical records?"

"He did."

"As you understood it, what prompted his request?"

"He wanted my views on why she died. Having been her conservator and guardian, he thought her true cause of death should come to light."

"Elliot Stone was not satisfied with the conclusions, if we can call them that, in Ms. Stillwell's death certificate?"

"He most assuredly was not."

One more in this vein and I'd be faced with objecting to my own statements as hearsay, had this been the trial it began as. A nice problem for the judge and a vexed one for me. Clever as hell, as was the strategy as a whole, how Kirwan had planned to use Leitner to win the case—the mystery defense we'd failed to guess. He'd have Leitner refute Longacre and throw the cause of death into confusion with his credibility underlined by my faith in him. And our credibility collapsing because of my doubts, *the plaintiff's own lawyer's doubts* about the "true cause of death."

The plan was for Leitner to use me against April, to save Stillwell with me. It might have worked, I saw from the consternation spreading among the eight mothers.

If the case had gone as planned, I'd be pissed as hell, objecting, maybe calling for a mistrial. It didn't matter now. Indeed it helped, but I could read another signal in Leitner's answers: screw with me on cross-examination and I'll come back on redirect and really bite you one. He'd reveal anything I ever told him as suited his interests. I was pissed as hell anyway, which would make cross that much easier, and the double-check chess move I was hoping to put in place.

Kirwan knew to go only up to the brink, to avoid the ultimate questions on cause. He took Leitner through Silverman's and Longacre's litany of possible head-injury complications. Hans destroyed them one by one, pulmonary embolism, pneumonia, aspiration of vomitus, heart problems, respiratory problems. Each was either definitively ruled out or completely lacking in any supporting data. Hans the master was utterly convincing. We well might have lost, had the case gone as planned. It also occurred to me that all of his testimony to this point was in fact how he saw it and factually true, as far as I knew. I stilled a spasm of fear that I might have gotten him wrong.

Hans headed into his wrap-up opinion, addressing the jury full on. They were buying every word. "No complication of head injury took June Stillwell's life." He spoke ex cathedra, with papal confidence. "Sudden death in a healthy young woman, albeit comatose, doesn't just happen without an intervention."

"Intervention, Doctor? Like the bus that hit the pedestrian?" Kirwan smiled dryly.

"A superseding medical cause," Leitner said, legal lingo that produced a thoughtful judicial frown and tapping on Otero's laptop.

"What ordinarily is required to identify such a superseding cause?"

"Autopsy. The Greek root means 'see for oneself.' Ever since Rudolf Virchow, the father of pathology, one hundred and fifty years ago, autopsy has been the unsurpassed and often only means of learning the cause of a person's death. Autopsy was the obvious and necessary way to see for oneself what really took June Stillwell's life."

"Did you make your views on the importance of autopsy known before Ms. Stillwell was cremated?"

"I did."

"To whom?"

"Elliot Stone."

"Were you successful in postponing the cremation so that an autopsy could be performed?"

"I was not."

Kirwan had reached what was designed to be his final point, the jackpot question. It would feed straight into the closing argument I could hear him giving at the easel: "We don't know for sure who or what killed June Stillwell, but this we know. There is zero evidence Dale Stillwell is responsible for the *superseding event* that intervened and took this healthy young woman's life. And we know this. The *reason* we don't know is April Mooney, who kept us from ever finding out. From ever seeing for ourselves."

So Kirwan went for the jackpot. "What and who prevented the autopsy you told Elliot Stone was essential to discovering the superseding cause of June Stillwell's death?"

Leitner eyed the jurors gravely. "Dale Stillwell, despite my urging, refused to permit the autopsy of his wife."

Break called, I checked the gallery. Quierin and Roybal side by side up front. On edge, it appeared from Quierin's measured hyperventilations. She came forward, flipped the gate, went to our table, handed me a *Denver Post*. June 15. STARR SAYS INVESTIGATING CLINTON STILL HIS JOB. QUAKE ROCKS MEXICO CITY. And already kicked to Section C, YUGOSLAV WITHDRAWAL ON SCHED-ULE AS NATO FORCE BUILDS.

I put the paper in a trial bag and caught a few breaths myself. Quierin and April took Roybal for a walk.

"Paige—"

"He teed it up for us. I can smell it. It's that close," she whispered through clenched teeth. "All you have to do is ask him, one, what caused June's death, and, two, who did it, and we slay Kirwan and go home rich."

"Paige, be strong."

"It's really hard, Elliot. I really like winning."

"You've done harder things than this. Childbirth."

"Falling off a log."

"You've got a great kid," I said. "A caring husband. A mostly virtuous life so far. Money judgments corrupt, you used to say. You don't need the corruption of a third of this disabled guy's annuities."

"It comes to four million dollars. Split with you, Elliot."

"Treasure of Sierra Madre. He's dead sure we'll go clawing after it, but it's dust on the wind."

"I want to cry."

"It just wasn't meant to be. Maybe it's not in your stars, a plaintiff's megaverdict."

"Not this time. By God, next time it will be."

"All rise."

Judge Otero settled into place with a troubled look. He opened his laptop and tapped the touch pad, reading his notes with a skeptical brow. He twisted a cheek. Had what just happened really happened? I fancied him thinking. And why? A man in whom unpredictability occasioned anxiety. At length he said, "Mr. Stone?" His invitation to cross-examination attended with an implicit question: What now? He hadn't seen nothing yet.

"Dr. Leitner. Elliot Stone, counsel for April Mooney. We know each other, do we not?"

"We certainly do, and have for a number of years."

"I'm unaccustomed to cross-examining you. Forgive me if this is a little—awkward."

"Understood." He smiled.

Time for the opening move. Something a little different. A knight instead of a pawn.

"What is phenol, Dr. Leitner?"

The judge straightened. "What did you say, Counsel? Phenol?" The jurors strained to hear.

"Yes, Your Honor. Phenol." I spelled it. "What is that, Dr. Leitner?"

"Chemically? Toxicologically?"

"An overview, if you would." Already it felt natural, the rhythm of lawyer and expert, offering Hans to educate.

He described phenol as a hydrocarbon in the benzene series, in its free state a colorless liquid with a characteristic odor. A caustic, toxic, and very dangerous poison that destroys tissue on contact and frequently has fatal effects.

"Its uses?"

"Fewer and fewer, fortunately. In this country in free form phenol has a few laboratory applications not relevant here. Formerly it was widely used to disinfect, principally in hospitals. Phenol has now been abandoned in most hospitals because of how hazardous it is. Some, to be blunt, backward institutions stock it still."

"Charity hospitals? Medicaid hospitals?"

"All kinds of hospitals can be backward."

"Colfax rehabilitation hospital?"

"Uses it with a vengeance, I fear. Colfax smells like phenol, and the smell is unmistakable."

I fixed a moment on his eyes. A reassurance prompt: You the man. Let's go there.

"At Colfax, did just anyone have access to phenol?"

No objection, though objectionable.

"Apparently so. Orderlies, janitors, anyone. It was in storerooms, on carts in the halls, everywhere."

"What would happen if"—a melodramatic wandering now was called for as I grappled with the unthinkable—"if someone poured a small amount of free phenol into June Stillwell's feeding fluid?" Kirwan stared in mock shock. The judge's shock was real.

"What would happen is what did happen." He described the horrifying cascade of injury leading to death much as Quierin had. I handed him the nurse's notes from midnight and 4 A.M., and the ambulance and ER reports. All consistent with poisoning by phenol. His rich voice occupied a courtroom that had gone dead except for reporters scratching notes. The judge sat stunned, his laptop stowed, his trial having left him in the dust. The account was mesmerizing, Dr. God at the top of his game.

"Dr. Leitner, in response to Mr. Kirwan's questions, you told us June Stillwell's death was not consistent with pulmonary embolism, aspiration of vomitus, heart or respiratory disease. That it was caused by a superseding medical event. An intervention."

"I did."

"Was her death consistent with intervention—by phenol poisoning?"

"Yes, it was." An intake of breath from someone.

"Without telling us what it is just yet, do you have reason to believe phenol was administered to June Stillwell the night before she died?"

"I do."

"In your opinion, was phenol poisoning the superseding medical event that took her life?"

"In my opinion it was."

Now even the reporters were still.

"How might someone have been able to administer phenol to this hospital patient?"

"Very easily. Anyone, in a matter of seconds, could have slipped a vial of phenol into her liquid food, left undetected, and what happened would happen."

"Anyone with access to her room?"

"Correct."

"And June Stillwell would be helpless?"

"Correct."

"To prevent her foul and most unnatural murder?"

"I agree with your allusion to Shakespeare, Mr. Stone. Ms. Stillwell's was not a death from natural causes."

"Shall we," the judge offered weakly, "break for lunch?"

The jurors were already chattering before their door shut, disregarding multiple admonitions not to discuss the evidence. Otero motioned us forward with ten bent fingers. "Gentlemen, what's going on? I don't like being kept in the dark."

"Nor do I," Kevin Kirwan said. "I need to confer with my

client about a mistrial. This was out of the blue, never disclosed. Hans," he said angrily. "Wait for me outside." Kirwan played his part well. Hans left the court with nothing yet showing Kirwan was in on the game.

"Dr. Leitner is the defense medical expert," I said. "I can't sandbag the defense with their own expert."

"I wouldn't think so. Where are you going?"

"I truly can't predict."

"I thought I knew what this case was about, Mr. Stone. I hate feeling stupid."

"None of us knew. I was more stupid than anyone. We're all still learning."

"Till one-thirty, then. I expect to be enlightened."

I passed on the La Placenta buffet. Too much to metabolize given everything else I had to consume. Trial bags in hand, Paige and I headed for the back door to Otero's chambers to avoid Leitner, whom Kirwan was supposed to detain, shadow, and pepper with questions and accusations while Edson hurried Stillwell away. Quierin and April waited by the back door to the courtroom. They took us to a windowless hearing room borrowed over lunch. April slipped me a burrito half and a plastic fork in a grease-stained sack. Paige locked the door. "Is it here?" I asked.

"We got it, horse." Quierin winked.

"Horse?"

"Greenhorn cowboy terminology."

"Can't believe he didn't ditch it," April said.

"He wouldn't. He's Dr. Medico-Legal. He knows destroying records when you're under suspicion comes back to nail you. Plus there's no way he could be sure I hadn't seen and copied a set. And he's relying on the *in limine* ruling. He's sure it can't come in. How'd it go with you guys?"

Quierin said she and Roybal had taken the "Authorization for Release of Medical and Therapy Records" I'd drafted and Stillwell had signed the day before to Ellen Vesco, Hans's virtual assistant, at her home office. Ellen knew the drill. The patient is entitled on written demand. Quierin said it was needed now, in court. Today. Roybal, in blues, lent authority and offered his cruiser. Ellen let them into Hans's office, plucked the chart, and handed it over.

"Has anybody talked with Millsap?"

"Charlie did," April said. "He's on board."

"How's the colonel doing his answers?" Quierin was curious.

"He thinks we bought the deal," April said.

Paige bit her lip and slowly shook her head. What a deal.

I unsnapped the bag, pulled out the *Post,* and opened the middle section. Inside the newspaper lay a color-coded manila folder. The treatment records of Dale Stillwell. I unfastened and handed the medication log to Quierin, asked her to find what she could on-line, and told April to come back at one-thirty to pick up tabbed pages for Kinko's. I now required an hour alone.

CHAPTER 9

"Dr. Leitner, I'd like to revisit your background a bit. You and I worked together in the former
Yugoslavia on a war-crimes prosecution."

"We certainly did. The Vukovar Hospital massacre. You
were lead prosecutor. I was a forensic witness."

"Not merely a witness, you supervised the exhumation and
identification of over two hundred hospital patients executed by
the Yugoslav army, did you not?"

"Yes, along with Quierin and others, as a member of your
team." He nodded in Quierin's direction. She smiled and
acknowledged him. Down her bench, a curly-haired guy looked
up from his reporter's notebook. Here was an angle, a potentially colorful interview.

"You are sought after as a forensic expert in war-crimes
investigations around the world, are you not?"

"I suppose that's true."

"You are a founder of Doctors for Human Rights?"

"Yes."

"Human rights and the prosecution of war crimes are of paramount personal importance."

"They are."

"Why is that?" I could feel the old rapport warming, Hans

and I, expert and lawyer, friends, professional teammates, kindred minds, as I once thought.

Hans employed his thoughtful, frowning smile. "As a physician and forensic scientist I can think of no higher calling than medical intervention for human rights."

"Than joyful participation in the sorrows of the world?"

He nodded gravely. "Those of us who aren't monks have a duty to engage the world."

"To travel outward."

"You're describing, correctly, the way of the bodhisattva. The way of participation."

"Human-rights activism is participating. Traveling outward."

"It is, in any event, the way of my participation."

"You are a medical doctor by career, but a human-rights doctor by calling."

He laughed. "I suppose I am. I suppose you have me there. But medicine is a humanitarian endeavor too, as Rudolf Virchow also taught."

"Our work took you to the former Yugoslavia and The Hague during what period of time?"

"Fall 1996 through summer of 1998, back and forth."

"Among other investigations for Doctors for Human Rights?"

"Yes."

"Bosnia, Africa, elsewhere?"

"Yes."

"Each lasting—weeks?"

"Up to two months."

"You are shortly off to Kosovo for an extended period?"

"I shall be heading a team assessing atrocities against physicians, patients, and health-care facilities." His eyes brightened at the prospect.

"You also gave congressional testimony in Washington in 1997?"

"Yes. Two or three times."

"Other time-consuming Washington work—NIH panels, HCFA?"

"Quite time-consuming, yes."

"You testify in criminal and civil matters as a retained expert? Paid by lawyers and others?"

"I frequently do, yes."

"How frequently?"

"I've given testimony in, I believe, over six hundred depositions and two hundred trials."

"You know your way around a courtroom."

"I didn't say that." He laughed. He loved the qualifications part of the exam. "No two trials are the same."

How right he was. I took a shot of water from a Dixie cup. "As a founder and past president of the American Academy of Legal Medicine, you have a sophisticated understanding of the legal aspects of medical practice, wouldn't you say?" I offered a nod to encourage affirmation.

"I suppose I'd agree."

"The whole legal gamut—criminal proceedings, malpractice, legislation—correct?"

"I'd say so, yes."

I thought I caught a sigh of impatience from the bench. This was supposed to be cross-examination; I was supposed to be attacking, not augmenting, the defense expert's credentials. But Leitner was playing along. He thought he knew what I was doing, building him up to bolster the account to come of Stillwell's confession.

"Tell us your rates as a retained expert witness," I said.

He sat back with a blink of surprise, not quite believing I'd ask the tired question all plaintiff's lawyers do.

"Much of my testimony is pro bono. For free. My work for Doctors for Human Rights, your war-crimes tribunal, others. For those who can afford it, corporations, insurance companies, I charge one thousand dollars an hour, sometimes seven fifty, in large part to subsidize my public-interest work."

"You have, it's fair to say, a national reputation. International."

"That's fair."

"Your reputation is important to you?"

"Of course."

"Do you have medical malpractice insurance, Dr. Leitner?"

Both Hans and the judge swung to Kirwan to object. I tracked their gaze. Kirwan sat motionless and mum, though I could feel a yard away the radiant heat of his repressed anger. Leitner was giving him a big-time screw job, his key expert not only failing to come through but knifing his client in the heart. Kirwan was more than ready for the unaccustomed measure of inflicting injury by silence.

No objection voiced, Leitner had to answer. "Yes. It's a requirement of licensure."

"What are your limits of liability coverage?"

"Why do we need to know this, Mr. Stone?"

I smiled and looked clueless. Kirwan said nothing.

"Five million dollars, for what it's worth."

"Have you ever been sued personally for medical malpractice?"

"No," Hans said, annoyed more at Kirwan, it seemed, than me. "Happily."

"Good for you. If you lost a high-profile malpractice trial, that could hurt your reputation?"

No objection.

"Theoretically."

"That might become a subject for cross-examination of you as a forensic expert witness?"

No objection.

"It depends." Like the judge, Leitner looked increasingly puzzled and pissed off. Kirwan kept his head down, jotting on a pad, radiating heat.

"Well, Dr. Leitner. High-profile liability for medical malpractice in fact could seriously impact your expert-witness work, couldn't it?"

A hitch of his head, guard going higher. "Perhaps."

"Mr. Kirwan asked you a number of questions about Colfax hospital last fall. I want to clarify that if I can."

"Fine."

"Every time Dale Stillwell went to Colfax, so did you?"

"That's true."

"How often did you go there in the five months June Stillwell was a patient?"

"Far more than I wanted. But not as much as you did."

"Seven, eight times at least?"

"At least."

"What did you do there?"

"As the court ordered"—He glanced up at Otero—"and as I reluctantly agreed, I accompanied Dale Stillwell when he visited his wife."

"But what did you do when you were there?"

Hans gave me a hard look, scrutinizing where I was going. "I arrived with Dale. We went in. Staff knew me as his doctor."

"Staff recognized you as a physician?"

"I believe they did. We went to June's room. Often, I left them alone."

"You weren't afraid Dale Stillwell might harm his wife?"

"It didn't cross my mind."

"You had no reason to be concerned he might cause her harm?"

"If you're talking about whatever happened July fifteenth—"

"Apart from that."

"No. No reason." An injured smile: Why are you badgering me?

"You insisted April Mooney not be with her mother during these visits?"

"You and I worked that out to reduce Dale's stress."

"It was your requirement, wasn't it?"

"I guess it was."

"Dr. Leitner, do you know Neil Hancock?"

"I know him as Mr. Stillwell's lawyer. Both at his 1996 trial and last year and again this year. I believe he's behind you now."

Heads turned. Hancock in the gallery, as promised, played his fingers in a limp wave.

"Did you ask Neil Hancock last fall whether Dale Stillwell's annuities would be protected if April got a judgment against him?"

Double take. Guard rearing higher. Now the white king would start to defend. "I believe I did, out of concern for Dale."

"Move to strike the unresponsive portion of the answer."

"Granted," Otero ruled. "Doctor, answer only the question that's asked. Jury will disregard the superfluous statement."

"What did he tell you?"

"I believe he said annuities from a personal injury case are exempt from creditors, including judgment creditors."

"Meaning April could collect virtually nothing from any verdict against Dale Stillwell."

"That's what I said. Judgment creditors can't collect."

"Except for what?" I turned my back to him, ostentatiously catching Hancock's eye. He needed a sign Hancock might be testifying next. I was impressed with Leitner's self-discipline at this point, suppressing the outrage that had to be starting to build. "Mr. Hancock told you about an exception. What was it?" I faced him again.

"Murder—I think he said." He aimed for off-the-cuff.

"Murder." He'd named it, the greatest of crimes. The crime that cries out for vengeance, as the book of Genesis instructs. *"Murder* was discussed, months before June Stillwell died?"

Leitner chuckled. It jarred. "Only by way of understanding the statute."

"You understood, then, that a personal injury claim against Dale Stillwell would not be viable so long as June was alive?"

"I suppose." His look turned inward.

"Do you recall also asking me if April planned to sue?"

"Vaguely."

"You wondered if she could reach Dale's annuities?"

"I don't really remember."

"Do you remember when I told you so long as June remained alive, April probably couldn't find a lawyer and your patient was safe from suit?"

"That would be obvious, wouldn't it?"

"Hancock told you the same."

His eyes shifted to the gallery. "Yes."

"But a couple weeks later you learned April *had* found a lawyer. Paige Jorritsma." I drifted in her direction. "Do you remember my telling you that?"

"Sure."

"That worried you. 'Bad news,' you said."

"I was concerned for Dale."

"For Dale? You asked again whether suing him was blocked. Remember?"

"Not really."

"I told you the suit was still blocked. I said we, Paige and I, were looking at *other options*. Do you remember?"

He cleared his throat. "It meant nothing to me."

I took a breath. It was time to castle.

"Dr. Leitner, did you acquire a set of Colfax hospital protocols last October?"

"Yes. You were interested in my thoughts."

"Move to strike the answer except for the word *yes.*"

"Granted. Doctor—"

"I know," Leitner snapped.

"Respond to the question," Otero said slowly. "That and no more. Do you understand?"

"I do, Your Honor." He lifted his eyes to mine, in a steaming fury at the coming double cross.

"Those protocols included the procedure for taking stomach-fluid samples each Sunday at midnight for lab analysis?"

"I have no idea."

"Take a look, Dr. Leitner. Permission to approach?" I asked the judge.

"Approach."

I handed them to Hans and passed copies up to the judge and back to Kirwan. "Did you send these protocols to me on October ninth, 1998?"

"According to the fax sender line at the top I did."

I opened them for her at the witness box to "Stomach-Fluid Sample" then went to the ELMO to illuminate a transparency so all of us could follow. Leitner acknowledged he'd seen it. For the moment I switched the overhead off.

"You became familiar with Colfax personnel, their routines, their hours?"

"Glancingly."

"You knew Dr. Silverman was there only on first and third Fridays."

"I believe you told me that."

"In response to your question?"

"Perhaps. I was helping you look into concerns you had."

"Move to strike."

"Granted. Jury will disregard."

"Dr. Leitner, it was essential for June Stillwell to remain in Colfax hospital, wasn't it?"

"I don't follow you."

"When Dale wanted June moved to a hospital he'd pay for, you convinced him not to, didn't you?"

A quiver of fear or surprise in Hans's eyes. "Dale is disabled. Should conserve his annuities."

"Do you recall telling me the lives of the irreversibly comatose were not worth the public benefits expended on them?"

"Certainly not, and I certainly disagree."

Out-and-out lie number one. Now he'd lie when he thought he could get away with it. I'd try to expose his lies. Now the game was engaged.

CHAPTER 10

Hans Leitner's flush cooled from slow burn to cunning. He saw me now as a mortal threat. He had to understand I wanted more than just to take him down with Stillwell, as the accomplice who was protecting his patient. I hoped my jumpy run of questions was just incoherent enough that he'd miss the double check planned for the endgame, the move that both attacks and unmasks a hidden second attack.

A swallow of Dixie-cup tap water for strength. A sweep of the gallery. Silbi stood out like a peony. I returned to Leitner's eyes. I tried a run of mind-control messages: I have way more pieces than you. The judge just heard about phenol; he'll give me slack. This is cross-examination. I hold the whip hand. With Kirwan not objecting I can ask damn near any question I want. I have a full row of pawns, corroborating witnesses and documents, and you don't even have your queen. A lawyer who'll let you explain on redirect. You're cornered, Hans, and headed for mate.

Messages meant less for him than to gird me for the contest.

"Dr. Leitner, June Stillwell died December fourteenth, 1998, at Platte Valley Hospital. Do you have privileges there?"

"Courtesy privileges only."

"What else do you do there?"

His eyes dropped to his hands, then lifted, as he considered then rejected saying he didn't understand. "I sit on the Quality Assurance Committee at Platte Valley and several area hospitals."

"You're familiar with Platte Valley protocols, as you are with those at Colfax?"

"Yes."

"What did you do the morning of December fourteenth, 1998? The morning of June Stillwell's death?"

"I went to the hospital, as I testified earlier."

"Platte Valley?"

"Yes."

"June Stillwell was not your patient?"

"Certainly not."

"But you asked for and reviewed her chart regardless?" Crucial test question—would he deny what he'd admitted to me, knowing I had a hospital witness to back me up?

"Yes." He figured he was trapped, on this one anyway, but also that he could explain reading the chart when given the chance.

"You dressed in doctor clothes—surgical greens, even though you were not providing medical care to anyone at the hospital that morning?"

A one-shouldered shrug. "I have no idea what clothes I was wearing last December fourteenth."

"You wore a physician identification badge?"

"I went to the hospital. I'm sure I wore a badge."

"You went to the ICU where June was and identified yourself as from the QA Committee."

He nodded. "Yes."

"Showed them your QA ID card?"

"Probably."

"Took June's chart under those false pretenses to the conference room on that floor?"

"A QA Committee member is authorized at any time to review any patient chart without prior notice to maximize patient safety and quality of care."

"Patient safety? I'm just asking whether you went to the conference room."

"Of course. I looked through the chart. I was concerned about June's condition."

"Move to strike as unresponsive."

"So ordered." Otero darkened, now intensely involved. Whatever he thought, he sensed wrongdoing coming to light. "Doctor, answer *only* the question put to you. Did you take the chart to the conference room? Yes or no?"

"Yes. I said yes."

"Proceed, Counsel."

"Dr. Leitner, did you see in the chart that heroic efforts were then under way to prolong June Stillwell's life?"

"That's what intensive care is." A little lash of contempt.

"Did you see that in the chart?"

"Of course."

"Did you see a gastric lavage had been done? Her stomach had been pumped?"

"Yes, as I've discussed that with you."

"Gastric lavage is done when poisoning is suspected?"

"Correct, as I explained to you."

"You knew from Platte Valley protocols a sample of stomach fluid would be sent for analysis to the Front Range Poison Center?"

"Yes." A little weary now.

"Front Range Poison Center has GC/MS—gas chromatograph/mass spectrograph?"

"I'm sure it does."

"The gold standard for identifying poisons."

"And any number of other substances."

"Had June's sample reached the poison center, phenol would have been discovered."

"It likely would have been."

"After reviewing the chart you returned it and walked down the hall past Medical Records toward the lab?"

"Yes." Unhappily spoken, self-discipline slipping as he wrestled in the testimonial straitjacket of my leading questions.

"You proceeded to the refrigerated drop-off for courier pickup of laboratory specimens—"

"I did," he interrupted, a little loudly, "and I took the Stillwell stomach-fluid sample intended for the poison center. Would you like to know why?"

"Doctor," the judge said sharply. "You don't ask questions. You answer them." Shock expressed as anger.

I raised a hand—let it stand. I stole a quick look at the jury. Eight mothers with stricken looks. They'd be mightily disappointed when they found out this testimony was intended for a different jury.

"Dr. Leitner, we'll get to why you did what you did in due time. For now, just confirm this fact. You intercepted the sample."

"I'm afraid that's correct."

"From reading the records you know Ms. Stillwell's stomach fluid was never analyzed for poison at Front Range Poison Center."

"That is also correct."

"Because you prevented that."

"Presumably."

"What did you do with the poison center sample?"

"Threw it away," he said sullenly.

From someone, "Jeez—"

"Where?"

"I emptied it behind my office."

An image rose of the peaceful pine glade at the foot of Flagstaff. Toxic ground.

"There was also a sample for lab analysis at Colfax, so you went there. Dr. Leitner?"

"Yes. I went there."

"The Colfax staff recognized you as a physician. You told us that earlier."

"I assume they did."

"June's weekly stomach-fluid sample had been drawn at midnight as the protocol requires." I switched the ELMO back on and highlighted the line from the protocol.

"Apparently."

"Some eleven hours before she died."

"I don't know. Roughly."

"June's specimen was in the unlocked green refrigerator awaiting pickup for MetPath labs." I highlighted *MetPath* on the next line of the transparency.

"In the refrigerator, according to that protocol."

"Along with the specimens of roughly eighty other Colfax patients in room-number order?"

"Whatever. I don't know." A dispirited tone. The feint was

working, questions so detailed he assumed I had witnesses ready to finger him.

"You took June's sample, Room 110A, when you thought no one was looking. Yes or no."

Otero at the ready.

"Yes—I did that."

"Later you threw it away."

"Yes."

"Poured it out behind your office."

"Yes, and I'd like to say why."

"Let's go back a moment to you in surgical greens in the small conference room at Platte Valley. Poring over June's chart. You use a black Bic ballpoint, don't you?"

"I have no idea," he said with a minute but detectable tic of alarm.

"Look in your pocket."

Lucky break. Black Bic. I motioned to Silbi. She approached, a melodramatic promenade, chin raised, spikes at attention, and handed me the Book of Books. I passed the original hospital chart to Hans.

"In June Stillwell's hospital records, Dr. Leitner, all doctors' orders were handwritten with a black ballpoint." I showed him, the judge, and the jury the originals. Hans agreed.

"Do you see the phrases 'DNR' and 'no cor'?" I put up a transparency with those entries highlighted and projected it on the screen. "Did you alter this chart by adding those phrases?"

"Certainly I did not."

"Really? Look at this." I projected a transparency of his letter to me with "Doctors for Human Rights" highlighted and handed him the original. "This is your handwriting, correct?"

"Correct."

"Compare the *D*'s, *R*'s, *n*'s, *o*'s, *c*'s, and *r*'s, in the chart and in what you wrote to me." I projected an exhibit Moschetti had prepared, six-inch-tall letters from each. Unmistakably the same hand.

"Yes?"

"Now compare them to the slanted, closed handwriting in which all of the other doctors' orders are written." Another Moschetti exhibit.

"All right."

"And consider this infrared photograph showing different black ink was used for 'DNR' and 'no cor.'"

Objectionable, but Kirwan wouldn't object.

"All right."

"Do you dispute the conclusion of the documents examiner, who is prepared to testify in this courtroom that 'DNR' and 'no cor' were improperly added to this chart, by you, Dr. Hans Leitner, doctor for human rights?"

Hans swiveled to the judge. "This must proceed no further without affording me legal representation." Kirwan wasn't doing it, so Leitner would argue for himself. "This is wholly unexpected and unfair cross-examination. Mr. Stone is not qualified to act as his own expert witness. Mr. Kirwan is not protecting me from these unfair attacks. I request an immediate hearing to determine my rights."

"Are you finished?" the judge asked quietly. He'd just learned June was poisoned and that the witness had destroyed the evidence. Leitner's complaint of unfairness wasn't going to go real far. "You are a witness, not a party. An expert witness, paid handsomely for your testimony, which you willingly agreed to give. Is he also under subpoena?"

Kirwan rose and fixed Leitner with a withering look. "He is." I heard April's pressured breath beside me, at least as hot as Kirwan's. The courtroom was a vortex of bridled accusations, at its center Leitner, who might feel most betrayed of all. Stripped of discipline, I hoped, and whipped to a foolhardy rage, while I had to empty myself of both umbrage and sympathy. Go cold with purpose. Draw a bead and squeeze.

"You are subject," the judge continued, "to court order by subpoena to appear and respond to questions put to you. Unless you contemplate invoking your right against self-incrimination, you have to respond to questions put under oath. You are under subpoena and you must remain in court. You may have a lawyer present in the gallery but not as a participant in these proceedings because you are only a witness, not a party. I would like to know if you are considering invoking the Fifth Amendment. Do you need to confer with counsel before responding?"

"I do not need to confer with counsel." Leitner's lips shrank.

"Do you think you may need to invoke Fifth Amendment protection in response to Mr. Stone's examination?"

The jurors, all of us, hung on the question.

"No. I just want a chance to explain."

"Be warned you must respond to Mr. Stone's questions without explanation unless invited. If Mr. Kirwan later asks you to explain, you may, but not otherwise. Do you want to reconsider?"

A frozen moment. "No."

"Would you like a few minutes to contact counsel?"

"No." Hans drilled me eye to eye. He meant I would have been his counsel except that I'd betrayed him. He also meant he'd fight this out alone, *mano a mano*. A staggeringly reckless move, deciding to play on, but not unexpected. The pride that goeth before.

"Proceed, then." Otero sat back, black sleeves crossed.

I looked off a moment at the portrait of Judge Horace Marler, a study in reproach. Again I justified to myself what I was about to do to a friend and colleague. I closed my eyes and breathed.

"Well, then, Hans. Dr. Leitner," I said gently. "Did you write 'DNR' and 'no cor' on four pages of June Stillwell's chart when you had it in that conference room?"

"Yes, I did."

I glanced at Paige, pretending to scribble in a pad to hide a thunderstruck expression. But I'd figured Leitner might admit it. His style of play was becoming clear. Rather than fight facts he thought I had the evidence to prove, he'd explain them later, so confident was he of his persuasive powers. But how could *this* be explained?

"It was—" he began. "Forget it." Detecting Otero coming forward in his chair.

"What does 'no cor' mean?"

"No heroic measures to keep her heart going if she was likely terminal or persistent vegetative."

"That's what it meant at Platte Valley?"

"Yes," he said hoarsely.

"As defined by your QA Committee there?" And as fed to me by Silbi.

"Yes."

"Heroic measures such as those you knew were in fact at that time being employed to keep June alive, as you testified?"

Another yes.

"'DNR' means?"

"Do not resuscitate."

"Do not revive June if she appears to be dying?"

"Yes."

I went a few steps toward the witness box and returned to the podium, walking off the tension, finger to my lip. Time to roll out the bishops. Go diagonal.

"Fall of 1998—you knew April had a lawyer, a good, tough lawyer. Paige Jorritsma." My eyes met hers, less melancholy now.

"I don't dispute that."

"But you knew she had no viable claims against Dale Stillwell and his annuities so long as June was alive. You testified to that."

He threw up his hands.

"Yes?"

"Yes."

"In combination these two facts—that Ms. Jorritsma was April's lawyer, and second, that claims against Stillwell were frustrated so long as June remained alive—these facts worried you a great deal."

"Nonsense. I don't know what you mean."

"A *deep pocket*—do you know what that means?"

"Of course."

"We all know what *deep pocket* means. You were afraid you and your five-million-dollar policy were the deep pockets Paige Jorritsma and April Mooney would eventually come after if they couldn't get to the deep pockets of Stillwell's twelve million in annuities since June was still alive."

"Utter nonsense." Of course he'd deny it, but now motive was on the table.

"If you could offer up, as it were, your patient's annuities to April's claims, Paige would never think about claims against you."

"Utter bloody nonsense." He hugged his elbows defensively. "What claims against me could I possibly have been worried about?"

"Well, let's see. You maintain a file of clippings about malpractice claims against psychiatrists and pathologists, your specialties?"

He couldn't deny it. I might have a copy. "I do. You know because you rifled my files."

"Move to strike." A test of how Otero was leaning. A judge might be interested in a lawyer rifling files.

"Granted. Doctor, I've warned you repeatedly."

"Your legal medicine academy," I said, "follows trends in malpractice litigation against psychiatrists, doesn't it?" A guess.

"There is a committee that does."

"On which you sit?"

"I do." He massaged the back of a hand.

"The most feared claim of psychiatric negligence is the failure to prevent a foreseeably dangerous patient from harming himself or others. Correct?"

"Perhaps."

"You keep clippings of just such cases."

"I'm sure I do."

"*Williamson versus Lipzin,* for example."

"Remind me."

"A psychiatric patient who was out of medication killed two people and was found not guilty by reason of insanity. The victims' families sued the psychiatrist, who'd retired without arranging for coverage of the patient by another doctor or providing for medication to be continued."

"I don't know if I have a clipping."

"You have clippings of similar cases?"

"I'm sure."

"There are lots of cases like that?"

"Unfortunately, there are."

"You've given risk-management talks at medico-legal meetings about just such cases." Another guess. He confirmed it.

"You've lobbied for tort reform immunity for just such liability?"

"This is completely irrelevant." Objecting for himself again.

"Answer the question." Otero grunted.

Hans looked from the judge to me, to the jury, to Kirwan, deciding on his audience but getting nowhere. His audience wasn't in the room.

"Our committee employs a spokesman," he said, "to present our views to lawmakers about the shakedown that malpractice suits are all about. Including suits like those you mentioned, Mr.

Stone, where someone tries to hold a *doctor* responsible when his patient hurts someone."

"Those claims are at the top of your lobbyists' list, aren't they?"

"It's where they belong. The patient should be responsible for his own actions," he said, his patient not being present. "The physician shouldn't be legally responsible."

"For everything his wacko patients do?"

"Put it as you wish."

"Number one on the lobbyists' priority list. Knock out claims for poorly treated patients who hurt themselves or others. Since that's the claim where you get hit with the big verdicts. When a negligently treated patient kills or maims."

"What's your question?"

"A living June Stillwell, with potential life-care costs of, what? As much as twelve to fifteen million. A verdict for negligently allowing that to happen to her could eradicate your career, livelihood, assets, everything."

"What possible claim could there be against me?" he said strenuously. He went to Otero. No help there.

"Psychiatrists are not immune in Colorado from liability for failing to prevent foreseeable harm caused by a dangerous patient, are they?"

"You are the lawyer, Mr. Stone."

"Are they?"

"Not in Colorado."

"Dr. Leitner, this morning you told Mr. Kirwan that Dale Stillwell has been your patient, under your care, for four years. But he has not been under your continuous care, has he?"

"He remains under my care."

I glanced at Kirwan and the back of the court. Still no sign of Stillwell and Edson.

"Your care of Dale Stillwell has not been continuous, has it?"

"Roughly continuous, yes, it has been."

"You told us you were back and forth between the Balkans, The Hague, Washington, elsewhere, again and again in 1997 and 1998."

"Do you want to go through it again?"

"During the eleven months between August eleventh, 1997,

until July twentieth, 1998, after June Stillwell was assaulted, how many times did you see Dale Stillwell?"

"I have no idea without consulting his chart." He clicked up to Otero, looking for *in limine* help. Otero just brooded at his laptop.

"You didn't see him a single time in that eleven-month period, did you?"

"That doesn't sound right. I'd have to look at the chart." Righteous indignation that failed to take.

"All right." I drifted across to Paige. She handed me the color-coded folder from a trial bag. I sauntered up to Leitner. "Here it is."

"This is impossible. The judge ruled *in limine*. This violates physician/patient confidences. *How did you get this?*" Legal arguments spilling over into rage.

"Counsel—a sidebar?" the judge suggested.

"Yes, Your Honor, after two more questions, if I may."

"Objection, Mr. Kirwan?"

"No, sir." Beaming coldly.

"Dr. Leitner, you read the *in limine* order?"

"I certainly did." Getting animated, which didn't work for Hans. He did best when most capacious—large, generous, thoughtful, wise. "And I know the case it's based on, *Jaffe versus Redmond*. I helped with the academy's amicus brief in *Jaffe*. And let me remind you, Mr. Stone, that the Supreme Court held the therapist privilege rooted in the imperative need for confidence and trust between health-care provider and client. Principles you appear to disdain."

"The patient must be able to trust his doctor."

"Which is why you're out of line." Still snappy. Otero letting it pass.

"Trust—the judge's *in limine* ruling discusses trust and confidence. It also says Dale Stillwell's therapy records remain privileged because 'he cannot assert a mental capacity defense, *having been found competent by this court.*'"

Otero hiked to the edge of his seat. I was cross-examining a witness about his own rulings. No judge wants to be evidence in his own case.

"It says as much."

"Whose doing was that? Who made sure Dale Stillwell would be found competent?"

"What are you talking about?"

"You testified to District Judge Otero in August of last year that Dale Stillwell was competent. That didn't do *him* any good. But it kept your therapy notes out of the hands of the DA, Paige Jorritsma, Kevin Kirwan too." These weren't questions. This was for Otero. Kirwan was letting me go. The judge was letting me go too. At the competency hearing, Leitner had also manipulated him.

I popped Stillwell's chart with my index finger. "You have some very good reasons for trying to keep these records from seeing the light of day."

"Mr. Stone," Otero finally interceded. "That's your fourth or fifth question. Enough for now. There's a lot to digest. The jury shall be in recess while we sort this out." We watched them amble reluctantly away, fingers gliding along the railing.

"Now," Otero said sternly. "Mr. Stone. You have a lot more convincing to do before I vacate my ruling, so make it good."

Going into the defendant's therapy records would indeed violate the ruling, I acknowledged, but the ruling was designed to protect the physician/patient privilege. The privilege is owned by the patient, not the doctor. The patient may waive it, and the defendant has. I handed him the authorization signed by Stillwell the afternoon before that allowed release of records to me and their introduction as evidence in his trial.

"Mr. Kirwan, your position?"

"I agree with him. It's a whole new kettle of fish, Your Honor. My client has waived. On with the show."

"I just hope the fish isn't one of your red herrings." Otero humor making a rare appearance. "You see, Mr. Stone, my problem is, as this witness protested earlier, what is the relevancy? Assume he committed malpractice. Assume that led to Ms. Stillwell's assault and eventual death. The doctor isn't a party defendant. How does his negligence relate to April Mooney's claim?"

A defense tilt now and it was all over. "I'll tie it up, Your Honor." I would, if everything fell perfectly into place.

"Your Honor." Kirwan stood. "The defense concedes the chart's relevancy and jointly with plaintiff moves you to vacate your *in limine* ruling. The records are relevant and they are no longer privileged." The showboat smoothly subordinate to opposing counsel, saving my ass and his string.

Otero studied Leitner. The witness had the boggled look of a man double-teamed, a steer caught short in team roping. The judge appeared to think better of discussing it further in his presence and said, "I want to hear from the defendant."

Kirwan went looking for him. They were back shortly at the double doors. Stillwell buttoned his tweed jacket. He approached the gate with gallows sobriety. Leitner avoided his patient's eyes, morosely looking away. The place felt suffocating in unhappiness.

Stillwell stepped to the well below the bench. He clasped his hands in front of him like a schoolboy. He told the judge he w-wanted the story of him and his d-doctor told to the w-world.

CHAPTER 11

With his patient watching and the patient's chart in my hand, a copy of the chart in his, a sheaf of abstracts Quierin had printed out in chambers, and a set of Kinko's transparencies at the ready, Hans had no choice. He could only be Hans the educator, the world's best medical expert. Let's talk about post-traumatic stress, I said.

"In 1996, at the trial of *Stillwell versus Western Pacific Railroad,* you testified that Dale Stillwell had the most severe case of post-traumatic stress disorder you'd seen in your career."

"At the time, it was. Later I went to Bosnia."

"Your career includes having been an original PTSD researcher at the West Haven VA Hospital in the 1970s?"

"Yes."

"And many scholarly publications on this disorder."

"Correct."

"And supervision of combat PTS wards at VA hospitals?"

"Yes."

"Dr. Leitner, what was the traumatic event that left Dale Stillwell with PTSD?"

"A railyard accident in which he was crushed between two locomotives with serious injuries, including a focal injury to the prefrontal lobe of his brain."

"Explain for us why these injuries resulted in PTSD."

By force of habit Hans addressed the attentive jury, though he had to know where this was bound. The effortless rhythm of expert testimony had him in its sway. I'd prompt; he'd expound. He couldn't resist, nor would he try; it was all there in the chart in his upright, open handwriting.

"Ordinarily," he said, "the brain protects itself from PTSD with a self-deception called retrograde amnesia. After severe trauma the brain erases its memory of events before as well as after the injury, and the victim has no retained knowledge of the horror of what happened to him. Unusually, Dale retained highly vivid memories of everything surrounding that extraordinary trauma, so much so that to remember the accident is to relive it."

"Are Dale Stillwell's painful memories any different from those all of us have?"

"Very much so. Dale reexperiences a trauma for which he has hypermnesia, or an excessively real and detailed recall. Psychologically, he has to split off the traumatic hypermemory in order to coexist with it."

Stillwell sat stock-still, occasionally nodding along. He knew this part well. Insight into his condition had been part of the treatment. April watched him intently, as though the two-dimensional projection she'd despised was turning into a full-fleshed human being before her eyes.

"Explain for us the concept of splitting, Dr. Leitner."

"I'll try. In severe PTSD the trauma is so painful it cannot be integrated into conscious experience. It is kept separate and given a kind of underground psychological life. The split-off traumatic event is always real, present, continuing. Like some horrible version of the *Groundhog Day* film, it never ends, it is never in the past. The sufferer actually splits into two streams of consciousness. One is his normal, integrated consciousness composed of memories, thoughts, feelings, desires under the control of a single self. In this world the trauma, in effect, never happened. The other is a never-ending living hell of, in Dale's case, the terror of being crushed alive by thousands of tons of steel."

"The patient is either in one world or the other?"

"The patient lives in the real world but arrives in hell by

momentary panic, by nightmare, and, most important, by dissociation."

"What is dissociation?"

"Certain triggers, trauma-related stimuli, cause a patient to dissociate, to flip into the other world and relive the trauma as though it were happening again. The nightmare comes to life and the conscious person—is temporarily lost."

"A different person."

"An altered identity in an altered reality. Dissociation can range from subtle distortions of time and changes in thinking and feeling to fugue states, with the patient sometimes hundreds of miles away, days later, with no idea what happened. In Dale's case, it usually took the form of a life-or-death struggle to repel the terror."

"And no memory afterward?"

"None. Amnesia is the hallmark of dissociation."

"If the trauma involved a head injury, how does that affect PTSD prognosis?"

"Serious head injuries often don't cause PTSD because of retrograde amnesia. But with hypermnesia like Dale's, our studies of combat PTSD in vets showed those with head injuries had far more intractable PTS and a much greater tendency to dissociate."

"Tell us now"—I skipped a beat—"about PTS dissociation and violence."

"Trauma is by definition violent. In everyone trauma can produce a fight-or-flight response. PTS dissociation usually takes the form of one or the other, depending on personality. Some go into a fugue state, flight, and literally flee to somewhere else. Some fight. What and whom they fight can be anything in their path, as if they're a trapped animal, or it can have a recurrent focus."

"Innocent people can be hurt. Even killed."

"Absolutely, but remember, the violent dissociative is innocent too."

Hans's eyes came to rest on his patient. A hand opened in mute apology. Stillwell shook his head, rejecting what? His doctor or his innocence?

"And the patient has no memory of any violence done?"

"Almost never."

"A risk like this requires vigilance on the part of the thera-pist."

"Yes."

"I'm sure you impressed your staff at VA PTS wards with the need to be on guard for dissociative violence."

"Always."

"Can you counsel a PTS dissociative to avoid violence?"

"No." He turned to the jury to explain. "The dissociative is helpless to control a fight or rage response when dissociating. You can't counsel changes of behavior. You treat them by taking steps to prevent dissociation, not to make them behave while dissociating."

"How do you do that? What is the treatment?"

"Psychotherapy, hypnotherapy, drug treatment."

"Hypnotherapy is—hypnosis?"

"Yes. Actually, hypnosis is dissociation, the same phenome-non. PTS patients are the most hypnotizable people there are. Hypnosis gives us a controlled way to access their other world. A structured way to reexperience the trauma without terror, and gradually, painstakingly reintegrate it."

"Was Dale Stillwell hypnotizable?"

Leitner checked the chart. "He had a very high score."

"How frequently did you employ hypnotherapy?"

"At every session once treatment began."

"With good results?"

"Yes. As you know from the chart, Dale stopped dissociat-ing."

"As a result of treatment? Hypnosis and medication?"

"That was my conclusion, as you've read."

"With hypnosis you were able to take Dale into the accident, in fact to induce dissociation."

"Yes, in a calm and controlled way, so he could face it. Begin to come to grips with it."

"When you took him with a trance back to the accident, June was there?"

"She was always there. The chart confirms that. She was the only other person. The engineer and the one who ran up after-ward. Hypnotized, he always saw June. The accident June, not June his wife."

"We'll come back to that shortly. First, let's talk about

your course of treatment. Dale Stillwell had been your patient since . . . ?"

"Since October 1995. At that time he remained in intensive brain-injury rehabilitation."

"Was his PTSD recognized?"

"Only that it was likely. The brain injury masked everything. We had to wait as he emerged to assess psychological damage."

"When was his PTSD assessed?"

"May twentieth, 1996." Leitner skimmed over the page. "His trial was approaching. I was to testify. A comprehensive assessment was due. The results were alarming."

"How did you evaluate him?"

"I tried to get a psychological history. I never learned much about Dale's life before the accident, just a few confused fragments of autobiography." Stillwell was, not just to us, but even to himself, a cipher. "Not unusual, by the way, in someone whose mind has been rocked by trauma like this. Remember, Dale is dealing with at least two psychiatric diagnoses. PTS plus personality disorder from traumatic brain injury. Terrible impulse control. The incoherence of his world. It couldn't have been easy—"

"For June," I said.

"Not easy at all."

"What else did your assessment entail?"

"For PTS specifically I did a structured interview and questionnaire called the SCID-D, and later, after the trial, I gave him a yohimbine challenge. In every way he was off the chart. Very, very severe."

"Yohimbine challenge? What's that?"

"The purpose is to determine whether the patient is a candidate for certain drugs. Yohimbine is an alpha-adrenergic antagonist. Give a true PTS dissociative a yohimbine injection and he may go to his other world. It's not a very nice thing to do and it can be a dangerous thing to do."

"What did Dale do when challenged on yohimbine?" I put the transparency of that day's notes on the ELMO.

"He had a full-blown dissociative flashback to his accident, which was very good news. It meant he would be treatable with an alpha-adrenergic agonist. Clonidine could close the same door yohimbine opened."

"What did he actually do?"

"He was in hell. The accident was happening again. He was being crushed between two locomotives. We were in my office, just the two of us—and he attacked me."

"He came after you, according to your notes." At the ELMO lightbox I painted orange Hi-Liter across the description.

"He was in a rage. A panic. He opened a cut on my head."

"With a stapler."

"He tried to beat me with a stapler, yes."

"Twelve stitches. You told him next session."

"He needed to know what he did."

"Why you, Dr. Leitner?"

"I was there. If you'd been there, it would have been you. It was—nothing personal." Leitner smiled. "When he looked at me, he didn't see a human being, much less his doctor. He saw threat incarnate."

"Had June been there—"

"She'd have gotten hurt."

"Worse than you?"

"Quite likely."

"It's important for us to understand why."

"I'm aware of that." Leitner hunched a shoulder. "And I'll tell you. There had been a couple of incidents earlier. One not long after he came out of his coma. June leaned over him as he lay on his back in a hospital bed. Dale looked up at her and went—crazy. Tore from the bed, chased her into the hall despite his condition, and was restrained after."

I'd reviewed the hospital chart as conservator in 1996. Delusional from brain injury, they'd thought at the time.

"Several times after, he was discharged home. She defended herself somehow. Occasionally Dale went into a fugue for an hour or so, but not for any three-day trails of destruction. Dale's episodes were usually brief and very intense, under a minute. Then he snaps to his senses. Has no idea what happened."

"Did the episodes continue?"

"The first week of treatment it happened again, full-blown. She came with him, in tears, and described it. I explained it wasn't Dale and it wasn't her. It was the train he was fighting."

"June was the focus of his dissociative violence?"

"I shouldn't admit this under oath, I know, but it's unmistakable when you read the chart."

"It is, indeed. June was in great peril if Dale's illness wasn't properly treated, wasn't she?" I put up a transparency.

"She was, as I wrote on that page."

"Why June?"

"Go to the facts of the accident. He didn't know her then. A stranger but the one in control, driving the train, when that cataclysmic thing happened. Hers was the face and voice he saw before and the first face and voice after being smashed between two engines with the breath, almost the life, choked out of him. He lay on his back, both lungs collapsed, a penetrating head wound open to the brain, eleven broken bones. Gasping, soaked in blood, but awake, hyperawake, horror-stricken. The first person to him, the face that bent over his, was that of June, who would become his wife, whom, in his other, integrated world he loved in his awkward, demanding way."

Leitner's and Stillwell's eyes met again, and again the hand opened. Forced to tell the truth, Hans would tell it well.

"Dale was resentful and terribly jealous, but he deeply loved his wife. And June . . ." Hans sighed. "June was the last person on earth Dale should have married. In his psychological underworld, June's face wasn't that of his wife but the face of the stranger at the controls. The face that loomed over his as he lay on his back, crushed and gulping for air."

"'June is the face of his trauma,'" I read from the August 30, 1996, therapy notes, projected in orange. "'She is the accident. June is the train.'"

CHAPTER 12

The witness was ordered not to leave the chair during the ten-minute recess. The bailiff came forward at the judge's direction, hand on the grip of his revolver. Leitner rolled his head back and stared at the ceiling. I needed a reality check, but reporters were massing at the gallery gate. Quierin sat back with the curly-haired guy, hand-talking like a European as the guy filled his pad. April, Paige, and I found the back door to chambers and the little hearing room.

April hugged me. Light in her eyes, but she looked strong. "I can't tell you how important this is."

"I know."

"What else have you got?" Paige asked.

"Not a whole lot. Five or six moves. Where are we, as you see it?"

"Where we are is poisoning—proved. Motive—proved. Opportunity—proved. Cover-up with consciousness of guilt. Proved. Plus the judge believes. Good going, Elliot."

"So far."

"But you're not there yet. No direct evidence."

"It's a circumstantial case. Like yours against Stillwell. Like theirs against April."

"You need more."

"He won't confess."

"I know."

"He did it."

"I know, but it has to be—plausible. Would this doctor really take a life to save his career? Would he really go to such lengths?"

"I know Leitner. That's what he did. It seemed like a logical process, all the way to poisoning. In his mind he wasn't taking a life. June's life was already lost."

"He thinks he knows you."

"He knows I know he did it."

"*Show* he did it, Elliot." A knock at the door. The clerk telling us to get back in court. "Somehow, you have to show he did it."

Otero put the trial back on the record and observed that the witness remained under oath. "Mr. Stone?"

I held Stillwell's chart with both hands like a preacher with a Bible.

"Dr. Leitner, this afternoon you told us you had no reason to think Dale Stillwell might harm his wife when he visited. Was that true?"

"It was. Dale has been carefully treated and medicated since July twentieth of last year, as you also know from the chart. He will not dissociate now and wouldn't have last fall. He visited June to grieve. Because he loved her." Leitner was looking square at April. He was talking, really, to her. "May I, Elliot?"

I took it to mean he had something to add for April's benefit. "Please."

"Dale's greatest fear was of losing June, and he saw April as a threat. He knew she hated him for taking her mother from her. He knew how attached June was to April, which is why he walled her out. His jealousy of April was pathological. I think he understands that. It continued even while June was in Colfax."

Stillwell was doubled over at the table, head on his arms. April's blue eyes shone with understanding.

"Dale came each Sunday to talk with his wife. Converse with her in his mind. To speak of his love and sorrow, and to apologize. And afterward he'd curse himself and his illness—for what happened."

"And no dissociation."

"None since last July."

"Dale is highly treatable."

"I see I wrote that he is."

Leitner's clinical skills were in fact impressive. The therapy notes revealed a subtle diagnostician with encyclopedic depth. A practical clinician changing his patient's life for the better, a visit at a time. But they also showed his Achilles' heel. His attention wandered. He loved puzzles, and solving one, he'd seek out another. Between the lines you could see him growing distracted, feel a vagrant need for stimulation drawing him away.

What a shame Hans lost interest in, or patience with, clinical work, healing individuals. That he left career for calling. Maybe that's what he meant when he warned me not to. That I'd be headed for a fall. Warning me based on his own example.

"You had one-hour sessions with Dale two times a week in 1996."

"Correct."

"In short order you were able to eliminate dissociative episodes from Dale Stillwell's life."

"Once we titrated, adjusted, the clonidine, which took a few weeks, Dale was in good shape. I could join you in Vukovar that September."

"You arranged for coverage then. Dr. Fagen was available if Dale needed him and for medication while you worked with me in Vukovar." A transparency confirmed it.

"Yes."

"That was your routine, to note in a patient's chart who provided coverage while you were away."

"That's standard. I have very few patients, not much of a routine."

"And you were busy with other things?"

"I was."

"Increasingly so?"

"Yes."

"After you returned from Vukovar, you continued seeing Dale two times a week, hypnosis each time."

"Yes."

"With good results?"

"He was more and more functional. In trances he confronted

the accident fearfully but without terror. His rage began to mellow."

"The clonidine prescription was quite regular, a one-month
bottle with one refill."

"Yes."

"But that changed. When?"

"On August eleventh, 1997, because I knew I would mostly
be out of state, I wrote it for twelve refills."

"Instead of one?"

"Correct."

"We'll need to come back to that."

"I suppose you will." He gave me an empty smile.

"Looking through your notes, there are gaps in your treatment schedule."

"When I was away."

"Sometimes coverage is noted. Sometimes not. Why is
that?"

"I don't know."

"Carelessness? Confidence he was okay on his own? Or you
just got busy?"

"Perhaps. Some of each."

"You'd solved the fascinating diagnostic and treatment challenges. You understood Dale Stillwell. You moved on to other
interests because you need new challenges. Your human-rights
works was paramount, you testified."

"If you wish."

"You saw Dale twice in May 1997, twice each in June and
July, and once in August, then not again until July twentieth,
1998, over eleven months later. Why?"

"I was gone most of that time. Part of it I spent with you in
The Hague."

"Nothing is charted about coverage then. Was no physician
covering Dale for you those eleven months?"

He pulled an ear. "Apparently not."

"You left Dale on his own with a year's worth of clonidine."

"I—" He allowed his head a single shake. "Put it how you
like. He was doing quite well."

"But, predictably, he was likely to start dissociating again."

"Only in hindsight."

"In foresight too. There were danger signs, weren't there, the summer of 1997?"

He glanced at the chart, flipped the page. A shoulder flexed, the faintest of shrugs.

"Clonidine has a serious drawback, doesn't it?" According to Quierin's MedLine research. "Tolerance."

"Tolerance is a problem."

"Looking back through your chart, don't you see signs of clonidine tolerance the summer of 1997? Increased nightmares. A panic attack driving in July. Disorientation, what you described as tunnel vision, an out-of-body experience. Dale's traumatic underworld was starting to intrude again, wasn't it?"

"It does appear he was developing tolerance to the drug," Leitner quietly acknowledged. "The therapeutic effects were weakening."

"What could you have done about that?"

The rhythm of question and answer, lawyer and expert, swept on irresistibly, the dance with his tormentor he couldn't escape. There was an answer to my question, he knew it, and he was helpless not to give it.

"One can substitute guanfacine for clonidine and usually restore the therapeutic effects, though tolerance to guanfacine develops too."

"Then back to clonidine."

"Correct. I didn't fully appreciate the tolerance problem at the time, I guess."

"You had a lot on your plate. Distractions."

"Such as your trial in The Hague." A dry, rueful smile.

"'Drug treatment of PTS dissociatives is challenging and fraught with risk. It must be carefully monitored.'"

"I have to agree."

"I'm quoting you. A letter to the *American Journal of Psychiatry,* August 1996, abstracted on MedLine."

"I recall it."

I walked to the front of the podium and leaned back against it. I shook my head with heartfelt regrets. He'd been a mentor to me, a sort of hero. Some stages of this process cut deep. Ten feet away Hans's eyes rose to mine as regretful and sincere. We could have been in someone's living room.

"Careful monitoring because of the risks," I said. "But,

Hans, you let Dale Stillwell's PTS dissociation and treatment go *unmonitored for close to a year,* with no other physician for him to turn to."

"It was in hindsight a mistake. Mr. Stone," he added pointedly.

"You crossed your fingers, gave your patient a year's worth of pills, and went off to pursue glamour and sainthood as a human-rights champion."

"That's a cheap shot, Elliot."

"I retract it." But it was where I had to go. "You told me earlier your treatment of Dale Stillwell has been roughly continuous. He's been your patient for years. He remains your patient."

"Yes."

"Physicians have duties that arise from the patient relationship. And patients have rights. Human rights, if you will."

He gave it a little thought. "I agree."

"A physician has the ethical duty to provide for treatment and medication coverage when he's away."

Now Hans sat straight and severe—impaled. "There's a Colorado ethics opinion. The AMA code."

"Especially when serious harm may happen otherwise."

"Yes." He sighed without sound. "I agree."

"You failed to meet these responsibilities, Dr. Leitner, during these eleven months."

"I did." What else could he say?

"Why?"

"I just—didn't do it."

"Your attention was elsewhere?"

"It obviously was."

I turned and walked back between counsel tables, to my left Dale Stillwell, April to my right. People who were harmed, whose rights were abused.

"What happened July fifteenth, 1998?" I asked suddenly. Stillwell stiffened. His eyes began to range. This was the part his doctor didn't tell him. April came forward in her seat.

"We'll never know for sure," Leitner said. "Dale has amnesia. June died. No one else was there."

"But you learned enough through hypnosis. You understood Dale Stillwell well enough to put it together, didn't you?" My fingers went to the chart.

"Some of it."

"Tell them, Hans. Dale and April have the *right* to know."

Sometimes Willie Mays misses, and sometimes moments of truth aren't: Stillwell on the bench by the probate window.

"Tell them the truth at last."

Leitner looked at his patient but couldn't bear it. He gazed away, distant, as though imagining that night. "I believe—" he finally said, unable to endure his own silence any longer, aware of where this would take us but unable to block it and perhaps not wanting to. "They were together in bed, and, I believe, they were making love. I believe June Stillwell cried out during love-making—" His voice broke. He'd seen April's shock and sorrow, heard Stillwell's strangled sob.

"Tell them."

"Dale was on his back. June's face rose over his and she cried out."

"And he dissociated?"

"He was there, fighting for his life. He threw her over, stood, and grabbed and raised an object as she lay cowering on the bed. And he hit her with it. He saw now, still not his wife, but an injured person lying bleeding, and not moving. He covered her in blankets, as he'd been trained as a railroad medic for shock. As he'd been covered that day in the railyard in the snow."

"He came out of it?"

"He came out of it with no memory. But he knew he must have hit her. The object was smeared with her blood. He couldn't rouse her and thought he'd killed her. He was horrified"— Stillwell let out now not a sob but a muffled sound of pain—"later to learn she was alive," Leitner finished quietly.

"Dale Stillwell thought he'd killed his wife and panicked." I continued the narrative for him. "He got rid of the object, the figurine, and we know the rest, I believe."

Paige held April, but no one touched a hand to Stillwell, now dark and swollen with anger.

"Dr. Leitner, when you found out this had happened, you were recently back from The Hague."

"Yes. I testified in your case."

"You and Dale had been out of touch almost a year?"

"Yes."

"You pulled his chart," I guessed, "from the left cabinet,

fourth drawer down. You read it first to last. It must have been a sickening exercise. Horrible injuries to an innocent person that could have been prevented."

"And I was responsible, you mean?" A short, bitter laugh and he shifted in the chair. His jaw knotted. He was taking a stand. Trading the understanding, compassionate pose, and the pitiable, defeated one, for defiance. He thought he'd seen the next deadly move and he had to put up a fight. "That is *not* how I felt."

"No? In this court, in this trial, you could have defended him. You had everything"—I slammed the chart on the table— "*everything* Dale Stillwell needed to be exonerated from the claim that he murdered his wife. Didn't you, Hans?"

He glared. "I'm not a lawyer. I don't think like you."

"But instead you fought it. You did all you could to keep this evidence"—I slammed the chart again—"exculpatory evidence, from ever being seen by a judge or jury. Or grand jury. Didn't you?"

"I don't accept that, Mr. Stone."

"*We all saw it,* Dr. Leitner. Everyone in this courtroom saw it. You were willing to sell your patient out. You were willing to incriminate him for murder when you knew he was innocent. *Why?*"

Why? The question he'd been ravening for all day, that would finally give him the chance to explain, and he saw it was a trap. That I *wanted* him to say Stillwell confessed to poisoning June because it would drive home my point, that he'd incriminate his own patient to save his reputation. That reputation meant more than life itself.

The white king's escape was blocked. Hans couldn't explain, and there was no one left but him.

Double check.

"Your Honor," he appealed for help. "This is—argumentative." Like a whiny lawyer.

Otero opened his hand to me: continue.

"*Why, Hans?* Because this chart, this evidence exonerating Dale Stillwell, would bring your malpractice to light?"

He made a ragged noise intended to sound derisive.

"If you were ready to send your patient up, even to death

row, to conceal your substandard care, to protect your practice, and your income, your reputation, *you'd—do—anything.*"

I was growling. I was close to the deep end.

"*You'd do anything.*"

Hans just stared.

"Where were you late in the afternoon last December thirteenth when Dale Stillwell was frantically looking for you, not me, in the White Spot diner?"

Leitner suddenly flashed on Stillwell, who might well testify next. He wasn't pleased with what he saw.

"I—don't remember. That's seven months ago," he added lamely.

"You were alone with June Stillwell, weren't you?"

He made a helpless gesture.

"With a can of mint-scented air freshener and a vial of phenol."

His silence felt complete. Permanent. As though it might continue the rest of his life, like the silence of a coma. He was out of moves.

Finally the judge spoke. "The record shall reflect the witness did not deny, verbally or otherwise, the last two questions put to him."

"No redirect," Kirwan said.

Triple check and mate.

CHAPTER 13

Quierin and Darwin were next door sharing a smoke with the exhibitionist when Roybal's cruiser eased to the curb. Quierin joined me on the porch, hand radio in a belt holster like in Boz. We sat on the wicker couch and waited. Another long, edgeless evening of cooling skies and air eddies, shadows of birds and bats, sounds of mourning. The moan in the canyon of the snowmelt-fed creek. The cries of jays. Across town the eight o'clock Burlington Northern freight. Two longs, a short, and a long. *Remember me—*

Roybal rounded his patrol car and opened the passenger door. Hans got out, twisted off his blazer, and dropped it on the seat. He cleared his throat and said nothing, standing on the walk as in a schoolyard challenge, head cocked and jaw at a jut.

"Your friend," Roybal called to us, coming up behind him. "The doctor here. Wants to know you got a minute."

I waved to them and Leitner led the way, heaving up the sandstone steps.

"What about the search?" I asked.

"Where we're headed next," Roybal said. Hans's office, where Millsap and company would be waiting with a search warrant. When Hans had finished testifying, Otero had ordered Lanny, the bailiff, to detain him while Otero conferred with the

DA. The spectacle of Hans in custody in a courtroom was more than I cared to sit through just then, and we had left. Roybal said Otero pitched a little fit when he found out Chief Judge Chambliss, who presided over the grand jury, had already issued the search warrant. "Otero says DA knows, plaintiff, defendant, Chambliss, all the trial counsel, and half the witnesses know. 'Everybody but you and me,' Otero tells the doc here. At which point Lanny," the bailiff, "pops up and says, 'I never knowed about him, Judge.'" Roybal doubled up laughing and whacked one of the turned Victorian stanchions on old Judge Marler's porch.

Otero's piques die off quickly and he's back to business. As Quierin had learned by hand radio, he had soon called his court to order and found probable cause to issue a warrant for Hans's arrest. He read Hans his rights and ordered him into Roybal's custody pending investigation and the gathering of evidence. They were now en route to the Flagstaff office where Hans would be joined, to observe the search, by the only available associate on short notice from the law office of Howard LaFond, whom Hans had called for representation.

I told Hans he should get out of here, proceed with the search. That Howie would forbid his talking with us if he knew.

"Fuck LaFond." Jaw forward as a prow.

I opened my hands, shook my head, and held the front door wide.

I'd seen the search warrant, damn near drafted it, organized it by the hanging file categories in his cabinets—articles, research, clippings. *The Disposition of Toxic Chemicals in Man.* The computer. Not much he could do about the computer. Too late to throw it off the Tallahatchie Bridge.

I could see why Hans wanted to postpone the reckoning by coming here. The search, then the grim procedurals, jail-or-bail hearings, a Boulder perp walk with a mountain backdrop, and, not just for him but his wife, medical colleagues, our side too, scandal-addled inquisitions by the cranky media come to town.

"You bastard," he muttered as he passed me, eyeing the Pis on the pedestal in the front hall. *Bastard* was mild. Life as he knew it was over.

Without speaking, we went to the scarred breakfast table

under Kathleen's portrait in beans. Leitner scraped his straight-backed chair to the table. Roybal stood inches behind him, grinning and slapping a thumb in his palm. I studied Hans's eyes, vacant of threat. He'd come for pity, I figured. "Drinks?" I asked. Roybal shook his head. "I'll save the celebrating for after the shift." I popped three Grolsches and poured shots of kosher brandy.

"Here we all are again." I served the drinks like a *konobar.* "Where's the Danube?"

Hans gave a lukewarm smile.

"Three years," said Quierin. "One more Balkan war come and gone."

Leitner lifted the shotglass of colorless liquid an inch or two, not quite up to the *zhivili.* Quierin supplied it. She maintained a toastmaster stance, arm reared. "I worshiped at your clay feet, Colonel. You make me so pissed when I think about you."

We each took sips.

"Pissed? Yeah. But nothing like me." He rubbed his mouth with the back of his hand.

"I didn't enjoy it," I told him. "Any of it."

"That's comforting, Elliot," he said sourly. "You'll be suing me next. That will be more fun."

"No, I won't. But Paige will."

"This case is over, I assume." He loosened his tie and opened his collar.

"It's over. April and Dale are having dinner right now, getting to know each other. Everyone in this case, all over this town, is having a beer and talking about your testimony. You couldn't help being the world's best witness, even testifying against yourself."

A wan sigh. "If I'd known—" He dropped his head and shook it slowly.

"You mean the Fifth? Yeah. I thought you might not take it. You're smarter than lawyers. You've creamed too many in court. For all the man-of-science business, you've got a reckless streak, Hans."

"Lawyers—" He twitched out a little smile. "I guess I need them now."

"You need a doctor," Quierin said.

Leitner rattled off a false laugh. He knocked back the shot, held a swallow in his mouth, then gulped it.

"I think I'll see Fagen. Fagen's good."

"With narcissists down on their luck?"

He laughed again, the same. "This is so unreal, Elliot. *Arrested,* because of *you.* They never even arrested Dale. This can't be—happening."

"It's happening, Doc." Roybal picked at a bump on his elbow. "Big old shit is coming down."

"You were why they didn't charge Dale, weren't you?" I asked him. "Russell Tucker's go-to guy for knocking out insanity pleas. He was afraid of you."

"I hope he still is. I want a lawyer he's afraid of too. What do you know about this guy LaFond?"

"Showboat. You can do better."

"What do you think I should do?"

"I'm sure not your lawyer."

"No kidding."

"But I'd say, tell the truth and commit the rest of your life to good works in the memory of June."

Roybal rolled his eyes, filled a glass at the sink. "Come a cold day in hell," he muttered.

Leitner abruptly looked offended. "I'm not admitting a goddamn thing. I'm not getting stuck with this. What you did was—devious. Unworthy."

"Had to get you under oath before you caught on."

"You're a pretty smart guy. So"—Quierin crossed a long leg, tamped out a cigarette from a crushed blue package. An acceptable time to break the rules—"we move like a burning house."

"This proceeding was—illegitimate," Leitner sputtered. "It's an illegal search. Illegal arrest, and I'll beat it, goddamn it."

"You sound like Belgrade politician," Quierin said, "dissing tribunal."

"You know it wasn't a fair fight."

"You nearly pulled it off. We got lucky."

"The banked tissue—" Leitner glanced up at Roybal leaning against the counter, legs crossed, arms crossed, and forearms flexing, smiling fatly back. I asked Roybal to leave us awhile so we might speak with a little less constraint. He headed for the front porch with a two-finger salute.

"Thanks," Leitner murmured. He wet a lip. "Guy's an ass-hole."

"Anyway, Colonel." Quierin lit up. She twirled the Bic in her fingertips. "Yah, sure, frozen tissue was lucky break. Plus you keep chart. Plus somebody sees you do naughty things."

"Who are these mystery witnesses? I'm entitled to know."

"They're entitled to protection," I said. Silbi was thinking of law school. Paralegal anyway. Leaving Legal for the real thing.

"Of course I kept the chart." He groaned. "He's my patient. I have to have a chart."

"You couldn't change it either," I said. "There's too much to change. You couldn't pencil in coverage by another doctor who'd deny it since it's a dump on him. Plus, the judge had ruled it stayed secret. Plus, you thought I'd read it."

"I know you read it." He pitched me a look, as though I were dirty as he.

"Nope. Didn't need to."

That struck him briefly dumb. "You're a sneaky bastard, Stone. I really never thought it of you."

"You keep making the same mistake, Hans. You're sure I'll never tumble because I revere you. I think you're so wonderful it could never cross my mind, and it didn't for a long time."

"That's not it. We were friends—"

"Means nothing in the context of what was done to June."

"Nothing?"

"Correction. It means everything—betrayal by a friend. I feel like I've been knifed."

"You couldn't feel worse than I." He smiled, an arthritic wince, then his face creased with pain. "Elliot, and Quierin, at least believe this. I understand how April and Dale were hurt. I hope you saw I tried to right that some today."

"Is this why you're here? Hoping we'll soften up because at last you were sort of honest with them?"

"I have no such illusions," he said in a monotone. He circled a shoulder and frowned. He put the glass to his lips.

"The first bad thing you did, and one of the worst, was not telling Dale. Not just hiding from him that he was innocent, but encouraging him to feel guilty. Telling him he struck June in anger. With that lie, the die was cast, wasn't it? After that you had to keep the truth buried, which led inevitably to what you did to June."

"You're full of shit, Elliot. And you will never trap me again."

"A foolish lie you couldn't get out of, that's what trapped you. You couldn't let Dale or his lawyers think he had a defense, because that would have exposed the chart, hence your malpractice, hence the lie. There was no turning back, was there?"

I studied his sunken, sullen stare, anger welling up.

"But what a thing to do to Dale," I said. "Exploiting his amnesia. Way worse than foolish. Shielding yourself with your patient, but there's also an element here of—what? Sadism, I think. Cultivating guilt feelings in that suggestible, grief-racked man."

"Sadism, Elliot?" Again, a smiled wince of pain. "What do you know about that? I may be arrogant, self-serving, vain, you name it, but—sadistic?"

I was the one being studied, I saw. He was still trying to get inside my head.

"The pathetic part," I said, "is that Dale was utterly dependent on you. Especially after June died, and he's bereft, and seeing you for bereavement therapy, of all the sick ironies. And he's overwhelmed with guilt you instilled. How did you keep him from killing himself and exposing your deep pockets again?"

"I'm Dale's psychiatrist, for Christ's sake. He'd have long been lost without me. Can't you see that too?"

"Wait. I know. You told him any thought of harming himself, any step toward it, would disappoint you terribly. You would leave him again. He'd be on his own, and look what happened last time when you were off in Europe."

That rang something inside. Leitner's chin dropped toward his chest. He lifted his eyes. "Dale would testify, I suppose?"

"Of course. As will Hancock, Edson, Kirwan, and I, and lots of others. You're fucked."

"Yah." Quierin knocked an ash in a Belleek Irish teacup of Kathleen's. "Where light won't shine. But you fight this anyway, don't you?"

"I sure as hell will. This is long from over. I don't like being tricked, Elliot. That's one reason."

He pushed his shotglass at Quierin to refill.

"What will you say? Will you still try to pass off the poisoning on Stillwell?"

"Yes. He confessed to me. That explains the missing samples. Plus, my investigation of Colfax. That's what I was doing there. Accompanying Dale was a pretext. I was penetrating Colfax's racketeering. I'll say all the things you wouldn't let me say today."

"You weren't investigating Colfax, Hans. You stumbled on that and you improvised. The HCFA letter doesn't mention Colfax. I think you did want Rico to disappear. He was too close to events. You actually used him to administer the phenol. You left an anonymous message with Colfax administrators, didn't you? Rico was going to the feds. But investigating Colfax? No, Colfax was a fallback villain if Stillwell didn't pan out."

"My explanations for my actions make sense." He frowned smugly. "You can't refute them."

"I can. You phonied the chart with DNR orders. Moschetti's got you cold. That doesn't track Stillwell as a poisoner or a Colfax investigation. There is only one explanation for that, making sure June died."

"In the presence of such ruinous damage it was wrong to prolong her life," Leitner said righteously. "No cor was a proper order. Arcenault should have entered it."

Quierin's walled eye slid to the side, an *Oh, bullshit* look that was often followed by *hah*. This time she said, "Nobody will fall down for that, Colonel. That is insulting us."

Wrong to prolong her life rubbed me raw. "You are ever the humanitarian, aren't you? The utilitarian. The rationalizer. Human rights justifying inhuman acts."

"Fuck off." He scraped back his chair and rose to his feet. "I'll see you in court. I'm pressing charges for the break-in, by the way."

He stood unsteadily but made no move to leave. Unconvincing; he could tell it, and that we knew why. Roybal waiting on the porch.

"Sit down," Quierin said. "We finish this."

"Did you come for an apology?" I said. "I apologize for last

Friday. Hell, for today too. For doing what I had to. I can give you that, as a former friend."

He dropped in the chair, heavy and bleak.

"There's more bad stuff, isn't there? Your hard drive. E-mails to Ellen Vesco. The perils of the virtual office."

"Why you come here, Colonel? To make us feel sorry for you?"

"To make us apologize?"

"To make us have mercy on you?" She searched his beaten face.

"I came," he said, "to talk."

"Okay." I smacked a fist. "Let's. How can the good do evil? The Serb conundrum, remember? That's what we should talk about."

"Let's start with the choice of phenol." The choice of phenol, as Quierin had explained, said much about the poisoner. "I suppose you had no other options?"

"Elliot, I can't talk this way."

"The poisoner had no other options."

He pulled at his chin. "What else is both guaranteed effective and available to anyone at Colfax? Not just Dale or April, but maybe, what? Thirty or forty people. Nothing I know of."

"And takes GC/MS to ID," Quierin said. "And nobody knows till it's too late. No yelling with pain 'cause comatose can't yell. Nurse can't rouse her 'cause severe CNS depressed— so what? She's a Rancho two or three. Normal she won't rouse. With coma, phenol's perfect."

"A poisoner"—Leitner knit his lips—"might think so. He might also think it's fairly low risk. He can even be a little sloppy. If the phenol's found, it probably won't matter. Schlepps like Silverman and Tucker won't go anywhere with it, but even if they did, they'd focus on Colfax neglect, or an in-house Colfax job, or a relative." Leitner's thin smile waxed sardonic. "Only one person might worry this poisoner."

"Two," Quierin said, "once I hit the town."

"You've changed, Elliot, in the years I've known you. You never were a zealot."

"I *made* this guy," Quierin said proudly. "He's my project. I first meet you two, Colonel's the big cat in the alley. Who's this beardy-faced railroad man? May have potential."

"Don't you think," I said, leaning back, hands behind my neck, "the poisoner might actually find this deed fairly easy to justify? Just balance the harms. On one side, the loss of a career and future contributions to science and human rights of a potentially historic dimension. The next Rudolf Virchow."

Leitner snorted.

"On the other, the loss of a scarcely sentient being whose life not only had no value, but negative value. Negative personally because what living really meant was unending misery, and not just her own. April's, Dale's, even mine, in a tiny way, a friend might think. A negative value to society as well. June contributes nothing but may consume millions that should go instead to those who might give something back."

"Ending June's life," Leitner said, "should not be thought of as an act of compassion and certainly not of altruism." He looked a tired version of the sage of old, helping brainstorm a problem, cautioning objectivity.

"No, but we could think of it as—advanced tough love, maybe. It takes courage to think beyond conventional sentiments and rules of behavior. It takes—scientific detachment. Intellectual clarity. Not an act of mercy, but an act of . . ."

He smiled and frowned, thoughtful. "Discrimination, call it."

"Is this how the good do evil? Detach from sentiment and moral rules, justify forbidden acts in the name of a larger good?"

"It was a terrible mistake," he said. "Whoever did it."

"Yah. It didn't work."

"When head and heart part ways," I said, "I think that's when the good go bad."

"There may be something to that." He took my measure. "Reason in isolation can be dangerous. Reason unrestrained by sympathy."

"Maybe at first he's just a doc scared of a malpractice claim, though not just any doc. A compulsive CV polisher, you have to admit, unnerved by the prospect of cross-exams about June and Dale Stillwell every time he takes the stand as an expert. And at first the idea may have seemed pretty reasonable. Stillwell has the dough, and he ought to be responsible. He's her husband and he destroyed her life."

"How you characterize the poisoner sucks but, broadly, you have a point. He rationalizes."

"And it's more than that. Each of his steps takes greater courage. He summons it to think clearly, logically, unconventionally."

"Acts of courage can be self-justifying."

"The poisoner is a man of sensibilities. He evolves a sense of mission, to do the right thing in the most complex sense. To follow a more complicated morality than rules on stone tablets, as you once said to me. To be capable of paradox. The wisdom to do wrong. That requires bravery and even, in a way, high-mindedness—"

"To be uniquely and ruthlessly moral." He passed on the brandy but accepted another Grolsch.

"Like a—Virchow. He was a radical, right? A visionary. Sort of a proto-human-rights doctor."

"The greatest of his age."

"You no Virchow, Colonel."

"Not even close." Leitner removed his glasses and held them away. "But I think you sense the issues you were dealing with."

"Yah. Except one thing. One thing about phenol choice I don't get. Is hideous way to die."

"Right," I said. "Right. I don't quite get that either, Hans. As the plan spun out, something else came to the fore, didn't it?"

"Phenol makes sense like you say." Quierin worked her expressive hands. "Has every advantage, just one disadvantage. Tortures before it kills. Ruthless moral guy says no way, right? But this poisoner says, hey, okay. Downside acceptable. Who is this poisoner really?"

In the heat of our stares shame rose in his face. "Who are any of us at heart?" Hans murmured. He dared for a second to catch my eye, then quickly lost it again.

"Radovan Karadzic." I leaned a fraction closer. "We've talked about him. Psychiatrist, poet, president."

"For whom I have contempt."

"I know, but he intrigues you, doesn't he? His poem, sitting on the mountaintop, playing the *gusla,* watching Sarajevo burn below as his army shells it, master of terror and death inflicted on an innocent city. What intrigues you, I think, is the idea of license. That he permitted himself to do such things."

Leitner bit a thumbnail, looking away.

"How does it go, what Emerson said? 'We permit all things to ourselves . . .'"

"'And that which we call sin in others is experiment for us,'" Hans said somberly. As he spoke, he didn't move at all, and I felt my neck prickle. "'For there is no crime to the intellect.'"

"Do you believe that?" I chased down his eyes.

"On some level."

"Was it an intellectual experiment, then? Head unconstrained by heart. An experiment in heartlessness?"

"What might such an experiment prove?"

"That it could be done, like Everest. Something authentically wanton. Gratuitous, purposeless cruelty, like murdering Vukovar hospital patients. Murdering a Colfax hospital patient after torturing her first. Could that partake of this majestic dark greatness you talked with me about?"

Leitner exhaled explosively. "A poisoner such as you postulate," Leitner said, "is the devil."

"You no devil, Colonel." Quierin waved her lighter admonishingly. "You just a want-to-be."

"You trivialized June Stillwell's life as expendable, but I know differently. I saw her strength. I saw how brave she was. Goddamn you, Hans"—I came forward, getting in his face—"reduced to next to nothing, June Stillwell was still a hero of mine. Goddamn you for what you did."

He laughed strangely, an unhinged, debauched sound.

"I think you wanted to take life, and not just wrongfully. Diabolically. Hell, you hinted as much at dinner."

He sighed through his nose. "Too many martinis."

"No, the martinis were to gull information out of me. I think you wanted me to sense, without understanding, your—experiment with June. You wanted your greatness appreciated. You honored me with a glimpse into your soul."

"Not there." Quierin pointed the Bic at his chest. "No soul in there."

"It got to be a head game, didn't it?" I leaned back. "You could draw on both your specialties, pathology for the physical effects, psychiatry to manipulate the players. It was a fascinating professional exercise, I bet. Applied forensic medicine. Medicine and law intersecting at June's hospital bed."

"I think Colonel gets a thrill ride on it."

He stared. I held it. "The intellectual challenge, staring up, thinking it through, but also the risk, the adrenaline. Not just thinking the unthinkable, but doing it, by God."

"And finally there was," Leitner said loudly with a sideways look, almost a leer, "the allure of pure evil, is that it? A human-rights doctor committing an atrocity himself to see what it feels like?"

We let his breathtaking declaration stand, irony vanishing like smoke in the silence.

"I'm tempted," I said, "to say you are monstrous. Your darkly great self would like to hear that. But you're no devil. No Virchow, either. Just a good doctor who happened to slip up. Malpractice and it cost a life and look where that led. You're not even really a physician anymore. What's left is the medical expert who feeds off lawyers and lawsuits. Hired gun, professional witness, parasite, whore."

I imagined him then with X-ray sight, the skeleton of Ovcara, nothing in his heart but a bomb, the true djinni at last. From booby-trapped corpse, to the mooing roommate, to tortured Dale Stillwell, to heartless Hans. The malevolent spirit finally arrived to deliver his message.

"Why you really come?" Quierin asked. "What you want here?"

"Forgiveness?" I asked. "Or impunity? Or what?"

"You want understanding," Quierin said. "Understanding, I think."

"What do you have to tell us?"

He stood again, more calmly. He looked at us in turn, ran his fingers through his pile of hair, and puffed his cheeks. "It could happen to you," he said almost tenderly. He turned for the hall.

No. Not what he'd done. I wasn't almost-him. Yet in the broadest sense he was right about what could happen. I could cause wrongful death and rationalize it. Like Mayor Jovanovic. Like the JNA. I was capable of a moment of cowardice or panic, a failure of conviction, of bolting for self-preservation and letting someone die, of watching rather than intervening, or a hundred other failings. Under enough stress of fear and need I could buckle and allow life to be wrongfully taken. Or even take it myself, and rationalize why, and cover up the evidence and pray it wouldn't be found.

"I hear you, Hans," I said as he walked away. "You've convinced me. There aren't any monsters. There's no such thing as an evil person. There are only evil acts. But you have to suffer for them, and you have to atone."

He continued out the hallway and the front door and onto the front porch. The door closed softly after him. The djinni's message trembled in the air—*It could happen to you.*

Until Quierin broke the spell. "Okay, horse." From behind my chair she looped her arms across my chest. Her lips grazed my neck. "Let's round up the wagons."

CHAPTER 14

The SuperShuttle barreled past the grama-
grass wetlands of South Boulder Creek, moiréed by the wind. It
downshifted for the long climb up Overlook Hill. Over the crest
lay what plain-speaking folk called the metro area. Costco, Target, a LEGO-land of look-alike houses, the future home of
Flatirons Crossing Mall—vast reaches of bare earth spinning
with dust devils, crawling with Cats—and in the distance, the
troubled skies of Denver. Queen City of the Plains. Quierin read
last week's *Camera*. I reflected on fortune's wheel.

The Queen City Trust was an investment cover for Russian
Mafia funds, my investigator, Beckwith, was finding out. The
front man, Doc, was Ivan Silverman himself. Doc would have to
be Silverman, I now saw, undistracted by the pull of Leitner's
menace. No way to run the scam except through the medical
director. And who better than Russians at the art of routing public moneys to the private weal?

Jasmine was fired the day the *qui tam* suit was filed. The U.S.
Attorney joined our case the following week. You still the
Watash? Rico wanted to know. Mr. Watash to the feds, I told
him. It helps they're on board. Good protection. Rico wanted to
ask Jasmine to be a co-relator in the lawsuit. Paige agreed to co-
counsel and to manage it while I took a few months off. She figured, green eyes glowing, we'd find way more ripped off than

the $6 million Rico guessed. Between Connor, the Colfax fraud case, and refiling for April against Leitner, Paige was planning on leaving railroad defense. Never was a more unlikely plaintiffs' practice born.

The trial of Dale Stillwell ended the morning after Leitner's testimony. Bernie Edson, rocking the podium, renewed his motion to dismiss with a twitchy smile. Paige acquiesced so long as April's rights to refile wrongful-death claims were preserved. The judge wanted to hear from the plaintiff herself. April stood and said it was her choice that her claims against the defendant be dismissed, and Otero granted the motion. Stillwell asked permission to approach Ms. Mooney. He left the defense table and shook April's hand. Formally reconciled in open court. Otero then sent eight frustrated mothers home without the chance to pass heavy judgment on the defendant's doctor. Another eight would, another day.

Before releasing counsel, Otero let us know he wasn't entirely happy about what had transpired. Tort claims a pretext for gathering criminal evidence. Plaintiff and defense counsel colluding to trap an unrepresented third-party witness in potential criminal liability. A plaintiff resting her case, then disproving her own claims. Unprecedented. Actually—bizarre. He wondered about the propriety of what he'd just presided over.

"We were reacting," I said, "to evidence not known until trial was under way in part because the doctor misled this very court last year."

"There was a lot misleading of this court," Otero said darkly.

"On discovery of this evidence we had duties that included informing the other side."

"But not me?"

"Getting out the truth necessarily entailed an element of surprise, Your Honor."

"Did your duties also require you to rifle the doctor's files, Mr. Stone, as he claims you did?"

"That? Well . . ." What could I say? I broke into his office, though I hadn't actually taken anything, or even read any confidential documents. Sometimes you just can't do it by the book. Some foes are too wily for that. If we ever get Milosevic to The Hague, it probably won't be pretty either, procedurally neat and constitutionally clean. Some bastards you've got to nail when you can.

"Never mind." The judge waved an annoyed hand, letting me off. "Dr. Leitner will raise it in due course, I'm sure. Anything else?"

"One item," I said. "Mr. Stillwell engaged counsel at a time when both he and his conservator, June Stillwell, were legally incompetent. Any agreement regarding legal fees is therefore not binding. Nor were their arrangements ratified after Mr. Still-well was declared competent. He told me this in a conversation at which defense counsel was present by telephone. I'm sure he would confirm it to the court."

I looked at Stillwell. He half stood and nodded. "That's r-right." Kirwan was mouthing something—what the hell?

"Since there's no contractual basis for their fees," I contin-ued, "defense counsel may be compensated only on a quantum meruit basis, that is, for the value of their services in securing a favorable outcome for their client. A hearing should be held. Excessive fees already paid should be disgorged. I understand they total over a half million dollars."

Stillwell half stood again and nodded.

"Paid by coercing Mr. Stillwell to assign to these three lawyers rights to future annuities you approved, Your Honor, in 1996, exclusively as compensation for brain-injury disability."

"He *assigned* his annuities?"

"In part and under the duress of an agreement they got him to sign before you declared him competent. I suggest the assign-ments may be void as well."

"Is this another new allegiance, Mr. Stone? Do you represent Mr. Stillwell now, after successively representing him, then his wife, then her daughter *against* him?"

"I bring it to your attention only as an officer of the court. This man has been taken advantage of enough."

Kirwan rose, incensed and threatening, but Otero ordered a hearing to review the validity of the agreements and assign-ments of annuities and the amounts of every bill and payment under the quantum meruit standard.

"The court reminds Mr. Kirwan," Otero finished, "his client's success in this trial was by and large not the doing of his counsel, who evidently never considered the doctor's culpability or a psychiatric defense. The court also notes the court itself was less than vigilant in protecting Mr. Stillwell's rights in the past. I assure you that will change. Set a hearing."

Kirwan accosted me in the hall afterward. "What the fuck." Lapse of eloquence.

"You're done with gouging this guy, Kevin." Which felt pretty good, all in all, the next best thing to ending his string.

I had a similarly unprofessional and somewhat less discourteous phone conversation with Millsap. After all, he and Tucker turned out to have been right to hold off charging Stillwell. April and Stillwell, once his targets but newly immunized, were putting it together for Millsap now—the banked heart tissue, the GC/MS, the therapy and pharmacy records, the string of witnesses. Darwin lent a hand. Add the transcript of my cross and we were giving it to him on a plate. Next time, Millsap, do your own work.

April and Quierin exchanged good-byes over dinner at the Indo-Ceylon. Still pretty tasty, but nothing like home Quisine. April was looking ahead. She spoke excitedly about finishing college and finishing the case. Grad school. "Then, something, science and law enforcement, or military? Medicine even maybe? Learning something, like, not really rotting bodies necessarily. But like what you guys do."

"Taphonomists are all girls," Quierin said. "Guys do paleo. Huge, ancient, macho brutes. For exhumation you need a big heart." Quierin nudged her.

April wanted to know when she'd see Quierin again.

"I ride the winds of misfortune." Quierin turned a theatrical profile. "Maybe blow me someday back." A little too theatrical.

The SuperShuttle highballed down the turnpike with us, three stiff-necked couples, a smatter of lounging students and business singles. Some of the passengers were in shorts. Three wore T-shirts. Two wore Walkmans. BRING IT ON, a T-shirt said. Another said, THE MOVE. Something to do with board sports. Two singles on cell phones. Insufferable diatribes you couldn't help overhearing.

Quierin, as usual, stood out. The personage on the bus. Black on black on black. Coy glances above her newspaper at me. The half smile half revealed. The incontestable promise in the cast of her face both of unexplored Indo intrigue and a charged enterprise of moment.

Outside, the premall wasteland flew past like a war zone. Gusts of dirt soiled the view.

"You come to America," I said, thumping the paper, "and never make it to Neiman Marcus. Never even make it to Dillard's."

"Yah, yah. Kentucky pop chicken, all those places."

"You'd like Neiman Marcus. Elegant gals spray perfume on you."

"Yah."

"Never did any really American things. Never tried to quit smoking. Never bought stock. Did we eat any Mexican food? I don't think so."

She half smiled, then snapped, smoothed, and folded a two-page spread of the paper, framing its photograph: Quierin in a modified *Vogue* cover pose.

"The article you're reading for the tenth time. How is it?"

"He do pretty good job." She smiled and peaked her brows.

"It's all about you, Quierin."

"Can I help it?"

"A little April. But Paige? Me? Not a word."

"Elliot." She shook her head with feeling. "You just don't have it."

"It?"

"Snap. Mystique. Celebrity."

"'Who would guess the tall, chic, Eurasian Ph.D. has investigated atrocities that would turn the blood cold?'"

"He got papers to sell."

"'How can I say this? Justice in America is weird.'"

"What about O.J.? What about Karla Faye? What about impeachments?"

"And, Quierin, in this country we have a presumption of innocence. When we speak for publication we say 'alleged.' We say we'll let the system run its course."

"No problem, horse," she said. "Leaving Dodgetown tonight."

The refineries of Commerce City flamed toward heaven. Chemical foam drifted in mats at the confluence of the Platte. Freeways likewise converged. Traffic thickened and slowed.

"We've got bodies to exhume in America too. You could find work here."

"Kind of bodies?"

"The Greenwood Massacre in Tulsa. Race riot. Mass grave near El Paso. Drug hits. You could poke around for Jimmy Hoffa. You could teach."

"Consult. I like consult."

"We could be a team. We could even—"

"Hah. Never. I'm not ready to die."

"Marriage isn't about dying." A lesson learned.

"Till death do you apart, right? Hold hands and walk off to die."

"Hold hands and live. Happily ever after."

"Hah." She broke into a full grin, superior and amused. "I try to see you as a husband." It came out *goozban*. Then the Quierin volte-face. "Only way I see it is Vegas ceremony. The real America. In casino with rolling coaster on the roof."

Out the tinted windows the last verges of Denver fell away before the landscape. In all directions treeless prairie fled to the horizons, shaped on the west by the ragged white wall of the range. All around was the clear and sunstruck land I'd longed for from flat, gray, damp, cramped, chill northern Europe. Alone in an empty prairie basin, the white tented canvas of DIA hove into view, swarmed by aircraft like wasps to a nest.

"This train," the S&L announcer informed us, "is departing for Concourses A, B, and C."

"The only places it can go are Concourses A, B, and C," I said.

"Now, Elliot."

"It's stupid. Stupid airport."

In the subway thousands of little pinwheels spun.

An efficient matron, a Swiss Air frau, asked mandatory questions about luggage without a trace of weariness with her job. Quierin required a window seat. The blue sky behind the Airbus nosed to the glass was just starting to blush.

Quierin loved flight. Airports new and old, the shuffle of humanity with wheeled carry-ons, youth with day packs, age with shoulder bags. She loved full-throttle takeoffs and dizzying views from little scratched windows. Waiting to board put her in a dreamy mood.

"I want to see ice floes under moonlight," she said, head resting on my shoulder.

"Now boarding rows fifteen through twenty-five," the frau announced. Quierin pulled me to my feet.

"Let's do it," she said. "The largest crime scene in the world is calling."

We fed our boarding passes into a machine and trundled down the carpeted Jetway.

"What you thinking?" she asked.

"I'm thinking, what now? What next in life?"

"Now—I take your hand." She did.

"And we walk off into the sunset?"

She raised a brow; the ambivalent smile. She swung my hand in a childish arc. "Why not? Why not have an American ending?"

"We go off together to track down the bad guys?"

"No, no, no. We go to the wild blue yonder."

Her fingers tightened. My pulse jumped to Quierin's touch—the thing worth living for.

"Happy ever after all."

AUTHOR'S NOTE

The idea for this story crystallized in spring 1998 on Louise de Colignystraat in The Hague with the intersection in my imagination of three worlds—the Republika Sprska in Bosnia, the International Criminal Tribunal for the former Yugoslavia, and brain-injury wards back home. Among those behind the idea, four deserve particular mention: Igor Motl and Mutic Sinesa, destined to be leaders of their generation, in Bosnia, in Serbia, or beyond. And Lisa Hammond and Gloria Lamar, young women whose enduring courage and humanity inspired my efforts to speak through the pages of a book.

Physicians for Human Rights, recipient of the Nobel Peace Prize and unequaled force for truth and justice in the Balkans and throughout the world, also merits special mention. My book's fictional Doctors for Human Rights and its fictional founder neither represent nor resemble Physicians for Human Rights, Doctors Without Borders, nor any other real agency or person. Physicians for Human Rights was an inspiration for and certainly not a subject of this novel.

The more difficult enterprise of turning the idea into a book could not have been carried forward without the uncompensated assistance of dozens, only some of whom I have room to thank: Toxicologists Gary Krieger, M.D., and Leslie Boyer, M.D.,

Louis Jares of the Donor Alliance and Mile High transplant bank. Heather Ryan, then of the Coalition for International Justice and Carr Center for Human Rights, for her thoughtful readings. Maja Poklevic, for educating me about the tribunal. Steve Briggs, Jack Olsen, and Diane Brown, for prosecutorial and judicial perspectives and reality checks. Sarah Flynn, for her sharp eye and good advice. Steve Napper, for railroad law and lore. The late Chuck Meyer, for help in understanding grief. Heather McLaughlin, for help in understanding therapeutic riding. Don Brenneis and Wynne Furth, for help in understanding anthropologists. Macon "Wheelman" Cowles, for The Devil's Advocate and voir dire showmanship. Hilary Kivitz, for explaining, and all our colleagues in the Prijedor OSCE class of 1997 for demonstrating the irreconcilability of Hume and Kant. Tom Hoh, as the model for Elliot's devotion. And all my kids' friends, plus April Rinne, whose names I appropriated. (The characters aren't you. I just love your names.)

Among the many writers I drew on I am especially indebted to my old teacher, Robert D. Richardson, Jr., and his intellectual biographies of Thoreau and Emerson; to Roger Shattuck, for his critique of infatuations with evil; and, not, by a long shot least, to Rebecca West.

A rocking team of pros brought my flickering idea and sputtering labors to reality. Lisa Drew, to whom I owe, in short, a career. Leslie Breed; my agent and friend, Margo Brown and especially Laura Folden, who made typescripts out of sows' ears; and Jake Klisivitch, who kept the trains on time.

I am indebted to my parents, Baine and Mildred Kerr, for the Matteson Cottage writing refuge, and my firm, Hutchinson Black and Cook, for both a sabbatical year in Bosnia and The Hague, and generous leave later to hole up on the Big Island and get the thing done.

But, first and always, to Cindy, for insisting that the cause be just and the course true.